RETURN TO THE HOUSE THAT FELL FROM THE SKY

PATRICK DELANEY

Illustrations and Cover Design by Wofford Lee Jones

Paperback

ISBN: 9781735525198

To the Juliet family

THE GREY WORLD UNIVERSE

Dante's Town of Terror

Dante's Wicked World

~~*Dante's Medley of Madness*~~

The House that Fell from the Sky

Silvers Hollow

Witch 13

Return to the House that Fell from the Sky

Crow Corp. (est. 2024)

Witch 13: Reborn (est. 2025)

RETURN TO THE HOUSE
THAT FELL FROM THE SKY
PATRICK DELANEY

PART 1: FALLOUT

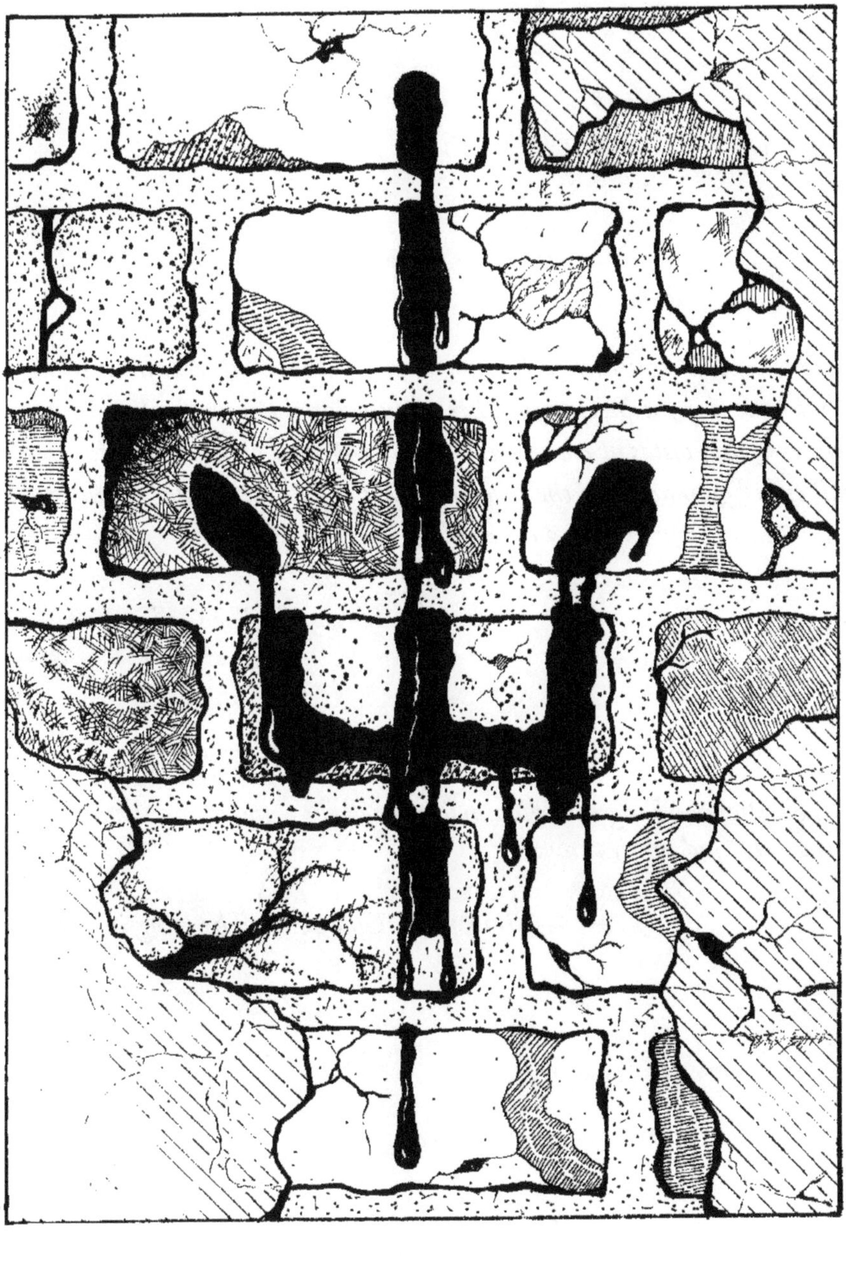

"The sciences, each straining in its own direction, have hitherto harmed us little; but some day the piecing together of dissociated knowledge will open up such terrifying vistas of reality, and of our frightful position therein, that we shall either go mad from the revelation or flee from the deadly light into the peace and safety of a new dark age."

— *H.P. Lovecraft, The Call of Cthulhu*

"for I knew that the King in Yellow had opened his tattered mantle and there was only God to cry to now."

— *Robert W. Chambers, The King in Yellow*

A HISTORY LESSON

THE HOUSE WAS death.

The structure had come to Winterview City, Connecticut, on a night not unlike any other. It had been mere days from All Hallows' Eve, when the world was slowly sinking into night. Pumpkins lined the sidewalks like ghostly lanterns, ushering the spirits of the dead on their way. Witches and ghouls of all sorts roamed the cold streets in droves, and anxious ghosts lurked in every dark corner.

Even the most universally suspect things went undetected, for Halloween had drawn nearer—and with it a blind eye because, after all, these things were to be expected. Welcomed even, by most. And while the air sang of fright and festivity, the rats burrowed deep into their dens in the sewers, the birds flocking to brighter, warmer places.

Stillness had set about the dark city when an explosion of blinding light and dreadful chorus gave birth to the thing on Seventh Street.

The police, summoned to the K District of Seventh Street, found a structure had miraculously overtaken several city blocks. What happened to the existing businesses was unknown, and any persons thought to be in the immediate vicinity were officially reported missing.

Some called it a house. Others say it resembled nothing of the sort.

But all eventually came to agree that whatever it was had brought forth a terrifying new reality. One in which the supernatural no longer existed only in fairy tales and books, but were in fact as real as the air they breathed.

The structure, christened "The House that fell from the Sky" by major media outlets, was over seven stories tall and spanned roughly 35,000 square feet. The architecture was infinitely complex, vastly superior to anything the world had ever seen, constructed of elements unknown to man.

On Halloween night, three days after the structure's arrival in Winterview, a YouTube vlogger named Brent Lowry found himself in the house for mere seconds. Upon his exit, a nearby National Guard patrol witnessed a now insane Lowry's suicide of a self-inflicted gunshot wound.

Two months later, a private business conglomerate known as the Crow Corporation obtained a federal injunction to seize control of the property.

As a pretense for discovering the truth about the house, the Crow Corporation hosted the Seventh Street Lottery, a drawing for Winterview residents guaranteeing three winners and a friend of their choosing the chance to win one million dollars should they spend one night in the house until dawn.

Five participants entered the house. They are:

Scarlett Vantassel.

Thomas Vantassel.

Hannah Maxx.

Jackson Briggs.

And world-famous magician Vincent Velladex.

Of the five that entered, only two returned.

To the public's knowledge, no one has entered the house since.

Until now.

Prologue: Part I
RACHEL

RACHEL WEBSTER SPRINTED over potholes and cracked concrete, towing the cardinal-red kite behind her, the fraying string taut in her small hands, angled up at the clouds. She laughed as the wind playfully batted it across the sky, and laughed harder when it began to fall only to get jerked back up again.

She spun on the balls of her feet and darted for the porch, all fifty pounds of her hopping up the steps (minding the one with the nail jutting out) and cranking the kite reel like she was hauling in a delicious bass.

Dad was asleep in his recliner inside, the one with the rips and the tears in the arms. He'd said they were going to upgrade to one that actually worked when he found a better job, but until then, she was content with it.

She peeked in through the living room window.

He was sprawled out there, one leg hanging off the broken footrest, a line of drool down the side of his face, a bag of Cheetos in his lap.

He was working the night shift again. He'd done it before in the past, but Rachel wasn't crazy about it. He was always too tired to take her anywhere, sleeping his days away like some kind of vampire. His eyes were always tired and red and he got that stubble on his chin that pricked her when he'd kiss her on the cheek before he left for work.

Rachel watched the kite dance across the sky, granting it more slack, and her smile waned. The air was crisp, tinged with the smell of wet concrete and glorious summer BBQs happening all over the city.

When was the last time Dad had barbequed? She thought this question over in her head but her thoughts moved like the kite, much too fast, shuffling in the wind.

Where did he even work again? He'd had so many jobs by now she was starting to lose track.

Her nose crinkled. She scratched her head, clutching onto the reel with her other hand.

The mall! That was it! He'd only been working there a few days now, and it was already "draining the life out of him." His words.

Sheesh. She hoped she never felt that tired. He looked like a zombie. But all this sleeping did have one small perk: lots of alone time. She could do whatever she wanted while he was asleep. Play with her dolls in the tub with so many bubbles you couldn't see the water. Speed the remote-controlled monster truck she got for Christmas around the apartment like her own personal racetrack.

Even go outside unsupervised. Something he never let her do while he was awake.

Her eyes dropped from the kite, finding a massive concrete wall stretching down the street in both directions. Their porch faced it, and Rachel couldn't help but think of it as a moody neighbor. She could see it out her bedroom window, but the shadow it cast made it hard to see anything on the other side.

She sighed, disapproving of the drab eyesore, but always remained curious what was on the other side. Dad had made her promise never to go anywhere near that wall, saying it was "dangerous," but she didn't see how. It was just a stupid wall. Their house was full of them. A big one, sure, but still just a wall.

They'd built it the end of last year, around the same time all the people in the city started coming down to their neck of the woods. Before then, people had wanted to stay as far away as possible. The slums of Winterview, apparently. But after the house showed up right around last Halloween, everyone magically had the urge to rush out and take a peek. She heard on the news they'd had some sort of contest not too far from their apartment, only a few streets down. But the contest came and went and then…nothing.

Then one day, not long after, ginormous trucks were driving up and down their street. People in yellow hardhats and neon vests were shouting and yelling and had their giant tractor machines going and Rachel thought they sounded angry. Sometimes they kept her awake all night long.

Eventually, they got in their big trucks and machines and they left, and it was like she was waking up from a dream. Or maybe a nightmare. She looked outside at the thing they'd been working on that had caused all the fuss and realized that big gray wall had completely cut the city in two.

Outside the wall, where their house and her school and friends were.

And whatever was *inside.*

She thought when the construction crew had gone that it was finally over. That the sounds would stop and she'd be able to sleep again like she did so well before.

But it wasn't over.

In the intersection right down the road, they had also built a little booth. It had glass windows and this panel with buttons and lights and a coffee maker. She didn't really know what it was for, but before long there were new trucks coming and going, always stopping at that little booth, saying hi to the man inside, flashing their little cards at him. Part of the wall would open up like a secret passageway and the cars and trucks would disappear inside. Sometimes there were bigger trucks with people in the back of them, crammed in there like sardines. People in funny masks with red eyes and these round canisters on the side.

A strong gust caught the kite and it spiraled into the sky.

"Oh no!" she said, but then clapped a hand over her mouth, fearing her dad might hear her.

The kite abruptly nosedived, crashing into a rusted antenna on a rooftop on the other side of the wall. She saw it shudder in the wind, struggling to get free, but the string was tangled. It might as well have been on the Moon.

She tried to reel it in and the string snapped with a *plink!*

A long creak.

She glanced down at the intersection.

The booth was empty. The door swayed in the breeze. The man who was once there was there no more. He'd wave at her some days when she'd get home from school, always smiling, tipping his head like they did in old black and white movies. *Gentlemen,* Sandi had called them. Sandi was her babysitter before. She'd bring her food and play games with her and keep her company when Dad was at work.

But she would be gone soon, just like everyone else in the Fringe.

Everyone except her and Dad.

The security booth door smacked the concrete pole next to it, the plastic banging over and over in the wind.

"Where'd they go?" she asked herself.

Traffic to the wall had slowed lately. She barely saw trucks go in there anymore. Maybe once a week? Or was it a month now?

She glanced back in the living room window.

Dad was still sleeping.

Curious, she set her reel down on the porch fence, then trotted down the steps, making her way across the street to the wall.

She eyed it suspiciously, her father's words echoing in her head.

It's dangerous. In fact, don't even go on that side of the street. Ever. You hear me, kid?

Weird plants were growing over the surface, hanging down like vines. Only they weren't like any vines she'd ever seen. These ones were weird colors, like they couldn't make up their minds about what they wanted to be. There was some sort of slime on it, too. Gobs and gobs of the stuff oozed down from the top.

"Gross," she said, making a sour face.

She tiptoed along the face, eclipsed in the shadow of the great wall, at last reaching the booth.

"Hello?" she called.

But it was no use. The man inside was gone just like everyone else.

A heavy grind, like a million pounds of rock being dragged along the road.

The wall began to shake, then move.

The door—it's opening!

She had to hide. She looked around desperately, trying to find somewhere, anywhere at all, but there was nowhere. No place to go.

She dropped down to her hands and knees as the door ground to a stop. She felt the earth shudder beneath her, her heart galloping in her chest. She peeked her head around the side of the booth, mind racing, imagining what might lay on the other side.

A gust of wind roared into her face, spraying her golden hair in all directions. The force almost knocked her over, but she latched onto the side of the booth, the vibrations rattling through her hands and feet.

She gasped as a shower of sparks rained in her direction. She recoiled away, watching as a black blur rumbled by on the other side of the booth.

A black truck. A monster. Bigger than all the others she'd seen come and go from this place in all the months the wall had been there.

A loud bang, like the ones that exploded in the night sky during Fourth of July.

Then another.

The truck weaved across the road drunkenly, narrowly missing the booth, strewing a trail of smoking wreckage behind it.

A flash of light lit up the rear of the truck with a crack so loud her ears popped. The truck groaned, swaying, then abruptly veered the other way, the engine screaming.

Her eyes went wide as the tires (which were as tall as her if not taller) jumped the sidewalk, the truck mowing down a row of parking meters in a hail of change.

She gasped, watching the amazing scene play out in front of her.

The truck collided with the barbershop's glass facade in a spectacular crash of metal, drywall, and glass, sending a shockwave of debris rolling down the street like an entire block had been demolished.

She ran into the street, into the dust and the smoke in complete and utter amazement, mindful of the debris littering the road, and stopping in the middle of the intersection. She looked down at the road and saw dozens of little pieces of metal, some of them scorched black.

She folded over and scooped one up in her hand, taking it between her fingers and holding it up to her face.

She squinted, her ocean blue eyes noticing the smooth metal was golden, so polished she could see her reflection looking back at her.

Heat. Building in her fingertips. She saw ribbons of dirty smoke coming from inside the brass casing.

Her fingers bloomed with white-hot pain.

"Ouch!" she said, flinging her hand, the thing flying back to the street. This was getting to be too much. But she looked at the wall again and remembered that nothing exciting happened here anymore.

Dad was sure to be up now. If the bangs hadn't woken him up, the crash would have for sure. Well, at least if she was going to get into trouble, this spectacle had been well worth it.

She started to make for the apartment and her foot kicked something heavy, nearly breaking her toe.

"Ow!" she shouted, limping on one foot.

She dropped down, massaging her toe, examining the thing at her feet.

It was black. No bigger than a suitcase. The container reminded her of some sort of a safe, where you'd put something valuable, like diamonds or money. There were machined panels reinforced with smooth round bolts all around the edges.

She bent over, reading the stark white paint stenciled on the side.

CROW CORP.

"Crow Corp…?" she whispered. What the heck was that?

She tugged on the lid, but it didn't budge.

"What the heck," she said, perplexed.

She looked up, scanning the streets, but she was alone.

The coast was clear.

She grabbed it around the edges with both hands, using her legs for leverage and flipping it over. Or so she thought.

The top half flopped open, slamming onto the road, and judging by how heavy it was, it might as well have been a box of bricks.

She gazed down into that hulking black container, a wash of brilliant gold bathing her youthful face like she'd discovered an ancient tomb.

Her pupils dilated.

Her breath hitched, caught somewhere in her chest.

Tucked inside all that gold housing was the most beautiful thing she'd ever seen.

And it was all hers.

Prologue: Part II
ISABELLE

THREE MONTHS LATER.

The jet punched through the clouds, rocketing through the dead gray sky like a falling star.

Ever since the day the house had come, Winterview had been submerged in perpetual winter. Ash constantly wafted through the air as if the city burned. Creeping mist wandered the streets. Tourists and Winterview residents alike thought twice before traveling down any alleys, or side roads.

Isabelle Busoni admired her reflection in the window. Flowing raven hair. Olive green eyes. Flawless tanned skin. And a figure most women would kill for. Truth be told, it was hard to imagine a time she'd looked better. Of course, looking this good wasn't hard with your own personal chef and trainer. One of the many perks of being born into a wealthy family.

It was like flying over an active volcano. In her mind, she was somewhere else. Somewhere exotic. She imagined looking out the window and seeing a shimmering sea of blue instead of the dreary world she'd come to know these last twenty-six years. The child in her stirred then, and a spark of excitement flickered in her heart. How many times had she left the country? She could count the times on one hand. Money wasn't the problem. So, what *was* the problem then?

The jet lurched and she nearly smacked her head on the wall. She looked around the inside of the cabin, quickly pulled back to reality.

The Eclipse 550 would have been incredible to anyone else, but to her, the novelty had worn off long ago. One of her mother's private charter jets, the aircraft seated five passengers (not including the pilot), sported leather seats, and had a max speed of four hundred thirty miles per hour. With a price tag to the tune of three million dollars no less. It was a smooth ride, though, she'd give it that.

She looked toward the cockpit, where flecks of ash fluttered past the windshield. She drummed her nails on her thigh as the glass of Chardonnay rattled on the pullout tray in front of her. She leaned closer to the round window and peered down, catching sight of the city below.

They were passing over Winterview City.

Dozens of skyscrapers formed the apex of a doomed metropolis, one with a cancer festering at its heart. The concrete world drifted in and out of hollows in the clouds, and the thought of the city disappearing entirely made her happier than she thought it would.

There was another break in the clouds and she squinted harder. Her father's former headquarters. She'd recognize that hideous building anywhere. Painted a dull gray and smothered in rust, it stuck out like a sore thumb, a once-beautiful thing that had rotted along with the rest of the city. Apparently, nobody had attempted to salvage it after her mother relocated their base of operations to New Haven.

She knew somewhere in her heart that her mother was partly responsible for what was happening. *Before* the house had come, anyway. Now she had been vindicated. At least in her own mind.

The plane dropped and she felt her stomach fly into her throat.

Her hands clamped down on the armrests like a vice.

The pilot, a silver-haired man in a baseball cap whose name she didn't care to learn turned back to her, confident as could be, and said, "Just a little turbulence, nothing to worry about."

She picked up the glass and swallowed what was left.

Goddamn you, she thought.

They shouldn't have come this way. Her intuition told her so and it hadn't failed her yet.

She'd left that morning straight from her penthouse in New Haven. Her mother had a private jet on standby and a chauffeur waiting to bring her straight to the airport. The world had been exquisite that morning, even by seasonal standards, but as they'd drawn closer to Winterview the skies had dulled to a steely gray. She was so wrapped up in her own head that she'd completely forgotten that her flight to Boston passed right over Winterview.

Her skin suddenly felt clammy. She shifted in her seat, turning away from the window.

A sweaty, plump hand laid itself on her own and a chill ran through her.

She looked up to see the flabby face of Paulie DeFalco leering at her. Dark eyes were set too far back in a face wrapped in the oiliest, saggy skin she'd ever seen.

"You got the jitters, Bell?" he asked. His New York accent was thick, and some part of her couldn't help but be amazed that he, by some fluke of nature, had passed the bar. His slicked back hair. Expensive, tan suit that virtually matched his complexion. A gaudy gold bracelet opposite a Rolex. The man didn't have a single redeeming factor about him.

Isabelle pulled her hand out from under his and shook her head, turning back to the window. "Hardly. Just eager to get this over with."

"Well, if you do, just remember, I'm right here," Paulie said with a wink. He ran his fat tongue over his flaky lips while he ogled her like she was the juiciest steak he'd ever laid eyes on, then went back to work on a glass of brandy.

She wondered: If her mother knew about his not-so-subtle advances, would she have had him killed years ago?

At this point, nothing would have pleased her more. But as fate would have it, her conscience had other plans. After all, Paulie DeFalco had gotten her family out virtually hundreds if not thousands of potential charges.

She thought back to the first time she'd been arrested. She was sixteen-years-old. Her and Nanette Engel, a childhood friend, had managed to sneak away from the home she'd grown up in. She'd intentionally left her phone in her bedroom and Nanette had her new convertible BMW waiting down the street. From there it was off to every fashion outlet they could find.

They ended up at the mall, where they spent a few hours hitting all the major spots before ending up at a Macy's. As the clock wound down and her anxiousness grew over her father's reaction, Isabelle stuffed a beautiful suede wallet, tag and all, into her jean jacket pocket.

They'd been not two steps from the exit when security had stepped out from behind the clothes racks. There was a shred of disbelief there, and as she was being arrested it was almost a surreal moment. Here she was, one of the richest, most spoiled teenagers on Earth who could have anything she wanted if she only asked, but instead, she'd went out of her way to steal it instead. If you asked her, she couldn't tell you whether it was because she liked the rush it gave her, or because of the power she felt doing it. But she knew one thing: she loved both equally.

Her mother and father eventually came to the station to pick her up with their entourage, Paulie in tow.

Paulie had walked into the interview room and seen her, ogled her with a funny look in his eyes, as if he'd noticed something different about her. She'd matured, grown in ways young women do, and by the way he was staring at her then, she could tell he no longer saw her as his boss's daughter, but a woman instead. She'd stolen something, broken the law. Made the decision to do something she *knew* was wrong.

And now Paulie DeFalco was thinking about doing something wrong himself.

The officer stepped into the room a moment later and Paulie did his thing, smooth-talking people and greasing wheels the way he always did. They were out within an hour, no worse for wear.

Paulie DeFalco was merely a façade. If he failed in legal matters, she knew her mother and father had other ways of handling their problems. But, Paulie was always their first line of defense. Even now, as she soared over Winterview ten thousand feet up, nothing more than a white streak in the sky.

She listened as Paulie slurped his brandy. The sucking made her stomach turn and his cologne was so overpowering she considered breaking the window to get some fresh air.

Isabelle still didn't think her mother would hesitate to kill Paulie herself if she were so inclined. No morality among murderers, only principles. At least the ones she knew. She could have this man killed right as they stepped off the plane at the snap of her fingers if she wanted. Paulie deserved it, if anything. She'd only heard snippets of what he did in his private life, but that was enough to churn any woman's stomach. The only thing stopping him from doing the same to her was knowing what her mother would do to him afterward. Because loyalty only goes so far in this business.

The plane lurched violently. The empty wine glass whipped through the air and exploded.

"Christ!" Paulie yelled out. "What the fuck is going on up there?"

The pilot turned back. "We're heading into a storm, might want to fasten your seatbelts."

"How about a little warning next time, asshole?" Paulie said. "Can you believe this guy?"

A burst of lighting clapped outside the window.

"I can't see shit on this side," he said, and she could see the seatbelt fighting to restrain his bulky body.

Paulie unbuckled his seatbelt, squirmed out of his seat, and leaned over her. His bulging stomach nearly rolled itself onto her breasts and the thought sickened her. His aftershave was so cloying her eyes burned. She leaned back in the seat and was on the verge of shoving him away when his expression softened.

He said, "Huh, well would you look at that."

She looked out the window and there it was, just like all the news reports said it would be.

The house that fell from the sky.

There was something hauntingly surreal about it. She'd seen it on the news, heard stories piled upon stories of the events that had transpired there, but until that day she'd never laid eyes on the thing. While others had flocked to the city to catch a glimpse of the house, she had remained indifferent. Because there were always more pressing matters in the family. There always were. And now, seeing the mythical mansion from this vantage point, all she could feel was cold, dead fear.

Against all instinct, she leaned closer to the window for a better view.

A massive wall snaked its way through Winterview City, cordoning the house off from the rest of the world. The structure itself was more vast than she'd ever pictured in her mind. From a distance, the surface was quite a bit darker than the rest of the surrounding neighborhood. Nearly black, by her guess. She thought of her father's tumor, the one that had been positioned right on his brain, and couldn't help but draw a comparison. This hideous, ugly thing set into healthy tissue.

At least, it had been. Until a bullet had passed through his skull.

Not long after, her mother took over. And ever since the house's arrival in Winterview, her business dealings had suffered considerably. The hit had made itself apparent everywhere in Connecticut. Because nothing was beyond the house's grasp, no matter how far.

"I can't believe that fuckin' thing actually exists," Paulie muttered. "Figured it was some made up bullshit for the press."

Paulie turned to her, their faces mere inches apart. He looked her in the eyes and smiled out of the corner of his mouth. His breath reeked of alcohol, and she could see the tartar crusting his bottom teeth like barnacles. She supposed the thought crossed his mind then of acting on his most violet fantasies with her, but he knew the consequences would be far greater than the conquest.

Not that she'd let it get that far, anyway. She'd die first. Or go down trying.

Paulie's eye twitched and he heaved his body away, plopping back into his own seat.

An electrical vibration surged in the walls, and Paulie's bulbous head lifted into the air. "What the hell was that?"

Isabelle looked toward the cockpit, where the pilot was leaning forward in his seat, flipping switches. The man grabbed the radio, checking the settings.

Paulie and Isabelle exchanged a confused look.

"Hey! What the hell is going on? What's that noise?" Paulie said. "Hey! Are you hearin' me, asshole?"

The plane jerked hard to the left. Paulie's glass of brandy launched through the air and crashed into the wall with a weighty thunk. Isabelle and Paulie were thrown against their seatbelts like crash dummies. Her head collided with the wall and stars twinkled in her vision. Paulie half-screamed, half-grunted, folding over the armrest into the aisle.

The power groaned loud and long, like the cabin was on the verge of tearing itself apart. The metal creaked, and Isabelle closed her eyes and waited for the inevitable.

To her surprise, the plane shuddered like a dying animal, struggling to right itself. The motion settled right as the sound of rain touched down on the front windshield.

Heart racing, Isabelle opened her eyes to find the cabin intact. Paulie's sagging chest heaved, sweat pouring down his face.

She watched as the pilot holstered the radio, then looked back at them, the relief on his face telling them they had been about two seconds away from dying. Paulie gaped at him, flabbergasted, and Isabelle couldn't shake the feeling that things were about to get a whole lot worse.

The pilot smiled, giving them an ill-timed thumbs up.

The engines sputtered.

Paulie's face went white. "Oh shit."

Ash. It swayed down from the sky like tiny black snowflakes.

Was she dreaming?

Isabelle lay on her back, staring up at the clouds, watching it lazily drift through the air, blissfully unaware of the white-hot pain sizzling behind her eyes.

A fire crackled nearby like a campfire. The sound brought her back to her parents' villa in New Haven. When she was a girl, she'd lie there for hours with Duke—her pet Shar Pei. She'd let the warmth melt the redness off her nose, watch as the snow fell outside the windows and the logs charred until they fell apart in blocks of ash.

A man murmured.

Paulie? She meant to say the word but nothing came out. Her throat was bone-dry; she could hardly muster the energy to breathe let alone put two sentences together. She tried again.

"Hello?" The word came out hoarse and broken.

Whispers reverberated all around her. They sounded more like a dream at first, far away, but they carried on, rustling on all sides of her. A long mechanical groan sounded like some sort of gigantic machine was waking up.

She reached up and ran her fingers along her face.

Ash?

The plane!

Her green eyes went wide and she gasped, sucking in a sober, giant breath. She tasted smoke and kerosene. She opened her mouth to call for help but pain flooded in and she let out a choked sob instead. Her eyes glazed over with red, wet and shiny.

She rolled onto her stomach with a grunt and glass shifted under her weight.

The crackling of the fire kept on. The heat was coming from nearby. Only it smelled different here. It wasn't that smoky, burning woodsy smell you got in the wilderness when you roasted marshmallows. This was metallic, and chemical. Caustic, and acrid.

Isabelle pushed herself up and pain flared in her shoulder. She screamed through her teeth, staggering on a teetering world, steadied herself on some wreckage, and looked down at her hands. Dried blood crusted her palms and between her fingers, bits of glass jutting out of her skin like tiny diamonds.

How long had she been out?

Holding her breath, she dug the shards out of her hands, then flexed them to make sure she still retained movement.

The wind stirred. A cool breeze caressed her face. Her forehead felt wet.

She reached up and ran her fingers along her skin.

Blood.

Not enough to be life-threatening, but blood still the same.

What the fuck happened?

The area was smothered with fog and smoke.

She couldn't see a goddamn thing. She looked to the sky, where she could make out the distant shape of an eerie red sun veiled behind partitions of fog. The mist rolled past her as if it was alive, studying this fun new thing that had come to play.

Another mechanical clack. The world rocked. Her head turned into a dizzying mess and she staggered directly into the mouth of haze.

She was completely blind now. Nothing but fog and smoke and her own heartbeat in her ears. She could hardly see her own two hands in front of her.

"Hello?" she moaned.

The vapor seemed to hear her and contracted, thickening before her eyes.

"Paulie?" she said with a shiver.

The sound of voices began to grow. She heard whispers all around her. They came from everywhere and nowhere, carrying on like a head full of ghosts. They grew nearer, increasing.

Isabelle spun, searching for anything that could tell her she wasn't dead. That she wasn't going crazy, losing her mind.

"Is anyone there? Anybody?"

There!

A pulse of red was buried deep in the mist. She locked onto it and stepped forward. The gray seemed to sense her and quickly solidified, concealing it once more.

"Paulie, is that you?" She hacked into her elbow, wiping her mouth.

Bloody hands held out in front of her, she started forward. She worked her way into the swirling mass, tearing through layer after layer. Her head reeled as she moved, throbbing like the worst hangover she'd ever had in her life. The wind began to pick up, and the fog surged faster.

The crimson glow ahead smoldered brighter, and she quickened her pace.

"Paulie? Paulie, is that you?" She was shouting now.

The silence cracked wide open with a ticking.

It was faint—distant, but it was coming from somewhere nearby. She closed the gap between her and the light, and the mechanical count intensified, pounded in her head, clacking against the inside of her skull.

It sounded like a gigantic clock.

She was running now. The fog was thinning, sweeping over her face and tousling her hair as if she were a child. Her breaths were shallow and fast. The air rushed over her teeth and dried her mouth and throat.

She pictured herself ripping free from a spider's web. Her momentum expelled her from the fog in a splendid gust. Her arms pinwheeled and she lost her footing, colliding with the earth.

She held there a moment, aching face pressed to the ground, letting her heart settle.

A contorted face stared back at her.

She screamed, recoiling.

Paulie DeFalco stared back at her, his eyes pried wide open in terror, his mouth twisted open revealing a mouthful of silver fillings and a plump, dry tongue. His flabby neck was severed in ragged strips of flesh, his body nowhere to be seen.

A fly buzzed past her, landing on Paulie's eyeball, scuttling across it.

Isabelle gasped, scrambling away from the severed head.

One final chime quaked the earth; she felt it waver beneath her, radiating through her legs, sending a tremor up her spine into her skull.

The fog fluttered away like thousands of gray moths, revealing the massive blood-red face of an ancient clock, and before her: the silhouette of a house.

Interviewer: ...*but I think I only have one big question today, and I'm sure it's the same one that's been on everyone's mind. What really happened inside that house, Scarlett?*

Scarlett Vantassel: (inaudible). *It's funny, you know? Ever since we went into that house and came back out people seem to think we have some sort of big revelation, some answer about what it is, or why it's here.* (A pause) *But that's the thing, isn't it? Because even after everything that happened in there, even after what happened to Hannah, Vincent, and Tommy...well, I still don't know much more than before I stepped through those doors. All I know is they were my family, and it took them away.*

Excerpt from *Good Morning America*, January 3rd, 2015

NICK

ONE WEEK LATER.

The bell rang. Nick Webster listened from the shoebox-sized office as hundreds of ghosts, pirates, vampires, and witches poured into the hallways in fits of spirited laughter and screams, wondering where he'd went wrong.

"I don't understand," he said.

Nick looked across the desk at Principal Jennings, the head of Winterview Elementary. Long overdue to retire, Principal Jennings' face was more worn than a catcher's mitt, with leathery skin, glazed-over eyes, and a mouth fixed in a frown. Nick was surprised she could even see him sitting there, three feet in front of her. He wondered if the city had done this to her, aged her like an old raisin.

God, she looked miserable. And then he reminded himself that he probably didn't look much better. The nightshift had a tendency to do that to you, suck your soul out one minute as a time.

Nick leaned forward, digesting her words. He hoped he appeared moderately shocked, because that sure as hell wasn't how he felt. Being honest with himself, he was more surprised it took this long to get the call. The disappointment was still painful all the same. He'd gotten the call from the school around noon that day, only a couple hours into sleep. He'd pulled a double the night before at the decommissioned train depot, finishing up his rounds at the abandoned Winterview Mall. He'd come home, offered Sandi (the babysitter) forty dollars she subsequently declined, then spent the next half hour picking up toys and packing Rachel's lunch for school. A Capri Sun, peanut butter and banana sandwich (or sometimes grilled cheese), and a bag of Cheetos, all perfectly organized in a plastic SpongeBob lunchbox. It wasn't the delectable gourmet meals they'd been used to living next door to Sandi, but it was edible and more importantly cheap and that was enough for now.

He turned and gazed out the little window in the office door. Rachel was slumped in a chair in the waiting room, legs dangling, her attention off in the clouds somewhere beyond reality. His heart swelled watching her sitting there so patient and innocent, and he wondered what he did to ever deserve something so precious. He tried to imagine a world where the one good thing in his life had done anything worthy of summoning him to the principal's office. His love began to simmer and, before he knew what was happening, it was positively boiling.

"What do you mean, *behavioral problems*? What problems?"

The principal cocked her head. Did she know he was lying? She pitied him, that much he was sure of.

"Over the course of Rachel's time with us, her teacher has observed increasingly disturbing behavior," the Principal said. "Frankly, certain unusual tendencies among the children have been more commonplace lately for…obvious reasons. In that vein, we as educators have been especially cautious about what we believe is worth mentioning to parents, and what isn't. That being said, I'm sad to report that Rachel's behavior falls in the latter category."

"I see," Nick said. He was impressed with himself, staying as diplomatic as he was despite the powder keg inside him that was on the verge of exploding. Was he suppressing his anger? Or was he just getting good at learning to live with disappointments? He couldn't tell which.

He asked, "So what exactly is the problem then?"

"I know this isn't easy. Believe me. Every time I have to call parents down here to have one of these conversations, I wish I'd chosen any other job in the world. But at the end of the day, it needs to be done." The principal's face fell heavy with misery. She picked up a manila folder from the side of her desk, holding it out in front of her. "These are drawings Rachel has done over the last few months. It appears she's quite the little artist. Her teacher, Mrs. Tanner, has been saving them." She opened the folder, then handed him the drawings.

His mind ran wild with ideas, and he noticed he'd stopped breathing.

It's not what you think. A misunderstanding, that's all, he thought.

He held the drawings up, studying them.

Shit. The wind left his sails along with all the anger burning in the pit of his stomach, and all that was left was a sinking feeling like his ship was going down.

"Do you know what that is, Mr. Webster?"

Nick nodded, wiping the sleep from his eyes.

"And do you have any idea what would have motivated her to draw all of these?"

Nick nodded, leafing through the drawings. The lines at first glance appeared erratic, but as he looked closer, the more he realized that the skill required to have illustrated these was well beyond anything Rachel was capable of. Black walls. Red oriel windows. There was an unsettling quality about how precise the lines were; how symmetrical the drawing was.

"We live on the Fringe," Nick said matter-of-factly.

Principal Jennings was taken aback. "Oh, I'm sorry. I wasn't aware."

"She's had..." he paused, "*is* having, a really hard time with it. We both are. Its..." He composed himself. "You have *no idea* what it's like right there, next to that wall."

"I can only imagine. I'm sorry."

"It feels like every month is worse than the last," Nick replied. "We...we don't have any other option right now. We're barely scraping by as it is."

Principal Jennings eased back in her chair. "Isn't there family you can stay with?"

"No. No one."

"Surely there's someone?" she repeated. "Rachel mentioned a neighbor who likes to cook?"

"Sandi," he said, with an uncomfortable smile. This just keeps getting worse, he thought. "Our neighbor. *Was* our neighbor, I mean. She used to babysit Rach. She still does sometimes, but I think it's gotten to her too, living out there. She moved to Silvers Hollow a few months ago."

"I see," Jennings said.

"I am all she has," Nick said. "There is no one else. Nowhere to go."

"And her mother?"

Nick nearly winced at the word. "She's not in the picture. She died last year," he said. *You can't stop lying, can you?* "She—it's not important. She's gone. It's just Rachel and I now."

Jennings' face fell sadder yet. She sighed.

Nick shuffled the illustrations into the folder and stacked them back inside, laying the folder on the desk. "Could be worse, though, right? I mean...they're just drawings, right?" he asked with a wan smile.

The principal wouldn't make eye contact.

"It *is* just drawings, right?"

Principal Jennings turned to him. "Yesterday afternoon, Rachel's teacher, Mrs. Tanner, said she saw Rachel sitting in front of the closet."

Nick waited, a crinkle in his brow. He didn't like where this was going. Because he *knew* where it was going. She didn't have to tell him.

Jennings continued. "While the other children were working on their assignments, she claims that Rachel was speaking to someone inside the closet."

The bagel with cheese he had for breakfast rolled in his stomach. He stood up, anxiously rubbing the back of his neck. Everything had gone tight, and he thought of his father dying of a heart attack at fifty-two. Pain began twisting in his chest and he visualized the muscle being crushed between a network of giant cogs.

"Mrs. Tanner told her to finish her work, but she wouldn't move. She stayed there, sitting in front of the door. Staring at it. Talking to it."

He peered at Rachel through the glass. She looked angelic, arms folded in her lap, backpack at her feet. He wondered: *If Jennings told you Rachel murdered someone, would you still see her just as innocent? Just as precious?* He put his hands on the back of the chair and his fingers bit into the wood.

"After a moment, Mrs. Tanner asked Rachel who she was talking to, and do you know what she said?"

Nick shook his head. "No."

"She said she was talking to the man who lives in the house."

HARPER

DOCTOR MIRANDA HARPER gazed upon the Dead Zone, arms crossed, face twisted up in apprehension. The steely light gave her auburn hair a blood red tinge, framing a pale, milky face. Her wide, expressive eyes were set farther apart than most, giving her a strange, alien beauty. Her fingers caressed a small medallion hanging at the nape of her neck of the patron Saint Christopher. A gift from Katie on Mother's Day the year before last. The necklace hadn't left her body since. Showering. Swimming. Sleeping. The small piece of gold had become a part of her. Katie said it was to protect her, to keep her safe, and Harper found it curious. Maybe because she didn't ever see herself as being in danger. If you control yourself and your surroundings, you never leave anything to chance. It's only when you relinquish control that you're in *real* danger.

Harper sighed, closing her eyes.

Morning had come after another night of light sleep, and by noon she'd gotten the call she'd been waiting for. She'd been down at the park, there but not there, taking in what little sunlight she could while watching a lone boy and his dog brave the chill in the wind to watch his kite tear across the sky. One of the last few calm moments before the walk into a place she wasn't sure she'd come back from. She thought about Katie, remembered what it was like dashing alongside her while that goofy banana-colored kite whipped through the air. Katie's laugh ricocheted in her head painfully and Harper's eyes pulled shut. The smell of the grass and the air kicked up in that hollow space in her mind. Autumn leaves fluttered through the air as the kite snapped at the sky and suddenly her mind was reeling a million miles an hour.

Mom?

The word hit her like a slap to the face.

Her eyes shot open, and the Dead Zone stared back at her.

Katie wasn't here.

Because of you. Because of what you did. She's gone, far far away.

She could make out the perimeter wall a few blocks away.

Harper breathed quietly, looking down upon the dreary city from Outpost 12, one of nearly a dozen government installations built near the Fringe. Flakes of ash swept past the other side of the window, and Harper thought this might be what the world looked like if nuclear war had broken out. According to what they'd told her at the briefing, there were outposts *inside* the Dead Zone as well at one time, although Harper couldn't fathom the purpose *or* the need. Even at this distance, safely removed from the proximity nearest the structure, she still felt the slightest beginnings of nausea and a faint strain on her eyes. God only knew how the personnel inside would have felt stationed that close.

She couldn't see much, of course, even from this high up. Towering office and apartment buildings rose into the sky beyond the wall, disappearing into the fog. Once prime real-estate, everything abandoned inside the perimeter wall was now cursed as far as the rest of the city was concerned.

Not long after the PR disaster that was the Seventh Street Lottery, the military thought it fit to erect a twenty-foot concrete wall around the area surrounding the house. A notoriously bad idea, Harper thought. They couldn't fix the problem, so they did the only thing they could think to do and lock it away from the rest of the world. This area, deemed to be extremely hazardous by the U.S. government, was designated the "Dead Zone," a restricted area kept under twenty-four-hour surveillance.

But all Harper saw was a melancholy, concrete jungle.

Let it burn. Was it a little coldhearted? Maybe. Maybe a little cynical, too, even. But Winterview was long past its expiration date. If it weren't for the alarming number of deaths, she wouldn't have come at all. Maybe that wasn't exactly true. After all, this was a chance for her to prove to the world that there was an explanation, that this building didn't just fall out of the sky and land here like everybody seemed to think. These suicides weren't a coincidence. Something emanating from that building was causing the nightmare unfolding on the city. Cause and effect, the natural order.

She just had to find out what.

The air was stale with cigar smoke. Apparently indoor smoking laws didn't apply here.

Harper watched another chip of ash carelessly flutter down and brush past the glass.

It wasn't ash. They'd already analyzed it back when the house first came. No, it definitely wasn't ash, but that's exactly what it looked like.

A buzz on the intercom.

The young secretary smiled and said, "The Director will see you now."

Harper didn't return his smile. She moved past him, splitting the mahogany doors.

A man as rigid as he was tall rose from behind a desk as she entered, extending his hand. "My my my, Dr. Harper. They didn't tell me you were so tall. Thank you for coming."

She shook his hand with a sober tip of her head. "Of course."

"Please, have a seat," the man said, waving at a chair.

The man sported a military flattop, graying at the temples. His face was hard yet fair, a weariness carved into the canyons around his eyes. His dress uniform was impeccable.

Harper gave the office a quick once-over. A grimy window ran the length of one wall. Another wall had a length of bookcases that were mostly empty. And with the exception of a few framed credentials, not much else. It was obvious the man didn't spend much time here. The room was more for show, like a model home.

"My name is Robert Dawson. I am Director of the Red Sky and all operations therein. I apologize for my lateness, but there were some matters that required my personal attention in the Midwest."

Harper sat with her legs crossed, hands folded in her lap, her face impassive.

"People all seem to think the world revolves around that big eyesore out there, but let me tell you, there's a lot more going on than they know," Dawson said. He got up and walked to the counter, holding up a glass.

Harper shook her head. "No, thank you."

He shrugged, "Suit yourself." He picked up a crystal decanter, pouring two fingers of brandy. His back to her, he took a few slugs, swallowing what was in the glass, then set it in the sink.

Dawson said, "I trust your training went well?"

Training, Harper thought. A joke is what it was. Part of the stipulations for joining the expedition inside the house was undergoing the Red Sky's personal training program, which included a crash course in first aid (for her colleagues more than her), firearms, and survival.

"More or less," she answered.

Dawson cleared his throat. "I was informed that you have been made privy to the details of this...assignment, and have accepted the terms. Can I assume that also means that you have been made aware of the situation inside the Dead Zone?"

Harper nodded.

"Well then, on to business," he said with an artificial smile. "What is it that you needed to discuss?"

Harper looked him straight in the eye. This wasn't a man that was used to being told no. She didn't see this conversation going over well.

"I think we should postpone the mission."

"Postpone it? Why in the hell would I do that?"

"Over the past three months, we've been analyzing the data you provided."

"And?"

"We've been unable to find anything conclusive thus far."

Dawson scoffed. "You're shitting me?"

"No. I'm afraid not."

"*Nothing*?" he asked, strumming his fingers on the desk. "And the subject?"

Harper's gaze fell away for a moment, then returned to him. "I've done extensive testing in the hopes that there was even a small chance of cognitive function, but all attempts have remained unsuccessful. The subject remains nonresponsive. I've spent hours with him but it's getting us nowhere. The patient has consistently failed to respond to external stimuli as well. We're wasting our time."

Dawson nodded as if he already knew and agreed with this. "Well, it was worth a shot. I'm sure you gave him a hell of a lot more chance than those other shrinks." She never did care much for the term.

Harper smiled, then said, "It is my recommendation that the expedition be postponed until further data can be collected, at which time we can reevaluate our options for how to proceed safely."

Dawson looked at her as if she'd gone insane. He laughed from the pit of his stomach, rising from his chair and pacing to the window. A silence fell over the room.

"Do you know why there's no cars down there in the street, Dr. Harper? Why there's no people? Do you know why this *building* is in fact empty at this very moment?"

Harper waited for him to speak.

"It's because nobody, and I mean *nobody* can figure out what the fuck is going on out there. The CDC. The Army. Nobody has a clue. I'm sure you're already well aware of this, but the government does not want to feed the stories surrounding this place any more than they have to, and I don't blame them. Especially after that circus that happened down the street. So, what do they do? They distance themselves from it by calling in a very special, very clandestine outfit for the sole purpose of babysitting this disaster. And what is this little organization called you might ask? You guessed it: the Red Sky."

Harper watched as Dawson turned around, easing back into his leather chair.

"I think it's safe to say that if you haven't figured out those samples you've been looking at; you're not going to."

Harper arched an eyebrow.

"You gave it the old college try, but if the United States Army couldn't do it, I don't think you had much chance either."

"Then if you don't mind my asking, what exactly are we doing here?" She masked the irritation in her tone well enough, but she was sure some of it must have spilled out.

Dawson leaned back in his chair, steepling his fingers. "You are here to investigate the structure and substantiate any of the claims made by Scarlett Vantassel and Jackson Briggs, and to assess the team's mental condition once inside the premises. That is all."

"Why are you sending us? Why not special forces?"

"This is strictly a 'scientific expedition,' Dr. Harper. There are no known hostiles, no confirmed threats, and thus, no known danger—other than ghosts, of course," he said with a crooked smile. "There will be no automatic weapons or trigger-happy soldiers running around. Just you and your wits and whatever the fuck it is out there."

"There's something you're not telling me."

"You're good." Dawson chuckled, nodding. "Let's just say that this won't be the first expedition inside the Dead Zone. *Or* the house. All previous attempts have been met with failure, and it has been decided by the powers that be that a less...*trigger-happy* approach is needed, which is exactly why you're the one sitting in that chair right now."

"'Been met with failure?' Forgive me, Director, but I presume that's a polite way of saying they're dead? Would this be due to the biological phenomena you've casually dismissed?"

Dawson shook his head as if he didn't know what she was talking about. He slid out his desk drawer and dug out a hearty cigar. Dawson ran it under his nose, inhaling. He grinned at her, lighting the end with a match. "One of the greatest things ever created by man, if you ask me. Smells a little bit like heaven."

"Surely you've noticed the particles carrying on through the atmosphere?" Harper said, motioning at the window.

"The air has been checked time and time again for carcinogens and every other potentially life-threatening pollutant known to man. Every one of them has come back clear."

"So, what is it?" she probed.

Dawson shrugged, casually brushing it off. "Don't know. But if it's not dangerous, then it's not my problem."

Harper craned her neck to the window, watching the black specks dance through the air. Something wasn't sitting right.

"Has it occurred to you that the atmosphere may be causing the behavioral changes in Winterview's population?"

"Sorry?"

"Seasonal affective disorder. In most people it's characterized by less-than-ideal amounts of sunlight."

"You think people are offing themselves because of the weather?"

"Not the weather itself, but the ash combined with the clouds and fog could be causing—"

"Whoa, whoa, whoa," Dawson said, holding his hands up. "Let me stop you right there."

Of course. He didn't want to indulge her by listening to important details. It was evident he didn't want to know anything at all. He was planted here to make sure everything went according to plan. A nice game of Pass the Buck. Do your job, and do it well, then it becomes the next person's problem.

"*Look*, Doctor, clearly people are not thrilled about whatever is going on out there. Hell, if I lived here I'd probably want to jump out a window, too. The people are scared. They want answers. So do we. So, barring any theories you might have, they are absolutely useless to us until you go inside and find out what the fuck is going on. Is that clear?"

"Crystal."

"Good. Then we're on the same page. I apologize if I'm curt, but we all want the same thing here."

Harper could see that buried somewhere underneath his callous exterior there was a sincerity too, regardless of how much of an asshole he pretended to be. It was the power. It got to their heads. A large number of the patients she'd had on her couch over the years told her so themselves. CEOs. Surgeons. Police Officers. People in positions of authority like the power that comes with it. Most didn't abuse it, but that's not to say they didn't enjoy it.

So, it was true, then. The government was just as desperate as the rest of the world to find out the truth.

She checked her watch. She was running late.

"I'm sorry, I have to go. I'm giving a keynote speech in an hour."

"Ah, yes, I heard on the news. That's a hell of a drive," Dawson said, standing. He extended his hand once more. "Thank you for coming, Doctor."

Harper nodded. "Good day."

"Doctor?" Dawson called out to her.

She turned and looked back at him.

"If there's anything you think you can do to save this city…" He paused, and she could see the fear in his eyes, however subtle. "Do it. Time is running out."

NICK

THE SCOOPER CARVED into the vat of Chocolate Chip Cookie Dough.

"What happened?" he asked. "I thought strawberry and vanilla were your favorites?"

Rachel shrugged, watching the girl peel up another mound of ice cream. "Chocolate is."

"Since when?"

Rachel didn't answer.

For an ice cream parlor, it was a lot hotter than Nick would have thought. His back was drenched in sweat. He unzipped his hoodie and stuffed it into one of their bags.

The shop was empty. The scent of sugar cones and sweets and frost lingered in the air, every vacant seat and table nothing more than a barren memorial to a once thriving business. The floor was faded checked tiles, the walls and furnishings fashioned in pink and brown. Perched on the top of the ice-cream freezer was a ceramic black cat holding a butcher's knife and a dead fish. At the opposite end was a hollow plastic skull stuffed with crumpled dollar bills and loose change.

He remembered bringing Rachel here as she'd grown. They'd stop by on the drive home from Hartford and get double scoops. Nick didn't like ice cream much, but he did love those few treasured moments with her, when he'd hand her the cone and she'd look at him like he was her own personal superhero.

And it was always one scoop of strawberry, and one scoop of vanilla.

Always.

He'd expected her to change as she got older and the hormones kicked in, but not *this* early. She wasn't even eight yet for God's sake. Puberty was miles off. So, what the hell was the problem then?

Nick and Rachel watched as the cashier—a scrawny girl in braces with a face angry with acne—peeled away globs of buttery ice cream, mounding them on top of each other.

She handed the second waffle cone to Nick, and he held the other out to Rachel. "Here you go, Spanky."

Rachel's disengaged face lit up. He couldn't ever imagine getting tired of seeing the wonder in her eyes. He hoped there never came a day when that went away, no matter how old she got.

Nick took the change from the cashier. "Thanks," Nick said with a weak smile, shoving two dollars in the tip jar.

They stepped out of the parlor into the gray afternoon. They sat down in the outdoor patio area, which was decorated with metal tables and chairs overgrown with rust.

Nick looked over at Rachel, the conversation with Principal Jennings agonizingly fresh in his mind.

How did things get this fucked up? he thought to himself. *You can't ignore it forever. And the worst part is you knew you couldn't but you went and tried anyway and look where that got you.*

Nick set the bags on the table and leaned back in the chair, feeling every sore muscle and worse: the damage to his paternal ego. Every parent thought their child was perfect, and he was no exception. But that gut punch moment when someone confirms otherwise? Well, that wasn't a feeling Nick wanted to get used to.

He took in a long breath, gazing at the horizon.

Where the sky should have been was a river of hostile clouds instead. He tried to recall the last time he'd seen the sun, but he couldn't remember. No, now all he could remember was the gray. A cold colorless dome had fallen over the city and never left, leaving them trapped inside a snow globe.

A horn blared, jerking Nick out of his musings.

The air was fresher here, away from the Fringe. Plus, at this distance from the apartment, he didn't have to worry about the ash. Sometimes it carried down to this block if there was a steady wind to ride, but for now the weather had died down.

They calmly watched vehicles pass by on the street. Rachel appeared fascinated, nipping small chunks out of her treat as traffic zoomed by, throwing sprays of fall leaves into the air.

After he'd picked her up from school that morning, they'd driven to the outskirts of the city so Rachel could pick out a costume. He'd promised her they could pick one out last month after they'd received mailers advertising Winterview's new plan for tackling Halloween. The school had sent out reminder cards about the school's annual Halloween carnival being canceled that year, so this was Winterview's contingency plan.

Nick thought maybe that would deter people from commencing with the celebrations, but as it turned out, it didn't make a damned bit of difference. While half of Winterview decided that it was in bad taste to celebrate All Hallows' Eve with the mounting deaths happening throughout the city, the other half apparently couldn't have cared less. They'd still carried on with Halloween traditions, carving jack-o-lanterns and hanging plastic skeletons from their porches as their neighbors offed themselves in record numbers. The city had spent a whopping 350,000 dollars to fund a massive Trick-or-Treating festival called the "Ghost Walk," where families could congregate and drink and dance as far away from the Fringe as humanly possible without having to remember what was lurking a few miles down the road. The event was to be held at the outdoor promenade along the pier for safety reasons. Dream Fair, the amusement park that took up residence on the boardwalk, had been closed since last year, and had been selected to be the perfect location for the event. Mayor Sloan had made the Ghost Walk his top priority in the hopes of reawakening life in the city, which at that point in time had died on the table.

Nick knew that regardless of the event there would be the usual mischief makers running amok in the streets, wreathing the trees with toilet paper and egging cars and windows. He'd done it himself back in high school, but those days were long past, and he had someone else to think about now. He wondered how much different his life would have been without Rachel. Would his life have been better? It was a shitty thing to think about. Did all parents ask themselves that same question at some point in their lives? Think about what could have been?

Don't think like that. It might be okay for some people, but not for you. You'd be lying dead in a gutter somewhere with a hole in your head if it weren't for Rachel. Quit feeling sorry for yourself.

He looked across at Rachel, watching her devour the ice cream.

Bribery. It was one of the most useful tools in a parents' arsenal. You need a child to cooperate, you bribe them with something. A new toy. Longer cartoon viewing time. Later bedtime. Or in this case: ice cream.

He was more than a little ashamed. But he'd tried everything else. What was he supposed to do? How many other parents had to bribe their kids to get them to listen? How many didn't? How many could ask and they'd oblige like perfect little angels, like they were living in some perfect world where everyone did everything they were supposed to do *how* they were supposed to do it.

Rachel had always been quiet. Even when she was a baby. She didn't coo and make cute baby sounds like most infants. She watched everything happening around her. Wasn't it only natural that she had an imaginary friend?

Principle Jennings' words replayed in his ears.

She said she was talking to the man who lives in the house.

A shudder ran through him. Jesus Christ.

Children have imaginary friends all the time, don't they? Maybe she's talking about a different house? No, he shook his head. *You know exactly which house she's talking about.*

Nick cleared his throat. "So, Rach," he began. "Do you know why

I was talking to your principle today?"

Rachel bit a chunk off the waffle cone, nodding.

"You do?"

"Yup. Mrs. Tanner thinks I'm crazy. The other kids do too."

Nick's mouth hung open. He wasn't expecting this kind of response. He figured she was oblivious, but apparently not. "Crazy can mean a lot of different things," he explained. "I think she's just a little curious about your imaginary friend."

Rachel looked at him oddly. "What imaginary friend?"

"The one in the closet. Your teacher says you've been talking to an imaginary friend in the closet."

Rachel giggled.

"What's so funny?"

"Mrs. Tanner," Rachel said. "She's so funny. I don't have an imaginary friend."

"Oh." Nick felt relief wash over him, his face spreading into a smile. "Yeah, right," he said, clearing his throat. "That's what I said too—"

"My friend is *real.*"

Nick's smile dissolved into a frown. His left eye twitched, and he had to stop to make sure he'd heard her correctly.

"What?"

"My friend," Rachel explained, "the one that lives in the closet. He's not pretend, Daddy—he's real. Sometimes he talks to me from my bedroom closet, too, when it's dark. He mostly only comes out when it's dark. He says he likes it when the world is asleep. When he can visit and nobody will bother him."

A snake slithered up his spine, the sweat coating his back icing over.

Rachel said, "He likes the dark."

"He?"

Rachel turned, nodding. He saw the sincerity and unabashed truth and it scared him to death.

"Mm-hmm..." she said. "He says his name is the Boogeyman."

The little food that was in his stomach dissolved to acid; he felt bile creep up his throat. His mouth hung open in a moment of incredulity.

"Daddy?"

Nick turned to her. He couldn't get any words out.

"Who's that man in the funny white costume in the window?" she asked with a giggle, pointing across the street.

Nick followed her eyes to the other side of the street, landing on an empty window in an abandoned apartment building.

"Where?" he asked. "I don't see anything."

"Oh," Rachel said, squinting. She paused from eating her ice cream, suspicious, then her eyes relaxed a little and she shrugged. "That's funny. I guess he left."

Oh, God. Is this actually happening? She's not only hearing people in the closet but now she's seeing *them, too?*

This had gone far enough. It was time to call someone. But who? What was the protocol for something like this? He didn't have the faintest idea where to start.

How about Google, you idiot?

A feeling of dread settled over him as Rachel finished the ice cream cone. She swallowed the last bite, then stood up and collected the smaller bags from the table, composing herself the way an older woman would, straightening her hair and sleeves and wiping her mouth with a napkin.

Nick's unease settled marginally. Rachel was surprisingly mature for a seven-year-old. Hell, maybe *that* was the problem? Maybe she was getting bored. Maybe what she needed was more stimulation in class. Something more advanced. After all, she always turned in her work on time and never missed an assignment. She never even asked him for help with her homework come to think of it. She was a good student if he'd ever seen one. A far cry from himself in school, thank God.

A model student and they're giving me grief for having an imaginary friend? Fuck it.

She needed to talk to a professional. Let them figure her out. Cleary whatever he was doing wasn't working for a damn, and at this point he was only going to exacerbate the problem.

He stood up, grabbing the rest of the bags off the table.

They began walking along the sidewalk, side by side, Rachel

humming to herself, him awkwardly trying to juggle the bags.

The shadow of an abandoned skyscraper spilled over them.

Nick felt the temperature drop a couple degrees as the world went a shade darker.

"Daddy?" Rachel said.

They slowed, stopping in the middle of the sidewalk.

"What's that noise?"

He glanced around the city streets.

Empty storefronts and buildings. Abandoned cars.

Wait.

There.

Now he heard it. It was faint at first. A high-pitched droning.

He scanned the sidewalk, glancing up and down the sidewalks.

"Yeah," he said. "What is that?"

The sound climbed, growing louder by the second.

He turned, peering around as it increased rapidly.

"I don't—"

The sound morphed into a scream. Nick turned his head skyward in time to see a writhing body break from the clouds. He instinctually ducked down, seizing Rachel in his arms.

The body, shrieking, broke through the clouds, colliding with a passing car like it had been hit by a meteor. The sheer force exploded in his ears and he felt like his eardrums had ruptured. The car's windows detonated, showering them with glass. The car horn instantly went off as the car swerved off the road.

Nick sprinted out of the way, swinging Rachel in his arms just as the car jumped the sidewalk.

The wreckage weaved past them, he could see the roof sunken in, a bloody mess of bone and human hair. The car careened forward, mowing a path through the ice cream parlor's outdoor patio furniture, where they'd been seated moments ago.

A muffled shriek escaped the shop. Nick spotted the cashier standing behind the front window, frozen.

Her eyes found Nick only long enough for him to see the terror there.

"Run!" he yelled, waving his arms.

She was too petrified to move.

The rolling mass of corpses and metal veered wildly toward her.

No time.

"Get outta there!" Nick screamed, his eyes crazy and frantic.

A magnificent clatter of glass erupted, followed by the sounds of a building giving way and, when Nick looked back, the front of the store was gone.

And the cashier was too.

HARPER

HARPER LOOKED OUT at the impatient crowd before her.

She was the guest of honor. Keynote speaker and *the* authority on the house. And playing for a packed house, no less. Far more than she'd ever seen in her career before. Every seat was filled, with some students even crowding the exits and standing alongside the staircases. The lecture hall reeked of sweat and cheap body spray and even though the air was nearly frozen, she could still feel beads of sweat skating down her stomach. The projector beamed at her with a burning white light and, standing there before them, she wondered if she'd made the right choice. After all, would it benefit any of them to learn more about something they could never truly comprehend?

"So," she began. She took in a steady, controlled breath, and her dark eyes blazed, "What do we know about the house that fell from the sky? And I don't mean what you heard from your sister's boyfriend's uncle's neighbor. I mean, what do we, the *scientific community*, know about the house?"

Dozens of hands sprouted from the sea of faces.

Her mouth curled into a pleased smile. *Well done, Doctor.*

Maybe she'd underestimated them? Maybe there was hope yet.

Harper pointed to a young girl in the third row.

"Um…that it's haunted?" the girl said with a valley girl twang. She giggled as she finished her sentence like she'd cracked a joke and the sound echoed loud in the auditorium.

A moment of silence hung in the air before the crowd erupted into fits of premature laughter.

Harper ran her tongue along her teeth and wondered if they'd noticed the unimpressed expression on her face. Her mood began to wilt like a dying plant and her face filled with blood. She couldn't see the girl's face all that well in the shadows, but she imagined her all the same. Blond, curled hair. Glossy lips. Perfectly manicured nails. The apple of every man's eye.

"Suppositions and hearsay," Harper said, "nothing more. Those are two things that have no place in science, and clearly, neither do you."

A collective gasp followed by a pause.

Harper waited, reveled in the silence, then said, "Get out."

She watched from the podium as the girl froze, clearly speechless. "But—"

"You've already wasted two minutes of our time together, and I'm sure your peers would appreciate the opportunity to hear what they've come here for."

Harper watched the silhouette. After a moment, the girl slammed her book closed and collected her things, storming through the packed aisles before the heavy metal door banged closed with a thud.

She'd dealt with this type before, the ones who liked to be the center of attention, make sly remarks all semester long then waltz in a half-hour late to lectures. She'd tolerated it the first three years of her career, but no more.

"Now," she said, "my time is valuable, as is yours. You are here for one reason, and one reason alone."

Harper took a small remote off the podium and the projector's shutter blinked, casting a wall-sized black and white panoramic image of the house behind her.

The restless students quieted, and she was left with nothing but the protracted moans of a harsh wind circling the campus. Harper beamed at their respect for the house, and her rotten mood began to freshen.

"I present to you, the house that fell from the sky. Or its actual name: the Halliday House."

Several stories tall, the house was a bizarre masterpiece of architectural genius, towering behind Harper as if they were right there on Seventh Street. The edges of the grainy image bled onto the connecting walls and awestruck faces in the aisles.

"I ask again: What do we know about this magnificent structure before us?"

More than a dozen arms shot into the air. Harper nodded her head at the second row.

A new female voice called out, "We know that it only opens on Halloween."

Harper nodded. "That's right. And can anyone tell me *why* it only opens on Halloween?"

The eager hands sunk back into the sea of bodies.

"No?"

Silence.

"Of course not. And that's because *no one* can. There is very little about the house that we know and even less that we understand. Even with all of today's advancements in technology, even with understanding the *tiniest* events happening right here in the universe," she pointed at the wall behind her, "we haven't even scratched the surface of what this building truly is." Harper turned to the wall and stepped forward, hands folded behind her, admiring the house.

She continued, "What we do know, is that exactly two years ago, on October 28th, two thousand fifteen, at approximately 3:00a.m., there was a light and notable seismic activity in Winterview. That's right, an earthquake, folks. *Several* earthquakes, more specifically, all registering above a 5.0 on the Richter scale, which, as any Winterview native knows, have been virtually non-existent until that night." She turned back to face them. "I myself was less than two miles from Seventh Street when the house appeared. The police drove right past my hotel window."

Harper paused, taking a few sips from a bottle of water resting on the podium.

"As of today, there have officially been a total of four people, *just four*, who have been inside the house and come back out," she said. "That we know of."

One of her students called out, "You're referring to Scarlett Vantassel and Jackson Briggs? The winners of the Seventh Street Lottery?"

Harper tried to discern who had spoken but quickly abandoned the idea.

"Yes, that's correct," she replied. "I'm sad to say that the only information we have been able to glean on the house has been pieced together from Scarlett Vantassel's abundant, and might I add, questionable interviews."

A round of murmurs fell in waves across the audience.

"I'm sure you've all seen them on YouTube. *Good Morning America*. Wildly entertaining, yes, I'll give her that. But, as you all know, she left the public eye and has been absent for some time now."

"You don't believe her then?" another student asked.

"Scarlett Vantassel was what we refer to today as an 'influencer.' Social media junkies. Some who even hold a dangerously large margin of power over their audiences. It doesn't help that her niche is horror fiction, which in itself damages her credibility."

Someone from the audience asked, "How does that hurt her credibility?"

"Come on, people, think about it. Beloved horror vlogger goes into an alleged 'haunted house' and returns with countless fantastic tales of terror. Ghosts. Monsters. Whole worlds of blood and flesh. Endless spooky things. Need I say more?"

"Her brother died in there. You really believe she did all that for publicity?"

"I've seen people do worse. And for the record, he is *presumed* dead. Which, as you know, is a hell of a lot different than actually *being* dead."

"You think they're alive?" the student pressed. "Hannah Maxx? The magician, Vincent Velladex?"

"There's nothing that says they're not drinking Mai Tais in Malibu this very second. After all, that little publicity stunt had a very substantial payout. Which is my whole point: It is irrelevant *what* I think. As I explained before, we need more than stories to find truth. And that is all Scarlett Vantassel has—stories."

"Some might argue that's better than nothing. Having someone with firsthand experience that's seen inside," another student replied. "Shit, you ask me, girl deserves a fuckin' medal."

Applause broke out in the crowd and Harper grinned.

"Maybe she does," she said with a tip of her head. "Maybe. But you all have to remember that science is about finding *empirical evidence*, something that, in this matter, has yet to be obtained. Don't get me wrong, I don't blame her. *Why*? Because our memories are terrible, terrible things. More often than not, the information we recall is flat-out wrong. Hugely inaccurate. Which, in Ms. Vantassel's case, makes for some messy interviews. Especially when they're live."

A quiet chuckle from her audience.

"How do you explain the photo?" a student's voice echoed down from the higher seats in the auditorium.

"Ah, I'm glad you asked," Harper said, clicking the remote and throwing a new image onto the wall. "The photograph. Found to be in possession of Scarlett Vantassel upon her exit from the house. Analyzed and confirmed by experts to be authentic, this photograph appears to be the single shred of evidence to substantiate her claims.

"According to Vantassel's testimony, these are the individuals responsible for the house's construction." She used a laser pointer to trace each as she went along. "Hugo Halliday. His wife Constance. Their daughter Vanessa. And this man in the derby is Hugo's brother, Herbert Bell. A brilliant architect in his days. All wealthy socialites in their time. The last evidence we have of them points to their disappearance in the late 1800s, long before the photograph is dated."

A twinkle shone in Harper's confident eyes. She had the audience eating out of the palm of her hand.

"I know what you're thinking. It is literally impossible for seven people to build anything even approaching this magnitude in anything shy of a century. And you're right. That's one of many things we don't know. But there's an even bigger, more important question: Where did it come from?

"And that is exactly why this photograph is so vital. Because it is the only shred of evidence that we have about the house's true origin."

Another question fired off from the audience, "Is it true that you're planning an expedition to the house?"

Harper put on her best poker face. She let them stew, relishing the moment, then said, "Yes, that is correct. Tomorrow, in fact."

Murmurs rose in the crowd.

Harper elaborated, "It's no secret that the house has caused considerable difficulties for Winterview City. As many of you know, last year the government erected a wall to cordon off the area most affected by the structure. While the military did attempt to control the situation there within, now known to us as the 'Dead Zone,' that control was lost due to unforeseen circumstances.

"To that end, the government has requested that myself, along with two other specialists, all experts in their respective fields, investigate the area, and more importantly, the house, to find out exactly what is happening there, and how those events correlate with what's happening in Winterview."

Another question fired off from the audience, "Why is the government sending a psychologist?"

It was a fair question. The same thought had occurred to her when she had first been approached about the expedition.

"I'm sure you all know by now that there is a certain...*stigma* surrounding the house."

"What stigma?" they asked.

"It is believed that those who come into close contact with the house experience varying degrees of psychosis."

The volume in the room began to ramp up, voices whispering. Speculating. Fueling the endless rumors about the house.

"However, as with most of the other information we have heard about the house, these theories are completely baseless."

"You still haven't answered the question."

God, they were impatient.

"My role on the team is to provide objective feedback on any and all data collected, and to monitor the mental health of the team and ensure that clarity is preserved while investigating the grounds."

A voice came from the shadows. "So basically, you're going to make sure no one goes crazy while you're there?"

More snickers among the onlookers.

Harper nearly rolled her eyes. "In so many words, yes."

"Dr. Harper, is it true you're an atheist?"

Harper rested her hands on the podium. "I am, yes. Although once again, my religious beliefs are completely irrelevant."

"You don't believe in God?"

"Next question, please," Harper said.

"What about the deaths?" The voice stood out amongst the rest. It was deeper, grizzled.

Harper froze. The Red Sky had instructed her not to make any official comment on the suicides. She had planned for this in her mind, knew it might happen. Probably best to avoid getting pulled into the grislier details surrounding the house, she thought.

"You conveniently left those out," the man said. He was older, maybe late-fifties, with a rasp to his voice, and Harper pictured tar-coated lungs and copious amounts of alcohol.

She peered into the darkness, watched a silhouette rise from the throng of bodies.

She decided to plead ignorance. "I'm not at liberty to comment on that at this time, but I will say that those are rumors, nothing more."

Spoken like a true diplomat.

"Over fifty men, women, and children died on Seventh Street on Halloween that year."

Harper shook her head. She brought her tone down a few octaves to let him know she wasn't wavering. "Again, those are unfounded rumors, nothing more."

"Another twenty-five had to be committed to Serenity Falls. That's the asylum in the Painted Mountains. That's where they sent the ones they found standing in the streets—staring up at the sky. There's rats in the walls there. In the cabinets with the food. It's a lovely place."

Harper began her rebuke, "There is no evidence that—"

"No evidence?!" the man snapped.

The man's sheer rage caught her off-guard.

"I'm sorry, I—"

"*No evidence*?" he shouted. A switch had flipped and his voice seemed infinitely loud in the lecture hall. The rest of the students were getting uneasy. She could hear their anxious movements. "And that's not even counting the suicides. What about those, Doctor. Harper?"

Harper tried to regain control, "The recession and cuts in Winterview's financial revenue have led to several tragedies. But that's *all* cities that have suffered through a recession all over the world. There's no proof—"

She could see the man as he shouldered his way past several students, arriving at the aisle. He was shorter than she imagined, wearing a filthy trench coat. She wouldn't be surprised if he'd rolled in off the street.

"Did you know that there were six deaths just this morning, Dr.? Six people killed themselves, and you think it's because of the *mall* closing down?"

Harper said, "It's easy to assign blame to—"

"These are the FACTS!" the man screamed. "Isn't that what you wanted?" He was moving down the aisle, advancing on the stage.

"Sir, I'm going to have to ask you to leave before I call security."

The man continued, "A mother cuts out her own eyes because she sees things other people can't see. Two more leap off rooftops right next to City Hall. Another man throws himself in front of the subway in front of nearly sixty people. His remains are smeared for miles along the tracks and, by the time they clean him off...well, there's nothing even left to put in the coffin for his kids to see. Nothing to bury. Nothing to mourn."

She felt her patience slipping but her hands had turned to wood and all she could do was watch him stalk closer to the stage.

"And today," the man said, climbing the stairs to the stage. "Today they find a seventh body, right here at the college." The man's voice trembled. He drunkenly stumbled out of the light and onto the stage, clearly exhausted and weak. Harper looked into his haunted, helpless eyes. He had a desperation in his eyes. A madness. One that she'd seen before. One that she recognized. The feeling terrified her. She tried but couldn't shake the thought she was about to die.

Harper attempted to speak, fumbling her words.

The man sighed, taking solace in her momentary loss of words. He decided that he was tired of her ignorance and indifference, reaching into his jacket pocket and pulling out a snub-nosed revolver.

Harper's eyes bloomed in terror; her heart began to shrivel.

A wave of gasps and panicked screams rose in the auditorium. Harper stumbled back, reeling with fear, colliding with the podium and falling to the stage. The microphone shrieked. Harper heard panicked breaths echoing in the high ceiling.

"You don't believe." The man stared down at her as he pulled back the hammer on the revolver with a hearty click and said, "But you will."

He put the gun in his mouth and pulled the trigger.

NICK

RED LIGHT WASHED over the destruction.

Daylight was escaping beyond the mountains, leaving the world gloomier by the second. The air buzzed and a chill crept over the city.

Nick stood on the sidewalk in front of an abandoned Verizon, a cellphone pressed to his ear, pacing through strobes of red. It was almost hypnotic, the whirl of the light. He listened as the other end of the line rang and rang.

"Pick up," he hissed. "Pick up pick up pick up."

An ambulance was parked across the street, obscuring the facade of destruction littering the ice cream parlor. The coroner's van was parked in front of that and beyond it two police interceptors.

Rachel sat on the rear bumper of the ambulance, watching the coroner wheel out a body bag on top of a stretcher, a blanket thrown over her shoulders.

Nick sighed, feeling the tension in his neck. *Christ, what a day.*

The phone line clicked.

"Hello?" a woman's voice answered.

"Oh, thank God. Sandi, it's me. Look, I know what you said, but I really, really need you tonight. Please."

A sigh. "We talked about this, Nick. Last night was the last time."

"*Please*, Sandi."

"I can't do this anymore with you." Sandi's tone was melancholy, tired. "Can't you call the agency?"

"Believe me, if I had any other choice I wouldn't be calling but I've been trying and trying and nobody will come out here. You know how it is, this entire city is completely fucked. People don't want anything to do with us ever since they built that wall. They're acting like we're goddamn lepers or something, and I don't know what to do."

A pause. Nick bit his lip. She was thinking about it.

Sandi Dornan. AKA, the babysitter. Before she was his babysitter, she was his neighbor. A chef by trade, she'd worked in some of the finest restaurants on the east coast including a few in Manhattan, where she'd racked up a reputation for her exquisite saffron sauce and insanely expensive white truffles.

Ever since the day he and Rachel moved in next door she'd been smitten. Sandi had a crush that put crushes to shame, bordering on stalking but never even remotely dangerous. The woman didn't have a mean bone in her body. In retrospect, maybe that was part of the problem. Since when did being nice become a character flaw? he thought. He didn't know what his type was, but nice definitely wasn't it.

He hadn't meant to lead her on. The babysitting thing wasn't even intentional, but he'd be lying if he said he hadn't taken advantage of her kindness a time or two. He'd even woken up with her a few mornings. She never appeared to mind. He always regretted it, blamed it on the drinks the night before. But that was how he was, impulsive as all hell, doing whatever he needed in that moment to minimize the hurt and get his mind off the bad things, gratify the needs that all people shared, Chef Sandi included. They'd wake up together and she'd look up at him with those amber eyes and white smile and he knew she wouldn't take the night back the way he wanted to. The fact was, he needed a helping hand with Rachel, and Sandi always seemed to be around. She'd pop up every time he stepped outside the door, was constantly bringing over fresh baked treats and new movies for him to watch. He didn't exactly twist her arm, either. She liked Rachel. She liked him. They liked her. Case closed. What was so wrong with letting her help out from time to time?

In the year since the house had come, Nick wasn't sure if Sandi had relocated to Silvers Hollow to get away from his chronic bullshit, or to escape the crumbling city. They'd been playing a game for years but she was getting tired of it. The house was merely the straw that broke the camel's back. He'd found it increasingly difficult to get her to watch Rachel as the months rolled on, and in an area condemned by the city no less. Sandi had floated the idea of bringing Rachel to her house in Silvers Hollow while he worked, but that proved impossible with the miles he was racking up on his truck. The money just wasn't there, and gas prices were skyrocketing. A week ago today, Sandi, caring woman that she was, had politely explained that she wasn't going to be doing anymore babysitting in the city, but left the option open should he change his mind. Last night was it. Or so she thought.

He'd taken her for granted. He knew that now. He'd managed to find an agency not long after she moved, but the rates were ridiculous and getting a sitter to come to the Fringe was next to impossible.

So here he was, throwing himself at her feet, pathetic beyond all hope and desperate to boot.

He pressed on, "I tried, Sandi. They can't get anyone to come on this short notice and they've barely got anyone as it is." He paused, running a hand over his buzzed blond head. "Look, I know what you said, and I'm sorry, okay? I don't have anyone else to call and I cannot miss my shift tonight, otherwise I may not have a job in the morning."

A pause on the other end of the phone.

"Sandi?"

An annoyed sigh. "Fine. I will do this and I will help you because I know you are trying to be a good father, but Nick—this is the last time. For real. This is not my problem anymore."

"Right, yeah. I understand. Thank you thank you thank you, Sandi. I owe you bigtime."

"Right," Sandi said.

"Wait," he said. "Sandi?"

"Yeah?"

"Thanks, Chef," he said.

Click.

Nick smiled and flipped the phone closed.

One problem at a time.

A gust of wind wafted through the road and over the sidewalks, dusting his eyes with polluted air laced with black flecks. The smell of rot and smoke drifted into his sinuses and his eyes watered. He held a hand up to his nose, fighting back the urge to vomit.

What the hell is that?

The breeze carried on through the street. The air hummed. His skin prickled with gooseflesh. The air was ice. The temperature felt like it had dropped twenty degrees in mere seconds.

He craned his neck up to a lamppost towering above the street. A swarm of large moths beat against the plastic housing around the bulb, making weighty little thumps. He zipped his hoodie up, checking his watch.

"Shit," he said.

When did it get so late?

He was going to need to get back soon if he was going to make it to work on time.

He watched as the shadows grew long and clouds suffocated the sunlight.

An eclipse?

The smell returned with a vengeance and he felt his body physically wince from the putridness of it all.

It was time to go. He needed to get Rachel.

His gaze fell from the sky.

The vehicles were gone. The streets were empty.

The wind stirred. Crumpled bits of debris tossed along the road past his feet. A newspaper slapped his leg, folding around it like a giant white bat.

He reached down and peeled it off.

His eyes widened. His pulse began to climb in his ears and he could have sworn he heard his blood moving throughout the network of veins in his body.

The front page of the *Winterview Times*.

Nick scanned the paper, finding a bold headline.

CITIES DEVASTATED BY CREATURES WHILE OCEANS RISE!!! Not far below on the same page was a second headline that read:

SUICIDES INCREASE WORLDWIDE!

"What the fuck?" he muttered. He pitched the newspaper away like some infected thing and it rode the wind down the road. He jogged forward, stopping in the middle of the street.

The wind breathed harder, cold and cruel.

Where the hell is the ambulance?

The lampposts flickered, threatening to cut out and leave him suspended in darkness.

He dashed forward, stopping in front of the ruined ice cream parlor.

The coroner and police were nowhere to be seen.

"Rachel?" he shouted. His voice echoed off the concrete buildings, fading, fading, gone.

The buzz climbed in his ears like two horseflies.

He flinched as the lampposts exploded one after another in shrieks of electricity, raining down tiny shards of glass.

"Rachel?"

An infinitely loud mechanical groan. He spun around, the faint whisper of a gasp escaping his throat.

The black sky pulsed into a blood-red ocean. He glimpsed ominous white hooded figures suspended against the crimson hellscape.

A shudder racked his body. He staggered back, nearly falling to the street. His mind couldn't rationalize what he was seeing, couldn't fathom what was in front of him.

The colossal wail rang out again, louder if that were even possible, and he sensed something enormous coming his direction.

The earth began to vibrate. He looked down and saw debris rattling, crawling across the road.

Glass shattered in the distance, loud and piecing. The faint sounds of destruction tore a path through the city. All he could do was stand and listen as it crashed through building after building as if they were nothing at all.

An animalistic, alien roar keened and his heart nearly exploded. The hooded figures remained unnaturally pinned to the sky, surreal and sinister.

A few blocks away, a building collapsed, groaning as it toppled from the horizon. A shockwave of dust and debris came toward him like a wave and, beyond that, the disturbing sound broke free from the obstruction, terrifyingly real and dangerously close.

And right as the thing emerged into view, Nick, standing paralyzed by hopelessness and fear, felt the cold bite into his hand.

A harsh snap in his ears, and then the world went dark.

HARPER

HARPER STOOD AT the intersection of Fourth and Hawkins, a black coffee in one hand, her cellphone in the other. It was almost dusk, and the fading sun warmed a gloomy sky, giving it an eerie scarlet hue.

Harper took a step forward.

In front of her: a twenty-foot-high concrete wall that spanned from one end of the street to the other.

The once busy intersection was all but deserted, sporting empty storefronts, sidewalks, and roads. The facade of a barbershop nearby had collapsed in on itself, a mess of rebar and wood. The only functioning vehicle nearby was her rental, which she'd left parked about a half mile back. She wondered at first if she'd been overly cautious, but reaffirmed her decision when she held up her cellphone and watched the screen erupt into an electronic seizure.

"I'll be damned," she said. "You were right."

She studied the screen, watched as it flickered with vibrant colors and hissed with static. She didn't normally carry a phone when she worked; too much chance for distraction. But, she'd brought it today merely to see for herself.

"Told ya," a voice said. "That means the options are going to be extremely limited. I'd be surprised if we'll get comms anywhere near the house. And even if we do, it'll be dead before we can use it."

Madison Park, a Korean biologist from Sacramento, California, was casually perched atop a rusted mailbox bolted to the sidewalk. She worked on a half-eaten cheese Danish.

"Mom?" The word was peppered with static, but the voice was unmistakable. Harper's heart nearly burst through her ribs, and she thought the world moved.

It came from the phone.

Harper held the phone up, disbelievingly watching the parade of lights breaking across the screen.

"Katie?" she said.

She quickly looked up to find Park eyeing her.

"What's wrong?" Park asked.

"I thought I heard Katie," Harper replied.

"Fuck," Park said. "I haven't seen that kid in years now. How's she doing these days?"

Harper smiled, finding the screen on the phone returned to normal.

"She's good, thank you." Harper wondered if she sounded as formal as she thought. Park didn't seem to mind, though. Maybe she had grown used to her after all these years collaborating together.

"Well, tell her I said hi. She grows a foot every time I see her again. She's going to be taller than you soon."

Harper shook the unease off like rain. She strolled further into the intersection, finding nothing but desolate buildings and empty roads. She stopped, standing in the shadow of the great wall, framed by a six-foot red symbol that had been crudely spray-painted across the concrete.

"Another one," Harper called back. "This is the fourth I've seen so far."

The red paint had faded considerably, washed out by rain and strained sunlight. Three vertical lines cut through a fourth, horizontal line, the center rising to a point like a primitive crown.

"Cultists," Harper said grimly. "As if the world didn't have enough problems already. Park, you ever seen this symbol before?"

"No, you?" Park talked with a full mouth, shouting from across the street.

"I believe it's the mark of the King in Yellow."

"King in Yellow? Isn't that something to do with a play?"

"Only in the vaguest sense," Harper said. "Tell me if you've heard this one; some abstract entity from some dark place in time. Causes madness in the minds of men. Drives people to do unspeakable things. Beyond that nobody really knows for sure. I think the King in Yellow is more of an idea, a concept, than anything concrete."

"Well, you'd know more about those wackadoodles than I would. I'm sure you've had a few of them on your couch at one point or another. They've probably got some sort of altar around here somewhere with goat heads and dead birds or whatever it is they do."

Harper chuckled. "And where exactly did you come by all this information?"

"Netflix, where else?"

"I hate to break it to you, Park," Harper said, her hands on her hips, "but most of those stories are made up."

"Tell that to that guy who got his head lopped off driving back from that wedding in Utah."

Harper pulled on a pair of nitrile gloves, carefully inspecting the unnerving wall art. "Most cults are sophisticated. Much more so than people would assume." She traced her index finger along the paint, the glove coming away with a long red smear. "People often misunderstand what they are. They're not about orgies and black magic and ritualistic sacrifice. They're about connecting with people. People who are like them. They're about finding meaning. Purpose.

"The majority are driven by religious and philosophical beliefs. But, it could also be race-driven, like the KKK. And then there's the infamous Satanic cults—although some might argue those aren't necessarily cults." Harper stood back, taking in the entirety of the sigil. "Which brings us to this lovely new addition: Doomsday cults. But the dangerous ones are few and far between."

"Tell that to Jim Jones." Park said. She dropped down from the mailbox and dusted off her hands, picking up a large nylon bag and walking into the street to join Harper.

Park said, "Um, question. What is it that you were hoping to find here, exactly? We've already been up and down this thing back to front."

Harper craned her head back to take in the summit of the wall. She surveyed the surface as she wandered along its base. "Who knows. Inspiration maybe. Confirmation. Maybe a feeling. Maybe nothing."

"Uh-huh," Park said. "I'm tellin' ya, lady, we have searched every square inch—"

Harper held up a hand. "Come here, look at this."

Park walked over, dropping to one knee.

Amethyst phosphorescent fibers carpeted a low section of the wall. Harper thought they looked like something you'd find in the deepest, darkest part of the ocean floor. A piece of nature that had no right being here.

"Some type of moss?" Harper asked.

Park took a step closer. "Looks that way." She pulled a pair of nitrile gloves from her pocket and slipped them on. "Different than the others. The guards that were stationed here mentioned organic abnormalities, but these guys don't look like any of the ones they catalogued." She unzipped her pouch, which included a case of chromed instruments and fished out a pair of long tweezers.

"I've never seen moss that wasn't green before much less bioluminescent, have you?" Harper inquired. She took a sip of her coffee, watching Park. The air was nippy, cold enough that she could see her breath pluming in front of her face.

Park shook her head. "No," she said, the tweezers biting down on a thick patch. "It's not impossible, though. Green's the one people see most often obviously, but I've seen others before—out in the field. Blue. Yellow. Even black on occasion. Usually a lot less common, though. Purple is new to me. Could be a new species."

High above the city, thunder rolled through an ocean of clouds. Harper folded her arms over her chest as the wind picked up.

Park tore off a piece of the moss and placed it into a small glass jar. As she began fastening the lid, her attention caught on another anomaly.

"Park? What is it?"

Park secured the jar with a label, peering closer at the wall.

Black slime oozed from hairline cracks in the concrete, webbing out and coating the surface in a network of vitreous vines. Harper thought they looked like a network of crystalized veins overtaking the barricade.

"Well, that's new," Harper said, leaning nearer. "It looks like the concrete is decomposing."

Park brought her face closer, inches from the wall. She lifted her hand, bringing the tweezers closer.

"I wouldn't touch that if I were you," a man hollered.

Harper and Park spun around.

Standing on the corner of the intersection across from them was a man and a little girl. He struggled to balance a surplus of bags in one arm, his other hand interlinked with the girl's.

Harper and Park exchanged confused glances at first, unsure how to proceed. This particular area of the Fringe was supposed to be empty. They'd told her it'd been cleared out months ago. The thought of there being people living this close to the wall made her skin go cold.

The child couldn't have been more than six or seven. She wore a glittering green dress with a lavender necktie and slippers.

Harper and Park studied her unusual clothing.

The man picked up on their confusion, glancing down at the girl. "Oh," he said with a sharp laugh. "She's Disgust."

Harper and Park stared at him.

"Disgust?" Harper repeated.

"From *Inside Out*?" he specified.

Harper shrugged, completely clueless.

"The *kid's movie*," the man said, raising his eyebrows. "It's Halloween tomorrow, remember?"

Harper and Kim eased, nodding along.

"Oh, right. I thought it looked familiar," Harper called across the intersection, even though she truthfully didn't know what he was talking about. "Great costume," she said anyway, giving Rachel a smile.

Rachel stared across at her, unflinching.

Jesus, was she *that* out of the loop? When was the last time she'd even turned on her television? Who knew if the damned thing even still worked? Who needed one when there were millions of books out there, waiting to be read?

And more importantly, when was the last time you actually read *a book?*

The little girl warily slipped behind the man's legs.

"Sorry, she's a little shy. I'm Nick," he said. "We haven't seen many strangers around here lately."

"Ah, yes," Harper agreed. "We were under the impression this area was abandoned."

"Abandoned?" the man echoed. "Who told you that? Ah shit, who am I kidding, I guess it is. Haven't seen anyone else out here for days."

Harper remained quiet, carefully regarding the man.

Sporting a five o'clock shadow and close-cropped blond hair, he couldn't have been a day over thirty. He had a kindness to his voice that was reassuring and, standing there, holding that little girl's hand, it was obvious that she was his whole life. As Harper watched them together, a great sadness resonated inside her, hollow and yawning. Katie was that small once. Not so much anymore.

"Mom?" The word replayed in her mind. She was positive she'd heard it come from the phone. She'd bet money on it. But that was impossible, wasn't it? There was no reception in the Dead Zone without a landline.

God, she missed Katie.

Not now. Focus, she told herself.

The man shifted his weight, fighting with the bags, trying not to break his hold on the girl's hand. "I've lived here all my life. Even before they decided to build that monstrosity. This is my place in all its glory," the man said, hooking a thumb at the stoop behind him.

Harper turned and peered behind them at the building, smiling. "Ah, yes, I see."

"What are you guys doing?" he asked, watching them. "You two don't look like you're from around here."

Park smiled artificially and went back to the wall to gather specimens, leaving Harper to do the talking. "We're collecting samples."

The man tilted his head. "Samples? Of what? That shi—" he caught himself, and Harper found herself smiling, "—*stuff* on the walls?"

Harper nodded. "We shouldn't be long."

The world flickered white with a deafening clap of thunder. Harper felt the street rumble beneath her feet like a subway train was passing below. "We should probably hurry this up, Park."

"Working on it," Park replied.

"You with the Army?" he asked.

Park eyed her over her shoulder.

"When was the last time you saw anyone come through?" Harper asked, pointing at two immense doors built into the wall.

Nick shrugged. "Had to be months ago, maybe more."

Months? Christ, it had been longer than she thought.

The girl tugged impatiently on the man's hand. "All right, yeah, here." He handed the girl his keys. She bounded away, speeding up the stairs and disappearing into the building.

"What's your name?" he called across to her.

Harper hesitated. She could feel Park's eyes burning into the back of her head.

The man waited as the wind howled through the street like rush hour traffic, the two of them staring across at each other in a strange, misplaced moment. When he could see she wasn't going to relent, he frowned and began to head inside.

"It's Harper," she blurted out. "Doctor Miranda Harper." She heard Park scoff behind her. Only a few days in and she'd already broken the first rule.

The man stopped. His face warmed into a smile.

She could see all of it there. The struggle. The loss. The pain. Everything she'd expect to see on the face of someone living in the decaying neighborhood closest to the house. He was struggling to find one redeeming thing left in the city, just like her. How could she deny him that?

"It's nice seeing some new faces way out here," he said. He started for the stoop, then called over his shoulder, "Some free advice, though, Doctor? Whatever it is you think you'll find on the other side of that wall? It isn't there."

NICK

THE LIGHTS FLICKERED.

Nick looked up at the kitchen ballast, and his eye twitched.

Unused Halloween decorations overflowed from a cardboard box abandoned to a dark corner in the living room. A bowl of candy corn sat untouched on the kitchen table. A tragic Dracula wall decal sagged toward the floor. Half the bulbs in the string of orange lights framing the front door were dark.

The tubes in the ceiling powered down one at a time, then sputtered back to life.

This was his new life. It had been for a while now. Anything functioning on a direct current of electricity was hit or miss, whether it be the television, microwave, or in this case, the lights. While they worked more or less, there were constant surges, hiccups where they'd go dead for seconds, sometimes minutes.

In the Fringe, anything functioning on battery power was dead almost instantly. Batteries were drained of life in a matter of minutes. Phones especially. He'd had to have an actual landline installed to be able to make phone calls again until he was far enough away. Cars were useless altogether. They didn't last. Gasoline operated vehicles worked marginally longer than electric, which died almost instantly once they got anywhere near the wall. Maybe a few hours, if that. Nick suspected it depended on how much juice they had. Heavy-duty batteries lasted longer than others, but he still parked far, far away. It was almost as if the house was draining the surrounding city of its energy, bleeding it dry like a bloodthirsty leech.

The lights stabilized as he finished pulling on his security windbreaker, straightening his tie. God, he felt like shit. His mouth was dry, and his throat felt like he'd inhaled smoke from a burning building. The skin felt raw any time he swallowed, or took a breath. He'd cleaned off the grime from that day right after they'd got home from the horror show that was the ice cream parlor, but found he was sweating by the time he stepped out of the shower. He hadn't had cold sweats in months, but Halloween was drawing nearer, and he knew things got especially weird in the Fringe around then.

Pull yourself together, shipwreck. You've got an eight hour shift ahead of you and you're gonna need to get your mind right if you plan on walking around an abandoned mall all night.

He had a knot in his neck the size of a fist. He twisted his head to the left, then the right. He waited for the crack, hoping to let some relief flood in, but it never came, the ache only compounding. He fumbled the kitchen cabinet open with shaky hands, head pounding, and swiped a bottle of aspirin, washing down a couple tablets with a glass of water. Pain flared like fire in his throat, reminding him that he could only ignore it for so long.

A clicking sound, like a car engine cooling down. The fluorescent lights hissed above his head, the orange lights framing the front door dimming.

He turned to the living room and saw the TV screen flash on and off rapidly. Rachel sat slouched in his beat-up leather recliner. He couldn't see her face from that angle, but he hoped she was asleep. An episode of *The Twilight Zone* was unfolding on the screen. It was the episode in the diner, the one where an alien was hidden amongst the patrons.

Hidden in plain sight, he thought.

He circled around the bar counter and picked up the remote.

Shit. She wasn't asleep after all.

Rachel's eyes narrowed in annoyance. She sighed, fluttering the strands of hair dangling in her face.

A soft knock at the door.

Rachel sprang from her chair.

"Hey, what're you doing?" Nick said, holding out an arm. "You know the rules: only Dad gets to answer the door."

Nick walked over, twisting the deadbolt and pulling open the door.

Sandi Dornan, a shapely woman with umber skin waited on the other side, two Tupperware containers in her hands. Her hazel eyes shimmered in the soft porch light like antique copper. Coils of springy black hair were highlighted with caramel ribbons, framing a round, warm face.

"Hey, Chef," he said, the corner of his mouth pulling into a smile. The pet name had started as an inside joke. They'd run into one of Sandi's old coworkers grabbing dinner one night and he'd overheard them address her as such. He'd repeated it in that teasing, flirty way he did, and it had just stuck. Sandi used to love it before, back when she thought it meant something special between them, but looking at her now, seeing the expression on her face, she could tell it never truly meant anything more than it sounded like.

Nick took one look at her and mouthed the words, "Thank you."

Sandi smiled, bittersweet.

Nick stepped aside. "Come on in."

Sandi walked inside, finding Rachel standing in the middle of the living room, straight as a pole.

Sandi glanced at Nick and he shrugged.

"Look who's here, Rach," Nick said. "I thought she'd keep you company while I'm at work tonight."

"Hey, Rach," Sandi greeted. She smiled, walking over to Rachel and getting down on one knee. "I assume your Dad had a frozen dinner on standby for tonight, so I thought you might want something homemade for a change." She opened the lid on the first Tupperware container and held it out.

The smell of parmesan and garlic steamed from a mound of angel hair doused with marinara and flecks of cilantro. Two perfectly formed meatballs were buried underneath the noodles.

Nick's mouth watered. God, he missed her cooking.

Rachel eyed the pasta for a moment with an odd look on her face.

Sandi gave Nick a strange look and he rubbed the back of his neck because he didn't know what else to do.

"It's your favorite; spaghetti with meatballs," Sandi announced. She leaned in closer. "And some chocolate tiramisu for dessert, but don't tell on me," she said with a wink.

Rachel didn't move.

Sandi reached out, gently tucking the loose strands of Rachel's hair behind her ear.

"Don't be rude, Rach," Nick said. "What do you say?"

Rachel stared at Sandi, her face emotionless, then said, "Thanks, Sandi. I'm not very hungry right now." She turned to Nick. "Can I finish watching the show now?"

Nick frowned. "Yeah…sure, Rach."

Rachel walked away, shoulders slumped, hopping back into the recliner.

"She doing any better?" Sandi whispered.

"Touch and go."

"Did you call that therapist? Dr. Graham?"

Nick rubbed the back of his neck. Sandi arched an eyebrow.

"You didn't call, did you?"

"Doctors cost money, Sandi," he said. He felt his voice raising and dropped it back down to a whisper. "I am doing my best—"

"There is something wrong with her, Nick," she hissed. "You need to get her into a doctor—"

"I know what she needs, *believe* me. I am doing my best here. I'm trying. Don't you think I'd drive her there right now if I could? We are *broke*, Sandi. We went on a shopping spree at the *Dollar Barn* for Christ's sake. I can barely keep the lights on in here. How the hell am I supposed to pay for a doctor on top of all that? If you have an answer, please, by all means, tell me what to do here."

Sandi frowned, and the knife twisted a little more. Pity was the last thing he needed right now.

Sandi wetted her lips, changing gears. She watched Rachel, sunken back in the chair, and he could see a stitch of guilt on her face. "Did you at least have the nurse at school take a look at her?"

Nick nodded. "Yeah. This afternoon. Nurse said she's been a little tired in class lately. She hasn't been getting much sleep." A beat, then, "Neither of us have."

The kitchen lights sputtered again like machine gun fire. Sandi grimaced and drew a step closer to Nick. Her hair smelled incredible, like coconut and strawberry. Maybe he'd gotten too used to smelling burned toast and stale Pop-Tarts, but having Sandi here in front of him was almost euphoric to his senses. She was clean, put together, well-manicured. Everything he wasn't. He breathed in, her zesty clean scent purifying the rot that had lingered in his sinuses since the ice cream parlor.

An image snapped into his forethought: It was the Fourth of July, and Sandi had helped Rachel orchestrate the entire menu for the evening. Hot dogs, barbeque chicken, cheeseburgers (with Sandi's skilled touch, of course). There was no such thing as simple when it came to Sandi and food. A cheeseburger wasn't *just* a cheeseburger to Sandi. It was masterfully prepared ground beef seasoned to perfection, with caramelized onions and American cheese. It was perfect temperatures and times and presentations. And she was damned good at it, too. So they'd cooked and baked while he'd finished up at the UPS warehouse for the evening before the annual Winterview fireworks, and before long, Rachel was asleep in her bedroom and he was sitting on the side of his own bed in the moonlight, looking over his shoulder at Sandi while she slept. He smiled out of the corner of his mouth and pulled the sheet over her because she deserved that, deserved to have someone that did nice things for her, even if it was only for a moment. He'd lightly pressed a hand on the side of her face, feeling the warmth radiating from her body.

What was so reassuring about having someone sleeping next to you at night? he wondered. Against his own advice, he noticed the evenings she spent the night he'd sleep better than when she hadn't. But why? Was it physical? Or something psychological? It didn't matter. When they'd awoken the next morning, he'd asked her to leave before Rachel had woken. She'd looked at him, heartbroken and confused, grabbed her baking pans and her knives and favorite skillet and left without another word. In hindsight, that might have been the moment everything began to unravel. The final indignity she was willing to suffer through. What else could he have done? She'd stayed before, but never when Rachel was home. If he'd let her stay with Rachel in the house, that would have meant commitment. Rachel would have seen her there and it only would have confused things, and it just wasn't the right time.

Sandi had gone, and a few days later, she told him she'd found a house to rent in Silvers Hollow. He'd felt betrayed, but he knew that was ridiculous. This was *his* doing. He'd made his bed and now he had to sleep in it. He'd convinced himself that they were better off, but was that the truth?

The morning after the Fourth of July was when things had gone from bad to worse, only he hadn't known how bad until he'd went to bed, feeling nothing but emptiness in the pit of his stomach, a hollow of loss and regret. The memory was raw, as raw as memories get. Thrice as painful as he remembered it being. Maybe because he'd consciously stopped himself from thinking about it? An alarming question came to him: *Did I make a mistake? No. Don't start doing that. No second guessing. You don't have the time. There's never enough time.*

This wasn't about him. This was about Rachel. He couldn't bring home any woman he felt like. What kind of parent would that make me? The *human* kind, he thought. But still. He had a responsibility to keep his daughter's life as simple as humanly possible, and he wouldn't force her to call some stranger "Mommy" just so he didn't have to wake up alone in the morning.

But was Sandi really a stranger?

The power groaned.

Sandi gasped, as if her breath had suddenly been sucked out. The television monitor shrieked with an earsplitting static, then cut dark.

The room was silent.

Sandi's hands were shaking.

Nick took the Tupperware from her, sealing the lid back on. "Look, Sandi, if you don't think you can—"

"It's fine," she interjected. "Just go before I change my mind."

Nick took a deep breath, nodding. He walked over to the recliner. Rachel stared straight ahead at the dark TV screen, unblinking.

"I think the show's over for now, Rach?"

When she didn't answer, he leaned down and kissed her on the forehead. "Be good, kid. You know the drill, do what Sandi tells ya."

Nick turned to leave, flashing a brief smile at Sandi.

"If you need anything, *anything*, call me. Okay?"

Sandi smiled. "I will."

And with a hasty goodbye, Nick opened the front door, disappearing into the night.

HARPER

"THEY'RE RIGHT. IT *is* getting worse."

Harper stood on the balcony with a beer, the curtains tossing softly in the wind, the gunshot ringing in her ears. Not much else came from the streets below save for the occasional car honk. Even the sirens were absent.

"About the city: it's getting worse," she clarified.

Park stood at the hotel dining table with a map of the K District, examining their route, engrossed in her work. "What is?"

Harper walked inside and polished off what was left in her beer, shutting the balcony door. "The suicides. The closer they live to the Fringe, the more likely they are to be affected. The question is, by what?"

Park looked at her, nodding. "Fucked, but true. I wish it weren't, but the numbers do not lie." Park circled the table, scribbling notes with a pen. "Where's Dirac?"

Harper shrugged. "I'm afraid he declined our offer to meet."

"Real shocker."

"I assume he's preparing."

"Then shouldn't he be here?" Park asked, arching an eyebrow.

"Maybe in a perfect world," Harper said with a smirk. "The phrase 'does not play well with others' comes to mind."

Park scoffed. "Yeah, this is going to be *real* fun."

"What are you doing?" Harper asked.

Park stood up, resting her hands on her hips. "I am charting the coordinates on the wall where we've found anything...irregular."

"You think there's a pattern?"

"I don't *think* there's a pattern, there *is* a pattern. See? It's more abundant on the western face. More specifically the spot we hit today."

Park had marked red Xs along the wall at varying intervals. On the western border, there were about twice as many as anywhere else. You had to give it to her, Park left no stone unturned. She'd expect nothing less. After all, her friend had graduated from Stanford at the top of her class. Park might have been slightly zanier than the professionals Harper was used to working with, but she was also the breath of fresh air she desperately needed. Harper admired that about her, because she was the exact same way. Dedicated. Driven. Independent.

"I wish you could have seen him, Park. His eyes..."

The image replayed in her head. The gunshot. The ringing. The blood. The audience scrambling out of their seats, nearly trampling each other in the process.

Park ceased writing and looked up at her. Park had never been good at this, consoling friends, but she was making an effort nonetheless.

"That sounds awful, Harp. Absolutely fucking awful."

"There was nothing left," Harper said. "No reason. No hope. Everything was just...gone. How far gone are we to lose hope?"

"I saw a guy walk in front of a bus," Park said.

Harper tilted her head. "What? When? You never told me that."

Park eased her palms on the table. "Yeah, crazy huh? Day before last. Literally less than five minutes after I got into the city."

"What happened?" Harper asked.

"There's this bus coming, out in front of the terminal and...he stepped right out in front of it. I can't get the image out of my head, Harper. He looked right at me. He looked right at me and smiled and I'll never be able to get that image out of my head now. Because of that *asshole,* I have to live with that the rest of my life. Lovely, right? A nice big *fuck you* from the city. Just roll out the old red carpet for good old Madison Park."

Harper smiled bitterly, opening herself another beer. "I'll drink to that."

Clink!

They needed to get back on track.

"So, where are we at?" Harper asked.

Park guzzled down what was left of her beer and wiped her mouth. "So, assuming these schematics are up-to-date, our best bet is to use this entrance for a straight shot to Seventh. That one we saw today. From there, it's about a quarter mile to the house, which, if history has taught us anything, should be wide open come midnight."

Park's mention of the entrance brought her back to earlier that day.

"You thinking of that guy and his kid we saw earlier?" Park asked.

Harper shook her head, chastising herself. "I should have known they'd feed us a load of bullshit. That area's not abandoned. I doubt it ever was. Why would they lie about it?"

Park shrugged. "You know how it is. There's a lot of politics involved when things get to this level. But, for our sakes, assume they're lying. Speaking of which," Park dug into her bag, tossing a stack of folders on the table, "that 'moss' we were looking into earlier? It's not moss."

"What do you mean?"

Park opened the folder and riffled through the pages, which had page after page of lengthy numerical sequences. "I analyzed the sample we took earlier at the lab and it's definitely not moss."

"You're sure?"

"One hundred percent," Park replied, handing Harper a page littered with numbers and a black and white micrograph.

"I'll take your word for it," she said, handing it back.

"None of these cells have chloroplasts, so photosynthesis is out. I had a theory that maybe they used chemosynthesis like the plants on the ocean floor, but there's no glucose for them to snack on so that's bunk. Or it could be some type of genetic mutation from their natural environment, whatever that is. I've also checked every database from here to Timbuktu and it's not listed among the any of the known species. And the Army didn't have them registered. *Before* they jumped ship, I mean. So basically, it's also new, which means there have been zero tests run."

"What are you saying?"

"I'm saying I don't have any clue what it is. Problem is—"

"It's spreading?"

"Bingo," Park said, hitting her with a finger gun. "And faster than we initially thought."

Damn, Harper thought. She was afraid of this. That meant that whatever was happening beyond the wall was escaping containment. It was only a matter of time. Fast or slow, it was inevitable now. This was what frightened her about the house the most. It wasn't the whispers of endless horrific things running rampant inside. Those were stories as far as she was concerned. Spooky tales for the media to spin for inquisitive, prying eyes. The real danger was the ecological disaster unfolding before their eyes. Regardless of how the house had come to the world or why, it had brought something else with it. A creeping environmental nightmare that threatened to destroy the city if they couldn't figure out what was behind it.

Park picked up the second jar and held it up at eye level. "And this other sample? Well, this one is completely off-the-charts. It's completely new. I mean, there isn't even a word for whatever is in here. Nothing even remotely comparable. It's some sort of crystalized mineral that changes its physical structure like a manic-depressive. The molecules are volatile and highly, highly corrosive. One drop of this shit melted through the slide, and then the base. And even a little bit of the table. It seems to be a byproduct of the 'moss' or whatever it is. It could be some vicious strain of cyanobacteria, so I guess there's that theory. If it hadn't melted my slide I could have checked."

And now it's eating through the wall...

Park held the glass jars up in front of her. "That means that both of these substances are completely unknown to science, Harper. Just like the others the Army found there." Park laughed, taking in a sharp breath, completely bewildered by it all, and it was like she was watching a little kid discover her love for science all over again. "The only question now is...where did they come from?"

"I don't know." Harper folded her arms, her face grave, the lines around her eyes somewhat deeper. "But I'm sure they're only the beginning."

Harper got that familiar sinking feeling in the pit of her stomach. While she could tell this was all very fascinating to Park, Harper surmised the girl might be overlooking the inherent danger as a result.

"Park, why are you doing this?"

Park cocked her head as if she'd misheard. "What?"

"Why are you going—to the house?"

"Why do you think?" she said, taking the jar and securing it back in her bag. "Um...hello? Does the name *Ghost Stalkers* mean anything to you?"

"So?"

"*So?*" Park parroted. "So, that show singlehandedly almost ended my entire career. I lost my job at the university the night the first episode aired. The youngest professor ever hired and the board revoked my tenure, Harper. Did you know that?"

Harper shook her head. "No. I'm sorry, Park. I didn't know."

"I didn't even think they could do that!"

"If you were so worried about your reputation then why did you keep filming it?"

"Because I believed in it. Just like I believe in what we're doing here. And you don't abandon something just because it gets hard."

Harper watched Park fidget with two beaded bracelets on her wrist, straightening them out. How could she not have known? It had been years since they'd seen each other, yet Harper hadn't so much as picked up the phone to check in on her friend, dodging her calls on numerous occasions.

"I should have called, Park. I'm sorry. I really am."

Park nodded, accepting her apology. She never was one for grudges.

She collected the papers back in the folder, organizing them.

"All that aside, we can't keep pretending like we're not going to find anything on the other side of that wall, Park." Harper put a hand on her friend's shoulder. "What I mean is, there is a very high likelihood that we might not come back out of there."

"Oh, you all of a sudden believe in this whole 'haunted house' charade now? I thought you don't believe in the supernatural?"

"I don't, but I think we need to be prepared for the possibility that once we leave there is no turning back, and it would be a mistake for us not to admit there's some cold hard truth to that."

"Are you trying to shrink me? Or warn me?"

"Neither. I'm trying to tell you that that silly TV show wasn't the end for—"

"Harper, listen to me," Park said. "That 'silly TV show' ran for two seasons. *Two years* of my life. I know you think it was some stupid phase or stunt or whatever, but it wasn't. Not to me."

Two years? Had it been that long?

"Those years were the greatest, happiest years of my life. And as stupid as it may sound to you, being there with those people made my life so much better. So much more bearable, like I was finally free to be myself. Not the version everyone else liked, or the version people thought I *should* be. The one that *I* liked. The one I should've been from the beginning. And I wouldn't take it back for anything."

"I don't want to see you get hurt, Park. That's it. That's my whole speech." Harper smiled at her friend and Park smirked. "You may be a *Ghost Stalker* to everyone else, but to me you're my best friend."

"What're you talking about? I'm your only friend, Harper," she said, and they both laughed.

A dreadfully long moment of silence passed.

"Look," Harper said, easing onto the table. "All I'm saying is that you have a choice."

"And I've made it," Park said. She hastily packed up her belongings and walked to the entrance door, opening it and turning back. "We all have our reasons, Harper," she said. "What's yours?"

NICK

NICK WASN'T READY.

The mall was deserted. It had been for years now. Hazy moonlight filtered in through an enormous skylight, lowlighting winding stretches of balcony that twisted around the bend in front of him. He walked along the third floor of the once grand Winterview Mall, a flashlight in his hand, taking in the gloomy storefronts and occasional pile of debris. Most the store entrances were shuttered with metal grates, others had been boarded up after being vandalized countless times.

He'd landed this little gem of job with the help of Rush Employment Staffing. It wasn't Wall Street, but it was a means to an end, and any job was good news at this point. They were a necessity that was gradually becoming increasingly rare in Winterview.

He stopped and peered over the balcony. Below, he could make out the shadows of the former food court. He'd eaten there back before the city had decided that the mall was no longer "economically viable," according to Mayor Sloan.

He was barely into his shift and energy drink two was beginning to wear off.

He gazed around, taking in the decrepit shopping center. Sad, deflated banners hung along the sides of the columns. Wilted plants galore. Frozen, deserted escalators. Sheets of broken glass.

How had things gotten this bad? Wasn't it only a few years ago he was here, soaking up a much-needed day off with Rachel? They'd stopped for a Cinnabon in the food court like he'd promised, then wandered around in search of a pair of shoes at the Dance Closet for her recital that week.

And now, all he could see beyond the front window was another chapter of his life swallowed up by loss. He thought about the drawings, thought about her teacher, Mrs. Tanner, watching her while she talked to the closet.

A chill rippled through him.

He lifted the flashlight and pointed it at the wall of glass. Inside, he spied torn up carpeting. Piles of wood. Wires dangling from the ceiling and walls.

Depressing is what it was.

Nick sighed, tapping the flashlight on the window. "Move forward, man, not back."

A clatter echoed from around the bend.

He began along the balcony, quietly moving toward the bend leading to the next straightaway. He heard two muffled voices as he reached the crook. He carefully slid along the railing and ducked down, listening.

Voices. Two men talking. They sounded like they were talking via walkie.

His blood pumped faster, harder.

Glass shattered, and he startled.

He scooted to the railing and glanced down.

Below, an old pickup truck was idling with its headlights on, parked with its rear-end to the facade of one of the department stores. Nick couldn't see which.

"Shit," he whispered.

He wasn't ready for this. When he signed up to work security, the most he figured he'd come across was a vagrant trying to take a piss. Or maybe some dumb kids trying to graffiti the copious blank walls.

But no. Instead, he had his very first thief. *Thieves*, by the sound of it. Just when he thought his luck couldn't possibly get any worse.

He pulled his walkie from his belt.

"Command, this is Eagle Five, come in. We have a 459 in progress."

A moment passed. The radio was silent.

"Command, this is Eagle Five, come in, over," he repeated.

He glanced over the balcony again. The truck's engine idled, letting off warm exhaust. A lone taillight glowed crimson. The driver had shut off the headlights, which were aimed at the entrance doors to the mall.

A clamor of metal down in the store below.

Glass detonated and Nick recoiled away from the railing.

"Command, are you there? Anyone?" He scoffed, shoving the radio back in his holster. He got clear of the truck and made his way back around the bend.

Two flights of escalator stairs later and he was right around the corner. He got low, stooping along a row of planters that led straight to the truck.

The sounds grew louder as he slinked closer. He listened as metal crashed into the bed in a spectacularly loud fashion. The figure, draped in shadows, disappeared back into the store.

Nick pressed his body to the side of the truck, edging closer to the rear. He shot a glance at the store.

Nobody was there.

He steeled himself, hooked his fingers around the bed, and pulled himself up.

Inside: piles of copper tubing and other scrap metal.

Nick felt the cold end of a pistol press into the back of his skull.

His breathing didn't slow; it stopped altogether.

"You got a death wish, city boy?" The man's voice was raspy, etched with a deep Southern twang. When he talked it sounded more like a growl, and it wasn't a stretch to imagine the man was born of the wild.

Nick froze. If he hadn't had a gun pulled on him in the past (numerous times in fact) he probably would have pissed himself right then. But he kept his cool. Told himself to listen and keep his mouth shut. To keep calm, otherwise things were going to go from bad to worse. Again.

"Can't imagine this shit job payin' you enough to get your head busted in."

Nick weighed his options. He could run. Get to a phone and call the police, let them sort out this hick. That was procedure, after all. Call it in. The mantra spoken time and time again at Command. Call it in. Call it in. But of course, the time he *does* have something to call in, nobody is around to hear it.

There was also option number two.

The man said, "Look, stranger, I don't feel much like hurtin' anyone tonight, so let's say you take your happy ass outta here and forget you ever saw me. Otherwise, we might have a problem, you and I."

The offer was tempting. He was an asshole, whoever he was, but he was right. Was it worth getting killed over a minimum wage job defending a dilapidated shopping mall?

The man continued, "If there's one thing this shit world taught me it's don't be a hero," He paused, then said: "It ain't worth it."

Nick decided it was.

He whipped around in the darkness, expecting the gun to go off, but discovered all the man held was a short length of steel pipe. Nick backhanded the weapon away and felt the bones in his hand light up with pain. The pipe whirled off and clattered on the tile, spinning away in hollow echoes.

He faced off with the stranger, who looked equal amounts unimpressed and annoyed. The man was tall and lanky, mid-forties, with deeply calloused hands and the scars to prove he'd taken a beating or two in his life. Greasy hair dangled down near his eyes, which had a feral, fearless quality about them. Either he was caught off-guard, which Nick didn't even remotely believe, or he simply knew Nick wasn't a threat. He guessed the latter.

Seizing the opportunity, Nick launched forward, throwing his shoulder into the man's body with all his weight. The back of the stranger's legs caught the tiled edge behind him and they spilled over the planter, flattening plant husks and toppling into the fountain with a frantic splash.

Fire lanced his left shoulder and he screamed, but his voice came out far away, drowned out. He tasted dank water and grime and knew he was underwater. His uncoordinated attempts to fight more closely resembled a struggle not to drown, and all he could think was *please God don't let me die in this fucking mall!*

While he thrashed about, the man mounted him, casually grabbing a fistful of his shirt collar and effortlessly hoisting him out of the water.

He sucked in a deep breath, choking on water, and all he could see was a black blur.

He heard a crunch in his skull and tasted copper. The force from the man's blow snapped his head back and, before he knew what was happening, he was underwater again.

HARPER

THE DEAD ZONE.

Two minutes. Precisely a hundred and twenty seconds until the clock struck midnight and the entrance doors to the Dead Zone opened, allowing them access to one of the most restricted and potentially dangerous places in the entire world.

Harper stood alongside Park and Dirac in front of two rusted steel doors embedded in the wall, their hot breath slipping out into the oppressed night. A blanket of fog flowed between their legs along the perimeter. The trio donned charcoal field jackets and military boots, all provided and funded by the Red Sky.

Night had fallen sooner than Harper had anticipated, and between the deserted streets and nonexistent vehicles, the intersection looked like something out of the apocalypse. Harper and Park each carried a black duffle bag and a transport carrier for their test subjects, four rats that had become Park's pride and joy. Additionally, Harper wore a custom rucksack crammed with a plethora of useful albeit unconventional equipment. Dirac preferred minimal gear, sporting a single duffle bag and, aside from that, nothing more than the spectacles on his face.

The air was sticky, overwrought with moisture, and Harper could feel the sweat on the back of her neck icing over. She pulled the collar up on her field jacket, and all she could think about were the specimens Park had collected from the wall.

To the side of the doors leading into the Dead Zone was a lone security booth. Harper gathered it once housed a sentry to monitor and allow military personnel in and out. The glass windows had been broken out; the housing vandalized with tasteless graffiti.

Must have been a lonely place to work, night after night...

A voice cracked the silence, "Not too late to turn back."

Park, naturally. She was more likely to ramble the more nervous and excited she got. Fear and excitement often go hand-in-hand and Park was one of the people who saw them as one and the same. She'd always been that way since Harper had known her. Thrill-seeking. Carefree. Not the stereotypical "scientist" by any means.

Dirac, on the other hand, was exactly that. At least to the naked eye. Ever since they'd met at the compound, she hadn't quite known what to make of the man. With wispy gray hair, caterpillar-like eyebrows, and a perpetually annoyed expression, Dirac was pretty much what she expected. A physicist by trade. Harper had heard stories about Dirac in her academic circles. An anecdote here. A complaint there. Even a laughable rumor about him and his TA fraternizing during his brief employ at a certain four-lettered Ivy League university.

But to her, at least for now, there was nothing even remotely memorable about the man. Whereas a personality often developed out of necessity to make up for physical shortcomings, his did not.

Dirac wandered over to the booth, investigating the damage. He scowled, shaking his head. "Animals," he sneered. "No respect for government property. No wonder this city is on the brink of total devastation."

"Something tells me they don't mind," Park said.

Dirac either ignored her or didn't hear her.

"One minute," Harper announced, checking her watch, an old automatic her father had given her for graduation. The time was close now. Harper's fingers slid over a holster on her belt.

In case of emergency...

Park dropped down to a large nylon bag, unzipping it.

"Air temperature seems to have decreased, just like they said," Harper declared.

"No surprise there," Dirac replied. His face was barely an inch from the security both, taking in every doodle and mark carved into it.

"Dirac, anything interesting?" Harper called.

Park squealed.

Dirac poked his head out from the booth. Park reached into her duffle bag, wrestling out three sleek rectangular devices. Dirac took an interest, pacing over.

Park said, "You guys are going to love this."

Harper's eyes fell from the doors. Her frown relaxed into a grin watching Park handle the equipment right there in the middle of the abandoned intersection.

The sky rumbled low and angry, reminding her where they were, and melancholia flooded in, her mood downshifting.

Park inspected the device, turning it over in her hands.

"I don't think you're supposed to be having this much fun," Harper said with a smirk.

"Until my dying breath, Harper," Park said. She stood up, twisting a dial on the side. A mechanical click and a hiss of gas. The hollow cavity inside sputtered, producing a flame so narrow it was practically a laser. Their surroundings brightened to a pale blue glow, their faces glistening with wonder. Ash drifted hypnotically through the air like black snowflakes, and Harper couldn't help but feel that none of this was real. That she wasn't here at all, but was asleep somewhere far away, Katie asleep next to her on the couch back home, a book in her hands.

"Excuse me?" Dirac's grating voice violated her peaceful moment.

Park slapped the object on the back and a handle sprang up. "For you, monsieur Dirac." She beamed, handing the lantern to Dirac, his mouth agape.

"You're joking?" Dirac repeated. "*Lanterns*? What are we doing, going camping?"

"Dr. Dirac, you were briefed before training, yes?" Harper asked bluntly.

"Well, yes, but—"

"Then you are well aware that neither solar nor battery-operated equipment will function for any given length of time in the Dead Zone *or* the Fringe."

"Yes, I understand that, but lanterns? Come on, people, *lanterns*? This is the United States Government. Surely, they have something better suited—"

"I'm afraid this is what we've been provided, Dr. Dirac. People have been using oil lamps since before Christ. I'm sure we can make do." Harper took the lantern from Park, pushing it into his waiting hands.

Dirac stood dumbfounded, gawping at the lantern.

Park turned on two more units, handing one to Harper. "For you," she said gleefully.

Dirac muttered something under his breath.

A loud shudder, dusty and mechanical, resonated from inside the wall.

The trio turned to watch as the doors juddered.

"It's time," Harper announced, a look of wonder on her face.

The doors split in the center, pulling apart with a heavy metal grind like a secret Egyptian passageway opening.

"Dr. Harper," Dirac said brusquely, "you asked me what was written on the booth, yes?"

She turned to find him considering her, his intense eyes magnified behind two thick pieces of plastic.

"I did, yes."

"Yeah," Park added. "Care to enlighten us?"

And Dirac said, "It says, 'Save us—from Hell.'"

NICK

A SCREAM SHATTERED the silence.

Nick's heart jolted like he'd been hit with 10,000 volts of electricity and all of the exhaustion from the day burned away. The sound rattled the silver fillings in his teeth and pinged his tired bones with a shiver that rolled over into a shudder. The pain in his face swelled from the sudden movement, and he was grateful he hadn't had any broken bones after leaving the emergency room earlier that night. A couple small stitches in his face and he was right as rain. Down a few hours in pay after he'd been sent home early, but alive all the same. The mountain man was long gone by the time the police showed up.

What time was it?

Had he fallen asleep?

His head swam. The room tilted like a carnival ride. He groggily fought to get his bearings, struggling to discern if he'd merely dreamt it.

Another high-pitched shriek ripped down the staircase.

Rachel.

Sandi shot upright on the couch, nearly tossing off the side, her shirt hanging off one shoulder.

"Rachel?" she moaned, still half-asleep.

Nick was out of the recliner before he had time to think. He knocked the empty energy drink off the TV tray, racing for the stairs. His clumsy feet caught a lip of hard plastic; he tripped over an assortment of toys and stuffed animals, barely staying on his feet. Sandi tailed him as he barreled up the stairs.

Rachel's wail pierced the night loud and shrill. He took the steps three at a time. He buttonhooked at the landing and dove over the last of the steps, half-falling, half-stumbling into the hall.

The white trim surrounding the doorway glowed like a funhouse entrance. Chest heaving, legs shaking, he stopped there as her cries broke for a moment. He saw himself as a child, waiting at the carnival in front of that creepy old entryway, the head shaped like a giant clown, jagged, splintered teeth exposing a funnel of darkness beyond.

A heavy crash in the bedroom snapped him back to the now. He blinked away the reverie, knuckling bloodshot eyes. He swayed, half-asleep, half-concussed, then broke into a sprint toward her terrified cries. He threw himself into the darkness beyond the doorway, whipping an arm out. His hand batted away the elephant lamp as he slapped on the light switch.

Light exploded on overhead.

Rachel was there, cowering in the corner of the bedroom opposite the closet. She screamed, high-pitched and helpless, a pillow held out in front of her like a shield.

Adrenaline on overload, his eyes darted about the room.

The bed. The dresser. The window. All undisturbed.

He rushed over to her and his knee caught an untucked dresser drawer. The force ripped it free, toppling over the small piece of pastel furniture.

Sandi hurried in the doorway behind him, chest heaving.

"Rachel?" he said, reaching down and taking her in his arms. The girl continued to wail as if she didn't hear his voice. "Hey, it's me! Rach, calm down, I'm here!"

Sandi waited at the door, stunned, a look of alarm on her face.

Rachel whimpered and he rocked her in his arms, moving about the room, searching for the source of the disturbance.

"I saw them, the ghosts! They were in my room!"

"There's no one here, baby," he reassured. He rubbed his hand along her back and noticed her pajamas were drenched in sweat. Strands of her hair were clumped together, pasted to her forehead. He felt her hands touch the back of his neck and a chill passed through him.

She looked up at him with wet eyes, like she was coming out of a dream. "Dad?" she murmured. She began to quiet at last, and he squeezed her tighter.

He turned and looked at Sandi over his shoulder and her face was grave. How much worse was this going to get? First imaginary friends and now night terrors?

"What is it, Rach?" he asked. "What happened, huh?" He pried open the blinds with his fingers, tugging on the window.

Locked. Nobody had come in that way.

Rachel didn't speak. He stood there cradling her in his arms, feeling the vigor slipping away along with any chance of sleep for the night.

"Goddamn it," he uttered. He moved toward the opposite side of the room with her nestled in his arms. As he rounded the post she burst to life, her limbs flailing to extricate herself from his arms.

"What?!" he shouted, fumbling her. He lost his grip and she landed on the hardwood floor with a thud, scampering under the bed.

"Jesus Christ!" he said, getting down on one knee. "What is going on with you, kid? Talk to me!"

"Nick," Sandi said.

He turned to her, and she raised her eyebrows. *"What?"*

She gave him a look that told him to take a breath and collect himself. He nodded, swallowing.

Just take a minute, man. Everyone needs to calm the fuck down.

He leaned down, peering under the bed.

"Rach," he said calmly, "there is nothing here, okay? It is just us. Just you and me and Sandi. There's nothing to be afraid of." A pause, then, "Right, Sandi?"

No answer.

"Sandi? Isn't that right?"

Behind him, a long, drawn-out creak from the closet.

Nick froze. His eyes widened.

He held there for a moment, listening to the sound of his own heartbeat.

The creaking stretched on and on, and right when he thought it might never stop, it did.

Rachel's eyes panned past him to the closet.

Why wasn't Sandi answering? Why was the closet door moving?

He listened to his heart gallop in his chest. He was paralyzed on the floor, adrenaline surging inside his body, too scared to look behind him.

Rachel broke into a scream and, before he could react, the world went black.

HARPER

HARPER TOOK POINT.

She cautiously strode forward, the lantern held out in front of her, a tight flame casting an eerie blue glow on the surrounding buildings. Park and Dirac flanked her, giving them a good amount of track lighting as they made their way forward.

"Oh my God," Park uttered.

The three halted, stopping in the middle of the street.

The Dead Zone was unrecognizable. Surreal, alien vegetation covered the city. Endless varieties of shrubs, weeds, and what looked like black glass trees had overtaken the storefronts, patios, and roads. The undergrowth carpeted most every surface, even climbing high on the skyscrapers and into the night. Long cords of black vines twisted overhead across the street like massive webs. The sheer luminosity of color was borderline visual overload.

The steel doors ground back to life, slamming shut behind them with a mighty clap.

Spooked, the group whirled around.

"No turning back now," Park said. She stepped forward, kneeling down, holding her lantern close to a plant similar in appearance to a lotus. The plant pulsed, as if absorbing the light from the lantern, revitalizing itself. She remembered Park's words from earlier that evening, that photosynthesis wasn't possible with the moss, and she assumed the same was likely true with the lotus. Some type of parasitic plant perhaps? That would fit. What was the host organism then? And where did the "ash" fit in?

Park's gaze held fast, mesmerized. She reached out, bringing her gloved fingers toward the blossom.

Just as her fingers were about to make contact, Harper clapped a hand on her shoulder. "Let's not touch anything yet, Park."

Park stood up, peering around. "Look at this, Harper. I mean...look at it! The plants; they're everywhere. It's like some bizarre version of Pripyat."

"And handled just as poorly."

Harper took a step forward, mindful of her footing, where beckoning blue weeds sprouted from hairline cracks in the concrete. They swayed hypnotically, and Harper thought they moved the way a plant does when it's underwater. A type of algae?

"Harper?"

Harper turned to Park.

"What do you mean?" Park asked.

"About Pripyat?"

Park nodded.

"It's like they've learned nothing. Chernobyl was one of the worst ecological disasters in history and here we are, repeating history. Come to think of it, this might even worse."

"How so?" Park asked.

Harper wetted her lips. She looked out at the city, watching as the ash drifted through the eerie glow of their lanterns like some sort of nuclear winter. She wondered how the people of Pripyat had reacted when they'd seen the ash the night the reactor exploded. They'd made a fatal mistake that night, ignoring the signs, and here was Winterview, essentially repeating history. The devastation wasn't as fast-acting of a pending nuclear blast worthy of swift intervention, but the damage to

Winterview was still great regardless, even if it was a touch more insidious.

Maybe this was what the world needed? Maybe humanity's lack of understanding and sheer ignorance was ultimately going to catch up with them.

Harper said, "When the house first came, everyone treated it like it was this thing that was here for our entertainment. The media. The news… Everyone wanted to see it, this beautiful, magnificent miracle. But as you know, some of the most beautiful things are often the deadliest."

Park looked at her soberly and nodded. "I guess that makes us the heroes going in to open the valves, huh?"

Harper smiled. "I guess it does."

"Did they live, the three that went down there?" Park asked. "Wait, don't tell me. I don't want to know how it ends."

Harper turned to find a haze of blue light ahead on the right. Dirac roamed ahead, inspecting an abandoned building.

"Dirac, what is it?" Harper called.

The pitch of her voice appeared to stimulate the vegetation. A gust of wind swept from the darkness, rocking the lengths of vines and rustling the plants sheathing the walls and street. Park took notice as well. It was like they were standing inside of a living, breathing throat.

Harper marched forward, stopping a few feet away from Dirac.

"What is it?" she repeated.

Dirac stepped back. "Outpost 31," he said ominously. He cautiously followed along the wall with his lantern, stopping in front of the entrance. He held the light up, his breath chilled by the night.

Outpost 31 had once been the military's primary base of operations within the Dead Zone. Their briefing had instructed the team to avoid investigating the premises. Harper found that odd.

"My God…" Harper said.

She resumed her pace, pushing through the mist with Park trailing behind her, admiring the various unknown species as if they were casually strolling an alien botanical garden.

Dirac stood trapped in the glow from his lantern before a mouth of darkness. Two large security doors to the entrance were pried open, blotchy with rust, cordially inviting them in. Harper and Dirac waited while Park jogged over, grimacing.

"Well, this looks promising," Park said, chipper.

"Outpost 31," Harper whispered. She raised her lantern out in front of her, the lifeless glow illuminating a damp concrete tunnel. Dark veins sprawled out of the corridor and up the front of the building like blood-soaked ivy, covering nearly the entire facade.

"No," Park said. "There's no way this happened in a matter of months. This was aggressive. This entire ecosystem… This would have taken at least a year, easy."

"Some light, if you don't mind?" Dirac said.

Park looked at Harper and rolled her eyes.

Harper shrugged.

Dirac took a step forward as Park raised her lantern.

The red vines webbing across the building were nearly translucent, coated with some sort of cloudy mucus. Dirac's haunted eyes pinched together as he examined the texture more closely. He pulled a pair of forceps from his bag, prodding the surface.

"Dirac!" Park said abruptly.

Dirac jolted awkwardly from her voice, the forceps nearly severing a section of the growth.

Park erupted in laughter and Harper couldn't help but crack a smile, even if she knew it was wrong.

"How on Earth am I supposed to do my job if you won't stop yammering on?" he snapped.

"Easy there, Doctor Dreadful. We're all on the same side here, remember?"

Dirac glared at her, shoving the forceps back into his bag in a huff before snatching the lantern off the ground.

"Oh, come on. I was going to ask what your first name was, that's all," Park added.

"It is a fair question, Dr. Dirac," Harper added.

Dirac gaped at Park like he was having a conversation with a dog.

"My name is *Dirac*," he growled.

"Is that your first name or your last?" Park said.

"Dirac," he repeated.

"*Dirac?* That's it? Like *Madonna*?"

"That's enough, Park," Harper said. "We don't have time for this."

"What?" Park argued. "We're going to be working with this guy for the foreseeable future, the least he could do is tell us his first name."

"*Doctor* Dirac to you," he said, pointing an accusatory finger at her.

Park flipped him off, unimpressed. "Whatever you say, *Cher*."

A sound like a metal pipe being dropped echoed from the entrance, bouncing off the concrete in high-pitched waves. The vines invading the building seemed to inhale all at once, contracting like an organic net.

"What in the hell was that?" Park asked.

Dirac turned his attention toward the darkness.

Harper stepped closer to the entrance, extending her arm beyond the threshold, the lantern burning away the humidity lingering in the air.

"Dr. Harper?" Dirac called.

She twisted around to face him.

"May I remind you that we have been given explicit instructions not to investigate these premises, or have you already forgotten?"

The yawning cavern leading into Outpost 31 waited before her, a stranger in an even stranger land, faced with potentially dangerous and unexplored territory. All of the intel she'd been provided with thus far claimed the compound had only recently been vacated in the last few months, so why did she get the feeling that it had been abandoned a lot longer than the Red Sky claimed?

She felt a flutter in her belly like butterflies, and she wondered if this was the first time she'd felt even remotely alive since Katie had left.

Park stepped forward. "The Red Sky didn't rule out looters."

"No," Harper said, "no they did not."

"Absolutely not," Dirac sneered. "Didn't you two hear that? There could be someone in there."

"All the more reason for us to check it out," Park said.

"They could be dangerous," Dirac replied.

A clatter ricocheted from the entrance again, shrill in the quiet night. Their heads snapped toward the sound and Harper felt her heartbeat quicken.

"You see!" Dirac hissed. "There's someone in there!"

Harper's eyes narrowed, and she began forward with Park in tow, their lanterns casting a familiar pale glow inside the threshold.

"Are you two out of your minds?"

The sound grew louder.

Closer.

Harper's heart fluttered again, and it only made her want to press further, deeper. It was reckless, but she knew she never would have accepted the offer in the first place if safety was her primary concern. Because there was nothing safe about being in the Dead Zone, or even Winterview for that matter. The concrete passageway reeked of copper and grease, and she sensed that the walls were no longer the walls they once were, that the city that had once been normal had been overtaken by a power nobody could explain.

She breathed in and nearly choked on the rancid air, holding the back of her hand to her nose. She could hear Park beside her, listened to the woman's heavy breaths in her ears, filling her head with adrenaline.

They stopped as the noise reached its apex, crashing down on them like a rain of metal shards, the lantern rattling in her hands.

And then it all stopped.

One second it was there, screaming in their ears, and the next, it was gone.

They stood side by side, peering into the well of darkness.

"What happened?" Park whispered. "Where'd it go?"

Harper's face was grim, unyielding. "I don't know."

Dirac's voice grated at them from the street. "What's going on in there? Dr. Harper? Dr. Park?"

"That man is unbelievable," Park said, hushed. "Chivalry really is dead. God forbid he check on us. Who invited him on this little adventure, anyway?"

Harper exhaled, shifting the lantern to her other hand and staring into the pitch black beyond. "Dirac may be eccentric, Park, but we need him."

"Says you," Park muttered under her breath.

"Dr. Harper!" Dirac's voice was more urgent now. "Dr. Harper I think you better come out here and take a look at this!"

Park exhaled, shaking her head. She used her free hand to knead her eyes, forcing them open wider.

"Are you all right?" Harper asked.

She reached up, but before her hand could get close, Park brushed it away.

"It's all this damn dust in the air," she said, hacking. "It feels like I'm breathing in a dead body that got cremated and shot out of a confetti cannon."

But Harper knew it was more than that. Park was most certainly feeling the side effects of the house. After all, they were only a few streets away now. Closer than she'd ever been. Even here, in this concrete fortress she could feel the house calling to her, beckoning her to come for a visit. She'd be lying if she said she didn't feel it herself, the dull ache like two nails behind her eyes. That was the worst of it. At this point, anyway.

Park looked at her and knew she could feel it too.

"It's nothing," Park said. "I used to get migraines growing up. I'd throw up, skip class, cry in my car. So, this? This is nothing, *believe me*."

"Well, let's hope it doesn't get worse," Harper said. "We're not even on the same street as the house, and if it's this bad at this range, God only knows how we're going to feel once we're inside."

"Dr. Harper, are you listening?! You and Park need to get out here *now*!"

"We're coming!" Park screeched, and even she was surprised how high-pitched her voice sounded. She and Harper shared a quiet chuckle. Park coughed into her arm, combing her hair to the side with her fingers.

"What now?" Harper asked, annoyed.

And as they started back toward the street, the beginnings of the house's sickness seeping into their minds, footsteps shuffled in the darkness only a few feet further in.

NICK

HIS HEAD WAS ringing. He could hear Sandi calling his name, her voice coming at him in waves like a fire alarm going berserk.

"NICK!"

His eyes shot open and he winced. His cheek was pressed against the hardwood, pulled to the darkness under the bed. He felt crumbs pressed into his skin like tiny pebbles.

Sandi was kneeled down at his side, shaking him.

"Nick! Wake up! She's gone!" she shouted.

He pulled himself upright and felt the world teeter sideways. He groaned and his hand went to the back of his head, finding a sheen of fresh blood.

"She's gone, Nick," Sandi repeated. Her eyes were swimming with tears and they looked like they'd witnessed something terrible. She didn't look hurt from what he could see, but there were two of her and he doubted he was right enough in his mind to make that call. He watched her mouth move, but couldn't hear anything but the ringing, the same high-pitched sound he'd heard before back in the street outside the ice-cream parlor.

Sandi stepped closer, seizing him by the shoulders and shaking him harder. His head went light again but this time her voice broke through.

"Did you hear me? Nick! Are you all right?"

Nick looked down at the blood on his hands, sluggishly registering her words. Two concussions in one night. Must have been his lucky day.

Sandi got down on her knees and took his face in her hands. "Goddammit, Nick! Wake up!" she snapped. "Rachel's gone!"

"What're you talking about?" he asked. His voice sounded like it was coming from the other room, but it was an improvement. He was coming to. Sandi's double was fading.

"What happened?"

"Rachel—someone took her!"

The panic set in fast after that. He felt all the pain in his skull retreat away, the throb in his eyes and nose going numb. He fumbled for the edge of the bed, woozily getting to his feet.

"What do you mean *gone*? Where is she? What the fuck happened?"

Sandi's eyes darted about the room. She had her arms folded over her chest and she was taking in giant, deep breaths, pacing back and forth. She wasn't Rachel's biological mother, but she played the part and then some. "I don't know what happened!" she snapped. "I don't know—I think someone took her," she said, fumbling her words.

"Rach?" he called, and his voice echoed. He launched over the bed, his weight ripping off the comforter and sheets. He jerked aside the curtains, then rushed over to the closet and threw open the door to find nothing but mounds of toys and a few empty hangers. He leaned in anyway, tearing through it all. A crash came from the closet like he'd smashed one of the toys. He reemerged, slamming the door closed. "Rachel?!" He pushed past Sandi, throwing a glance into the bathroom before rounding the stairs, leaping over the steps.

He heard Sandi moving behind him, trailing him through the apartment. The space seemed so much more lifeless without Rachel, and it was quickly becoming obvious how much worse things would have been without her in his life.

Don't talk like that. She's fine. She's here somewhere.

"Rachel?" He swung open the downstairs' closet door, then ran into the kitchen and flung open the small door above the refrigerator.

Sandi arrived at the bottom of the stairs right as Nick produced an oiled wooden box from the cupboard. He heaved it onto the kitchen table and cracked the lid at an angle, revealing a cavity of red felt home to a polished revolver, blued steel. A Colt Python. One of the biggest, meanest handguns on the planet. The weapon had walnut grips and a mirror shine and he remembered telling Sandi in bed one night that it had been the only thing left of his family with any real value. Because while the steel would tarnish, it would never die the way his family had. Never get reduced to ash and memories like the stuff blowing all over the city.

He inspected the polished cylinder and counted the cartridges, then palmed it closed, meeting Sandi at the landing in the living room.

That was when they both noticed it: the front door was hanging open. The wind was calm. Beyond the threshold, the city was silent. It dawned on him then how isolated they were in the Fringe, more than likely the last ones left, easily a half a mile or more from anyone else.

His fingers tightened around the pistol. He took a steady breath, then stepped forward. "Rachel?" His voice trembled. His chest was tight and the weight of the situation was so smothering he could barely breathe.

"We need to call the police," Sandi said. She snatched the phone from the cradle, punching in the number. She pressed the headset to her ear and listened while Nick hurried to the open front door and braced himself there in the night, taking in the blackness beyond the entrance as if it were outer space itself.

He hastily scanned the road before rushing down the porch steps into the street.

"Rachel?!" he screamed, his voice echoing down the concrete wall separating the Fringe from the Dead Zone. He spun on his heels, pacing in the street under the moonlight.

"Rachel!"

His screams were swallowed by the night.

She was gone.

He rushed back into the apartment, slapping the revolver down on the table. He stayed there hunched, his palms pressed onto the table, out of breath. They'd already lost too much time.

"She's out there, isn't she?" he asked, sniffling. "Someone took her, Sandi. Didn't they?" A beat of silence passed. "Sandi?"

When Sandi didn't respond, he turned and looked over his shoulder.

Sandi was staring down at the phone in her hand, grimacing.

"Sandi?" he said, swallowing. "What's wrong? Did you call them? The police?"

Sandi met his eyes and he could see how frightened she was. He understood it because he felt that same fear now pumping through his veins. The same dread and horror. The same fear of the unknown.

Eyes wide, Sandi took the bottom of the phone's plastic cord and held it up in the air, the curly length barely a foot long.

The line had been cut.

HARPER

DIRAC WAS DOWN the street about twenty yards, waiting near the mouth of an alley. He waved his hands with the vigor of a child, and Harper wondered if perhaps he was younger than he appeared.

Park trailed behind her, stopping every couple of feet to take in a new species of reed that had sprouted up from a sunken section of the street. Twinkling heliotrope spores carried up from the reeds, up through the night, floating away into the darkness like fireflies. The alien beauty of it all was easy to get pulled into, and Harper had to force herself to remain detached, dispassionate. After all, the danger was as real as the beauty if not more.

"It's beautiful, isn't it?" she asked.

Park turned and looked at her, nodding, mystified by the amazing world they'd found right here in the middle of the city.

"Almost like we're on another planet," Park said.

"Maybe we are."

Park eyed her like she might have been on to something. After a tense moment, her face relaxed into a smile and she laughed. "Was that a joke?"

Harper grinned, setting down her duffle bag and the transport and folding her arms across her chest. "I guess I'm out of practice."

The two held there a moment, admiring a city transformed, watching the lazy spores drift through the air, sprinkling the night with a little bit of magic.

"We need to move, Park," she said.

"Right behind you," Park replied, closing up another sample jar and tucking it into her duffle bag.

"Will you two *please* hurry up?" Dirac hissed. He was whispering for some reason.

They met him at the throat of the alley. Dirac stood with his lantern held up in front of him like a ferryman to the afterlife, and his eyes sparkled with an unsettling glint.

"What is it, Dirac?" Harper asked.

"While you two were off fiddling about, *breaking protocol* no less, I took it upon myself to survey the area and—"

"Get to the point, Dirac?" Park interrupted.

Dirac glared at her. "I have never—"

"That much is obvious," Park said, "now out with it already."

Dirac fumed, shaking his head. "May I direct your attention there?" He shifted his light and the air was abruptly sucked out of Harper's chest.

A pickup.

The engine was off, but it was there plain as day.

Harper and Park wandered into the alley, their lanterns held out in front of them, revealing a network of variegated ivy overtaking the walls.

One second, they'd been in the city, the next an alien wilderness, and Harper thought that if she hadn't lost her faith a long time ago, she might have even called it a miracle.

The green-blue shimmer from their lanterns stirred the plants to life; they swayed and danced and welcomed them into the darkness. The vegetation was so dense overhead it formed a canopy, almost like a forest. No, that wasn't right, Harper thought. But it wasn't a jungle either. So, what was it then? And that was the whole point. It was something unheard of, a completely new ecosystem forming right here in the city, the rate at which it grew outright alarming.

"What the hell is this?" Park's voice. "A pickup? Here?"

The truck wasn't like the other vehicles they'd come across in the streets. That much Harper *could* tell. It wasn't overgrown, hadn't been reclaimed by nature the way everything in the Dead Zone had. No, this truck had only arrived recently. Only there was no telling *how* recent. There weren't any immediate signs of tracks either, almost as if it'd materialized out of thin air.

Harper rounded the rear, letting her eyes acclimate to the dark. She reached under a plastic tarp covering the bed and there was a clatter.

She reemerged, dusting her hands, and said, "It's scrap metal. There must be looters in the area. Keep an eye out."

Dirac perked up at the word, eyeing the spirited fog wandering by.

With the truck's passenger window down, Harper poked her head inside, nosing about. Her arms disappeared in after her while Park and Dirac listened to her fumble around inside the cab.

She abruptly broke into a coughing fit and pulled herself out, wrestling a cardboard box from inside. "God, whoever it is has been smoking enough cigarettes to kill an elephant."

"Looters? Here? That's impossible," Dirac said.

"I'm afraid so," Harper replied. Cradled in her arms was an overstuffed box nearly bursting with jewelry. Necklaces, watches, earrings. Even a music box with one of those miniature spinning ballerinas. Harper casually plucked a watch from the mounds of gold and silver and tossed it to an unprepared Dirac.

He fumbled it in the air, narrowly dropping it, but recovered. He glared at her before bringing the timepiece closer to his face. The papery skin around his eyes crinkled as he scrutinized the watch, running it through his hands.

"Looters," Dirac said.

"The thought crossed my mind, but I guess now we have confirmation," Harper said.

"Well, that's just perfect, isn't it?" Dirac said. "They've sent us here without an ounce of protection and now we have to contend with criminals as well. As if I didn't have enough to worry about already."

"Don't worry, Dirac, I'll protect you," Park said, slapping him on the shoulder.

Harper watched curiously as Park rummaged through the box, retrieving a polished gold bracelet. "Huh," she said.

"What is it?" Harper asked.

"Correct me if I'm wrong, but…I'm pretty sure this is a fake."

"How can you tell?" Harper asked.

"An excellent question, Dr. Harper. How on Earth would you know, Dr. Park?" Dirac sneered.

"Well, for one, the 'gold' is flaking off." She held it up for them to see. A glint of dulled silver beneath a thin gold coating. "Also, I had a friend that used to sell knockoffs from time to time online. Sort of a side hustle."

"Uh huh. A 'friend,' you say?" Dirac said with a dry laugh. "Peddling illegal forgeries? Why am I not even surprised? That would be right on par with what I've seen of you thus far, Dr. Park."

"And what's that, Doctor Dreadful?"

"There are volumes to be said about the way you, a supposed 'professional,' conduct yourself. I've always said friends are a reflection of the individual, and in this case truer words I do not know."

Park scoffed. "And that is so easy for you to say, isn't it? You know, being that you *have* no friends."

"That's enough," Harper scolded. "We need to move if we're going to stay on schedule." She lobbed the box through the pickup's open window, starting away.

"No, wait!" Park said.

Harper turned back to find Park's eyes big as silver dollars.

"What is it?"

"Look," Park murmured.

The gold watch remained suspended in the air between Dirac and Park, easily five feet off the ground.

"Oh my God," Dirac stammered. "That's impossible."

"That seems to be the theme tonight," Park replied.

Harper cautiously approached, seeing the watch as something comparable to plutonium. God, it was incredible, the gaudy gold-plated timepiece floating, completely ignoring the laws of physics. She felt like they'd discovered an ancient relic from a lost civilization. The trio watched it waltz through the air, and Harper refused to believe her own two eyes.

"Dirac," Harper said, "I believe this is your field?"

"Is it now?" he said. "And how did you come to that conclusion?"

"You *are* a physicist, aren't you?" Park said.

"Contrary to what you may think a physicist is, I am by no means qualified to explain the unexplainable."

Harper reached out, plucking the watch from its lonely orbit. She held it in her palm, Park and Dirac staring down at it like they'd struck gold.

"Something tells me we're not in Winterview anymore."

NICK

HIS HEAD WAS a pumpkin on the verge of exploding. He moved quickly, following along the wall, careful not to let the substance coating it touch his clothes or skin. After all, he knew the sorts of things that had taken root on the other side, and he didn't want it anywhere near him. The air smelled like salt and brine, he caught whiffs of it every time he stopped to scan the nearby windows and porches.

He could hear Sandi struggling to keep pace behind him, her voice calling out to him; it carried down the concrete in waves like the tide, and it sure as hell wasn't helping the throb in his head.

"Nick! Nick, will you please slow down?!"

He didn't have time to slow down.

Someone had taken her. His little girl. His life.

No. He needed to move. He'd heard about situations like this on the news. Seconds could mean the difference between life and death.

"Will you please hold on!"

Nick moved faster, arriving at the entrance.

Sandi jogged up behind him, barely staying on two feet.

"Jesus, Nick, can we just take a minute!" she snapped. She was bent over, her head hanging between her knees.

He ignored her, stepping inside the abandoned security booth. "We have to get it open," he said.

"What? What're you talking about?"

"The doors; we need to find a way in!"

"If you would stop for a minute and listen to me," Sandi said, panting, "I could have told you not to waste your time."

Nick turned to her, his blood thrumming in his ears. "What the hell are you talking about? Why not?"

Sandi hooked her thumb to the left.

The entrance door was already open.

HARPER

"I SMELL KEROSENE," Harper said. She had for the last three blocks or so. She didn't intend to address it, but the scent was only getting stronger the further into the Dead Zone they went.

"Yeah, me too," Park added. "Where's that coming from?"

They'd been making excellent time. Navigating through the fog with the lanterns hadn't been nearly as difficult as she initially thought. It had slowed their pace a bit, but not by much.

"I can't tell," Harper said.

Park stopped, stepping to the edge of the curb. She shifted the duffle bag slung over her shoulder behind her, waving her lantern through the face of the fog. The mist had become noticeably denser here, virtually opaque now. Harper could hardly see ten feet in front of her, let alone the buildings rising into the sky all around them. Sections of the atmosphere appeared off, like seeing panes of vibrating glass, but it was difficult to confirm her suspicions in the weak light.

After they'd moved on from the truck, they'd mostly remained quiet. Even Park was at a loss for words, something Harper had rarely seen. Wandering through the darkness and the sea of fog flooding the Dead Zone almost made her miss Park's banter with Dirac.

Almost.

She didn't know what to make of the watch. To her knowledge, nothing invented thus far would explain what they'd all seen back there. But the novelty had worn off quickly once they'd found other things drifting through the streets. Cars. Rubble. A city bus. Even a mummified cat. The fog made it hard to see much for very long, but every time something new passed overhead they'd watch it together, marveling not only as researchers but as human beings, too. And then it would be gone and they'd compartmentalize what others would call a miracle, file it away in their heads in a place that made sense. Because they had a job to do and, despite their differences, they were going to do it.

They'd collected and cataloged the gold watch along with Park's other samples, stowing it in an airtight specimen container and organizing it in the biologist's black bag. True, the containers were normally reserved for biological samples, but who was to say the watch hadn't been contaminated by something organic? Either way, there had to be some sort of logical explanation. A shred of empirical evidence she could extract from this overgrown graveyard.

The group carefully stepped off the sidewalk, roaming into the intersection. She squinted, spotting the silhouette of a traffic light overhead camouflaged in the fog. She couldn't read the metal street sign creaking in the wind, but her intuition told her it read SEVENTH STREET.

Harper took the lead, with Park behind her and Dirac taking up the rear. Harper assumed Park had him pegged for a coward, and right now she was inclined to agree.

"You've been awfully quiet back there, Dr. Dreadful," Park said. "We've got a legit *floating junkyard* over our heads and you've got nothing to say? Call me crazy, but that seems a little suspect."

"Park," Harper said.

"Seriously, though," Park said. "You'd think a renowned physicist—even *Dirac*—would have some kind of thought on the matter. Discovering weird floating antigravity shit should be like discovering plutonium for one of these guys, don'tcha think?"

Harper didn't answer, only kept walking.

"I guess between the electrical interference and the fog there's not much room for footage of this place, otherwise it would have been all over the five o'clock news," Park said. "Personally, I think it's the Meissner Effect."

Dirac couldn't take anymore of her yammering, apparently. "Do you even know what the Meissner Effect *is*?" he asked.

"Uh, duh," Park said. "A superconductor expelling a magnetic field."

"Indulge me, Dr. Park. What here would constitute a magnetic field?" Dirac asked. "I'm curious."

"How the hell should I know?" Park said. "*You're* the physics guy."

"The ash," Harper said, the words out of her mouth before she even realized it. It made sense. "The ash is more concentrated here. It might be acting as a superconductor, generating a magnetic field strong enough to lift the vehicles. The Red Sky have indexed it, but they haven't tested it in large quantities, only trace amounts. And let's not forget the house itself. It's comprised of dozens of unidentified metals. The phenomena happening in the city could be caused by any number of factors."

Her supposition was enough to silence Dirac for the moment.

They kept walking.

The fog was frost on her face, inviting icy tendrils into her lungs. Her chest burned. She slowed, a large dark shape materializing in front of her.

"What is it? Why are we stopping?" Dirac's voice, grating and loud.

"Shh!" Park hissed.

The mist slid away like a silver veil, revealing a scorched car burned down to its bare metal. Most the surface was carpeted in the same purple moss they'd seen on the outer perimeter wall along with a web of blood-red vines. A charred skeleton was at peace in the driver's chair. A few strands of singed hair fluttered in the breeze, caught on shards of glass teeth framing where the front windshield was. Harper wondered if the driver had died on impact and been killed instantly, or been burned alive in the heap of gnarled metal.

The air cleared further and Harper's breath caught.

She saw now; the intersection had become an automobile graveyard, home to dozens of burned-out, mangled vehicles overgrown with all manner of flora, ranging from bioluminescent mushrooms to pale, barbed stalks with black bulbs. The city had brought ruin to nature, but nature had taken it back. She tried to imagine the chaos that had fallen that night, visualized the panicked crowds and frightened people rushing to escape. Women and children trampled as they attempted to flee whatever had transpired that night. Winterview citizens crushed by automobiles piloted by drivers overtaken by group hysteria. In other words, complete and utter devastation. She pondered if the ash had played a part in the madness, but knew she could do nothing more than speculate until the samples were analyzed.

Dawson said it was perfectly safe, but she knew better.

The world stirred; a draft picked up, rolling the fog toward them in undulating waves.

The trio froze.

"Park, do you hear that?" Harper whispered.

Fluttering. Like a bat's wings.

"Yeah..." Park set the black box down and came to stand beside Harper, gazing into the abyss. "What is that?"

A hollow bell tolled, deathly loud, ricocheting off the concrete surrounding the intersection, rocking the earth.

Dirac started, falling back into a car and throwing his hands over his ears. "What is that horrible sound?!"

"Midnight. We must be close," Harper announced. "The house should be open. We need to move. That way." She jabbed a finger north.

The toll ceased and a flutter of paper broke free in front of them.

Harper and Park jumped out of the way as a flurry of crumpled flyers were expelled from the mist. One of them slapped against Park's leg; she reached down and peeled it off her shin. The rest of the wrinkled papers continued past Dirac and down the street, swallowed once more by the fog.

When the wind settled, Park flattened the sheet out as best she could, holding it up. Harper and Dirac stood at her side, examining it.

"'Enter now," Harper read aloud. "One-million-dollar cash prize for three lucky winners.'"

"'The Seventh Street Lottery,'" Park continued. "'Survive one night in the world's most haunted house and come out a millionaire.'"

"'Brought to you by the Crow Corporation,'" Dirac finished.

Park scowled at the paper, crumpling it up and hucking it into the fog like a deflated softball.

"Some contest," Dirac said, almost sympathetically, to Harper's surprise. The scientist bent over and reached down, scooping up a small bronze keychain from the street shaped to resemble the house's facade. He ran his fingers over the metal, feeling the weight of it in the palm of his hand. "Look where it got them." He held it up to his face and blew the coating of dust off, taking it in his fist and hurling it away.

Harper heard it get swallowed up by a puddle down the road.

"Nothing but a legacy of death," Dirac said.

A second flutter, a weightier one.

While Park and Dirac scanned the intersection for impending threats, Harper turned her eyes skyward.

"There," she said, pointing.

High above their heads, a street-wide vinyl banner was tethered to streetlights at either end of the road with loose cords of rope. The wind picked up, and when the banner thrashed faster, Harper could have sworn it sounded like clapping. Like the house knew they had come.

WELCOME TO THE HOUSE THAT FELL FROM THE SKY!

NICK

"WE SHOULDN'T BE here, Nick."

Sandi was doing her best to keep up, teeth chattering, arms folded across her chest, desperate to keep the cold away. He felt bad that she was here, following him into No Man's Land. He knew it was selfish, maybe even a little coldhearted, allowing her to tag along, but his mind wasn't exactly functioning rationally despite his best efforts.

Nick slowed, shrugging off his jacket.

"Here," he said.

"I'm fine, Nick," Sandi protested.

"C'mon, take it," Nick repeated, more sternly this time. Sandi relented without much of a fight, slipping her arms into the oversized coat.

"Thanks," she said with a wan smile.

"I'm sorry," he said. "You didn't want to come here and I knew it and I still made you anyway."

"You didn't *make me* do anything, Nick."

"Well, either way, thank you—for coming out here with me. This place gives me the fucking creeps."

Sandi smiled again and somehow it seemed more genuine, bringing a warmth to her face. Her coppery eyes twinkled with a sincerity few people had. He was surprised he hadn't seen it before all those nights when they'd lain together. Maybe it was because he had never *wanted* to see it before. Or maybe he just hadn't been ready. Whatever the reason, he was glad he saw it now.

Sandi started walking.

"Wait," he called out.

Sandi stopped, looking back at him. Half her face was cast in shadow and he suddenly got a sinking feeling in the pit of his stomach. A weight he couldn't explain.

"You don't have to go," he said. "It's okay."

Sandi cocked her head. "What're you talking about?"

"What I mean is, it's okay if you want to go—home. You've helped me more times than I can count and I don't want you to do this because of me. You can turn around and go. I won't hold it against you. No bullshit. I promise."

"Your ego is astounding." Sandi said. She looked past him toward the entrance, the hulking doors open, giving them one last chance to turn back. The lights of Winterview were dim in the distance, and Nick couldn't help but think of all the people awake in the city, completely oblivious to what was happening in their little corner of the world.

Sandi sighed, shaking her head. "I'm not doing this for you, shithead. I'm doing it for Rachel."

"Right," Nick smiled, embarrassed.

"Let's just find her and get the hell outta here."

"Yeah, okay. Good plan," Nick said. He pried himself away from her tired eyes, taking in the entrance to the Dead Zone. He took her cold hand and her smile brightened. "All the trucks I saw coming and going from here followed this road straight down. I say we keep going this way until we find something."

"Why do you think it's open?" she asked.

Nick shrugged. "I don't know."

"Well," Sandi said, motioning toward the entrance. "After you."

"Chef," Nick said, and Sandi smiled the way she used to, back before things had gotten so screwed up between them.

The Dead Zone had been abandoned a long time; that much was evident. The duo could barely make out the buildings all around them. And what he said *was* true; he hadn't seen anyone coming or going for months. Maybe even longer. Right around the time of that crash near the intersection had leveled the barbershop. So, the question now was: what the hell happened here?

The air was thick with humidity. Nick felt the hairs on his arm stiffen. A tingling radiated over his sweaty body like a thousand fingertips caressing his skin.

"I can't see anything," Sandi hissed. "The fog is everywhere. I can barely see two feet in front of me."

As if the fog was listening, layers of gray peeled away, revealing glimpses of exotic foliage overtaking the city.

"What in the hell is this?" Nick muttered. He let go of Sandi's hand, straying ahead.

"It's like it turned into some fucked-up forest or jungle or something. Look at all the colors," she said. Sandi sounded more worried than curious.

Nick didn't know what to think. He carefully approached a car abandoned in the middle of the street for a closer look. A dark-colored moss—the same kind growing outside on the wall—had crept up from the street, overrunning the hood and fenders as if the vehicle were a tree. An alga resembling kelp sheathed the moss in layers, swaying in the midnight breeze.

A strong draft kicked a cluster of pale stalks about; they bobbed and bent and danced in the moonlight. That was when he noticed it again: that smell like rotting flesh. He remembered it well from the street, when he'd seen that blood-red sky, heard that colossal sound knocking down the city one building at a time.

"Oh my God, what *is* that?" Sandi asked. She cupped a hand over her nose, her face scrunched up in disgust.

He looked down to see he'd nearly touched one of the stalks. "Don't come over here," he warned. He pulled the tip of his sweatshirt over his nose and mouth, backing away from the car and, as he did, he could have sworn the stalks had tried to reach for him.

"What is it?" Sandi again.

"Don't touch anything," he warned. "There's something growing all over everything. Some sort of fungus or…or *something*."

Nick heard a papery crunch and stopped in his tracks. He bent down, picking up a relic from days gone by.

"What's it say?" Sandi asked.

"It's an advertisement for the Seventh Street Lottery." He'd heard the stories. Murmurings of what happened here only a year ago. But it was as though the event had been erased from history, hardly a shred of evidence left behind other than what lay hidden in the Dead Zone and the concrete bunkers implanted around the city.

"Jesus!" Sandi shrieked.

"Sandi? What's wrong?"

She didn't speak, only stared past him.

And what he saw then he couldn't explain. His mind couldn't comprehend what he was seeing any more than it could comprehend the infinite universe or the creation of life itself.

The mist had retreated into the city, where the haunted heart that was the Halliday House awaited visitors to wander its corridors and get lost in oblivion.

"Oh my God," Nick said.

Rusted cars drifted overhead like ghost ships; he listened as the metal groaned, some scraping along the surrounding buildings like icebergs before vanishing into the sky. Rocks and debris hung suspended in midair. Sandi reached out and lightly touched one with her fingertip, sending it spiraling away. Strange plants pulsed and throbbed all around them, clearly alive and restless; he looked closer and noticed fleshy suckers lining the underbelly of a select few.

"Where are you, Rach?" Nick whispered.

Sandi laced her fingers through his, squeezing tight, and as much as Nick wished it would bring him some form of comfort, all he felt in his bones was cold, wet dread.

"What's happening, Nick?"

Nick stared up at a world gone mad, his face mapped with stitches, bruises, and blood, and said, "We're on a highway to Hell."

HARPER

"WHAT IS IT?" Park asked.

The trio stood before a mass of charred wreckage. Dirac used a splinter of wood to poke at the debris while Park circled around to the side.

Harper sniffed at the air.

Kerosene. The same smell from before. The smoke seeping from the wreckage was baked into the spongy tissue of her nasal passages. In the daylight it might have been easy to discern what was in front of her, but at night? Not so much.

"It's a plane." Park's voice bounced around from the other side of the ruins. The heap of metal groaned, shifting, and Park reemerged with a section of mangled propeller.

"A plane?" Dirac was incredulous.

"A small one, but yeah, afraid so." Park said. "Can't tell if there was anyone in there—it's too burned up."

"Well, isn't that wonderful?" Dirac added.

"I thought planes use diesel?" Park said.

"Kerosene," Harper said. "Lower freezing point means lower viscosity. Won't clog the engines."

Park heaved the propeller onto the charred remains, then started around to the other side.

"Leave it. There's no smoke and no sign of any survivors which means there's no point in wasting any more time on it," Harper said. "It must have been here a couple of days minimum. If anything could have been done for the passengers, well…that time is already long gone. We need to focus on our mission."

"That's preposterous," Dirac said. "A plane doesn't plummet into the middle of the city and vanish. If there was a crash, *someone* would have come."

Harper turned to him. "Like who?"

"The authorities, of course. The FAA."

"Your so-called 'authorities' have no jurisdiction in the Dead Zone, Dr. Dirac. The only authority here is the Red Sky, and they have sent the three of us. Either whoever was in that plane died when it crashed or they escaped, in which case they might still be nearby. If they are, we'll find them."

Harper started away and Park shrugged.

"We have to report it at least for God's sake!" Dirac shouted.

"I hate to admit it," Park said, "but Dirac has a point. Shouldn't we call someone?"

"You both know very well that we can't."

Park said, "I could rough it back; hell, it wouldn't take—"

"We will report it," Harper interrupted, "once we get back. But for now, we've got a job to do."

"Someone could be dead, Harp."

Dirac watched them disapprovingly.

Harper nodded. "I know, but a whole lot more people are going to die if we don't figure out what's going on here. We need to find out why people are dying in this city, and we need to do it now."

Park goggled at her like they were strangers, and Harper realized she was pushing too hard too fast. She needed to switch gears, downshift for the sake of her companions. And for her own soul, too.

She put her hand on Park's shoulder, leaning in close. "You? Me? Him?" she said, glancing toward Dirac. "This is our purpose, Park. They chose us because we are the only ones who can stop this city from ripping itself apart. Everything we do tonight is for the greater good, and every second matters. We can save this city. We can save these people. But we all need to be on the same page. Our priority is the house. Our research."

Park looked her in the eyes, reading her, and Harper didn't so much as blink.

"Okay, yeah. You're right."

Harper smiled. "Thank you."

A high-pitched wail broke from the quiet.

Harper wasn't sure she heard it at first. The noise was faint, drowned out by the disorienting atmosphere flowing through the streets.

Park turned, eyes wide, confused. Dirac instinctually took a step back, his gear nearly collapsing his rail-thin frame.

Harper was steadfast before the shimmering silver veil, listening to a potential ghost. She was skeptical. Unconvinced. Her mother used to say she was the most suspicious baby she ever met, and that meant something coming from a world-renowned pediatrician.

A second, shriller cry echoed down the lonely street. The sound hit her like an electric jolt, jumpstarting her heart.

A baby. The sound was unmistakable yet impossible at the same time.

"Uhhh...did you guys hear that?" Park muttered.

The mist had multiplied, completely submerged the street in a foam of gray.

"What was that?" Dirac said. "An infant? *Here*?"

"Who the hell would bring a baby down here?" Park asked. She took a step toward the fog, listening closely. "Well...I don't hear anything now. Maybe it was the wind?"

Another shriek pierced the buzzing night air.

Harper's heart seized.

"Christ!" Park yelped, clutching her chest with one hand.

Harper lifted her lantern high and started forward, engulfed by the greenish-gray fog.

Park quickly grabbed her duffle bag and lugged it over her shoulder, hefting the rat carrier from the street with Dirac reluctantly following behind, each of them disappearing into the blanket of smoke.

Harper could barely see a foot in front of her, using the lantern as a means to break apart the haze in the air. The baby's cries rode waves of the mist, coming from everywhere and nowhere. Her eyes felt like they were turning to two stones in her head.

She heard Dirac's voice lost somewhere behind her. "Blast it! I can't see a thing! Where are you going?!"

"Harper! Slow down!" Park yelled. "Damn it, will you please wait a minute!"

The infant's sobs grew louder and louder, amplified like they were being broadcast from megaphones all around the city. The cries clawed at her ears and she slammed her eyes shut, her hands trembling.

She stopped, taking in a slow, deep breath. She willed her heart to slow, letting the tremors work themselves out of her hands while the mist slithered over her neck.

She couldn't even hear Park and Dirac anymore, their voices completely drowned out.

Then…quiet.

The fog was gone; the world silent again.

Suddenly she was standing at the foot of a structure not of this world.

Park and Dirac tore free from the fog like flies from a web, crashing to a stop beside her, both of them panting, the color drained from their faces.

"Have you all gone mad?!" Dirac snapped. His boney fingers locked around Harper's arm but she was unfazed; her attention belonged to the house now. "I have never worked with lesser professionals in my entire life!"

When Harper didn't react, he wrenched on her arm harder, screaming at her like a petulant child.

"Dr. Harper? Are you listening to me?!" Dirac might have appeared somewhat threatening if he hadn't been wheezing so badly. A strong breeze might have even taken him out at this point.

Harper calmly breathed in the night air, exhaling frozen white smoke. "Dr. Dirac," Harper announced, "welcome to the house that fell from the sky."

Dirac gasped, realizing his error and stumbling back. He squealed as the weight of his gear threw him off-balance, his arms pinwheeling wildly.

Without looking, Harper's hand shot out and seized the shoulder strap crossing his chest, anchoring him. Her icy eyes found his own and she said, "There is nothing here with us other than our own imaginations. Please control yourself, Dr. Dirac."

Dirac's lips trembled, contorting into an embarrassed smile. "My apologies." His eyes rolled sideways in their sockets, widening as they drank in the darkness eclipsing them. "Oh my God," he uttered. "The house." His voice was but a whisper, his cantankerous inflection burned away, rendering nothing but pure unbridled wonder.

"It's here," Park said with a gulp. She removed the shoulder bag, carefully lowering it to the ground. "I didn't believe it… But it's really here."

They all knew it would be, and yet somehow, they were all equally amazed to find it waiting, hidden away from the rest of the world.

Park cheered, whooping with excitement. She threw her arms around Harper, squeezing her and hooting. "We found it, Harp! We're here! After all those years stuck in those mind-numbing research labs and we're finally here. The fuckin' House that Fell from the Sky and we're standing right in front of it!"

Harper smiled, conceding to let herself enjoy the moment despite her natural inclination to doubt. She reluctantly wrapped her arm around Park and gave the young woman a squeeze. Even Dirac's sour face broke into a congenial grin.

"We did it, Harp!" Park sounded like a kid in a candy shop. She was right to, because despite their differences, as scientists they all shared the same dream, the same hope to change the world for the better, to leave their mark so that when they were gone, their names wouldn't be forgotten. They would be remembered.

And now, standing before the house, she knew they *would* be remembered. The heroes of Winterview City.

"It's incredible," Park said. "Just like I imagined."

Harper could only make out hints of the structure's puzzling design; glimpses afforded to them when the fog permitted. The Halliday House was a crushed black silhouette against velvet moonlight, surgically stitched into Winterview City in one of the most bizarre and outright fantastic spectacles she'd ever laid eyes on. Charcoal onion domes. Cyclopean stone turrets. And long, serrated spires puncturing the cold vacuum of space above.

The feeling was indescribable. Everything she'd seen, every miracle or fledging thought of the universe, nothing could have prepared her for the beauty that was the house.

She knew then that she had made the right choice to come.

This was the answer she'd been looking for.

And the time was now.

She unshouldered her pack and set it on the street.

"Let's get to work."

NICK

"I'M NOT GOING in there."

A length of pulsing black veins had subdued most of the stencil painted on the side of the building, but Nick was still able to make out OUTPOST 31.

Sandi waited a few feet away, arms still crossed, teeth chattering.

"Outpost thirty-one," Nick said. He took a step toward the entrance, which might as well have been a tunnel to hell as far as he was concerned. Two immense rusted steel doors were pried open like someone had taken the jaws of life to them. The plants had crept over the archway of the entrance, forming a natural canopy.

"We can't go in there," Sandi said. "That's government property, Nick. If you get caught they'll send you back for sure. For *good* this time."

A shiver ran through him.

"Yes, thank you, Sandi," he said. "What a perfect time to remind me of that fact."

Cheshire Correctional Facility, aka The Bane of his Existence. For a split-second he hesitated as visions of his old life clawed their way to the surface. The world suddenly felt much smaller. He could smell the urine. Taste the blood. Feel the cold bite of the iron. The tremors in his left hand had never truly left him. Even now, years after he'd left Cheshire in his rearview mirror and never looked back, he knew he'd never truly be free of that nightmare.

"You go in there and that's trespassing," Sandi said. "*Trespassing*, Nick. You told me yourself your PO said he was looking for any reason he could to send you back. Do you really want to take that risk?"

Nick looked over his shoulder at her, annoyed. "What do you call this?" he said, gesturing around at the city. "I hate to break it to you, but we were trespassing the second we stepped past that entrance."

"If you want to scour the streets then fine, I am all for that, but I am also a *good citizen*, and I am not breaking in there and throwing away my reputation."

"Fine, stay here," Nick said, beginning forward.

The wind howled abruptly, carrying on in the cool night. The streets seemed to stir, the copious vegetation rousing to life around them.

Sandi darted from her spot, hurrying over beside him.

"Fuck it, I'm going with you."

The corridor ran at least twenty feet straight back into a well of dank, stone darkness. Nick and Sandi felt along the damp walls for a switch but found nothing.

"I can't see anything!" Sandi hissed.

"You're preaching to the choir," Nick replied. He waved the gun through the air, touching nothing but more air.

"Hello?" Nick's voice carried away, lost. "Is anyone there?"

"Maybe we should turn back."

Nick stopped. "Wait…I see something." He took Sandi's hand and started moving faster, shepherding her along.

"What is it?" Sandi asked. "What do you see?"

A light. It was faint, but it was there. About fifteen feet ahead.

"Nick?"

He ignored her, picking up speed. "There!" he said. His voice boomed, amplified in the corridor.

They stopped at the top of a flight of stairs. Dim fluorescent track lights followed below into the unknown.

"Stairs?" Sandi said.

"Looks that way."

"Where do you think they go?"

"Probably an underground lab where they run experiments on crazed mental patients," he said.

"Nick," she said, unamused, "I am not even in the mood right now."

Nick snickered, starting down the steps towing Sandi behind him. To his surprise, she didn't protest this time around. He thought maybe being out of the wind momentarily was enough to give her some sense of safety.

They descended each step, listening to the world behind. The ruthless wind, shrieking like a banshee. The heavy lull of the thunder high above the city. And the creaks of the decaying institution that was Outpost 31.

The base of stairs stopped at a long hallway with countless doors and windows dotting the walls on either side. The air was heavy with moisture. Nick breathed in wet cement and was pulled back to Cheshire. He remembered the rain seeping in through the cracks in the walls. The rats that would scurry across the floor in the middle of the night. They climbed, too. Some nights he'd wake up and they'd on his pillows, eating away at his lips.

He shuddered, forcing the memory away.

"Nick?"

He turned and saw Sandi's face looking back at him.

"Are you all right?" she asked.

He shook it off, peering around the lengthy hall. The stained carpeting was littered with glass, the long rectangular windows accompanying the rooms destroyed. Pale emergency lights mounted high on the ceilings cast a sickly green tinge over the underground.

Nick took the revolver out of his waistband, holding it down at his side. He craned his neck and noticed the ceiling tiles running the length of the hallway had been stripped away, exposing a network of mangled pipes and insulation. A single bead of sweat glided down his temple, cutting across the stubble on his jaw.

"Nick, look," Sandi whispered, pointing.

On the floor in front of them were dozens of lengths of copper pipe, messily cut and bundled with twine.

Nick quickly stepped to the nearest broken window, leaning in and glancing around.

Inside, two desks were pushed together. He spied an overturned chair. Sheets of paper littering the carpet. And a phone receiver dangling from a curly cord connected to the wall.

"Nick!"

He found Sandi two doors down in another office. This one was even more of a mess. Someone had taken a few chunks out of the walls and part of the ceiling had collapsed like wet paper from water damage. He could smell the mold they were breathing in, taste the moisture in the back of his throat.

Sandi was still, reading a dry-erase board hanging on the far wall.

"What is it?" he asked.

Sandi raised her hand, pointing at a chart on the wall.

"Look at this. This last entry was almost five months ago."

"Five months?"

"Yeah. Last spring."

"No, that can't be right," Nick said. "I saw trucks going in and out of here just a few months back. August maybe?"

"I don't know," Sandi shrugged. "That's what it says." She grabbed a clipboard dangling from the chart, skimming it. "It says here the final security inspection was signed off by someone named Dawson last May. The Director of the Red Sky."

"What the hell is the Red Sky?" Nick asked.

Nick's attention was drawn to a tattered map of the Dead Zone laid across a lone desk. The schematic of the city detailed every side road and alleyway down to the manhole covers. Hundreds of handwritten notes were scrawled across the map in red ink.

"Sandi, look at this," he said.

Sandi dropped the clipboard, wandering over. "A map of the city? What's all that writing?"

Nick leaned down, attempting to decipher the cursive.

"Look at this," Nick said, pointing to the north end of the map. "Electrical failure…twenty-five meters. November sixth, two thousand fourteen. This address…that's where that Italian sandwich shop used to be, isn't it?"

Sandi nodded; her voice nostalgic for her old life. "Piatto Preferito Deli. My dad used to take my sister and I there for panini's after school every Friday. Every blue moon they made this sandwich I was obsessed with called the Godfather. Five different kinds of meat. Provolone cheese. Mayo, mustard, tomato. The works. We must have eaten there a hundred times, Nick. The flavor was… It's why I became a chef in the first place." She paused, reminiscing, and Nick thought she looked happy there, in her memories. Happier than she ever had in life. "My dad used to tease us, tell us that the owners used to be mixed up with the mob. That the deli was just a cover-up."

Nick was quiet. He knew to keep his mouth shut.

"There were always these people picking up packages there. People who didn't look so nice. We always thought he was joking, but thinking back now, I'm not so sure…" She turned to him. "I bet you met a lot of people like that in Cheshire, huh? A lot of different kinds of people."

Nick nodded. "Yeah, Sandi. I did." A stretch of silence drew out between them, and he felt them get farther and farther apart.

Sandi's eyes fluttered, and it was like she had boxed up the bad thoughts, the notion that Nick might have been just the same as the bad people she and her family had seen while they ate lunch all those times at the deli.

Sandi reread the note in disbelief. "Electrical failure?" She noticed a small set of digits was scribbled to the side of the note: *002.* "These numbers…do you think they're chronological? The order of the occurrences?"

Nick examined the map for the other reported outages, locating each of them. "Yeah, that looks right. The dates correspond with these numbers."

"The power..." Sandi muttered. "The outages must have spread too fast. They weren't prepared for it to spread outside the Dead Zone so quickly. That's why this place was abandoned: they couldn't function here without electricity."

"But there *is* electricity," Nick said, gesturing at one of the emergency lights.

"No," Sandi said, shaking her head. "That's like back at your place. It's on but...*barely*. That wouldn't be enough here, not to keep the power on for a place this size. Especially if there are others."

"Hey, look at this one," he said, tapping his finger on the map closer to the house. "First encounter...December twenty-fifth, two thousand and fourteen."

"First encounter?" Sandi said. "Christmas?"

"Encounter with what?"

They shared an ominous look.

"I'm not sure I want to find out," Sandi admitted.

While she attempted to interpret more of the map, Nick strayed further into the room, taking in everything from generic workplace safety posters to a register of all staff members and their corresponding departments contained in Outpost 31.

He came to a punch clock and stopped in his tracks.

Wait. No, that was wrong. He'd never seen one quite like this. This wasn't the modern digital time clock he'd been accustomed to seeing most his life. This one was metal, olive green. He noticed a small cache of punch cards to the side and picked one up, reading it.

"Anna Dunn," he said quietly. "What the hell were you all doing here, Anna? What were you looking for?"

Nick respectfully set the punch card back on the shelf and continued on. He came to a set of metal bookcases and stopped, reading the text printed prominently on every spine.

"The Red Sky, Outpost thirty-one."

He tugged a random binder from the shelf and read the title:

"Department of Electrical Engineering."

He flipped open the cover, fingering through the pages, finding dozens upon dozens of redacted lines and whole sections of the manual torn out altogether.

"Anything useful?" Sandi asked. She quickly gathered the map from the table, crudely folding it up and shoving it into the jacket pocket.

Nick shook his head, shoving the binder back on the shelf. "No. Just more about the power issues they were having. We're wasting time; I don't think she's here."

A clatter of metal, loud.

The pipes!

Nick threw his arm out, pushing Sandi against the wall and flattening himself.

The light radiating from the hall flickered, dimming a shade. It was hard to see now, but if the lights were any indicator, soon they wouldn't be able to see at all.

With his back to the wall, Nick raised the pistol, sliding to the edge of the busted window. He drew in a deep breath and looked out, scoping out the darkened hall.

"HEY!" he shouted.

Sandi nearly jumped out of her skin as he rushed into the hall.

"Don't move!" he warned.

At the opposite end of the hall, an ominous figure in a white cloak waited, the hood casting a shadow over a bone-white mask.

Nick's mind raced, his body overloaded with adrenaline. Everything had gone quiet. The thunder. The wind breathing in from the entrance. Everything but his own beating heart.

"Who are you?" he asked, and he realized his voice was wobbly with fear.

"Nick?" Sandi hissed. "What do we do?" She was still hiding back in the office, watching the scene play out in front of her like her own personal horror film.

"Stay there," Nick reassured, holding a hand up.

The walls moaned, the lights flickering.

He took another step forward, squinting, and realized the mask resembled that of a doll. Almost cartoon-like in a nightmarish sort of way. Emotionless, hollow eyes. Flat, thin lips. No smile, or frown. No trace of sentiment whatsoever, the porcelain glossed over with a sheen of bleached white paint. And the blank, seemingly detached behavior of the individual behind the mask only made it that much worse.

"What are you doing here?" Nick asked. His patience was slipping. "Hey! I said, what are you doing—"

The shape sprang to life, sprinting straight at him.

Sandi screamed so loud Nick thought the windows might have shattered if they weren't already broken.

A flash of bright light lit up the hall.

The figure dropped to their knees, a quarter-sized spot of blood blossoming across the fabric. A piece of metal thudded to the ground and he saw the glint of a blade.

Nick could hear someone wheezing beneath the robe, fighting to breathe. Fighting to lunge at him even with their dying breaths.

Another flash. The gun kicked in his hands in a deafening clap; the hooded figure's head whipped backward; the body thrown to the ground.

Nick was frozen in place, the gun held out in front of him, hands shaking. Licks of smoke rose up dreamily from the barrel. His mind had gone blank. Was he in shock? He'd never killed anyone before. Sure, he'd heard stories while he kept his mouth shut and did his time, but he'd never expected it to feel like this. So...*numb*.

Before he had time to react, a blunt pain speared into his lower back. His eyes instantly watered; he tried to force a scream but couldn't; the air had been ripped from his lungs. An arm coolly wrapped around his neck, locking down on his throat. He choked out a garbled scream, his entire body contracting. The gun tumbled from his hand, somersaulting to the floor.

He listened to Sandi screaming bloody murder in the background of this horrible dream where he was being strangled and stabbed simultaneously. He collapsed to the floor, struggling to pry the arm from around his neck. The forearm around his throat flexed; the blade twisted in the tender muscle, grazing against bone. He screamed and strings of spittle flew from his mouth. His vision began to blur, darkening. Darkening. Why couldn't he see? The pain subsided for a moment then came roaring back. Tears slipped from his eyes as the life began to retreat from his body.

There was an audible thud and the pain ground to a halt. Not completely gone, but not nearly as excruciating as two seconds ago. Now it was just cold.

The pressure around his neck released instantly, granting him momentary relief. But without the assailant trying to tear his head off, he had nothing to keep him upright. His body buckled, collapsing to the floor.

The next seconds were like a dream. He watched them play out in a blur.

His attacker—a second robbed assailant—was yanked backward like a rag doll, folding in half as his savior threw a concrete fist into their stomach. The man effortlessly manhandled the cultist, clutching them with both hands and spinning them around. He threw a knee up and the shape grunted as teeth smashed. The man rocked them back, using the momentum to launch the body through the air into the open office window.

Sandi yelped as the body landed on the windowsill, impaled by the serrated shards lining the frame.

He watched as his guardian angel walked over and folded his arms around the cultist's neck. The body flailed like a dying fish, the limbs weakly kicking as the man leaned in, twisting until there was a dusty *snap!*

The body went limp, limbs falling lifelessly at their sides.

The man released the corpse and pushed himself upright, taking a deep breath.

Nick's pulse weakened, slowing in his ears. He thought he heard rain in the distance, back out in the streets. He thought about Rachel, screamed at himself to get up, get moving. To find her while there was still time.

He watched as the stranger, the man who had saved his life, reached into his shirt pocket and took out a brass Zippo. The man snapped his fingers and the flame danced to life, lighting a cigarette and sucking in a long drag. He blew the smoke out of his nostrils while he considered the corpse, snapping the Zippo closed and shaking his head. God, it smelled heavenly. He knew one thing: if he made it out of this alive, he was having a fucking cigarette. He didn't care if he'd paid a thousand dollars to quit (back when he could afford such luxuries).

"What's wrong with you?" the man asked curtly, and Nick realized he'd completely forgotten about Sandi. "Ain't you never seen a dead body before?"

That voice...there was something familiar about it.

Nick's consciousness was fading and returning, his mind dipping in and out of a dream.

Eyes half closed and powerless, he watched the man flick the glowing cigarette butt at Sandi. She yelped, scrambling to brush the ashes off her clothes. "Asshole!"

The man began walking toward him and he feared the worst, defenseless and bleeding out like a stuck pig. The man stopped short, leaning down and scooping up the bundles of copper pipes in his arms. He casually walked over, getting down on one knee and using a free hand to pry open Nick's eyelids.

All he could make out was a blurry face steeped in shadows.

Nick groaned, fighting to pull away as the man rolled him onto his side and felt around his back. He wheezed; his body pulling away as the man hastily inspected the wound.

The man took something small out of his pocket and he heard a plastic *pop!*

White-hot pain flared again as heat thawed his back.

His breathing weakened.

He was weakening.

"He'll live," the man quipped to Sandi. He stood up with his pipes and began climbing the stairs. "I'd get out the city if I was you. Dead

Zone ain't no place for a gimp and his broad."

And with that, he was gone.

Sandi rushed out of the office, coming to his aid.

"Nick? Nick, can you hear me?" she asked, panicked.

The numbness hemorrhaging into his body was spreading like he was being submerged in ice water. Pockets of blackness began pooling everywhere he looked, bleeding together until there was nothing but darkness.

HARPER

THE FIRST TEST had been a failure.

At some point during their brief journey to the house, two of the rats had perished. Harper attempted to mask her irritation as best she could, but Park still detected it anyway.

"It wasn't your fault, Harp," she said, sealing them into specimen containers and logging them in her journal. "They were obviously sick. No one could have known they weren't going to make the trip. Sometimes these things happen."

"I *know* it wasn't my fault," Harper said, "but we're down two subjects now, which means we're already deviating from the plan and we haven't even stepped foot inside the house yet. At this rate I'd be surprised if we're able to salvage any useful data at all."

Neither Harper nor Park nor Dirac could find any medical explanation as to why the rats had died. Christened Harry and Sally respectively, Park had procured them herself from a lab in Boulder, Colorado, two weeks before the expedition. Insured to be in immaculate health and masterfully trained, the team was surprised to find them both dead by the time they'd arrived at the house.

"I'd say this mission is off to a splendid start. Wouldn't you, Dr. Harper?" Dirac sneered.

Harper ignored him, centering the lengths of clear tubing leading across the threshold into the house. They turned sharply at the top of the porch steps, angling down to the street like a long, miniature waterslide. "Dirac: the starting chamber."

Dirac sighed, making no effort to hide his contempt, then picked up a small plastic box with a hatch on the top and handed it to Harper, who met him at the bottom of the porch steps. Harper set it on the ground at the foot of the steps. She screwed two tubes to the front ports, and stood up.

"And what exactly is it that we are supposed to learn from these rodents, Dr. Harper?"

Park was crouched down over the second transport container. "We *should* be sending you in there first, Dirac, but apparently the Board of Ethics favor tenure over personality." She reached in and removed two small white rats.

Harper lifted the lid on the starting chamber, and Park carefully set the rats inside, one in each chamber.

"Good luck, guys," Park said with a smile. "Don't embarrass me."

Harper closed the lid, then slid open a small door separating the tubes from the starting chamber. "According to the Red Sky, any living organisms that have breached the entrance to the house have come back out in one of two ways. The first? Extreme shock followed by a catatonic state that has thus far has been deemed irreversible. Not a single one has recovered."

"Riveting," Dirac deadpanned. "And the second?"

Harper continued, "Whereas the others have slipped into a form of coma, the others suffered a complete psychotic break not long after. Violence. Aggression. Sadism. They've become a danger to themselves and others. Deemed worthy of twenty-four-hour surveillance by the Red Sky."

The two rats scurried into their respective chambers, and Harper slid the plastic door closed behind them.

"I am more than familiar with the ghost stories, thank you," Dirac said.

"And let's not forget the third possibility," Harper added.

Park followed along the tubing, trailing along as the rats moved further down the pipe. She climbed the steps as the rats scurried up the tubing, cheering them on.

"The third option," Harper said, standing eye to eye with Dirac, "is you walk out of there before sunrise without losing your fucking mind. Tragically, the least likely outcome here tonight if history has taught us anything."

Dirac scoffed. "That's nonsense. I don't believe a word of it."

"Fortunately for us, for the next ten minutes anyway," she smirked, "these two subjects will be scouting ahead to determine the house's environmental conditions. Their likelihood that we don't lose our minds inside."

"Their *names* are Willard and Wendy," Park growled.

Harper watched Willard and Wendy scamper further, nearly to the slice of darkness running across the entrance. "The year of the house's arrival, two men went inside," Harper said. "The first was a civilian. He killed himself right here on this very porch. And the other man? The guard? Well, he probably wishes he was dead."

"I've known that for years and it still gives me the chills every time," Park said, standing up.

"Yes, we all know the tales of supernatural horror surrounding this house, Dr. Harper," Dirac said.

"You don't believe it?" Park asked.

"Are you dense?" Dirac scoffed. "Of course I don't believe it. That's pure rubbish." Dirac pointed at the structure towering over them, a funnel of moonlight casting him in a spotlight. "Every morsel of information that has been released about this building has not only been strategically controlled but also sensationalized by every conspiracy theorist, paparazzi, and failed dime store writer in a desperate—and might I add *poor*—attempt to turn a profit."

"Then what are you doing here, Dirac?" Park asked. Her candor caught him off-guard. "I mean, if you don't believe in all this, why come here?"

Dirac rolled his eyes. "I am here because, like you both, I am the best at what I do. However, I still am not convinced of your supposed qualifications, Dr. Park, but I digress. I am also being compensated with a considerable payout as are you both. Why else do you think I'd be standing here with you two in the middle of the night babysitting these rodents?"

"I don't buy it," Park blurted out. "No way you're here just for the money."

"Says you," Dirac replied.

"He wants to prove there's nothing here," Harper said curtly.

Dirac smirked.

"Isn't that right, Dr. Dirac?"

"I don't know what you're talking about," Dirac sneered.

"You're abrasive, pragmatic, callous. Impatient. You exhibit antisocial tendencies yet you're revered in your field. I've learned much during my time in academia, and if there's one constant that stands out above all, it is that talent will take you far in science, but personality takes you further, which tells me that perhaps you're not quite as miserable as you make yourself out to be."

Dirac glared at her.

"That true?" Park asked. "You a big softie in there somewhere, Dr. Dreadful?" She reached up and squeezed his cheek.

Dirac went to speak but stopped before the words could escape his mouth.

"Hey. Earth to Dirac," Park said, waving a hand in front of his face. "What's the matter?"

Harper and Park followed his line of sight, turning to the fog.

"What is it?" Harper asked, expecting something to come barreling out of the mist.

Dirac blinked his eyes, confused. "Nothing," he said, his voice soft. "I thought I saw something."

"What did you see?" Harper asked.

Dirac seemed to grow agitated then, like she'd kicked the hornet's nest. "Nothing, I said. Now can we get on with this?"

"All right all right, easy old timer," Park said. "Okay, let's see where they're—"

Park's notebook fell to the porch, her pencil bouncing down the steps. She dropped to her knees, bending over the two clear tubes feeding into the house. "Oh my God, Harp! Look!"

Harper dropped down across from her, peering inside.

Willard and Wendy were out. But more importantly, they were alive. They casually scurried back toward the starting chamber while Harper and Park watched in stone-shocked silence.

"What's going on?" Dirac asked. "What *about* them?"

"They're out, Harper. They're alive." Park crawled on her hands and knees, following them back to the chamber. She pulled open the panel, letting them scurry back into the box. "They're not showing any signs of distress. No physical damage. How is that possible, Harper?"

"Excuse me," Dirac said. "What exactly does that mean?"

Harper leaned back and rest on her knees, chuckling. "I don't do animals, Park. That's your department."

"Hey!" Dirac yelled. "Will someone please explain to me what's going on here? What are you two yammering on about?"

Harper watched as the rats stirred in the box, separated only by a clear plastic wall yet clearly interacting with each other. It was the second miracle of the night. She shook her head, riveted. "It means that something has changed," she declared. "Something unprecedented."

"Holy shit," Park said.

"I know," Harper began. "If the rats are alive that means—"

"No," Park interrupted, pointing.

Harper turned and looked down the steps.

And Park said, "People."

NICK

THE FOG BROKE apart like a cloud: two women and an old man stood on the porch of a house unlike anything he'd ever seen. Him and Sandi caught glimpses of it through holes in the fog, never revealing its entirety, yet revealing just enough to raise goosebumps on their arms.

There were two long clear tubes running down the porch steps, and a bunch of gear piled down on the street. Black bags and all variety of scientific equipment. And by equipment standards it appeared ridiculously expensive.

He limped along, moving slow, Sandi faithfully at his side. He felt the pull of his skin anytime his torso shifted, the glue holding up well enough. Sandi hadn't gotten a good look at the guy, but it didn't matter. He was long gone by the time they'd gotten outside. Sandi had made use of the map, navigating their way to the house. Turns out she couldn't read well in the dark and he couldn't walk well after being stabbed in the back, so progress had been painfully slow. Literally.

He'd unloaded two rounds already from the Python, which meant he had exactly four bullets left to protect them until they were clear of the Dead Zone. And he assumed those cultists weren't random attacks, which meant there were more than likely others watching. Waiting.

The trio spotted them and they slowed, coming to a stop a short distance away in the street. He strained in the moonlight but couldn't make out their faces.

That was when the taller of the two women walked out and he recognized her immediately.

"Dr. Harper?" he called.

Harper took a cautious step down the porch stairs.

The same dusty red hair. The same dark, oversized eyes. Skin as white as milk. Standoffish yet curious. It was her, all right.

"Nick?"

The second woman emerged from the shadows, standing beside Harper. Her stick-straight hair barely reached her shoulders, her eyes unassuming yet striking, a shade of green like a glass marble. She was Asian, that much he could tell, although from what region he couldn't be sure. She blinked, and Nick could see she appeared more inquisitive than alarmed. Almost like she was amused by the whole thing.

"Wait—you know them?" Sandi asked, shocked.

"They were outside my apartment earlier today," he said. "They said they're with the military."

"This is Park," Harper announced.

The Asian woman gave a short wave, smiling awkwardly.

"And this is Dirac." The man had a scowl on his face.

Nick gestured to Sandi. "This is Sandi."

"Nice to meet you!" Park yelled, and her voice bounced down the steps to greet them.

"Have you guys seen anyone here tonight?" Nick asked.

Harper arched an eyebrow. "You mean besides you? No."

"We're looking for my daughter," Nick said, his voice sounding ten times louder in the warped streets. "Someone attacked us earlier tonight."

"What're you talking about?" Harper asked, beginning down the stairs. "Attacked by whom?"

Before he could answer, a scream broke out to his left.

"Uh," Park uttered. "Did anyone else hear that?"

Another agonizing wail sent a shiver through him.

Nick turned, and Sandi did too.

Everyone did, in fact, and when they had all joined together in the middle of Seventh Street, a group of strangers in the night, they heard it again, that sound.

A baby.

PART 2: FORGOTTEN

SCARLETT

"YOU'RE A HERO, Scarlett."

The air was frozen. Scarlett Vantassel looked down and noticed her bare nails tapping away on the chair, and forced herself to stop. Her attention span had never been great. Her memory was one thing, but her attention span? Well, that was a completely different beast altogether.

Captain Hillard, the woman in charge of the Training Division of the Long Beach Police Department, sat rigid on the other side of an immaculate metal desk, her thick black hair pulled back in a tight bun, her uniform free of wrinkles and stains. A woman who took pride in her work. She also happened to be the shepherd of forty starry-eyed cadets that had come from all over the country to partake in twenty-seven grueling weeks of nail biting, action-packed law enforcement training.

Scarlett blinked, caught in a daze, suddenly all too aware of her current state. Her uniform shirt was half untucked, part of her collar smashed vertical, long creases cutting diagonally across her left leg. The truth was, she was a fucking mess.

You're a hero, Scarlett.

The words echoed in her head. Fluorescent lights buzzed overhead while stale air was pumped into the room. Was it the lights making that sound? Or was it in her head, injected into her mind by her time in the house? It always got worse the closer the days got to Halloween. The buzzing rose in her ears as she watched Captain Hillard's mouth move in slow motion, looking across at her with pity.

"I'm not," Scarlett choked out.

The buzzing stopped; her clarity swimming back.

Captain Hillard raised her eyebrows, leaning forward in her chair.

"What's that?" the woman asked.

"I'm not a hero," Scarlett cleared her throat, groping for her collar and flattening it, making a poor attempt to tuck her shirt in. "People say that, they tell me that day after day and, to be honest, I don't even know what that word means anymore."

There had never been a moment, not a day nor second where she believed herself to be a hero. What she was, was a survivor. And just like that, she was right back where she started. Her eyes followed down her chest, finding her name badge crooked, one side sagging noticeably.

"I doubt there's a single person in this academy that doesn't believe you to be a hero," Hillard replied. "That being said, in *here*, you're not special. You're just like everyone else, and it is my responsibility to make sure you are treated as such."

"I don't know what you want me to do. I don't...I don't even know why I'm in here."

"You don't?"

Scarlett shook her head.

"Well, allow me to enlighten you." Captain Hillard leaned back in her chair, steepling her fingers. "Scarlett, your...*celebrity status* has made things very challenging for us all here at the academy."

"Celebrity status?"

"I remember seeing you on the TV the morning you walked out the front doors. Both of you looked like you'd been through a war and then some, all covered in dirt and blood. And the truth was, my heart ached for you. Everyone out here thought it was some big publicity stunt, that lottery they had going over there in Winterview. We all did, me included. And it worked, to a degree. Hell, I can't remember a time when that city got more attention than Manhattan, but it did." Hillard took a breath. "But when you walked out of that house there was something so…genuine, in your eyes. Something so real, and raw. I knew then that you weren't some actress, that the whole thing wasn't some big charade for the news stations. But you know what I *didn't* see?"

Scarlett shook her head.

"I didn't see a victim" Captain Hillard exhaled, hooking a thumb toward the window. "I saw a survivor."

Outside in the academy parking lot, a circus made up of news vans, paparazzi, and fanatics were restless. She didn't mind the media so much anymore. After a few weeks she'd gotten used to them popping up here and there, shoving microphones in her face and blasting her with questions. But the fanatics…well, something about them didn't sit right with her. Maybe because they were true believers. People who wanted answers. And they were more relentless than a bucket of starved rats.

Scarlett sighed, running her tongue inside her cheek. "Oh. *Them.*"

"Make no mistake, your entourage are definitely an inconvenience, but they are not the bigger issue here." Captain Hillard exhaled again, shaking her head. "I think it's time we address the elephant in the room."

"I'm sorry, I don't—"

"How old are you, Scarlett?"

"What does that have to do with anything?"

"The average age in here is twenty-two. What're you? Thirty?"

"So…what? Are you saying I'm too old? I've been running laps around some of those guys. I almost got blinded yesterday with pepper spray for fuck's sake."

"Language," Hillard said.

"Sorry, Captain," she said, flashing a toothy smile.

"On the contrary," Hillard said. "There are hundreds of people that have passed through here and went on to decorated careers in law enforcement."

"I'm struggling to see what that has to do with anything?"

"Scarlett, *listen*," Hillard said. "Shut up and listen."

Scarlett nodded.

"You're right. Some are older than others. Age doesn't matter in the grand scheme of things, but they *do* all have one thing in common."

Scarlett listened.

"Most join because they see a future doing what we do. Protecting the city. Helping people. Maintaining order, and balance. Keeping the peace, as they say.

"Suffice to say, this may or may not have always been their dream. Everyone has their own reasons for joining, whether it's money or a common interest in what we do here. But, the one thing that they all have in common is that at the end of the day, they're here because this was the path they chose."

"So, what are you saying? That I'm not meant for it? That I'm not cut out for it?"

Hillard leaned forward, resting her arms on the desk. Despite the direction the conversation was headed, Hillard still somehow managed to maintain her objectiveness, a trait Scarlett assumed was part of what made her so proficient at her job.

"Scarlett, I've been reading over your evaluation, and while I won't bore you with the details, every one of the range officers overseeing your progress has expressed that your focus has become a serious cause for concern."

Scarlett leaned back in the chair, blindsided by the accusation. "My focus?"

"It's no secret that there have been a few…how can I put this delicately…"

"Captain?" Scarlett said. Her body tensed. The cords in her neck tightened, the beginnings of a migraine warming the base of her skull. "I don't *need* you to put anything delicately. You said yourself I wouldn't be treated any differently in here, so if there *is* a problem, I would appreciate a little honesty from you of all people."

"Of course." Captain Hillard smiled, nodding her head. "As you're well aware, a few of your fellow cadets have expressed concern after the incident this morning. I trust you *do* remember what happened this morning?"

"Yes." Scarlett blinked her tired eyes. "I have nightmares

sometimes."

"The house?"

Scarlett nodded.

"Must feel pretty damned real. They say you were screaming at the top of your lungs."

Scarlett swallowed, brushing a loose strand of hair behind her ear. "Lots of people have nightmares, Captain."

"But you're not just anyone now, are you, Scarlett?" Hillard shrugged. "I have seen lots of men scared in my life. Grown men reduced to sobbing messes when they're hauled off to county lockup. I guess it sort of comes with the territory. But your colleagues? They are genuinely terrified of your behavior. Enough so that it is actively disrupting their ability to properly focus on the program here."

"Like I said, lots of people have nightmares. It doesn't mean anything."

"Well, I suspect your history with the supernatural writes whatever story people want to believe when they meet you." Hillard hooked her thumbs into her leather duty belt, gazing out at the media frenzy in the parking lot.

"I'm sorry." Scarlett shook her head.

"Well, be that as it may, this is the latest in a long list of strange occurrences since you landed on our doorstep."

Hillard rose from her chair and walked to the window, leaning against the frame. "I'm not a religious woman," she said. "I don't believe in aliens and ghosts and the supernatural. Heaven and Hell." Hillard sucked in a deep breath, grabbing her jaw and the back of her head and twisting until a sandy crunch rang out. She twisted her head, loosening up. "Unfortunately, not everyone here thinks like I do, and these instances have compounded, causing more rumors in these halls than a damn high school locker room."

Scarlett felt the tinge of disgust on her tongue. Why couldn't people mind their own business? Why'd they have to throw fuel on the fire instead of a bucket of water?

She thought of Tommy then, wondered what he would do if it were him sitting here across from Hillard. He always knew the right thing to say, always knew how to make Scarlett feel like what she was going through was only a bump in the road. He listened, made her feel valid, like she mattered. He was always the optimist. Always brave.

And now he was gone. What would he say if he were here now? she wondered. She saw an image of him smile in her mind's eye, and the cold doom that was creeping into her head pulled away. God, she missed him.

Hillard turned, looking her in the eyes. "I do, however, believe that something *did* happen in that house. I don't know what, and I don't want to know. Frankly, anything happening outside of the city of Long Beach is not my problem. But you are here, which makes *you* my problem."

"They seem to find me no matter where I go," Scarlett replied, motioning at the crowds outside.

Hillard folded her arms, standoffish yet receptive.

"I thought after the first few months maybe they'd start to thin out a little bit, but no matter what I do, they're always right there, following me."

"One of the perks of being famous," Hillard said.

"What would you do if you were me?" Scarlett asked.

Hillard casually sauntered back to her desk, easing into her chair. "They'll tire of you eventually. News only stays news for so long."

Scarlett nodded, her head down.

"I noticed that prior to coming here you had previously interviewed with Winterview Police Department. Is that true?"

"Yeah."

"What happened?"

Scarlett coughed up a laugh, fidgeting in her seat. "They denied my application," she said. "They thought I had too much 'history' with the city. The house and all. They didn't think it was a good idea."

"Huh," Hillard said. "Probably for the best. If it's this bad here I don't even know how you'd walk outside in Winterview. You probably dodged a bullet anyway with all the shit going on over there."

"What do you mean?"

"It's been all over the news for months. Don't you keep up?"

"I don't use social media anymore."

"Really?" Hillard asked. "The 'queen' of TikTok and Instagram? My daughters say your YouTube channel broke every record in history. They said you even got some sort of red diamond because of it."

"The Red Diamond Play Button," Scarlett said. "And yes. But that's my old life. I gave all that up. I try to keep a low profile now, stay off the grid when I can."

"Why?" Hillard asked bluntly. "Why would you give up all that up?"

And she said, "To cling to any semblance of a normal life while I still can." Scarlett reflexively began chewing a hangnail, blinking her curious eyes. "What happened—in Winterview?"

Hillard reached down behind her desk, shuffling through papers. "Haven't you heard?" She reappeared, slapping the front page of *The Long Beach Post* on the desk.

Scarlett's eyes widened. Her heart beat harder. She felt an alarm like a cyclone picking up speed in the pit of her stomach. She snatched up the paper, standing up, her eyes trailing over the big bold letters scrawled across the front page beside a black and white photo of the house.

WINTERVIEW SUICIDES CLIMB, EAST COAST UNDER SIEGE

Dad.

Her first thought. Panic swelled in her chest. How long had it been since she'd called home, checked in on the one person who'd been there since it all started? Since the beginning.

Scarlett skimmed the article while Hillard's words fell on deaf ears. The buzzing was back, climbing, climbing. How had things gotten this bad in Winterview? How could she be so careless? Had she learned nothing from before?

"Scarlett?" Hillard's voice, stern and unshakeable.

Scarlett turned around, grabbing her jacket off the back of the chair and starting for the door. Her fingers were on the knob, twisting.

"Scarlett!" Hillard was right behind her now.

Scarlett turned around, eyes blazing.

"I know that you have been through something extraordinary. I wish that I could tell you that I understand, but I can't. What I *can* say is that we have come to an impasse. A place where if things don't change soon, I am going to have to make a very difficult choice," she put a hand on Scarlett's shoulder. "And I don't want to have to do that, Scarlett."

"You don't have to—I already made it."

JACKSON

THE OCEAN BREEZE was heavenly. Jackson Briggs smiled as the salty air caressed his face, softly tousling his feathered black hair. He smelled brine and seaweed infused with suntan lotion and barbeque. It was fall, but the weather was still nice, and the community had no intention of letting it go to waste. Everything about being back on the Pacific Coast made him feel right at home, from the endless beachgoers dotting the shimmering sand down to the parade of vibrant kites dancing across the sky.

He had it all. Everything he'd ever wanted. Thousands of miles between him and his father, Chief Todd Briggs of the Winterview Police Department. Canyons and rivers and mountains between him and the house. He had an apartment with an ocean view, more horror movies than he could get his hands on, and best of all, he was in love with the one person in the world who meant more than any one of those things combined. The person he'd literally walked into hell for and somehow emerged unscathed, give or take.

Scarlett Vantassel. His friend. His lover. His other half.

So why did something still feel off even now? Almost like everything he held in the palm of his hand was only an illusion that could crumble away at any moment and turn to the same ash blowing around

Winterview this very second.

"Jackson Briggs?"

He tore himself away from the kites fluttering against the horizon to find a tall balding man looming over him.

"Present," he said with an obnoxious smile. "Just joking."

The man frowned, unimpressed. "Come with me," he said, starting inside.

He'd never dressed so formal in his whole life. A navy button-up shirt (Scarlett had picked it out at TJ Maxx). A silk tie. Even dress shoes with a mirror shine with the exception of a small scuff on the inside right toe. Truth was, he felt like a circus attraction. Step right up, get your tickets to see the amazing Jackson Briggs blow another fabulous opportunity!

And all for what? A job he didn't even want in the first place?

The sunlight dimmed a shade as he stepped into Blackbeard's, a seafood junkie's dream. The air dripped of deep-fried batter and grease. He ran his fingers over a stained wooden table as they passed. This place definitely had the costal vibe down. At the edge of each table was a small lighthouse painted with its respective table number. Stark white paneling with blue accents glowed from the sun burning through the front windows. He'd eaten here once with his mother and he-who-shall-not-be-named when he was little, but they'd never returned. And, standing on the nautical star in the middle of the restaurant, he suddenly knew why.

The man zigzagged between a mess of blue chairs, guiding him through a graveyard of plastic meal baskets and shrimp tails before stopping at a booth tucked away in the corner. He held out his hand, and Jackson scooted in on one side. He thought about the Nighthawk Diner then, nostalgic for the past. It may have been a booth in that it had two bench seats, but other than that, it couldn't have been more different.

The man snapped his fingers in the air at two workers talking by the kitchen. He pointed at a flood of soda and ice pooled on a nearby table and the two employees groaned. "Not tomorrow, *now*," he barked.

"Nice place," Jackson remarked. He nodded his head at a basket on the table across from them. "Hushpuppies?"

"Yes."

Disgusting is what they were. Fried batter over fish guts.

"My name is Randy Stevens," the man said. "I have been the manager here for the past eight years and sixteen days."

"Wow. Down to the day." A laugh unintentionally caught in Jackson's throat and the manager's eyes narrowed. "Sorry," Jackson said, "throat's a little dry."

The manager eyed him suspiciously, splaying a packet of paperwork on the table.

"So," Randy said, flipping through the pages. "Mr. Briggs."

Jackson's jaw tensed. *Mr. Briggs.* His father's name as far as he was concerned. He'd abandoned that name the second he'd left Winterview in his rearview mirror.

"This says here that you worked for Ramsey's Pub for…ten years?"

"*Rowdy's,*" Jackson corrected.

"What's that?" the manager asked.

"It's Rowdy's Pub."

"I see…" Randy the manager flipped the page, looking confused. "It seems that you forgot to list your previous job experience, Mr. Briggs."

That name again…

"No, I didn't. That's all there is."

"I'm sorry?"

"I…well, you see, the thing is," Jackson said, shifting in his seat. "I haven't had any other jobs besides Rowdy's."

Randy's eyebrow arched. He flipped through the pages as if there'd been some sort of mistake. The clock on the wall ticked down, down, down.

"I see…" Randy said.

"I'm good with people," Jackson said. He knew it was a mistake the second the words left his mouth. Randy somehow looked even less impressed if that was possible.

Randy's eyebrow arched higher.

Strike two, he thought.

"Most the time, anyway," Jackson said with a pained smile.

"Your resume says you relocated from Winterviel City?"

"*Winterview*," he corrected.

Randy smirked, nodding. He leaned forward, beckoning him with his index finger as though he was going to share a secret.

Jackson looked around, confused, and leaned in to meet him.

"You may want to give your resume another spellcheck," he whispered. He winked, then smirked. "Just a thought."

"Right," Jackson said. "Thanks."

Jesus, what a disaster. He couldn't even get the resume right and here he was trying to find his purpose in life? And in place called "Blackbeard's" of all places?

"Winterview City..." Randy muttered. He lazily leaned back and the booth's vinyl seat creaked. He ran his plump fingers over his tongue and smoothed his mustache. "Where's that again?"

"Winterview?" Jackson asked.

Randy nodded.

"Oh," he said. "It's over on the east coast. Connecticut."

Randy stopped stroking his mustache. "Connecticut? What brought you way the hell out here?"

Clearly this man wasn't one to keep up on current events. If Jackson had to guess, Randy probably spent more time in Blackbeard's than in his own home.

"I'm originally from here," Jackson replied. "We moved around a lot when I was a kid. I was sort of an army brat growing up. Before Winterview, I mean."

Randy made a gun out of his fingers and pointed at Jackson, clicking his tongue. "Ah, gotcha."

A crash of glass to his left.

Jackson turned to find one of the employees standing a few feet away, gawping at him like he was Santa Claus himself. Tall and lanky with a pair of coke bottle glasses, a face angry with acne, and nest of frizzy red hair, the kid couldn't have been a day over eighteen. Jackson had never considered himself one of the "cool kids," but he'd be surprised if this kid had ever spoken to the opposite sex let alone rounded first base.

"Nelson!" Randy snapped. "What the hell are you doing?"

"It's you!" the teen named Nelson, his voice ecstatic. "From the TV."

Randy looked at Jackson and Jackson played it cool. "Sorry, kid, I have no idea what you're talking about."

"Of course you do, you're—"

"Nelson!" Now it was Randy yelling. "You better get yourself under control unless you want to go have a little chat in the office when you're done cleaning up this mess."

"Oh, blow it out of your ass, old man," Nelson said.

Jackson erupted into a fit of laughter, and Nelson followed suit.

Fuck it. He didn't need a job that badly.

"It's time to go," he said to himself, swinging out of the booth.

"No, wait!" Nelson said.

He heard Randy screaming out at him, berating him.

"Suck a dick, you fat prick! You can choke on this disgusting food, I quit!" Nelson shouted over his shoulder at Randy.

The front doors split in front of him and then he was out. The burnt grease scent whisked away, replaced by the cool ocean air.

He smiled, untied his tie, and slid it off, wrapping it around his hand. He skipped down the steps, rolling up his sleeves and checking his watch. Scarlett wouldn't be home for an hour; he had some time to kill.

He stood on the sidewalk, closing his eyes and looking up at the sun, feeling the warmth on his face. He listened to the sounds of the city. Carefree voices. Dogs barking. The gentle lull of the ocean waves.

He couldn't help but smile.

He opened his eyes, drawn to the pier down the beach, and started forward, jogging across the crosswalk.

He stopped when he reached the wet sand, bending over and slipping off the dress shoes he hated so much and lobbing them back on the beach. He rolled his slacks up to his knees, then peeled off his dress socks, letting his toes sink into the wet sand.

The warm saltwater swept across his feet, splashing up against his ankles and shins. The smell of the ocean was all but euphoric, and he felt so overcome with happiness he thought he might faint.

True, it was another blown opportunity, just like he knew it would be. A complete and utter disaster truth be told.

But when it came down to it, he couldn't have cared less.

Maybe because he knew he had the only thing that mattered to him. Or maybe it was being home again, a place that would always be here, waiting for him.

But then again, maybe it was that cool million dollars sitting in his bank account.

A half hour later he was sitting on the pier, legs dangling off the edge, sprinkles of sand matted to his feet, his contented face staring out the railing separating him from the great big blue.

Clouds had begun to form on the horizon, but they were hours away. Nevertheless, a handful of beachgoers packed their folding chairs and beer coolers into their cars, marching across the sand like lines of ants.

"Holy shit."

Oh no.

"It *is* you! I knew it!"

He looked up to find Nelson's stringy silhouette blotting out the sun.

"You following me?" Jackson asked.

"Me? Shit yeah!"

Jackson rolled his eyes, thumping his head on the bars. He exhaled, his hands tightening around the iron. "This is sort of my quiet time, *Nelson*, was it?"

"Holy piss, he remembers my name!" Spoken as if he'd heard God Himself. Nelson laughed, giddy with excitement, and sat down next to

Jackson, making himself at home and sliding his legs out between the railing like they were old buddies.

"Will you join me?" Jackson said sarcastically.

"The guys down at the Matrix are never going to believe this," Nelson said.

"The Matrix?"

"Oh," Nelson said, as if he'd made a faux pas. He used his middle finger to push his glasses up on the bridge of his nose. "It's the game store down the street. Magic the Gathering. Pokémon. Warhammer. All the best shit."

"Great," Jackson replied. He let his eyes fall closed again, tried to phase out Nelson's voice.

No escape.

"So, do you come here often?" Nelson's speech slowed as the sentence came out. He must have realized how dumb a question it was because without missing a beat he added, "Can I ask you something?"

Jackson groaned. *God, get me out of here.*

"What was it like?" Nelson asked. His face was brimming with anticipation, his mouth hanging open exposing a set of surprisingly white teeth.

"What was *what* like?" Jackson repeated.

"You know… I mean, when you walked out of there—like a fucking boss by the way—did you already have that whole thing lined up?"

Jackson gaped at him. "Have what whole thing lined up?"

"Come on, my man, that whole fucking charade at Blackbeard's! Did your agent set that whole thing up or was it your idea? That was absolutely genius! Fucking with Randy's head and then BLAM-O!" Nelson slammed his fist into his palm.

Jackson stared at him, his mind reeling, confused beyond all belief. The corner of his mouth hooked into a smile. "You are one strange little man."

Jackson breathed in the crisp ocean one last time, soaking up what little sun was left. "Well, Nelson, it's been weird, but I've gotta head out." He stood up, starting down the pier.

"Come on man!" Nelson shouted behind him. "At least tell me if you're going back next season?"

Jackson stopped in his tracks. "Why would I ever go back there?"

"What're you talking about? That place turned you into a fucking legend! Why wouldn't you go back?"

Jackson stared at the kid with pity in his eyes, shaking his head. "Don't take this the wrong way, kid, but get lost."

"Ah shit! My bad!" Nelson jogged to catch up with him, nudging him in the shoulder. "You're probably under some sort of NDA, right? Don't mind me, I'm probably acting like a complete idiot after listening to Captain Blackcock screaming at me back there. I gotcha, though, loud and clear. Sorry man."

Jackson stopped, putting his hands on Nelson's shoulders. Nelson's face lit up like the Fourth of July and Jackson thought the kid might pass out. "Nelson?"

"Yeah?"

"Have a nice life." Jackson smiled, lightly slapping him on the cheek and starting away again.

"Wait!"

"I'm leaving now," Jackson said, making his way down the pier.

"Can I get your autograph before you go?" Nelson asked.

Jackson slowed, turning back to him. "My autograph?"

Nelson's eyes went wide as his hands slid into his pockets, frantically turning them inside out. "Oh, come on! Are you kidding me?"

Jackson shook his head. "C'mon, dude, you don't want—"

"Got it!" Nelson held out a crumpled-up napkin.

Jackson stared at Nelson as if he was playing a prank on him but the kid didn't flinch. Nelson was one hundred percent serious, sucked into Jackson's aura of stardom that apparently was only visible to Nelson. He smoothed out the napkin, a warm, puppy dog smile plastered across his face, and held it out for Jackson to sign.

Jackson couldn't believe it. How sad must this kid's life be to want a nobody's autograph? Because that's exactly what he felt like—a nobody. A connection stirred as Nelson stared at him with baited breath, waiting for him to sign his sad little napkin, remembering his own struggles years before the house. The depression and loneliness. The struggle to even want to get out of bed in the morning.

"Got a pen?" Jackson asked, smiling.

Nelson's eyes seemed to grow before his eyes, blown up to triple their size behind the half inch plastic lenses. "Ah shit," he said, resting his head on the fence.

Jackson smiled. "No sweat, man. Maybe next time, huh?"

That was when he noticed it: the napkin's logo, he'd caught a glimpse of it when Nelson was smashing it flat and knew it looked familiar.

He reached over and took it from Nelson's hand, pulling it taut in his hands.

"Hallowed Grounds?" he whispered. "Where'd you get this?"

Nelson lifted his head up, squinting his giant eyes. "There's a coffee place a few blocks down. They have all sorts of coffee imported from all over the world. It's expensive as shit but I don't care, I'd rather die than drink that freeze-dried garbage."

He still had twenty minutes or so until Scarlett would be home. He could swing by and pick up a bag of her favorite coffee and be home before sunset. It was the perfect plan.

"Nelson?" Jackson said.

Nelson blinked at him and Jackson grinned. "You still want that autograph?"

SCARLETT

JACKSON WAS GONE when she arrived home. Granted, she was a few hours earlier than expected, but it was still curious. He'd mentioned an interview at a restaurant in the afternoon, but he should have been home by now, shouldn't he?

"Jackie?" No echo. No sound.

Silence.

Scarlett tossed her keys on the table and shrugged off her windbreaker, hanging it on the coat hook. She could still smell his cologne in the air fused with the coconut conditioner he used every morning in the shower. Scarlett's well-loved Teddy Ruxpin sat slumped in a cozy accent chair in the corner of the room, his fur singed by the flames that had nearly taken her life, patches of it stained from the smoke. Her face melted into a smile seeing her oldest friend.

"Jackie? You home?" she called.

She pushed open the bedroom door to find nothing but an unmade bed and a pile of books on the nightstand. The heavy wool curtains on the other end of the room fluttered, drawing her attention.

The balcony.

She quickly sidestepped piles of clothes and nearly tore the curtains off the rack.

The tranquil swell of the waves greeted her from below, lapping at an endless stretch of beach. The horizon blazed, a wonderful tapestry of all the beautiful colors.

"Shit," she muttered, sliding the curtains shut again. She tugged a sweater out of the closest and zipped it on, pulling the hood over her head. The media hadn't found them here yet, but it was only a matter of time.

She swiped her keys off the table, jogging back down to the street.

Her vintage Mustang gleamed from the curb; the blood-red paint polished to a near mirror finish. She smelled water and concrete and glanced at the next yard over to see the neighbor's sprinklers drenching the sidewalk along with the rear end of her most treasured family heirloom. Somehow, rather inexplicably, the Mustang had eluded the media. They drove her sedan mostly. She'd used it to go to the academy and back since they'd arrived in the city while the Mustang stayed home corralled in a private garage far away from any potential prying eyes. But not today.

She took her phone out, dialing her father as she unlocked her apartment mailbox.

Dale's voicemail clicked on again.

"Dad, it's me. Look…call me back when you get this. It's urgent. I'm going to try the shop again." She hung up, redialing as she swung open the mailbox door. She reached inside, finding a single postcard.

The postcard was postdated three days prior. The front was a stylized cityscape of Winterview, in all its metropolitan glory.

She flipped the card over to find a message from her father.

Scarlett,

Hey, kid. I hope you're enjoying your time on the coast. I miss your cooking but I'm sure you don't miss mine. Christmas isn't the same around here without you kids. Nobody to decorate the tree. I miss you a lot and I know your brother does too.

Love,
Dad

P.S. Say hi to your friend for me

A droplet splashed the postcard, the ink bleeding. She ran her fingers across her cheek to find tears. His handwriting was atrocious but you had to give it to the old man, he knew how to get a point across.

"What's that?"

She turned to find Jackson standing next to her, a paper bag in one hand and his dress shoes in the other.

"Scar? What's going on?" he asked. "You okay?"

Scarlett sniffled, wiping her eyes. "Yeah—no, I'm fine."

"What's that?" he asked, reading the card in her hands. "Your dad? How's he doing?"

"That's kinda what I wanted to talk to you about..." she said.

"Everything okay?"

Scarlett nodded. "Yeah, let's talk inside."

"Sure, all right." Jackson whipped his head, tossing his hair out of his face. "After you."

Jackson closed the door behind them, then set the bag on the table, brushing the dried sand off his feet. While Scarlett eased back on a bar stool, Jackson walked to the refrigerator, taking out two beers. He twisted the caps off and handed one to her, taking a long pull.

"Just like mom used to make. So, what's up?" he asked.

"I'm going to ask you something, Jackie, and I need you to be straight with me."

Jackson looked at her, concerned. "You know I will."

Scarlett put her hands on his knees, taking a breath. "You remember how I said I wanted to stop social media? Shut down my channel and my accounts? Tune myself out of all the shit going on in the world? You know—complete radio silence?"

Jackson nodded. "Yeah, of course I do."

"Captain Hillard pulled me into her office this morning."

"What? Why?"

"She said I've been having nightmares again."

"Oh." Jackson frowned. "Anything serious?"

"I don't know. I mean, they're obviously concerned if they feel the need to make a big deal about it. But that's not what this is about."

Jackson took another few swallows of beer, setting the bottle down on the counter. "It isn't? Then what are we talking about here?"

Scarlett picked up her backpack, unzipping it and wrestling out a newspaper.

"Where in the hell can you even find a newspaper anymore?"

Scarlett folded the paper over, handing it to him.

Jackson froze, grimacing.

"Did you know about this?" Scarlett asked.

Jackson couldn't look at her.

"Jackie, *tell me* you didn't know about this."

Jackson folded the newspaper closed, chucking it onto the counter. He groaned, tapping his beer on the counter.

"How long have you known?" she asked. If the betrayal in her voice wasn't evidence enough the look on her face sure as hell would be.

"Scarlett—" he began.

"How. Long."

Jackson relented, throwing his hands in the air as though he'd been caught. "A while. Okay?" He bit his lip, shaking his head. "Man. And here I was thinking this was going to be a nice quiet weekend together."

"Why didn't you say anything, Jackie?"

"Do you remember what you said to me that night, Scar?" Jackson asked. "After that guy showed up at our apartment? Do you remember the promise that we made to each other?" He raked his fingers through his black hair, brushing it back. "We made a promise that whatever happened, we wanted to leave that part of our lives behind us and focus on moving forward. That house was so fucking big it was like we couldn't get out from under its shadow. What happened there…it took over our entire lives until there was barely anything left."

"My father lives there, Jackie! Shit! Yours does too! How could you not tell me?"

"Because I knew you'd get sucked back in!" he defended.

She stayed silent, wondering what other skeletons he might be keeping in his closet.

"I mean, Christ, Scarlett! Don't you remember what it was like? Those interviews you did on live TV? They treated you like some sort of freak show and they threw me in there too just to boost their ratings. Getting phone calls at all hours of the night from these religious nut jobs asking me questions I don't have the slightest fucking clue how to answer. Having them show up at our apartment in the middle of the night, leaving those demented voicemails."

Jackson got down on his knees, taking her hands in his. "I didn't tell you because I don't want the house to be the only thing our lives are about anymore. I didn't tell you because I want our future to be *our* future, and no one else's."

"But it's more than that, isn't it?"

Jackson blinked his beautiful eyes and her heart ached.

"Something's wrong, isn't it?" she asked.

"What do you mean?"

"You feel it too, don't you?"

Jackson stared at her; his face troubled. "What is it?"

"I don't know... I wish I could explain it, but I can't." She took his hand and laid it on her chest. "I have this horrible feeling inside that something is wrong. Like *wrong* wrong. And I can't pretend that it isn't just because we want our perfect fairy tale ending. No matter how much you and I both want it."

Jackson sighed, nodding. He laid his head on her lap and her fingertips brushed his bangs away from his face.

Scarlett lifted his chin, kissing him softly.

"I'm scared, Jackie. I'm scared for my dad. I'm scared for your dad, and our friends. For Winterview. There are so, so many things that scare the hell out of me," she said. "But our future together has never been one of them."

Jackson smiled at her, and everything was like it was before.

A knock at the door.

Scarlett stood up so fast Jackson lost his balance, thumping to the floor.

"Whoa, easy!" he said.

"Who's that?" she asked, taking a step back. "They found us."

"It's fine, I'll get it," he said, using her as a brace to stand. "Don't worry about it."

He quietly walked to the door, his back pressed flat to the wall, his eyes tethered to Scarlett's.

She pointed and he nodded his head, the message received loud and clear. His fingers slid down the bookcase, wiggling a hardcover loose.

His fingers tightened as another series of knocks rocked the door on its hinges.

Scarlett watched as he sucked in a deep breath, raising the book over his head. "Wait," she said. She reached down and grabbed a golf club resting against the bedroom door frame, getting into position. "Okay," she mouthed.

Jackson held his breath and grabbed the knob, throwing the door open.

A gust of fresh ocean air tore through the room, fluttering Scarlett's hair.

Standing outside was a tall, skinny teen.

Jackson breathed a sigh of relief, lowering the book, his chest rising and falling.

"Nelson?"

SCARLETT (cont'd)

"FRIEND OF YOURS?"

Scarlett was still posed like a golf mannequin, the 9 iron up over her shoulder, her torso twisted, feet planted firmly on the ground, her chest heaving.

"He's more of an acquaintance," Jackson said.

Nelson stood in the doorway, oblivious. He hadn't even had the sense to duck or run.

"Don't shoot," Nelson said, holding his hands up in the air. "Or swing. Or whatever."

Scarlett exhaled a sigh of relief, lowering the club and tossing it against the wall. She approached, walking up beside Jackson. "Who's this?" She turned to Nelson and he smiled. "Who are you?"

Jackson set the book back on the shelf. "This is Nelson."

Scarlett made a face like he was speaking gibberish. She looked the stranger up and down, eyeing him suspiciously. "Who. Are. You?"

Jackson snapped out his stupor. "Sorry, uh, yeah. This is Nelson. We met earlier down at the pier. He's a fan."

Jackson looked as confused at this point as she was.

"Oh?" she said, hooking an eyebrow. "You brought home a stranger from the beach?" She turned to Nelson. "What a coincidence, we were literally just discussing this very topic."

Jackson grinned. "Ha, no. It's not like that. I, well—here, it's easier if I show you." He grabbed the paper bag he'd brought home, holding it up in the air.

Scarlett looked at him curiously, squinting. "Hey…why does that smell familiar? What is going on?" Her nose crinkled. "Wait a minute. That's not…?"

Jackson glanced at Nelson, who was watching them from the apartment corridor as if Scarlett had gone insane.

Scarlett snatched the bag out of Jackson's hands, tearing into it like a present on Christmas morning. She squealed, then launched herself onto Jackson like a spider, nearly knocking him over.

"Hallowed Grounds' Coffee!" she said. "You sneaky little person you! Is that why you got home late?"

Jackson twisted his body but Scarlett was hanging on tighter than a kraken on a ship. She pummeled Jackson's cheek with kisses in rapid fire succession. "Oh my God, this smells amazing. They need to make this a cologne." She sucked in a long breath of Hallowed Grounds' finest coffee beans, her eyelids fluttering like butterfly wings.

"I'm going to make a pot right now." She zipped into the kitchen, ripping open the bag.

Jackson stepped aside and Nelson wandered into the apartment, amused by Scarlett's antics. Nelson peered around the apartment, a confused look on his face. "Your crib isn't quite what I expected," he said. "Thought you'd have gold toilets and a pet leopard. And a butler."

"Nope," Jackson said. "Just good old fashioned porcelain toilets."

Scarlett knocked through the cabinets, unburying the filters and a dusty coffee maker.

"Someone's got a hard on for coffee," Nelson whispered out of the side of his mouth.

"You have no idea," Jackson said.

Scarlett watched as the coffee maker did its thing, filling the apartment with the scent of rich coffee grounds.

"Funnily enough, she doesn't actually drink coffee; just likes the smell of it. More of a tea person."

"Right..." Nelson said. "That makes a lot of sense."

Scarlett whirled past the cutout in the drywall dividing the kitchen and living room with the bag of coffee cradled in one arm and a steaming red mug in the other.

"She loves that place," Jackson said.

"Yeah, I feel like that about the Matrix," Nelson answered, his eyes still wandering the room.

"The movie?" Scarlett asked.

"The game store," he said. "They do Commander tournaments on Fridays and the winner gets a gift card to Vincenzo's. It's my safe place."

"Vincenzo's?" Scarlett asked, breathing in the mug. "What's that?"

"Only the greatest pizza ever made," Nelson said.

"Where in the hell did you find this, Jackie?" Scarlett asked, holding up the mug. "I've looked everywhere on the West Coast."

"Funny story, but Nelson here gave me a hand with that."

Scarlett froze, marching out of the kitchen. "Nelson?"

Jackson nodded. "Yes. Nelson." he held his hands out toward the teen as if he were introducing a new model car. "Remember? This person standing in our living room."

Scarlett took a step forward, holding up the coffee bag. "You're the one responsible for this?"

"He was the one who told me where to find it, aren't you Nelson?"

"Oh, yeah. Damn straight." Nelson said. He pushed his glasses up on his nose. "I love coffee. Especially the French Roast. I can't get enough of that shit."

"Whoa," Scarlett said. "You kiss your mother with that mouth?"

"Oh," Nelson stuttered, his cheeks flushing red. "Sorry, I—"

"Wowwww," Scarlett said. "I'm messing with you, calm down."

Nelson laughed, deflating.

"Well...*Nelson*. I guess you know what this means?" Scarlett took a step closer, her face emotionless, her eyes boring holes into Nelson's soul.

Nelson gulped.

"Welcome to the family, amigo," she said, laughing. She threw an arm around Nelson, squeezing him like a bunny rabbit while Nelson attempted not to be awkward. "Anyone that brings me coffee from Hallowed Grounds automatically gets my stamp of approval, I don't care how crazy they look." She released him, linking arms with Jackson.

"Thanks?" Nelson croaked.

"Man, those puppies are thick," Scarlett said, tapping her finger on the lens. "Can you see out of those things?"

Nelson recoiled from her fingers and his glasses went sailing off his face. "Ah shit, not again."

Scarlett gracefully plucked them off the floor, handing them back to him. Nelson breathed his hot breath on the lenses, polishing them with his shirt. There was something endearing about the kid. An indefinable quality she couldn't quite put her finger on. Scarlett couldn't help but draw comparisons to Napoleon Dynamite minus the moon boots and dance moves.

Nelson straightened out his glasses. "If I can get that autograph now, I'll be going."

"Autograph?" Scarlett parroted. She looked at Jackson, confused. "What's he talking about?"

"He recognized us from the TV, I guess. He said he had some baseball card or something he wants me to sign. We made a deal. The coffee for an autograph."

"Baseball card?" Scarlett said. "When were you ever on a baseball card?"

Nelson's gangly frame collapse down to the ground, digging through a long cardboard box he'd brought with him.

"Uhhh…that's a little weird, isn't it?" Scarlett asked.

"You got your coffee, didn't you?" Jackson said.

"Touché."

"Here is it," Nelson exclaimed. He stood up, a small card in his hand. "It's freaking mint. I have two so I can get the other one graded, maybe trade it if a Black Lotus ever comes up."

Jackson snapped his fingers, Scarlett's signal that apparently a light bulb had gone off in his head. "Wait. Nelson, I've got an idea. Don't you know who this is?" he asked, motioning at Scarlett. "You might as well get two for the price of one while you're here."

"Will you cut it out? I am not signing *anything*."

"Uh… No?" Nelson said, as Scarlett and Jackson exchanged hushed words. "She kind of looks like that that girl from *Juno*, though, minus the baby."

They both stopped midsentence.

Jackson blinked, looking at Nelson curiously. "This is Scarlett."

Nelson leaned forward, squinting his giant eyes behind the spectacle lenses. "Hi." He couldn't have cared less if she was the President of the United States.

"*Scarlett Vantassel*," Jackson clarified. "*The* Scarlett Vantassel."

Nelson was quiet, his eyes ping-ponging back and forth between them while they waited for him to respond. "I don't know what I'm supposed to say right now. Vantassel? What is she, part of the royal family or something?"

Scarlett couldn't help but laugh. She put her hands on her hips, cocking an eye at him. Nelson was definitely an odd specimen. She set her coffee grounds and mug on the kitchen table and folded her arms. "Wait. You don't recognize me?"

"Not really." Nelson asked. "Why? Should I?"

Scarlett gaped at Jackson. This was outright bizarre. Not recognizing Jackson was one thing. He did everything he could to stay out of the public eye, actively went out of his way to avoid doing interviews or taking photos in public. She, on the flip side, had granted nearly every one of the requests and opportunities thrown her way, up to and including *The Tonight Show Starring Jimmy Fallon*.

"You don't recognize me?" Scarlett asked, unconvinced.

"No," Nelson said, annoyed. "Sorry. I don't know who you are, but I'm sure you're very important." Patronizing didn't begin to describe the tone in his voice. "All I want is my autograph."

Scarlett scoffed, throwing her hands up. "Wow. Unbelievable."

"I don't understand what's happening here," Nelson said. "I thought we had a deal? You said you would sign this if I helped you find that coffee?" he said, holding out the card.

Scarlett stifled a laugh, slapping a hand over her mouth.

And in a matter of seconds, everything was clear as crystal. Judging by the expression on Jackson's face, the painful truth had hit him, too.

"I have all of his rookie cards, too," Nelson said. "And a lenticular one from his season with the Bandits."

She took the card out of Nelson's hand, examining it.

"Excuse me," Nelson interrupted. "That's for *him*."

Even she had to admit, he did look quite a bit like him. The pitcher for the Winterview Watchers, Daryl Duke, had the same build as Jackson. The same hair. The same disarming brown eyes. But his smile was where the similarities ended. Nobody had a smile like Jackie's.

Scarlett erupted into a fit of a laughter as Jackson stared down at the baseball card in disbelief.

"What's so funny?" Nelson asked.

Jackson shook his head, handing the card back to Nelson.

"I hate to break it to you, dude, but that is not me."

Nelson took the card from him, peering down at the picture.

"Yes it is. Daryl Duke. You won MVP for the Winterview Watchers three years straight. You hold the league record for fastest pitch in MLB history."

"Yeah, he does," Jackson said. "*I* however, do not."

"You're not Daryl Duke?"

"No."

"Then who are you?"

"My name's Jackson," he offered with a smile. "I'm an everyday guy like you—more or less."

Nelson held the card up to his face, squinting, then looked back at Jackson in disbelief. He touched his forehead and his eyes pinched shut as if he'd caught a brain freeze. "Dang it."

"Jackie does sort of look like him if it makes you feel any better," Scarlett said. "Your giant ice block lenses probably didn't help, though."

Nelson frowned. "They're prescription."

"*Outdated* is what they are," she said. Scarlett shook her head, walking back to the kitchen to check on her coffee. "Poor soul."

"Sorry, man." Jackson opened the front door while Nelson collected his cardboard box, goggling the card in silence like he couldn't believe the colossal mistake he'd made.

"Hey—Nelson," Scarlett yelled from the kitchen.

Nelson turned and looked over his shoulder.

"Thanks for the coffee, though. Really." she said, sincere. "Sorry about your card. That sucks."

And then Nelson was gone.

JACKSON

THE SALESMAN'S ROLEX obnoxiously winked at him.

Valiant Jewelers wasn't your everyday dime store jeweler. It was an exclusive club reserved for society's elite. The gold accents were polished to a mirror shine. The glass countertops were sparkling and flawless. Not a single loose fiber could be found on the black velvet displays home to some of the most exquisite jewelry ever designed. One couldn't merely stroll in and wander aimlessly with no real destination in mind, no.

Valiant Jewelers was by appointment only, and Jackson had made this particular appointment on this particular day because he knew Scarlett would be preoccupied. He'd damn near orchestrated the entire plan himself. Luckily, he'd been able to talk her down after she'd found out about Winterview two days earlier. No easy feat after she'd seen that front page announcement in the newspaper. Thankfully Dale had phoned later that night, reassuring her that he was all right. In fact, he was more than all right. The old man had won three hundred dollars off a Bingo Lottery scratcher and bought himself a new flat screen television, an appliance in the house that hadn't been updated since the eighties.

In the days following the events at the House, both Scarlett and Jackson had received a plain black envelope delivered to their homes. Miraculously, the Crow Corporation had made good on their promise.

Inside those sleek black envelopes was a check for one million dollars and a small foil card embossed with the Crow Corp logo. The juggernaut had receded into the shadows after the catastrophe that was the Seventh Street Lottery, but they weren't really gone, he knew. They were only staying out of the news long enough for people to forget what happened. The people who died that day. Hannah. Tommy. Vincent. And a hell of a lot more who had been lingering outside the house. He'd heard a bunch had been taken away to Serenity Falls, too, the sanatorium nestled high in the Painted Mountains.

Scarlett had attempted to gift her father everything from a new Toyota 4Runner to a modest house far away from Winterview City, but the stubborn old man couldn't be bought. He'd made his home and he was going to die in it, whether from old age or the apocalypse itself (which Scarlett felt wasn't far off). Jackson had to admit, Dale *was* resilient. Lord knows Jackson wouldn't have been able to refuse Scarlett's copious offers if he hadn't already become wealthy himself. But that was Scarlett's old man for you, stamped from the factory line of a different generation, operating by a completely different set of rules. And those rules decreed you can have handouts when you're dead. Until then, you work and earn your own way.

Jackson's father was similar in that way. "I'll sleep when I'm dead," his father used to say like a mantra. And maybe he secretly wished he *was* dead. Why else would he go to such great lengths to avoid his wife and son?

Bastard, Jackson thought.

After the coffee from Hallowed Grounds and Dale's phone call, Scarlett had let herself calm enough to think rationally again. And what was the best way to make sure she would continue to think rationally? By reminding her of the things that made her happy. Conveniently, Jackson so happened to spot a sun-bleached flier pinned on the pier's bulletin board advertising Long Beach's Silent Book Club. He had no idea what a "silent book club" was, but if it involved books, he knew Scarlett wouldn't be able to resist. And like a mouse to a piece of cheese she'd taken the bait and signed up to make an appearance. Their privacy was something to consider, but as long as she kept her hood up and her head down, she had been able to go to and fro for the most part within the city limits.

Which brought him to here. To now. Valiant Jewelers.

He stood at the counter watching Stan's mouth move, the finely trimmed gray mustache moving along with it, and he couldn't help but feel like he didn't belong here. Despite having more money in his bank account than he'd imagined in his wildest dreams, something about being in a place this swanky felt wrong.

"Mr. Briggs?"

Jackson blinked, resurfacing from his daydream. Stan, the salesman, was a reflection of the store itself. Immaculate pinstripe suit. Slicked back hair. White satin gloves. It was almost too much, like some sort of an illusion.

"Jackson," he said.

Stan smiled. He reached down into the glass display. "This is a stunning princess cut two-carat diamond. We got it in from Switzerland—yesterday, in fact. The clarity is top tier, very *very* nice."

Stan wasn't lying. It was nice. But that's all it was. *Nice.* And nice might be adequate for some women. But not for Scarlett.

"Sorry," Jackson apologized. "I thought this would be easier."

"That's all right," Stan reassured. "It's a big decision. Maybe the biggest. Not everyone gets it right the first time. Why don't we try this; why don't you tell me a little bit about the special lady? Maybe I can help pinpoint what we're looking for."

"About Scarlett?"

Stan nodded.

"Oh, well. Where do I even start?" Jackson said with a lighthearted chuckle, sitting back on the padded stool. He placed his hands on the glass countertop, his eyes rolling over hills of glittering silver and gold jewelry. "She's...*different* than other girls."

Stan smiled warmly. "Different how?"

Jackson reached back in his mind, diving into a shimmering trove of memories buried beyond the beach, beyond the tide, swimming deeper.

"Back when Scarlett and I were in middle school, I remember we had this dance one year. It had this fairy tale theme where you had to dress up like your favorite character. You know, Hercules, or Snow White; you get the point. It was kinda this thing they were doing to raise money for the local theater back then. I went as Robin Hood. I had these horrible green tights and this godawful fake leather quiver. So Scarlett's brother, Tommy, and I get there, and all the kids at the dance are just sort of standing around staring at each other."

"Is that right?"

"I shit you not, Stan. It looked like we had shown up at a funeral. That's how unbelievably sad this thing was," Jackson said, snickering.

"Sounds like quite a party," Stan said.

"About twenty minutes later, Scarlett rolls in." Jackson paused for a moment, blinking his eyes, hopelessly lost in his old life. "I remember she had this red cloak, and this big red hood over her head. And she just walked in like she owned the place, you know?"

Stan was quiet.

"Scarlett didn't say a word. Didn't come over to her brother and I. Didn't go stand in the corner like the rest of girls, or huddle together like us, the scared little boys. She looked around the joint like she was confused. Like she didn't understand why everyone was standing around being miserable. She was looking at all these other kids like they were wasting their lives being afraid. They just didn't know it yet."

Stan swallowed, folding his arms on the counter and leaning forward. "Afraid of what?"

Jackson smiled. "Life."

"Hmmm…"

"And do you know what she did, Stan?"

"What's that, sir?"

"She walked straight out onto that dance floor and she danced her fucking ass off."

Jackson had had feelings for Scarlett since before even he could remember. But that precise moment at the Fairy Tale Dance was the moment he'd went from innocent childhood crush to falling madly in love. And had it not been for his denial, he might have realized it sooner.

The pier was virtually deserted by the time he arrived at the beach. It was on the way home anyway, so why not? Most of the street vendors had gone, the shops closed up with metal shutters and steel fences.

He tried to make it a habit to visit at least once a day. Their apartment was only a few blocks over on a street called Grand, a brisk ten-minute walk if that. Scarlett had brought her Mustang out to California, but they'd kept it locked up most the time to avoid any more attention. Their rental was their main form of transportation, but Jackson preferred to go it on foot in the city when he could. The streets here were just so damn enjoyable compared to Winterview. The parrots singing in the palm trees. Breathing in the salty ocean breeze that cascaded over the rooftops like rolling waves.

He strolled down the pier, his hands stuffed in his pockets, watching the seagulls circle above the shore. He skimmed the little bronze plaques on the wooden benches bolted to the pier, wondering if he'd have one with his name one day. The thought was morbid yet made him surprisingly hopeful at the same time. Scarlett would understand, he knew. She always did.

Jackson breathed in the fresh air and took a small velvet box from his jacket, taking it in his hands and folding the top open.

His breath hitched; his eyes widened.

Sparkling inside was the most beautiful ring he'd ever laid eyes on. Big but not outrageously big. Elegant yet unique. And the best part? It was one of a kind, just like Scarlett. The sunlight beaming from the horizon caught inside the stone like fire, a dazzling kaleidoscope of brilliant colors. She was going to love it. The only question now was, when?

A protracted moan washed in on the waves. A hard jolt shook the boards beneath his feet. Then another.

He shut the box and tucked it back in his coat, glancing around the end of the pier.

Nothing. No people. No animals. The wharf was completely empty.

A grinding sound, like something heavy being dragged across the dock. He sidestepped to the edge and looked over the railing.

Down below, an empty boat was caught in the tide, lazily crashing into the pier's wooden supports. Intrigued, he quickly made his way down to the beach, following along the shore, crossing over into the shadows below the pier.

The boat was a few feet away, bobbing up and down with the break of the waves.

Jackson peered under the dock.

Shafts of warm sunlight brimmed between the columns. Seaweed clung to the wooden supports like party streamers, hives of barnacles reaching from the water. The calm lapping of the waves eased his nerves.

Jackson

A whisper.

His heart punched the inside of his chest. He stumbled back into the water, backing into one of the wooden supports.

"Hello?" he called.

Only the soft breaks of the water.

"Is anyone there?"

Silence.

You're losing it. Pull yourself together.

Pathetic. You're out. You got out.

He shook his head at himself. And that was when he noticed it.

A splash of red in his peripheral vision.

His jaw fell open. He craned his neck, his eyes pulled upward, widening.

Painted beneath the rotting planks of the pier was a sprawling mural of the house, with its towering spires and crimson windows. Coated with the same oily black residue as the house itself, the painting was a panorama of monstrous, ancient creatures gliding across time and space. Endless labyrinths of blood-stained stone. Ghastly scenes of mutilation. Stomach-churning gore. And illustrations of madness so depraved he felt himself getting drawn into them. There was horror. There was violence. And at the center of it all: a figure concealed in silhouette. The entity behind everything. Whether a man or something else entirely, he couldn't be sure.

A dark cloud began to swirl in his heart.

His vision began to blur.

His fingertips went numb.

His eyelids grew heavy.

The light began to recede, fading to blackness.

"What are you doing?" a voice asked.

A crack, like glass splintering.

Jackson screamed, his heart nearly jumping out of his chest and landing right there on the sand.

"Nelson?!"

"Yeah, Nelson. Who the heck did you think it was?" Nelson was staring at him from out in the evening twilight, watching him curiously.

"Fuck, man," Jackson laughed, relieved. He let his head fall back on the wood. "I never thought I'd be this happy to see you again. What the hell are you doing here?"

"I saw you walking on the pier," he said matter-of-factly. "What the heck are you doing down there? The lifeguards say not to go down there. It's dangerous. Broken bottles and syringes and all sorts of nasty crap."

"No shit," Jackson said, his voice riding the foaming tide. He exhaled, leaning back against the column, breathing hard. He didn't dare look up again. "I saw this boat down here. I thought someone might be hurt. Wait." He reached down and tugged off his shoes and socks, wadding through the water. He quickly grabbed the boat, towing it through the waves until it carved into the wet sand.

"Grab that end," he said.

Nelson looked at him curiously, hesitating a moment, then took the other end and began pulling.

Jackson clenched his teeth, hauling one side of the craft while Nelson carried the other. Together, they wrestled the boat out from under the pier into the light, dropping it on the shore.

Nelson stood in the sand wheezing. He put his hands on his hips as the breeze ruffled his red curls.

"Thanks," Jackson said. He dropped to his knees, peering inside the boat.

"What the heck are you even doing?" Nelson asked. "Whose boat is this anyway?"

"I don't know," Jackson answered. He reached in, finding a plastic cooler tucked in the bow.

"Hey; what's that?" Nelson asked.

Jackson popped off the lid, peering inside. He grabbed out a huge Fuji apple. Then a flattened sandwich sealed in plastic wrap.

"Someone's lunch," he said. "Guess they weren't hungry."

Nelson squinted. "Where the hell are they? Beach is cleared out."

Jackson looked at him ominously. "I don't know." He leaned back in the sand, resting his hands on the rim of the boat. Something slick and cold touched his skin.

He withdrew his hands, strings of a viscous substance stuck to them. He held his palms up, finding his skin coated with an oily black substance.

"Shit," he said.

"Gross! What is that?" Nelson asked, stepping next to him. "Oh my God, is that puke?" he said, howling with laughter.

Jackson shoved him away, quickly standing up and walking down to the ocean.

His feet sunk into the wet sand. He bent over, letting the cold water rinse away the substance glazing his hands. He scrubbed until his skin was raw, then let the water run over them a minute more for good measure.

Convinced he'd gotten it all off, he toweled his hands dry on his shirt, turning to find Nelson squatting next to the boat, his face inches from the rim.

"Don't touch that!" Jackson yelled.

His voice startled Nelson; he fell back on his butt in the sand and Jackson couldn't help but snicker.

Something slimy brushed against his ankle.

He jerked his head down at the water in time to glimpse a pale shape retract into the darkness like a bungee cord.

He looked up at the horizon just in time to see something colossal slip below the surface.

SCARLETT

THE SILENT BOOKCLUB might have been the greatest thing since sliced bread, but Scarlett was never going to find out. Now that she was free of the academy, she'd spent the afternoon treating herself, traveling back in time, back to when she'd been her truest, most unadulterated self. First, she fished a vinyl out of her collection that Tommy had gotten her for Christmas. Blink-182, *Enema of the State*, a limited printing of only 500 pressed, half translucent orange, half translucent green. The edition was a thing of beauty. She'd slid the record out of its sleeve, set it down on the platter, and dropped the needle. iPods were all the rage right now, but apparently, she was the only person on the planet who thought records still sounded better. More authentic. And while "All the Small Things" blared from the turntable, she'd began by dyeing a few blood-red streaks into her thin brown hair, the same kind she'd had when she and Luke Taylor met at Rowdy's Pub. The same as when Jackson and she celebrated her birthday with a couple of chilled Funfetti shots. They tasted like shit (cake vodka was a crime against alcohol), but they looked incredible and suited her to a tee. Silver nail polish because why the fuck not. A new pair of midnight black Chucks. A cherry-red hoodie (her last one had been confiscated by the hospital). And the final touch: her mother's cherished leather jacket. The same one she'd wore to the house. The same one that felt like a suit of armor every time she pulled it over her arms and around her body. She took comfort in knowing it was her mother's once. That it had protected her. Watched over her. And that now it was hers.

The music had stopped and the needle lifted, the record spinning to a stop.

After Jackson had gone on his way, she'd fired up the Mustang, veering off the path to Mystic Beach Books and ending up at the local library instead. She'd had to dodge a news van that happened to be passing by on the next street over, but she'd made it unscathed. When she and Jackson had agreed to cease all social media for the sake of their mental health and sanity, that pact had included ridding themselves of their laptops as well. Scarlett had simply left hers behind with Dale while Jackson had never owned one to begin with.

Maybe she'd overreacted a bit when she'd seen the newspaper. Maybe she hadn't. She shared a very personal connection with Winterview after everything that had transpired, and her father staying behind only complicated matters. Dale had never been one to lose his cool in an emergency, so there wasn't any easy way to determine the true state of Winterview.

With the exception of the one thing she'd vowed to stay away from at all costs: the world wide web. Her following days had been spent playing catch up, learning about Winterview's skyrocketing death rate. The strange, erratic changes to the city's environment, including the ash sweeping across the city that seemed to be worsening by the day. Burgeoning reports of widespread malaise and illness. Overwhelming and oftentimes irrational fear. The city had become worse off in every way since they'd picked up and skipped town.

Dusk. The sky glowed orange, licks of pink touched down on the horizon. Clouds as black as space slinked across the heavens.

Two funnels of light bounced into the gloomy parking lot, the Mustang screeching into an empty space.

Scarlett killed the lights and cut the engine, tugging the hood over her head.

The library, a concrete structure shimmering with tempered glass and gleaming metal, was surrounded by perfectly manicured grass islands, recently rebuilt from the ground up courtesy of a hefty grant from the city. She'd seen few buildings in Winterview this swanky, up to and including City Hall.

The driver's door thumped closed.

Scarlett gazed up at the hulking building, watched the sunlight brighten the massive glass panels, setting the building on fire.

"When you feel homesick just look up," she said softly. "Because the moon is the same wherever you go."

The Goldfinch by Donna Tartt. Her father had said that to her the day she and Jackson had left for the coast. When she'd asked where he'd heard it, he'd simply smiled and said, "Your mom said that to me once. I guess to remind me home is never far away." Inquisitive as she was, Scarlett had looked the quote up not long after, subsequently devouring her first novel since the events at the house.

Dale admitted early on in her childhood that her mother had always been the reader between the two of them. The old man had done his best to keep up with them, but he knew and understood that he could never fill the shoes left by Scarlett's mother, a woman with a voracious appetite for stories. Even in Scarlett's earliest memories of her mother she had carried a book with her, tucked in her back pocket or her purse. She would read to Scarlett and Tommy at night, sometimes for hours, narrating fantastic tales of magic and mystery. In the Vantassel household, trips to the library were adventures, Scholastic book fairs a cause worthy of celebration. Because books were knowledge, and knowledge was power. At least according to those little bookmarks their school used to give out. Scarlett still had the first book her mother had ever given her, *Green Eggs and Ham*, safely tucked away in a dusty box in her closet back in Winterview.

And standing here now, in the shadow of the Long Beach Public Library, Scarlett could only think of home.

No matter how many months had passed in this sparkling city with its clean sidewalks and industrial street sweepers, she couldn't shake the feeling that it felt wrong.

Because the only home she knew, would ever know, was the one from her dreams. The ones where she and Jackson were in the park, her laying on the grass with her head on his lap with a book in her hands, while Jackson gazed up at a cloudless sky, his hair tossing in the breeze.

Not Winterview City, but Silvers Hollow.

Not Long Beach.

Not Dallas, or Kansas City. Not Portland or San Diego.

But she'd try for as long as she could because she was happy. And as much as she needed Silvers Hollow, and as much as she needed her father, she needed Jackson more.

The front doors slid open automatically and, for a brief moment, it was as if she'd stepped into the future.

Great Scott!

If only she had a DeLorean Time Machine now...

Tommy and Hannah would still be here. Vincent would still be performing impossible feats at the Arkham Theater. They'd buy tickets and go and watch him and their lives would go on as they should have from the very beginning.

She stepped into the library lobby, surveying the spacious interior. An elevator and a flight of stairs led to a second story. A sleek waterfall cascaded across a stainless-steel logo of the city. Marble tile floors were freshly polished; she caught a glimpse of her reflection looking up at her.

A security guard watched her from an alcove tucked to the side of the lobby.

She kept her head down, pulling the shoulder strap on her backpack tight and making a beeline for the stairs.

The security guard tracked her with his eyes; she felt them following her as she swung onto the stairs, climbing, climbing.

At the top of the steps were endless metal shelves jam-packed with books of all shapes and sizes. A warm nostalgia came over her thinking about the old card catalogs of her youth, all the hours she'd spent flipping through them, jotting down some obscure numeric code before venturing off in search of whatever book she was on the hunt for.

But those days were long gone. In their place? Computers. Simply type in the name and *voilà!* (as Vincent would have said). There was something to be said about accessibility when it came to computers. They were convenient, yeah, no doubt about that. But impersonal.

Scarlett scanned the second floor.

The bookcases circled a substantial section of computer terminals for public use. Scarlett marched past them, finding a lone desk on the other side with a woman pecking away at a keyboard. She looked up as Scarlett approached.

"Can I help you?"

"Nope," she said hastily, rushing by.

She glanced over her shoulder to make sure no one was following her, slipping into a club chair next to the plate-glass window and setting down her backpack.

"I didn't think you were going to show," a flinty voice across from her said.

She looked up to find a woman in her late forties.

"Sylvia," Scarlett greeted, the taste of disdain on her tongue.

"Scarlett."

Sylvia Sharpe, the former newswoman for Silvers Hollow Channel 9, sat cross-legged in the club chair opposite her, slick as oil. Designer tortoise frames. A sleek pinstripe pantsuit. Black and red Louboutin stilettos. And a bleached million-dollar smile. All the hallmarks of the enemy.

After telling herself time after time she'd never speak to the press again, here she was, staring across at the one person on the planet she despised above all others. They'd harassed her, made her life a living hell for months, but maybe she could turn the tables, make them work for her for a change.

"You've got a lot of nerve showing your face here," Scarlett said.

"You're the one who asked *me* here, remember?"

"That doesn't make it any easier to look at you."

"You should be thanking me," Sylvia said.

Scarlett scoffed. "For what? For making me look like a crazy person?

For dragging my best friend's name through the mud? For making my dad relive what happened to Tommy?"

"You wanted people to know the truth. *Your* truth. And I quote, 'I tell them what happened, you take care of the rest.' Those were *your* words, Scarlett, not mine," Sylvia said without missing a beat. "You were the voice and I was the microphone. But those other shows?" Sylvia sneered. "*Howard Stern*, Scarlett? *Joe Rogan*? What did you expect to happen? Did you think you were just going to go on, babbling about your little adventure in front of millions of people and expect everyone to believe every little word you said? Newsflash Scarlett; they don't. You could have a goddamn spaceship sitting two feet in front of them and they would *still* question it, because that's how people are."

Scarlett glared at her.

Sylvia continued. "The problem with you is, you want to believe people are something that they're not." A beat passed between them. "A word of advice? Don't ever take people at face value. You'll only end up hurting yourself."

"Is that slice of wisdom straight from that microphone circle jerk you've got going now? What was it called, 'Trashy Reporters Dot Com'?"

"No." Sylvia was unfazed. "It's a cold hard fact of life and you better get used to it fast. Not just in this business. In *life*. It's eat or be eaten. Otherwise you're going to spend the rest of your days creeping around in your Little Red Riding Hood getup with these Jesus freaks chasing you around with their crosses throwing holy water at you."

Scarlett's nails bit into the armrest. "You know something, Sylvia?" She learned forward, her voice low. "You can buy all the designer handbags you want. You can wear your thousand-dollar shoes, drive whatever luxury car you paid off with mine and my brother's story, but you are never going to be anything more than a parasite feeding off of other people's lives. And you know what the real tragedy is? It's that you'll never have one of your own."

"Ouch," Sylvia snickered. "That's the spirit."

Scarlett scowled.

"If you loathe me so much, why ask me here?" Sylvia asked.

"Because you owe me," she answered. A moment of silence settled between them, and Scarlett glimpsed a flicker of humanity, a chink in Sylvia's proverbial armor. "*And*, because despite what you did, I want to believe there's still a human being buried underneath all that makeup. My mom always believed in you. I don't know why. I don't know what she saw in you, and maybe I never will. But I keep telling myself that if she trusted you once, there must have been a reason."

Sylvia's face softened. She sighed, shifting in her seat, gazing out at the city. "Well then, I guess it's a good thing San Francisco is only a few hours away then, isn't it?"

Scarlett's rage soothed, her adrenaline settling.

"I didn't have many friends growing up. Hard to believe, I know," Sylvia admitted. "I still don't. But your mom…she was my friend. And despite how you may feel about me, Scarlett, I genuinely *was* trying to help you. And while you may not understand this, press is something that has to be carefully orchestrated. Planned. You can't run around blabbing every little thought or impulse that pops into your head to complete strangers."

Scarlett rolled her eyes.

"You read, yes?" Sylvia asked.

It was rhetorical, but Scarlett nodded anyway.

"Can you imagine a book written like that? Firing off any little thought that comes into your head? Of course not, right? Stories have to be carefully curated, edited." Sylvia held her hand up, inspecting her nails.

"After everything I've been through—"

"*Especially* after what you've been through," Sylvia interrupted, like she couldn't believe Scarlett could be so naïve. "People can and *will* twist the truth any chance they get no matter who you are. You have got to protect yourself, and you do that by being smart. Strategic. Patient. And above all, ruthless."

Sylvia was quiet a moment. She looked around the library, her eyes wandering. "Haven't been in one of these places since college. Interesting choice for a rendezvous."

"I like the quiet."

"So," Sylvia nodded, "I just drove six hours straight to meet you here. Are we doing this or what?"

"What's wrong, your helicopter run out of gas?" Scarlett asked.

"Unavailable," she said offhandedly. "There's a wildfire over in Berkeley."

"Oh." Scarlett said. "So…San Francisco?"

Sylvia smirked. "Quite a change from Silvers Hollow Channel 9, I know. I suppose I have you to thank for that. No more fetching coffee, playing errand girl, fucking producers for screen time or raises. Now I'm my own boss. I've even got my own assistant getting coffee for *me.*" Sylvia's voice trailed off, almost as if she were wistful about the days before she'd gone national. "No, without 'Scarlett Vantassel and the house that fell from the sky' I'd still be the same pathetic failure I was my whole life, stuck in that little dead-end town."

Hearing Sylvia speak about Silvers Hollow grated her nerves.

"Well, I'm so glad I could help you further your career," Scarlett sneered.

"Cut the shit, Scarlett. That judgment in your voice doesn't suit you," Sylvia said. "Besides, if it wasn't for my little *promotion,* I wouldn't be here helping you now, would I?"

The woman did have a fair point.

"You bring what I asked for?" Scarlett asked.

Sylvia grinned, reaching into a leather carryall resting against the side of the club chair. She pulled out a folder, holding it up. "As promised."

Scarlett went to reach for it and Sylvia pulled it back.

"Your turn," Sylvia grinned.

Scarlett exhaled, looking around to make sure the coast was clear. She reached into her bag, pulling out a plain white envelope. She held it out and Sylvia took it, opening the flap to find a bundle of crisp hundred-dollar bills. Sylvia ran her thumb along the edges, fanning through them.

"It's all there," Scarlett said.

Sylvia smiled, sealing the envelope and tucking it into her purse. "They say money can't buy happiness. Maybe they're right…but it sure fuckin' helps."

Scarlett held out her hand.

Sylvia handed her folder, and Scarlett snatched it out of her hand. "This is everything we talked about?"

Sylvia nodded. "Everything from the last two years. Anything connected to the house since its arrival in Winterview."

Scarlett shoved the folder into her backpack, zipping it up. She tugged the backpack onto her lap, slipping one of the straps over her shoulder and standing up. "It's been fun."

"There's more," Sylvia said.

Scarlett stopped. "But you said—"

"Something not in the papers. Strictly off the record."

Scarlett eyed her suspiciously, unslinging the backpack and dropping it at her feet. She fell back in the chair. "Tell me."

"The military have been sending people into the house. *Lots* of people, in fact."

"That's impossible," Scarlett said. "It's only been two years. We were the only ones that went in that night. The year it came, Brent went in. That solider. But that was it."

"No," Sylvia said, infallible. "There have been others."

Scarlett's mind suddenly flashed back to the house. The dead soldiers. The bullet casings. The briefcase with the hollow inside.

"Crow Corp.," she whispered.

"What's that?"

"Who?" she asked. "*Who* went inside?"

"Researchers. Soldiers. Hell, I don't know."

"How do you know all this?" Scarlett asked.

The side of Sylvia's mouth hooked into a smile. "I have my sources."

"Why?"

"Word on the street is that not too long after you left Winterview, the military enlisted the help of a special division to deal exclusively with the house."

"What division?" Scarlett asked.

"They call it the Red Sky. Apparently, the custodian of all things happening within the Dead Zone."

"The Dead Zone?"

Sylvia nodded. "The condemned part of the city surrounding the house. That's what they refer to it as these days."

Scarlett brushed her thumb across her bottom lip, thinking.

"And that's not all," Sylvia confessed. "There's even talk of some kind of doomsday cult operating within the city. I believe they're being referred to as 'The Dolls.'"

"Jesus," Scarlett muttered. "Wait—the suicides? Do they think there's a connection to the house?"

Sylvia shrugged. "Depends on who you ask. Everyone has their own opinion. There're almost too many theories to keep track of."

"And the Crow Corporation? Did you find anything about them?"

Sylvia's smiled widened. "Actually, yes. I did."

Scarlett leaned forward, resting her elbows on her knees.

"Do you remember a woman named Elizabeth Crow?"

Scarlett nodded. "The spokeswoman from the TV. She was there that night—before we went into the house."

"Yes, that's right," Sylvia said. "As it turns out, she wasn't just the face of the company's public relations. She was also the daughter of the enterprise's founder, coincidentally, and happens to own a large stake in the company."

"The name gave it away."

"But what you may not know is that her body was never recovered. Her helicopter was there, burned to a crisp, but no body. Strange, don't you think?"

"You think she's alive?" Scarlett asked.

"Don't you?"

Scarlett fell back in the chair, tapping her fingertips on the arm rest.

"Scarlett, listen..." Sylvia began. "I've heard things about this...Crow Corporation."

"What things? Like what?"

"I covered that story back when I was with Channel 9. The healthcare. Their mission to *save* Winterview. I think it was all bullshit. Some sort of smokescreen."

"For what?"

Sylvia leaned forward, peering around the library, her voice low. "People have been talking. Important people. They say Crow Corp. isn't some altruistic enterprise trying to save the world. They say it's a cover for their true purpose."

"Which is what, exactly?" They were bordering on conspiracy theory territory now.

"I don't know. But they say Crow Corp. has been searching for something. Some sort of artifact."

"The Oblivion Stone?" Scarlett asked.

"No," Sylvia laughed mockingly. "Not your silly little rock. I don't *think*, anyway. But I have been wrong before. My guess is something else. Something worse."

"Worse?"

"I heard they have entire facilities filled with all sorts of weird shit they've found," Sylvia whispered. "State-of-the-art archives miles underground housing these...*things*."

"What kinds of things?" Scarlett asked, swallowing.

"The kinds of things you can't explain," she said. "The kind you keep locked up behind steel doors six inches thick and guarded with automatic weapons. The kind you want to keep far, far away from people."

Scarlett's eyes were wide, her palms sweaty, the fabric itchy on the back of her fair skin.

"Kind of like the house," Scarlett said to herself, frowning.

"And I hear they're not the only ones," Sylvia said with an impish grin. "I hear there's more of them out there. Collectors. People combing the planet for whatever is roaming around out there. In fact, I hear someone very, very rich even owns your entire wardrobe from that night at the house, minus that jacket you're wearing. Jackson's too. They went for millions, Scarlett. *Millions.* Probably have them on display in their own little museum somewhere. It's insane, there's a whole little underground society dedicated to collecting this occult shit."

"No fucking way," Scarlett uttered, her mouth hanging open. "You're not serious."

"Very. And you didn't hear this from me, but there's even talk about some clandestine agency that deals exclusively with all sorts of weird paranormal shit. Not the military. Not the Red Sky or Crow Corp. I'm talking about something that's so secret that, as far as I can tell, has no name...*yet.*" She put her hand to the side of her mouth. "Although that's a developing story, so you didn't hear it from me."

"This is insane," was all Scarlett could say. Her mind was reeling with possibilities. Was it possible a whole subculture dedicated to the supernatural and all things that go bump in the night actually existed?

"That is the name of the game," Sylvia said. She collected her purse, standing up. "I heard you quit the academy."

"News travels fast," Scarlett said.

"You've wanted to be a detective for as long as I can remember." she said, straightening her pearl necklace. "This may come as a shock to you coming from a woman you detest, but I did too—once."

This caught Scarlett's attention. "You did?"

"Of course. Why do you think I became a reporter in the first place?" Sylvia replied.

Scarlett stood up, slipping on her backpack and pulling her hood over her head.

"I think it's in our nature to want to solve puzzles," Sylvia said. "I'm sorry things didn't work out at the academy. I really am. I know what it's like when life doesn't turn out the way you thought it would."

"Thanks," Scarlett said, and for the first time in years since she'd seen this woman, she found herself warming up to her.

"Remember something, Scarlett," Sylvia said.

Scarlett watched as Sylvia blew the dust off her glasses, placing them back on the bridge of her nose, and then smiled.

"You don't need a badge to solve a mystery. You just need a reason."

JACKSON

"I KNOW YOU." Nelson blinked, and Jackson felt attacked.

"Dude, you really don't," Jackson said.

The sky was violet, combed with streaks of tangerine. He and Nelson stood under a taco truck awning, a cloud of steam drifting from inside. Jackson could smell the meat from here, strips of seasoned beef sizzling alongside diced onion.

"What are we doing here?" Nelson asked offhandedly.

"I don't know about you, but I need to eat."

Nelson gawked at the chef perched in the inside as if he'd never seen a taco truck before.

"Two, please," Jackson said, flashing two fingers. "And a Corona," he said, laying down a twenty.

The Hispanic gentleman nodded, flashing a friendly smile before disappearing behind the counter.

"Yes, I do," Nelson argued. "You and the chick that doesn't like coffee… Scarlett, that was her name! You both went into that haunted house, the one that appeared in the middle of that city." Nelson scratched his frizzy red hair. "Didn't you?"

Nelson stared at him, a curlicue of red fuzz on his head wobbling in the wind. His mouth hung open, waiting for an answer.

Jackson was quiet. He didn't want to get anyone else involved in anything even remotely pertaining to the house, let alone a kid who appeared to be completely clueless about most of life's common knowledge.

"Nelson, what are you doing here?" Jackson asked.

"What do you mean?"

"I mean, why are you following me around? Don't you have somewhere you need to be? Where's your parents?"

Nelson pondered this question perhaps deeper than Jackson assumed he would, then said, "I don't know. I thought you might want to talk about it. My grandma always said talking about your traumas can help you get over things."

"My traumas?" Jackson asked, confused. "What traumas?"

"You know. The haunted house or whatever."

"You don't know what you're talking about." Jackson shook his head. "Go home, Nelson. Or go to that game store you like. I don't care what you do as long as it's far away from me."

The taco truck's bell dinged; the cook handed Jackson his tacos on a grease-soaked plate along with a Corona and a wedge of lime. He walked over to a plastic table covered in graffiti and sat down, chugging half the beer in one go.

Nelson peered around as if he was trying to avoid Jackson's detection, slipping into the chair across from him.

Jackson exhaled in annoyance. "You know I can see you right?" he said, his mouth half-full. "You're not a fucking ninja, dude. And I hate to break it to you but you're pretty tall for a high schooler."

"I'm twenty-two," Nelson said brusquely.

Jackson stopped chewing, stupefied.

Nelson looked down at Jackson's tacos and blinked behind the giant lenses.

"Here," Jackson said. He pulled a twenty out of his pocket and handed it to Nelson.

Nelson looked at the cash suspiciously, then carefully took out his wallet, pocketing the bill inside.

"Uhhh…that was for you to buy something to eat?"

"I ate before I came down here. Not hungry." A fly dive-bombed his face and he swatted at it, pathetically uncoordinated.

"Unbelievable," Jackson said. He took another pull from his beer. "Why are you following me, Nelson?"

Nelson shrugged. "I don't know. You seemed like you could use a friend."

Jackson exhaled, swishing the beer around in the bottom of the bottle.

"What did you see out there?" Nelson asked.

"Out where?" Jackson asked. He shoved the last bite of taco into his mouth, wiping his lips with the napkin.

"Back on the beach. You saw something out in the water, right? What was it, like some kind of sea monster or something?"

"I didn't *see* anything," Jackson emphasized, polishing off the Corona.

"Yes you did," Nelson said. "And you saw something under the pier, too." He raised his arm, pointing across the street at the pier.

Like lightning, Jackson snatched Nelson's wrist in a death grip.

Nelson grimaced, trying to tug his hand away.

Jackson realized what he was doing, and quickly released him.

"Hey, what the hell!" Nelson yanked back his arm, massaging his wrist. "That wasn't cool, man."

"Look, I'm sorry," Jackson said, leaning in close. "Just stay away from the pier, okay? It's not safe down there."

"Why?" Nelson stared at him, cradling his hand. His eyes wandered, Jackson following his gaze to a wall scored with faded graffiti.

The Halliday House. Straight across from where they sat was another rendition of the house. Significantly cruder and sketched hastily, the house's black silhouette had been scratched out, marred by sets of erratic, frenzied lines.

The words seemed to melt before his eyes, bleeding down the wall.

All hail the King in Yellow

"What's down there?"

Nelson's voice saved him for the second time that day.

Jackson snapped out of it, forcing himself to look away.

Nelson noticed, doing a double take. He squinted toward the wall art, trying to read the words. "All hail the kid in yellow?"

"Jesus," Jackson said. "You really are blind. *King*."

"Oh," Nelson said. "King in Yellow. What's that?"

He dodged Nelson's question again, wiping his mouth with a napkin and crumpling it up, lobbing it into the trash can. "Where's your parents, Nelson? Shouldn't you be at home with your family right now having dinner? What're you doing here, sitting here with me?"

Nelson shifted uncomfortably in his seat, his posture painfully stiff. "My parents left when I was born. It's just my grandma and I. And Wanda."

"Wanda?" Jackson asked. "Your girlfriend?"

"My fish."

"Oh."

"I got her down at Petco. She's a rescue. Tomorrow's her birthday. She'll be seven years old, I think. That's like thirty-five in human years."

"Is that right?"

"It was you on the TV, wasn't it? You and crazy-coffee-girl?"

"Oh, I guess the goldfish story is over," Jackson muttered under his breath. He nodded. "Scarlett. Yeah."

"Yeah, her. You guys are like famous or something right?"

"Something like that." Jackson stood up. "I need another drink. You want one?"

"My grandma says alcohol is bad for you," Nelson said. "She says it dries you out like a raisin. She says that's where shrunken heads come from."

"More for me," Jackson said. He waltzed over to the truck, returning with a fresh beer and a nonexistent buzz and sitting down slightly more relaxed than he was ten minutes ago.

"You get one question, Nelson."

Nelson squinted, pushing up his glasses. "One question? What the heck do you mean?"

"You're here because you want to ask me about the house, right? So, I'll give you one question. If I were you, I'd make it count."

Nelson turned his face toward the ocean, watching a flock of seagulls circling over the shore. Jackson could still see the boat anchored in the sand where they'd left it.

"Did you see anyone there—in the house?" Nelson asked. His tone softened; it didn't carry the same monotonic weight. He met Jackson's eyes. "I mean—was anyone in there…that you lost?"

"Like clockwork," Jackson uttered. He shook his head, taking a swig off the beer and setting the bottle on the table. "Always the same question."

"What do you mean?"

"Ever since we escaped, people always want to know the same thing. You'd think there would be a million questions they'd want to ask, but no. It's always the same."

Nelson furrowed his brow. "What question?"

"The same question you just asked. The same one that got her killed," he said, realizing his slip.

"Got who killed?"

"My friend, Hannah," Jackson said wistfully. "She asked me that very question herself once. She had lost someone and she couldn't get past it. She thought maybe the house was magic or something. Like it could bring her back somehow. Make the pain go away."

"Did it?"

Jackson shook his head. "No. That's what people don't understand. You can't get rid of the pain. Nothing can. You just have to try and learn to live with it."

"Oh," Nelson murmured. "That sounds awful."

"Yeah," Jackson agreed. "I wish I had a better answer. People always leave disappointed."

A beat of silence settled in, the duo watching the sun melt into the horizon. Lines of customers were forming at the taco truck. Steam was billowing out, wafting in Nelson's direction. His lenses fogged; he began coughing, swatting away the smoke in front of his face.

"What people?" Nelson asked innocently.

"Just people. The news. Everyone, I guess."

"Like those two people that have been following you?"

"What?" Jackson's awareness multiplied times a hundred, a panic wailing in his ears. "What did you say?"

"Those two people that have been following you. What, you didn't notice?" His tone had a simplicity that was outright alarming.

Jackson leaned forward on the table, scanning their surroundings. "What? Here? There's someone watching us?"

Nelson casually looked around, twisting his long torso and checking behind him. "No, I don't see them now. I guess they're gone." He took off his glasses, cleaning them with his shirt, his lids squinting so much Jackson could barely see his eyeballs.

Jackson felt the tension ease, laughing to himself. "What're you saying, you can't see anything, you're blind as a bat."

Nelson put his glasses back on, unimpressed. "There was two of them," he said, holding up two fingers. "I saw them watching you the other day at the pier, too."

"Uh-huh. So why didn't you say anything then?"

"I don't know. I thought they were fans too. Like me. I mean, back when I thought you were Daryl Duke."

A second later a vintage blood-red Mustang roared up to the curb. The horn honked, drawing their attention.

"Who the heck is that?" Nelson asked, putting a hand to block out the sunset.

"Well, this has been…*weird*, Nelson," Jackson said, standing up. He tossed the soiled plate and empty beer bottle in the trash. "I can't sign your card. I can't give you any advice that's gonna save your social life. And I sure as hell can't tell you what's waiting for us when we check out."

The horn went off again, and Jackson waved.

"You're a cool guy, Nelson. Weird, but cool. I'll see you around."

Jackson tipped his head and climbed into the car. The Mustang didn't waste any time, peeling out and leaving two trails of smoke behind.

Nelson waved, choking as the cloud of smoke blasted apart, a sleek black SUV passing by.

"Told you," he said.

SCARLETT

"YOU DID WHAT?"

Scarlett could see the disappointment on Jackson's face. He didn't need to say anything else, she knew this was going to be an uphill battle.

Night had come. The Mustang was idling in the alley behind Dunkin Donuts, the taillights glowing in the night. Mist crept along the concrete, wandering by while people scurried past on the busy city streets.

"Look, Jackie, I know what you're going to say," Scarlett said.

"Christ, Scarlett. You went alone and met up with that psycho?"

"I know how it sounds, but look," Scarlett said, handing the folder to him.

"That woman nearly ruined *both* our lives and you're out having coffee with her?"

Scarlett turned on her selective hearing, opening the folder on his lap. "This is every article that's hit the news since the house appeared. Anything even remotely related."

Jackson exhaled, placing his hands on the dash. "We. Made. A promise, Scarlett," he said, lightly bumping his fist on the dash to emphasize each word.

Scarlett frowned. "I know, Jackie. I know we did. But hear me when

I say that something is going on over there. Something big. Something bad."

"Stop. Just stop." Jackson pivoted in his seat. "Scarlett, listen to me for a minute, okay? Winterview was falling apart a long time before the house was there. You know that. The city didn't fall apart overnight. That place has been dying for a long time. The house was just the straw that broke the camel's back."

"What about all this other stuff?" Scarlett said, fumbling through the articles on his lap. "Suicides. Reports of fucking monsters coming out of kids' closets. Cults. People getting sick and dying and nobody knows why. It's like ever since the house came—"

"I don't care," Jackson interrupted. He pinched the bridge of his nose, massaging out the tension. "I do not care. The *house* is not our problem anymore."

Scarlett stopped, staring at him.

Jackson rolled the folder in his hand, holding it up. "All of *this*? It doesn't matter anymore, Scarlett. We do not owe that city anything. Why can't you let go of it?"

Scarlett was quiet. She took the folder from Jackson, straightening it out. "This was a mistake." She reached onto the back seat and grabbed her backpack, shoving the folder back inside.

"Yeah," Jackson said. "It was."

"When are you going to admit that this was never about the house?"

Jackson looked at her, confused. "What do you mean?"

Scarlett sniggered. "You know what I mean. Don't act like this was ever about the house."

"I don't know what you're talking about."

"When was the last time you talked to your dad, Jackie?" Scarlett asked. She lifted her backpack off her lap and lobbed it onto the backseat.

Jackson looked away. "I haven't."

"That's the whole point!" Scarlett said. "You are great at a lot of things, Jackie, but there's one thing you're absolutely atrocious at: lying."

Jackson turned to her; his soft expression turned to something harder. "What are you saying?"

"How many times has he called you since we've left?"

Jackson was silent.

"How many times has he tried to apologize?"

"That is none of your business," Jackson said.

"You want to ask me why I can't move on? Well, what about you, huh? He's called you half a dozen times now. I know you try and hide the screen but you suck at it."

Jackson shifted in the seat, his fingers strumming his knee.

"So what about you?" Scarlett pressed. "Why won't you talk to him, huh? You ask me why I can't move on, so what about you? Why can't *you* let go?"

"Because I hate him!" Jackson snapped.

Scarlett froze, her eyes pried open in shock.

"You have any idea what it's like celebrating your birthday parties by yourself? My eighteenth birthday I came home and there was an envelope on my bedroom door with my name on it. Happy birthday, Jackson. Right?" he said in rapid-fire delivery. "Wrong. It was a *bill*, Scarlett. A fucking bill for rent!"

"I know things weren't easy for you growing up, Jackie," Scarlett said.

"Christmas morning. I'm six. I wake up, walk downstairs, and do you know what my Christmas gift was that year?"

Scarlett shook her head, regretting her decision to mention his father.

"My mom—leaving us. I woke up that morning and she was already gone. That woman, the same person who was supposed to love me, left!"

"I'm sorry, Jackie," Scarlett said. She saw tears slip down Jackson's cheeks. She reached over, taking his hands. "I didn't know."

"He had this picture in his office. But I couldn't look at. I couldn't stand to look at what he'd ruined." Jackson was breathing faster, his chest rising and falling. "And do you want to know what the worst part is?"

Scarlett was quiet.

"The worst part is that I can't even remember what she looks like anymore."

"Sometimes people don't know how to cope with things. They can't make sense of it in their head so they do the only thing they can think of. They run away." Scarlett said. "I'm sure she loved you."

Jackson shook his head. "No. She didn't love me. You don't leave people behind that you love. And that's why I left. I don't need him."

"You don't mean that," Scarlett said.

Jackson squeezed her hands, looking into her eyes. He reached up, resting a warm hand on the side of her face. "You think I can't let go, but the truth is, I did a long time ago. Tommy. Hannah. *They* were my family. I don't need him anymore because *you're* my family now, Scar. Haven't we suffered enough?"

Scarlett nodded. "Okay," she said.

Jackson looked at her. "Okay?"

She didn't have to say anything more. He knew. They both knew.

Scarlett nodded and Jackson's eyes closed in relief. He exhaled, smiling.

Before she could lean in to kiss him, a pair of gloved hands shot through the passenger window.

A crackle of electricity and a blinding light.

Jackson shrieked, his teeth gritted, his body flying into judders.

Scarlett twisted the keys to the ignition.

The Mustang's engine roared to life.

She threw the car in gear right as two muscular arms slid around her waist and wrenched her out of the driver's side door.

She threw her legs out, pushing off the side of the car and shoving her attacker off balance. She watched the dark buildings in the alley whirl by, transforming into the night sky.

She felt her body go weightless for a fleeting moment, and the next thing she knew she was crashing down on top of someone in a spectacular clatter of garbage. She grunted, flailing her legs, trying to free herself from the arms locked around her waist. The vacant Mustang rolled away, the driver's side door hanging wide open.

"HELP!" she shrieked.

A large hand clamped down hard over her mouth, muffling her

screams.

Scarlett watched as a shadowy figure calmly walked over to the open driver's side and leaned in, shifting the car to park.

She heard the Mustang's engine cut out.

This was her last chance or she was dead.

She released the arm around her waist, grabbing the hand over her mouth. She bit down as hard as she could, her teeth scraping over bone.

"*Fucking bitch!*" the man screamed, ripping his hand away. The metallic taste of blood filled her mouth. The hand around her stomach slackened. Without thinking, she whipped her head back and heard a hard crunch followed by a grunt.

She was free. Adrenaline pouring into her bloodstream, she flailed off of the assailant's large frame, awkwardly finding her footing in the pile of garbage and standing up. Her eyes tracked to the other end of the alley, where she could see people casually walking by in the crosswalk.

"Hey!" she said, trying to flag down someone. But it wasn't enough. In the commotion the air had been squeezed out of her. Her cries of help came out in a whisper.

"Naughty girl," a velvety voice said.

Scarlett turned in time to see a black fist smash into her face.

The impact whirled her like a top—she spun around, her back slamming into a dumpster with a hollow thump before she collapsed to the ground.

Her view of the stars turned to solid black.

The silhouette of a woman stood looming over her. Further to the left she heard the man climbing out of the pile of garbage.

"Put them in the car," the woman commanded.

Scarlett willed her body to move. Screamed at herself to get up, to get going. Move! Do anything! But her head was light, fluffy with clouds and warmth. Her body was immobile, her vision swimming.

"Jackie," she moaned. Everything was slowing down. The world was tilting on its axis, and she wondered if she would drift away into the beautiful night sky.

"You're a mess," the voice said with a cruel laugh. The woman had an accent. European. The lithe shadow got down on one knee, reaching out and brushing a few blood-stained strands of hair to the side. Scarlett winced, trying to pull away but paralyzed from the blow. She watched as the woman reached into her coat. "Time to go home, Scarlett," the voice whispered.

A seizure of white light and a hiss of electricity.

Then: absolute, beautiful darkness.

SCARLETT (cont'd)

IT WAS COLD. Too cold.

Scarlett's eyes peeled open to find a wall of grimy glass overlooking a city skyline. It was night. The room was dark, the only light a soft glow from the windows below. They were in some sort of suite, on top of the world.

"Winterview," she whispered. She'd know that city anywhere.

She let her clarity refocus, seeing her warm breath escape into the cavernous room. She moaned, feeling the left side of her face flare with pain. She tried to speak and realized her mouth was stuffed with a rag. Her hands were bound behind her. She attempted to wiggle them but couldn't. The circulation in her hands was damn near being cut off.

A quiet groan from her right. She twisted at the waist to find Jackson in a chair beside her, his hands bound behind his back as well, his head slumped down, resting on his chest.

"Jackie?" She heard it clear in her head, but it came out garbled, virtually unintelligible.

Jackson was coming to—albeit more slowly than herself.

She tried to speak but the rag dampened her voice to nothing.

A sharp gasp to her left. She twisted to the opposite side, finding Nelson tied to another chair. She blinked hard, disbelieving.

Nelson??

Two heavy doors creaked open behind them. She listened as the sound of heels clicked across the tile, fast approaching.

She watched with bated breath as a beautiful woman in her mid-forties casually strolled into view. Easily six feet tall and slender, Scarlett could have genuinely said she had never seen this woman in her life. With high, chiseled cheekbones and a bronzed hue to her skin, the woman carried herself confidently, perhaps even dangerously. She stepped forward, tugging the gag out of Scarlett's mouth, her piercing blue eyes transforming Scarlett's soul into an icy snowscape. The woman grinned and two gold incisors glinted at her, enhancing an already flawless smile.

Scarlett glanced at Jackson, who had come to. He was quietly watching them, assessing the situation.

The woman snapped her fingers and two figures behind them moved down the line, cutting off their restraints. The man and woman from the alley casually flanked the woman, quietly watching them.

Now that they were out of the shadows, Scarlett was able to get a good look at them both.

The first, a man called Enzo "The Beast" Astley, was positively formidable, dressed in an Italian navy-pinstripe suit that could barely contain his hulking frame. He almost would have been handsome if it weren't for a crooked nose and a brow like a Neanderthal. His greasy hair was slicked back, and hostile, black eyes gave Scarlett the impression he must be showing incredible restraint to not have killed her already.

The woman was easily half the man's size. Coined Morgana "Nightmare" Venditto by her peers, the second figure was petite, with a high ponytail as black as a horse's tail and skin like snow. Scarlett discerned an eerie similarity to herself, almost as though the woman could have been her mirror image had she been raised in a darker world. An uglier, more brutal one. A handful of pink scars were etched into the woman's expressionless face, one of them tracing over her right eye, the black pupil split open like a crocodile.

The blond woman took a step forward, eyeing Scarlett. "Good

evening, and welcome back to Winterview City. About now your heads are pounding, your bodies are probably a little tingly. You're scared. Confused." She abruptly stopped speaking, marching over to Nelson.

"Who in the fuck is this?" she asked.

"Nelson Rockefeller," Enzo said. A thick accent.

The woman rolled her eyes. "What the fuck is he doing here?"

"He's a friend of theirs," the man replied. "He saw us—we didn't want any lose ends."

The woman's dissatisfaction was obvious.

"Do you know who I am, Scarlett?" she asked.

Scarlett shook her head. "No."

"You're probably wondering who I am, so let's get that out of the way now. My name is Katya Carlisle." The woman breathed deeply, gazing out at the city lights. "Over a hundred years ago, my husband's family immigrated here from Sicily. They worked for decades, building this city brick by brick with their own blood. Their own tears. Everything they had to give their children an empire. A future."

Scarlett and Jackson looked at each other.

"This high-rise once served as his base of operations." The woman pressed her index finger to the window, dragging it through a coating of dust. "Some of the biggest decisions of his life took place in this very room."

Katya turned around. "And now look at it. Nothing more than a monument for all the souls who died for a dream that was never realized."

"What does this have to do—" Jackson began.

The hulking man in the suit threw his weight, cracking Jackson across the face so hard his chair toppled over.

Scarlett launched out of her seat.

Morgana cut between them, a blade in her hand, the tip jabbing into Scarlett's throat.

Katya stepped up to Scarlett. "*Do not* interrupt me again. Now sit."

The man seized Jackson, throwing him back in the chair and firing off another fist into his ribs for good measure, Jackson folding over on himself.

"My husband…he was a cruel man," Katya continued, like this was business as usual. "And, like many men, his penchant for violence often clouded his judgment. Before long, his hold on Winterview began to slip."

Morgana's attention was fixated on Scarlett.

The woman continued. "As the years passed, I discovered that his influence over the city was slipping. His volatile temper left many fractured relationships in his wake, including some very important people. Obviously, I couldn't let him destroy our reputation and everything his family had built for generations, so I did the only thing I could—I killed him. I shot him in the head right over there," she admitted, her smile morphing into a devilish grin. She coolly leaned back against the window, crossing her arms across her chest.

"Not long after his death, an unbelievable structure unlike anything anyone had ever seen before appeared, driving the city to the brink of total financial ruin."

Scarlett's eyes narrowed. She used her shirt sleeve to wipe dried blood from her nose. She stole a glance at Jackson and saw a string of blood dripping from his chin.

"All operations in the city were ceased. All ships immediately required an inspection. All deliveries. Cargo containers. Money. All of it *frozen* while the government scurried about the city like bloodthirsty rats.

"So, rather than watch our fortune burn to the ground, I relocated our operations to New Haven for a fresh start, so that he may die with his family's pathetic legacy.

"Like with any move, there were obstacles at first. People that had their own opinions about me. People that didn't share my vision for the city, whether it be New Haven or Winterview, which was dying by the way," she said, with a playful tone. "I have a gallery now, as a tribute to them: the ones who dared to question me."

Scarlett looked at her, intrigued.

"*Skulls,*" she said matter-of-factly, alleviating Scarlett's curiosity. Katya walked forward, running a finger across Scarlett's cheek. Her body quivered, fighting every impulse she had not to slap the woman's hand away. "There's something beautiful about them once you strip away all of the skin, and muscle. The little pockets of fat. There are no more games. No more lies to tell or truths to speak. Only exquisite silence."

Scarlett swallowed.

"I hear you've seen things other people only dream of. Nightmares so horrifying and magnificent they can make you go mad."

Scarlett nodded her head, not breaking eye contact.

"I envy you," she confessed, and the sincerity in her voice was enough to make Scarlett's blood run cold.

Katya walked back to her place between her two associates. "Exactly three days ago, my daughter, Isabelle, was on a jet chartered for Boston."

Scarlett looked over at Jackson, who had his head down, staring off into space as the woman kept on. He wanted no part of it. She didn't need to hear him say it to know.

"The last communication from the plane was a mayday sent by the pilot, transmitted seconds before the signal was lost." Katya turned back to Scarlett and her blood chilled. "Hours later, for a very brief moment, the plane's black box emitted a weak signal, deep inside what has come to be known as the Dead Zone. As you both know, this is also the location of a certain structure that is heavily monitored by the government, making it very difficult for my people to search."

"If it's in the Dead Zone, the military would have found her by now. They wouldn't have missed a plane crashing into the middle of the city."

The woman began to step forward but Katya waved her away.

"For whatever reason, the military has made no attempts to enter the area, and seems to be observing the situation from afar."

"What about the police? Can't the police try and—"

"Since relocating to New Haven, our ties to Winterview's police force have diminished considerably. We're in no position to ask favors of them. Besides, like you said, the Dead Zone is controlled by the military now."

"So…what?" Scarlett asked. "It's been *years* since we went anywhere near that house. You want to send us all to our deaths?" It was a little dramatic even for her, but she had to try. Jackson would never survive another trip to the house. She doubted she would either. "Look, I understand why you think we know, but I'm telling you—we don't. If there's one thing I understand about the house, if you've heard anything I've said over the last year, it's that you *can't* know it. There isn't any consistency once you're inside. There's no way of navigating it or…or beating it."

"What are you saying?" Katya asked.

"I'm saying that it just *is.* The only certainty we have is not to go anywhere near it."

She looked over at Jackson, a dark bruise mapping the left side of his face. He shook his head, caught somewhere between hell and limbo.

"I'm sorry for the confusion," Katya said, sniggering. "This is not a request. You, and you alone have an intimate knowledge of the house."

Scarlett shook her head.

"You've met my associates," Katya said, holding out her hands. "They will accompany you to the house to find my daughter and return her to me."

"What about you?" Scarlett asked. This caught Jackson and Nelson's attention.

"Darling, don't you think I would if I could?" Katya asked, patronizing her. "I'm afraid I've been called away for a very important business meeting with some very important people. Maybe next time, love." Scarlett got the feeling she wasn't bluffing. She had no doubt the sociopath would go if she were able.

"And if we say no?" Scarlett asked.

"Yeah, if we say no?" Nelson repeated.

All the faces in the room panned to Nelson, stupefied.

"Your father lives here in the city, yes?" Katya said. She sauntered over to Jackson, lifting his chin. "Yours too."

"You'd be doing me a favor," Jackson said.

"Dang man," Nelson said, "that's cold."

Katya tilted her head, surprised at Jackson's callous remark.

"Somehow, I doubt that. But I suppose we'll find out, won't we?"

She walked to Scarlett, crouching down in front of her. "Your father wasn't hard to find," Katya said. "'Vantassel's Royal Automotive.' It has a nice ring to it. He has no idea who I am, and I hope for your sake he doesn't ever have to."

Scarlett jumped up and Morgana was there in an instant. She grabbed Scarlett's shoulders, shoving her down in the chair and leveling a blade across her throat.

"Don't worry. He's fine…for now," Katya said with a sly smile. "I can feel your rage. Your hate. Burning in here," she said, holding a hand to her chest. "You remind me of myself. So full of…fire. That's good. You're going to need it where you're going."

Katya stood tall, looking at each of them and chasing it with a sigh, as if she knew the expedition was doomed before it had even started. She started for the exit, her heels clacking as she made her way to the door.

Her voice echoed in the empty suite, bouncing off the concrete.

"Go to the house. Find my daughter. If you fail me, you'll all be dead by sunrise."

JACKSON

THE DARK WELCOMED them with open arms.

The air was damp with moisture. Jackson could smell the wet earth and the vegetation peeking out from the cracks in the walls. His clothes were sticky, grating against his skin. Scarlett was ahead, Morgana trailing two steps behind, and Nelson behind her. Then him. And at the tail, the man who had rearranged his smile with a single fist to his face.

They were in some kind of underground access tunnel, that much he was sure of. They'd entered through a basement door in an abandoned Italian restaurant a mile back. Their two taskmasters wielded flashlights but the rest of them walked on blindly. Every so often Nelson would bump into a wall and Jackson would help straighten him out. A crack like a lightning bolt ran through one of his lenses.

Jackson wasn't sure how Katya knew about their secret route. He had heard whispers about hidden passageways in the tunnels below the city when they'd take the train over from Silvers Hollow, but as he'd grown, he stopped speculating. Stopped believing.

The reality was far more depressing than the fantasy. Always was.

"Um, guys?" Nelson asked. "Where are we going exactly?"

"Keep a lid on it, kid," Enzo snapped. He shoved Nelson from the back and Nelson lurched forward, falling on his hands and knees.

"Hey, dickhead!" Jackson shouted.

"Ow," Nelson said, exaggerated. Jackson rushed over, taking his arm and helping him up. "What'd you do that for?"

The hulk went to raise his hand again and Scarlett planted herself between them, narrowing her eyes.

"You want our help? Fine," she said. "You want us to risk our lives to find some girl? Fine. But you lay another finger on him, or any of us, and you can find out what's inside that house without us. Got it?"

Jackson had to hand it to her, she was small, but she was no pushover. Scarlett glared at the man then turned to Nelson, brushing the dirt and leaves off his clothes.

"Freaking goons," Nelson said. He cleaned his lenses off with his shirt, walking again.

"We're here," Morgana announced. Without hesitating, she mounted the ladder, quickly climbing to the top.

They listened as the manhole cover ground onto the street above, a funnel of weak light shone down the ladder like a stage light.

"*Up*," the Enzo ordered.

Scarlett looked over her shoulder at them, and Jackson nodded. She disappeared up the ladder first.

Nelson lingered at the bottom like he was looking into the sun. "Geez, it's bright up there. Isn't the power off?"

"Come on," Enzo ordered. "You next. Get your skinny ass up that ladder."

"Fuck, man, I'm going, geez. I have a bad hamstring, okay?" Nelson hooked himself onto the ladder, working his way up, absorbed by the light.

The man waited, staring at Jackson as if this were another Friday night.

"Don't waste your time," Enzo said. "Hey, I get it. You wanna do the right thing: Save that idiot. Get the girl. Walk out a hero, right? *Wrong.*"

"I don't know what you mean?" Jackson said.

The goon walked over to the ladder, leaning against the bottom.

"This ain't my first rodeo. I've been doing this a long time. Decades now, since I was a little punk like you, and I can already tell what you're thinking by that stupid look on your face. Let me save you some time, kid. There ain't no room tonight for hero shit. Not here. You don't know her like we do. Everything you think you know about her? Forget it. You ain't seen shit, buddy."

"I don't follow," Jackson said.

"Katya. It's a front. A façade. She might come across like some high-powered business dame—and she is—but you run out on us and she will kill you and everyone you ever cared about—put your skulls in her fucked up little museum and then fuck your headless corpse." He lowered his voice, his face grave. "One time, she found out one of her crew was working with the Feds as a situated informant. A phone call from Katya and four hours later he was on a steel table, completely paralyzed. She likes to keep a bunch of shit like adrenaline on hand to make sure the poor bastards don't black out."

Jackson's face scrunched up with disgust.

"Katya asked Morgue to take care of it. She cut off his eyelids first. She told me it was so he got to see everything she was doing. *Everything*. Capeesh? Katya likes to watch. She gets a rush like it's sex or somethin'."

He'd heard enough. He approached the ladder, stepping on.

"You want my advice, kid?" Enzo asked.

"Do I have a choice?"

"You want to get out of here with your little girlfriend? Keep your mouth shut and use your fucking head."

Jackson laughed, eyeing the brute. "Well, don't forget, my 'little girlfriend' did that to your face."

The goon glowered as he started up the ladder.

It was like climbing into another world.

An ocean of thick fog blanketed Seventh Street.

He broke free of the mist, its tendrils clinging to his clothes. Scarlett stood alongside Nelson, taking in their surroundings.

"Move," Morgana ordered.

Jackson stepped aside as she watched Enzo ascend the ladder, emerging from the hole in the ground.

Nelson strayed away, abruptly stopping, his nose inches from a wall. "Guys? Where are we?" He backed up, bumping into a tree. He rotated, finding a trunk formed of translucent black glass. "What the heck is this? It looks like one of those glass sculptures." He lifted his hand, his fingers reaching out to feel the surface.

"Don't touch it, Nelson," Scarlett shouted. "Don't touch anything."

Nelson retracted his hand and sighed, wandering back.

Morgana and Enzo conversed amongst themselves, glancing their way ever so often.

"What do we do?" Scarlett whispered.

Jackson watched the enforcers talking, thinking it through. "Nothing. Don't do anything."

Scarlett gaped at him. "What are you talking about?" she hissed. "We have to do *something*—these people are gonna kill us the second we find her."

"What'd you say?" Nelson's voice cracked the quiet street.

"Nelson, will you *please* be quiet?" Jackson whispered.

"I think that'll do." Morgana was a foot away, quiet as a church mouse. Jackson hadn't even seen her. "Which way?"

Scarlett stepped to the center of the intersection, looking both ways down the lonely road. The wind stirred, pushing the fog past their feet.

"That way," she said, pointing.

"Lead the way," the woman said.

Scarlett began walking. Jackson and Nelson rushed to catch up with her, the two henchmen flanking them.

Nelson looked to the left, taking in the towering façade of the house.

"Is it really haunted?" he asked.

"Hey," Enzo barked. "I'll ask the questions, four eyes."

Nelson acted as though he didn't hear the man, kicking rocks on the street.

"Is it haunted?" the man asked.

Jackson and Scarlett looked over their shoulders, the woman wearing an amused smirk.

"No," Scarlett said. "I don't think that's what it is at all."

"But everyone on the news—" Nelson began.

"They haven't been inside, Nelson. *We* have," she said, waving her thumb at herself and Jackson. "Don't believe anything the news says. They're full of shit." Jackson couldn't help but wonder if those last words were directed more at Sylvia Sharpe than the media.

"Someone's touchy," Enzo said.

"Assholes," Scarlett muttered under her breath.

The moon flickered as they passed down the road through the twilight, the light filtering through the house's countless eaves, onion domes, and widow's walks.

"Hey," Scarlett said softly.

Jackson looked over at her.

"You all right?" she asked, pointing to his face.

He touched his cheek, nodding. "Not as bad as it looks."

Scarlett smiled, and it was enough to warm the street.

"Chicks like guys with scars, right?" he asked.

Scarlett chuckled. "Oh, absolutely we do. I could never be with a guy if I knew he couldn't take a punch."

Jackson laughed, and for a brief moment it was as if they were back in Silvers Hollow, their arms linked, strolling along the sidewalk into the sunset.

"Looks like you got a nice shiner yourself," Jackson added with a tip of his head.

Scarlett winced, as if she could feel the hit again, and Jackson noticed blood had begun to bleed across the whites of her eyes.

"Fortunately I can take a punch, too," Scarlett said.

Jackson's hands worked themselves into fists but he shook them out, knowing they were being monitored.

"So, what's your take on these two?" Scarlett asked, glancing back. The enforcers were keeping their distance; calm as could be.

"They don't look worried, so I guess we've got that going for us." Jackson sighed, wiping the dried blood from his lip. "I don't know. Something tells me they're not going to be easy to shake. That guy is built like a fucking tank. I doubt all three of us could take him."

Scarlett quietly walked alongside him.

"Hey, string bean, stay on the sidewalk." Enzo again.

They looked over and saw Nelson hop back onto the sidewalk.

"What about her?" Scarlett whispered.

"What *about* her?"

Scarlett crossed her arms over her chest. "I don't trust her."

"No shit, Scar," Jackson replied. "They're fucking murderers, why would you?" He neglected to mention Enzo's story about Katya using her as her own personal torturer.

"No, it's more than that," she argued. "She's hardly said two words all night."

"Yeah, so?"

"I don't know. I just have a bad feeling… Did you see all those scars all over her face? I mean, what has to happen to your face to look like that, Jackie? Can you answer that? Because I would love to know."

Jackson looked over his shoulder and the woman noticed him watching her. She grinned, waving menacingly, and a cold washed over him like ice water.

"She gives me the fucking creeps," he said.

"Hey, guys. What's that?" Nelson's voice. He slowed on the sidewalk, hands in his pockets, and hurried over to the middle of the street.

"What?" Jackson asked.

"You don't hear that?" Nelson asked.

"Hear what?" Scarlett asked.

Even the two enforcers had stopped in the middle of the road.

"What's the problem?" Enzo shouted.

"Shhh!" Nelson snapped, and even the man was shocked. "Listen."

Jackson took a few steps further, the mist crawling up his waist, whole sections of the night shimmering like panes of glass.

"Holy shit," Enzo said.

Morgana was stone silent, her piercing eyes scanning the dark buildings surrounding them for the source of said disturbance, a sound that appeared to be audible to everyone but Jackson.

"That can't be real," Scarlett asked, flustered. "Can it?"

"All right, everyone, calm down," the man directed. "Don't do anything stupid."

"It's coming from over there, I think," Nelson said, pointing in the direction they'd been walking.

And that was when he heard it.

And in an instant, things went from bad to worse.

The sound; he heard it now. It was faint, but it was there, lost somewhere in the night.

The color drained from his face.

A baby.

SCARLETT

"THAT'S A BABY out there!" Scarlett yelled.

"Holy shit. A baby?" Nelson said. "What the heck is it doing here?"

"I don't know, but it's not our problem," Enzo replied.

Scarlett listened to its cries echoing in the night, buried somewhere in the layers of fog and darkness. "We can't just leave it out there!"

The man stepped forward, raising his voice. "I'm getting tired of listening to you—"

"She's right," Morgana interrupted.

Everyone turned and looked at her in surprise.

"The infant's cries will draw unnecessary attention," she finished.

Scarlett smirked at Enzo and he responded with a grunt.

"Fine," he said. He marched forward, shouldering Jackson aside.

Before he could get more than ten feet, two orbs of light began to glow in the fog.

Enzo stopped, shielding his eyes as the light intensified.

"What now?" he uttered.

Nelson was farther ahead. Enzo jogged ahead, catching up with him.

"Everybody back," Morgana ordered.

"Nelson, get back here!" Jackson said.

But he was already too far ahead. Enzo grabbed Nelson by the collar, jerking him closer and shoving the gun against Nelson's kidney.

Morgana slipped a pistol from her coat. "Get out of the street. Now."

Scarlett grabbed Jackson, quickly pulling him behind a wall while Nelson stood stock still in the middle of the road, the goon's gun shoved into his back.

Morgana ducked behind a car abandoned on the side of the street while an old pickup emerged from the mist as if straight out of the 1950s.

Enzo waved, flashing a phony smile as the vehicle approached.

"Don't do anything stupid, kid," Enzo said. "Just follow my lead."

The truck slammed on its brakes, skidding across the wet road to a stop mere inches from him.

Enzo exhaled, and Jackson already knew what he was thinking.

That was close.

The truck idled, the engine sputtering, the headlights blinding Enzo and Nelson.

"Hi there," Enzo said with a friendly wave. He turned and looked over his shoulder at Morgana, shrugging. Nelson was frozen next to him like a store mannequin.

The headlights cut out, leaving the streets bathed in the same bluish-green gloom from before. The engine sputtered to a stop; the driver's door creaked open.

A man stepped out of the truck, and Scarlett didn't need to be standing close to see he was plenty pissed off. His dark hair was greasy, dangling over his eyes. His skin was tanned as though he spent most of his time outdoors. One of those outdoor survivalists where they're dropped off in some remote part of the world with only the clothes on their back and a knife. He was lean but muscular, his clothes dirty and worn. On his hip was a leather sheath concealing a large hunting knife.

The man strode forward, his dark eyes quickly assessing Enzo.

"You wanna get run over, shit-for-brains?" he asked, and Scarlett hoped his brains were as big as his balls.

Enzo chuckled, attempting to play naïve.

"Sorry about that. My son and I are a little lost, and I wondered if you could give us some directions."

No way he falls for that bullshit, Scarlett thought. She ducked down, peeking out from behind the wall as the scene played out. Morgana watched her like a snake, cool as could be, hidden behind the wrecked automobile.

"That right?" the wild man asked. He looked Nelson up and down and scoffed. "How old're you, kid?"

"Twenty-two," Nelson replied.

"Mother fucker, you look forty."

"Screw you, man!" Nelson said.

The stranger looked at Enzo suspiciously. "Why ain't your hair red?"

Enzo snickered. "My old lady is a ginger. We're tryin' to find our way back to the city," he grinned. "The *good* part of the city, I mean."

"Ain't no good part of the city left."

Enzo looked over the man's shoulder, finding a blue tarp crossed with rope concealing the cache in the bed. Nelson mirrored him, squinting.

"What'd you got back there?" Enzo asked.

The wild man stepped closer. "A whole lot of mind your own fuckin' business."

The goon wasn't intimidated, but Nelson sure was. His hands shook, and the cold moisture in the air had coated his glasses with a thin layer of frost.

Enzo's grin widened. He straightened his posture, standing up to his true height, and it was as if his body had grown right before their eyes. At this rate a brawl was about to happen in the middle of Seventh Street.

"Come on, man, don't be stupid," Scarlett whispered.

Without missing a beat, the wild man took another step forward, and it was clear neither of them was going to back down. Enzo moved the gun away from Nelson's side, hiding it behind his back.

"Me and my son here, you see, we're lookin' for someone."

The stranger breathed deeply, his eyes narrowing. "I don't give two shits who you're looking for, old man, and I have a feelin' that ain't the first lie you've told tonight."

Enzo scoffed, his eyebrows arching. "*Old man*?" His fingers tightened around the pistol. Scarlett looked over to find Morgana had snuck closer, pressed flat against a mailbox, within striking distance. Or firing range.

Just as the tension became overwhelming, the baby's wail broke across the street again.

Enzo and the wild man broke eye contact, peering around the street.

"I think it's coming from over there."

She didn't recognize the voice. Someone new. She could tell the man from the truck didn't recognize it either. Which meant someone else was here. And not one person—but many. Enzo had noticed, too, along with the man from the truck.

They turned, letting go of their grudge for a moment, listening as the voices approached.

The whispers climbed higher and higher, ricocheting off the buildings and the house, amplified by the cold, hollow silence.

Until they were right there.

Scarlett stumbled out from behind the building into plain sight as five dreamy shadows wandered out of the fog.

Simultaneously Enzo discovered the source of the sound, walking past the feral man, his gaze locked onto something unexpected lying in the middle of the street.

"Holy shit," he muttered.

"People," Scarlett said out loud. "Why are there people here?"

Jackson shook his head, and Scarlett knew this was a bad sign. People wouldn't be this far out here if they didn't have a reason. And of all the reasons to be here, none of the ones that came to mind were good.

Jackson climbed out from behind the building, Morgana close behind.

Scarlett and Jackson walked side-by-side as the strangers began to emerge from the fog like survivors seeing light for the first time. This was the moment. This was everyone laying down their cards. No more hiding. No more secrets. Their two captors were already far off their scripted plan. If they wanted to get away, now was their chance.

Morgana flanked her and Jackson, keeping her distance while the man from the truck and approached the thing in the street.

Nelson stayed put as Scarlett and Jackson moved past, stopping at the sides of the two men.

The baby shrieked again, and Scarlett's heart skipped a beat.

The approaching voices immediately ceased.

Scarlett hesitated, breathing out the chilled night air, then took a step in front of the group, watching the voices emerge one by one, their faces becoming clearer.

A tall woman with alabaster skin and blood-red hair was at the forefront, flanked by a young Asian woman and an ornery older man with wild silver hair and a scowl on his face. Not far behind them, a man in his mid-thirties with a buzz cut limped forward, a Black woman with bright eyes helping him along.

Scarlett and the tall woman locked eyes, regarding each other curiously while the baby's cries calmed before quieting altogether.

The woman blinked her big eyes before lowering them to the street.

Swathed in a golden fleece blanket, left to die in the middle of the cold, fractured face of Seventh Street, was a baby.

HARPER

"WHO ARE YOU?" Harper asked.

There were six of them. Complete strangers trespassing in the Dead Zone.

First these two and now this.

Not to mention the infant lying at her feet.

The girl didn't speak, draped in shadows. She looked over her shoulder at a burly man in a suit. The man shook his head and the girl nodded. Clearly something was afoot.

"This is a restricted area," Harper said.

"Yeah. It is," the man said. "What the fuck are you all doin' out here? Taking an evening stroll?"

She didn't care for the language.

"I might ask you the same question."

That was when it hit her like a bolt of lightning.

"You're Scarlett Vantassel," Harper uttered, absolutely floored. "And you're Jackson Briggs." It had taken her eyes a moment to adjust in the moonlight, but it was them, not a shred of doubt in her mind.

Harper looked at Park and Dirac, who, as far as she could tell, were in just as much shock as she was.

"What are you doing here?" Harper asked.

Scarlett stared at her, and Harper detected an acute desperation in her eyes.

"My name is Dr. Miranda Harper," she said, introducing herself. "These are my associates, Dr. Park, and Dr. Dirac. We're researchers working with the government."

The hulking man stepped forward. "And what about them?" he said with a jerk of his head.

Harper glanced over her shoulder to see Nick facing away, leaned up against a car with no doors. Sandi—a woman far out of her element, whose gentle nature had so clearly allowed her to be dragged way out here—was rubbing his back, attempting to reassure him. Sandi obviously cared deeply for the man Harper now knew as Nick Webster, but she wasn't so sure he shared that same sentiment. Sandi saw them eyeing her and whispered something in his ear, hurrying over to the crowd of people in the street.

Harper looked at the man. "We've only just become acquainted. They say they were attacked," Harper told. "They claim someone's been taken."

"Attacked?" the man asked.

Harper nodded. "Yes, that's right."

"*Taken?*" The man laughed mockingly. "By who?"

"It's true," Sandi confirmed. "They stabbed him," she said, nodding to Nick. "He lost some blood but I think he's going to be all right."

Park stepped forward, drawn to the cooing, a tiny hand peeking out, the rest of the newborn buried in blankets. "Um, guys, I know this may not be the best time, but there's a freaking baby in there, and the city is borderline freezing right now."

"She's got a point," Scarlett said.

She went to move forward and the man grunted, stepping in front of her and shaking his head. "Whoa, easy there, toots." He put a hand on her shoulder, walking her back.

Harper looked at Park curiously. They exchanged a look, noting something was amiss.

The baby began wailing, shrieking louder than before even.

Time slowed to a crawl.

Every beat of her heart and breath she took dialed up to ten.

Another man lingering nearby that Harper could only describe as feral lost interest in the events transpiring and attempted to walk to a truck parked about fifteen feet down the street. One that looked remarkably like the one they had encountered earlier that night filled with stolen goods.

The man in the suit noticed his brisk exit and said, "Where do you think you're going?" Clearly agitated, the man began shoving his way through the others in the group, chasing after him.

And lastly, Sandi, who's interest in helping others would prove to be a grave error, lost her patience with introductions and said, "Oh for Heaven's sake. Haven't any of y'all seen a baby before?" With a warm, motherly smile, she dipped down and gently picked the baby up, rocking it in her arms. The infant's cries died down as she swayed, carefully unwrapping the blanket covering the baby's head. "You poor thing. What are you doing way out—"

Sandi froze.

Harper saw Nick look up, shrugging off the pain searing the nerves in his back and taking notice of the new silence settling over the night. He groaned, pushing himself off the car, getting his bearings back. The blood looked like it was coming back to his face. Some of the color had returned to his cheeks, Harper thought.

"Sandi? What is it? What's wrong?" he asked.

Sandi's eyes went wide with horror; her breathing stopped and Harper saw her bottom lip quiver.

Sandi peeled back the blanket covering the baby's face, as if unveiling the curtain of an exhibit.

A collective gasp.

A plastic doll stared back at her mockingly, one of its weighted eyelids broken, drooping down, part of the plastic forehead molted with burns.

Sandi reached into the blanket, pulling out a small black device and holding it up for all to see.

The two groups exchanged looks, confused to all hell, listening to the tiny speaker expel the haunting sounds of a newborn.

Scarlett stepped forward and the hulk grabbed her by the collar, jerking her close. She looked at him and yelled, "It's a trap!"

Before Harper could register what was happening, a thin steel cable snapped taut around Sandi's ankles. She went to scream but all that came out was a gasp as her feet were ripped out from under her. Her body folded back through the air; Harper glimpsed Park's hands straining to catch the girl, but she didn't have enough time, snatching handfuls of air instead.

Sandi's face slapped the pavement hard with a weighty thud, like a sack of potatoes had been dropped. A gush of blood shot out of her mouth along with some teeth, scattering onto the concrete.

"Sandi!" Nick screamed. He broke into a sprint, pushing off the car.

Before anyone could react, the cable snapped tight with a metallic crack. A sound like a fishing reel whirred to life and Sandi began skidding across the pavement, moaning as her face ground against the earth.

Scarlett dove through the air, her hands grasping; but she was too late. She landed on the wet road with a grunt, rolling past Dirac's feet.

Sandi let a scream out as she was swallowed by the fog.

Harper couldn't be sure how long she stood there. Could have been seconds. Could have been hours. Everything happened so fast it was like time was going on, whizzing past her while she stood letting her mind try to play catch up.

The time for reticence was over, apparently, because in the minute since Sandi had been pulled screaming into the darkness, the two groups had merged.

All except one.

The man with the hardened eyes and the grease-slicked skin. He stood at the rear of his truck, eyes scanning his surroundings.

Harper glanced over and saw that Scarlett was still on the ground, sliding back on her butt, staring into the fog. Harper hastily stepped over and offered a hand.

Scarlett looked at it, and Harper saw the gears turning in Scarlett's head, weighing the choices she was going to be forced to make before she had to make them.

"What the hell was that?" Jackson was standing next to them, his hair wet with sweat.

"What the fuck is going on?!" the hulking man yelled. He had a gun out now, held down in front of him. "What the fuck was that?" he repeated, pointing into the fog.

A woman in a long black coat was already at their rear, calmly surveying the structures closest.

"SANDI!" Nick shouted. His voice was robbed of hope, as though he knew Sandi wouldn't be coming back no matter how much he willed it. He broke into a run and Park and Jackson stepped in front of him.

"Hey! No! You do not want to do that," Park said.

Nick struggled forward and Jackson restrained him while he shouted for Sandi.

"Get the fuck out of my way!" he snapped.

"Relax man!" Jackson argued, holding him back. "You can't help her!"

"Who in the fuck is that?" The hulk's voice killed the commotion.

Nick stopped resisting.

The group turned one by one to the yawning streets and the fog.

Harper didn't know what she expected to find that night.

Maybe some insight into the supernatural.

Maybe some shred of evidence identifying the catalyst for the biological phenomena happening in the Dead Zone.

Maybe even the truth about why she came tonight.

What she *didn't* expect, was to find figures in white robes waiting motionless in the streets.

Murmurs began to cultivate within their numbers.

Whispers. Panic, and alarm.

Harper turned, taking in her surroundings. A sense of alarm was climbing in her chest. She had been able to suppress it, keep it under control after years of dedicated training. But she was losing control. She could feel it.

The figures weren't only in front of them—they were everywhere. Watching from the windows of empty buildings. In the streets, where the fog gave them glimpses of their true numbers. There weren't a few. There were dozens. All watching, waiting. In their hands: Axes. Knives. All manner of rusted metal instruments that could be used to maim and mutilate.

Harper shook her head, amazed at her unbelievably bad luck.

"Cultists," she said, a trace of irritation in her voice.

Scarlett was silent beside her, her brown eyes wide open, soaking up the horror, her breath pluming into the frigid night. Harper could read people well by this point in her life. Anger. Fear. Even indifference. But what she saw in that girl's face was something completely unexpected. Confusion. Scarlett had been in this situation once before, so maybe she had expected the events to play out the same, assumed she had one up on a house that had gotten the best of her once before.

Only that wasn't true at all. Things had changed already, and she hadn't even made it through the front doors.

New rules.

The man the world knew as Jackson Briggs stood tall beside his love, slightly more terrified than he had been five minutes ago and a little sicker in the face. Harper saw their fingers slip between one another, and she wondered how long it had been since she'd held someone's hand herself in that way. Felt a connection to anything meaningful.

She chided herself for falling face first into self-pity. She needed to change gears.

The man in the suit wrestled his way to the front of the group, his pistol at the ready. A power play to scare away the strangers, no doubt. And a poor one at that. Even if he managed to kill some of them, the others would have more than ample time to hack off his limbs one by one. The woman in black had receded into the shadows, lying in wait with a pistol out at the ready as well, although she wasn't nearly as obvious about flaunting it. Harper assumed the weapon was meant more as a deterrent than a scare tactic.

"Harp, what do you think they're doing?" Park asked.

Harper shook her head. "I don't know."

"I don't like this," Jackson said. "Something doesn't feel right."

"No shit," the hulking man sneered. His eyes were near popping out of their sockets, utterly confounded as to how he had ended up in this bizarre predicament. He grunted, wiping a bead of drool from his lips, then withdrew from the front lines to converse with the woman in black.

Dirac scoffed, as though he couldn't trust his own eyes. "A joke. Plain and simple."

"That ax look like a joke to you?" Park asked him.

"They look pretty damn real to me," Jackson added.

Dirac sneered at them as if their collective IQs had dropped suddenly. "A *prop*. They're all props. What's the matter with all of you?"

"Uh-huh," Park said.

"They don't look like they're joking to me," Scarlett said, and Harper noted a nervousness in her tone.

"Are you all really that gullible?" Dirac asked. "Dr. Harper?"

He looked at her and for the first time since they had arrived at the Dead Zone that night, she felt like he saw her as an equal. Not a subordinate, or a friend. But a colleague. Someone whose opinion he would respect.

"I don't know," she said simply. And with that, any professional impression or whisper of credibility she had made on Dirac was gone.

He scoffed, his wiry skeleton springing to life. "What is the matter with all of you? You can't seriously believe these… these…*hooligans* are actually dangerous?"

Scarlett looked at Harper, and Harper could see she was two steps away from ripping Dirac a new one. She shook her head. Don't bother. It's not worth it. Let him be.

Scarlett acknowledged her, biting her tongue, and instead Park did it for her.

"Why don't you go find out?" Park asked.

Nobody thought he would take her seriously, but take her seriously he did.

"I will," he exclaimed proudly, puffing up what little chest he had and holding his head high. Harper thought maybe she misheard him at first but then remembered that people will do irrational things when they're afraid, especially when faced with life-threatening situations.

Like an army of robbed figures wielding an assortment of sharp and blunt instruments.

Dirac flashed a smirk, accepting Park's challenge. He shrugged the strap of the black bag on his shoulder, securing it, then rocked on his heels, strolling into the fog as if it were any other brisk winter night.

"Wait!" Park shouted. "I was joking!"

HARPER (cont'd)

HARPER'S PROTECTIVE INSTINCTS kicked in. She started forward and Scarlett reached out, putting a hand on her shoulder.

Harper stopped in her tracks. She looked back at Scarlett, and Scarlett shook her head. Don't do it. Dirac made his bed, now let him sleep in it, her face said. Maybe there had been a window, a very brief window in which Dirac could have been stopped, but the truth was, every one of them was so perplexed by so many strange events converging at once that they had simply failed to act.

Harper glared at Park, her sly quips crossing a line by putting one of their own in jeopardy.

Park held up her hands, feigning innocence. "What? I didn't think he was *actually* going to do it." Harper didn't have to say anything else. The young biologist already knew that whatever happened now was on her and her alone.

"Hey!" Jackson shouted. He had his hands cupped to the sides of his mouth. "Don't go over there, man!" His voice bounced down the street. Harper half expected the white shapes to scatter like doves in a magic act but they didn't. They simply waited.

Dirac calmly strolled down the street, passing the stoic mountain man and his fossil of a truck. Dirac was whistling a tune from that old show on late-night television, even tipping his head at the man as he passed like he wore an imaginary cap, and Harper could see that even the mountain man was as baffled as they were.

Enzo and Morgana had stopped talking. She'd overheard their names in hushed voices. They too now watched as Dirac attempted to initiate what at least in his mind were a form of negotiations. Enzo's mouth was agape, either charmed by Dirac's fearlessness or astounded at his stupidity, and Morgana was as cool as ever, her icy gaze betraying no secrets. No emotion. No fear.

"We have to do something." Nick was at Harper's side, a hand pressed to the small of his back, his face scrunched up in pain.

But no one did. They simply watched as Dirac moseyed out of the safety of their numbers, approaching the cloaked shapes.

Nick looked down and inspected his hand. Dried blood. Whatever they had done to patch the wound had worked. For now, at least. He had a smear of red across his cheek that looked like war paint.

Harper stood with baited breath as Dirac slowed, mere feet from the figures. He came to a stop, and it was as if the reality had caught up with him. His jaw went slack. He cleared his throat, head held high in that pompous way only Dirac could.

The mountain man turned and peered over his shoulder at Harper. A shiver ran through her. The man didn't look worried. It was more like he was trying to figure out his course of action if things got hairy, working out his escape route in his mind.

"He's fucked." Everyone looked over at Nelson, the tall, frizzy-haired misfit of the group. His ill-timed commentary caused Harper to shake her head. Not only aloof but utterly clueless as well.

Dirac waited. The ominous hooded figures were silent. Their white robes flapped in the wind like angel's wings. Harper couldn't even see their chests moving, almost as if they weren't alive at all but rather some form of bizarre ornamentation for what remained of Seventh Street. If the cultists hadn't been standing right there in front of her, Harper never would have believed they were real at all.

"Good evening," Dirac said.

And that was all he got out.

The figure closest him animated to life, heaving a large ax over their shoulder. Harper saw an expressionless white mask shimmer in the moonlight.

Dirac's eyes widened. He took a step back, realizing he had made a grave error, and gasped.

The ax pitched through the air and there was a thud, like it had hit the trunk of a tree.

Harper recoiled into Park and Scarlett. Nick stepped forward, like he couldn't believe what he was seeing. Harper shared that sentiment.

Blood spit from Dirac's gaping neck, misting the stark white robe of his attacker. The old man fell to his knees, the ax still embedded in the side of his throat, the wooden handle protruding into the air. His chin began to droop to his breastbone, the others watching in crippling terror.

"DIRAC!" Park shrieked. She lunged forward and Harper and Scarlett grabbed her, pulling her back. She sobbed, tears streaming down her face, and it was then that Harper noticed she was crying too.

Dirac held there for a moment on his knees, looking up at the one who had buried the ax in his neck, not even afforded the courtesy of seeing his face one last time. Clumsy, uncoordinated fingers groped across his chest, finding the rusted ax head buried in his throat. Dirac's face fell into a warm smile. He mumbled something to himself while a torrent of blood flowed down his left arm, splattering on the street.

The cultist didn't bother to retrieve the ax. They reached into their robe, and Harper saw the moonlight catch the blade of a very large knife. Her mind went to some variety of machete.

Dirac's breath vanished. He moaned one last time, fighting to hang on, then collapsed to the street, the ax handle jutting out of his neck like a tombstone marker.

A moment of silence lingered. Mere seconds of quiet ticked past while the fog wandered the roads and the tattered banners of the Seventh Street Lottery beat in the wind.

Then, all hell broke loose.

The cultists scattered like frenzied birds.

Harper heard screams. The group crumbled into factions. She and Park dove behind a nearby car while Scarlett and Jackson bolted in the opposite direction, back toward the house's entrance.

"Run!" Scarlett yelled over her shoulder, warning them. "Get inside!" *Easier said than done*, Harper thought.

The cultists reached the mountain man first. He was still near his truck, caught further out in the road. The first one slashed at him with a serrated blade of some kind. The man sidestepped it and grabbed their wrists, coiling himself around them. He grunted like he had a throat full of gravel, using his leverage to pull the blade into their jugular. There was a sound like wet paper tearing and a subdued gasp. He released the body and it fell to the ground, the white robe soaked with blood.

Another cultist threw themselves onto his back, jarring him forward. He caught himself before he fell, reaching behind him and wrapping an arm around their neck. He used their weight for momentum, heaving them over his shoulder and launching them into the side of the truck face first. He didn't waste any time. He threw open the truck door and slid into the seat. Another cultist dove for the driver's side, slashing at him with a knife. The man dodged the blade, grabbing onto their arm and yanking it through. He seized the door handle, slamming the door hard enough for Harper to hear bone break. She watched the body launch back like it had been ejected from a jet. The truck's antique engine sputtered to life. The mountain man threw on the headlights and illuminated dozens of the cultists rushing the vehicle. Harper watched as they swarmed the truck, climbing onto the windshield, two or three of them scampering into the bed. The engine revved, the rear tires burning out in two clouds of smoke.

Harper watched as it lurched not forward, but back, the glowing taillights veering wildly in reverse.

She looked over to see Morgana dash away.

The truck collided with a car broken down in the middle of the street. The truck's rear windows detonated as the three cultists in the back were launched into the air, careening onto the pavement twenty feet away in a jumble of bloody robes.

The truck stalled, out of commission for the moment.

The cultists began their assault on the others, charging forward.

"I didn't sign up for this shit!" Enzo said. A robed madman emerged from a building across the street and ran straight at him, cutting across the street. The white fabric fluttered against the wind like a ghost was flying at him.

He raised the gun; a flash accompanied by a clap of thunder.

The assailant's head snapped back, throwing them off their feet.

Enzo turned in time to see another less than ten feet away. He whipped the pistol to the left and fired again. The bullet caught them dead in the shoulder but they kept coming. Enzo pulled the trigger again, and this time they went down.

He fired off a few more rounds with surprising accuracy, knocking down more of the cultists.

The gun clicked.

Enzo turned to see Scarlett and Jackson fleeing past.

"Harper!" She heard a voice crying out somewhere in her head but it was too far away, lost somewhere between all the screams and gunfire.

Nick was standing a few feet away, watching the carnage unfold, the Python in his hand. He turned this way and that, unsure what course of action to take. He turned around to see a machete flying at his head. He recoiled, dodging it narrowly, but lost his balance and went down hard on his ass. The Colt went spinning into the street.

A wall of solid white rose, blotting out Harper's view of the skirmish, and it was then she realized someone was right in front of her, on top of the rusted car. The figure drove an intricate double-edged blade down at her head.

They were too close; she didn't have enough time to get clear.

She held her shaking hands in front of her, prepared for the inevitable, and the thought came to her how utterly ridiculous she must have looked.

She watched the blade cut through the night, the mirrored tip catching the moonlight in a silver starburst.

Park was there in an instant, shoving her out of the way. The blade caught Park's upper arm and she howled as it sliced through skin and fat and muscle, grazing the bone. The missed opportunity caused the cultist to lose their balance; they rolled forward face first, toppling off the car onto the street.

The knife went clattering to the pavement.

Park fell to her hands and knees, throwing a hand over the wound.

"Get the knife!" she screamed.

Harper's eyes zigzagged over the road, desperately searching for it.

The cultist scrambled to get back up. Harper couldn't tell the back from the front, the stark white robes like some sort of optical illusion. She spotted Nick wrestling with another, fighting for his life while a second shape was fast approaching. And for the first time that night, she thought to herself, *I'm going to die.*

The cultist struggled up. Harper could see a spot of blood on the shroud covering their face. *Good*, she thought.

The cultist spotted the knife. They made a move for it and Harper didn't hesitate. She threw herself hard, tackling them to the street. She mounted them while they flailed, fighting and clawing tooth-and-nail. A pair of hands shot out of the robe, locking around her throat.

Her teeth bit down. Her eyes watered and tears slid down her cheeks. She felt the cold fingers cinching around her slender neck. She looked over to see Park's arm doused with blood, coming back to reality.

Park saw what was happening and winced, struggling up, getting to her feet and shuffling forward.

Park slid on her knees, scooping up the knife.

Harper felt her vision begin to go black. She wrenched on the hands but it was no use; they might as well have been stone.

Parallel to her, Nick was on his back, engaged in his own battle. He threw a punch, cracking the cultist in the head. The body collapsed as if the life had left them the moment a second attacker arrived.

Her view darkened, then brightened again. Fading. Fading.

The second cultist hauled an ax through the air. Nick used the corpse laying on him as a shield, pushing it out in front of him.

A hollow *thump!*

Nick blindly kicked out at the robes with his foot; Harper heard a crunch as the cultist's ankle folded in half.

Nick slid out from under the corpse, jerking the ax out of the cavity. The cultist wasn't ready; Nick whipped the ax through the air like a baseball bat. A heavy metal whoosh and the cultist's head went sailing, knocking off the truck's rear-end in a splash of blood.

Harper's sight dimmed.

"Watch out!" Park's warning tore through her ears, grazing the deepest darkest parts of her subconscious.

Harper sprang back to life.

Park dropped to her knees beside them. She slashed the blade across the cultist's wrist. The hand immediately released and the air rushed back to Harper's lungs.

The life poured back into her body like liquid fire. She seized her second wind and turned the tables, digging into the robes and finding a neck, letting her hands close around their throat. Soft and fleshy. Cold. No Adam's apple. A woman. The cultist seized her wrists, resisting, and Harper looked at Park desperately, struggling to maintain her hold.

Park stared at her helplessly, unsure what do it.

"Do it!" she screamed. "Now!"

Park looked impossibly at the knife, the blade covered in blood, and shook her head as if she knew what she had to do but would have given anything not to do it. She sucked in a deep breath and squeezed her eyes shut, plunging the knife through the air.

The blade bit into the fabric right about where an eye would have been. A wet squelch followed by a crunch, where she assumed the blade had broken through the socket.

And for the first time that night, Harper screamed.

JACKSON

HE WAS RUNNING. Scarlett too. Seeing someone get murdered in front of you seemed to have that effect. It wasn't like the movies. It didn't feel romanticized, or staged. It was brutal. Raw. Terrifying.

Jackson was trailing behind her, dodging the crazy people in the white robes at every turn. Scarlett had tried in vain to warn the others to get to the house. Told them to get inside while there was still time. But the cultists had multiplied. No one could have seen it coming. They were just too fast, and more importantly, there were far too many of them. They swarmed from the fog like locusts, expelled from the darkness, pouring out of abandoned buildings in droves, coming at them from all directions at all angles, surging in faster than the hulking Italian guy could shoot them.

Enzo spotted him and Scarlett running along the façade of the house. He dropped one oiled magazine to the street and slammed in another with his meaty palm. His eyes narrowed.

"The entrance!" Jackson said. "The house!"

Enzo looked at him like he was confused.

Scarlett turned back, appalled. "What the hell are you helping them for? They're trying to kill us, Jackie!" she snapped.

Jackson shrugged, smiling guiltily, and Scarlett rolled her eyes.

He saw Enzo start in their direction and wondered where Morgana had gone.

A flutter of black in the street. A silent, stealthy predator in a sea of predators. To his and Scarlett's surprise, Morgana wasn't running from the crazed religious fanatics. She was running *at* them. One had a baseball bat full of nails up in the air, ready to swing, sprinting straight at her. Morgana darted forward, low on her heels, and ducked with the grace of a cat. A burst of silver and a screech of metal as she side-stepped the cultist. The body slowed, the white robes pooling with red. They took a few more steps, staggering drunkenly before falling to the road.

That was the first time they both realized the degree of lethality of which Morgana possessed, her practiced, effortless movements like those of a world-class ballet dancer and master assassin all rolled in to one.

Scarlett tugged his hand and that was when he saw it: the entrance to the house. The two immense skeleton doors looked exactly the same as they had a year ago. Inside the doors was an entire universe of intricate moving parts enchanted with a golden luster. He remembered the Clockwork's Gate, remembered seeing his best friend for the last time standing in this very spot, and wondered if he would find him waiting somewhere inside.

"Come on, Jackie! We've gotta go!" Scarlett's voice rescued him from his thoughts.

He looked up at her silhouette against the moonlight. Her shoulder-length hair and dyed cherry tips, the same as she'd had in high school. The milky, pale color of her skin. The sprinkle of freckles across her nose that had become more pronounced since they'd moved West. Thin, chapped lips. He watched her warm breath escape into the night and admired how much life she still had left in her. How much she had to live for. How much *he* had to live for. He suddenly remembered the ring. His hand went to his coat pocket and he felt it there, the small rounded velvet box tucked inside. They'd knocked him out, dragged him all the way back to Winterview via private jet, and yet somehow, by some fluke of time and space, hadn't found the ring. That, or they simply didn't care enough to take it.

Scarlett waited, looking at him in that way only she could, and he fell in love with her all over again, realizing there wasn't another person on God's green Earth he'd want by his side right now.

A white blur emerged over her left shoulder.

"Look out!" he yelled. He reached out reflexively, shoving her out of the way as an ax whirred past. His arms cleared its path in the nick of time; the weighty head cracked against the concrete in a shower of sparks.

Jackson didn't think. He gritted his teeth. His fingers curled into a fist so tight that his nails broke the skin. His fist was lightning, battering the cultist in a solid connection to the face. His knuckles flared with white-hot pain; the force knocked the shape off their feet, down for the foreseeable future.

Scarlett gawked at him, impressed, then shifted her eyes to the street, looking around. "Wait—where's Nelson?"

Jackson looked back to see Harper and Park on their feet headed their direction. The good doctor had a backpack in her hand, running for her life. Nick was right behind them, whacking a machete through the air threateningly like some sort of primitive caveman, attempting to ward off the advancing cultists.

Jackson didn't see the hillbilly. After the truck had crashed in spectacular fashion no one had emerged from inside. For all he knew the man was already dead.

Nelson was nowhere to be seen.

"He must be inside already," Jackson said.

Jackson and Scarlett began picking up speed, reaching the long mouth of steps leading to the porch. He looked up at the house, begrudgingly reunited, and it was like not a single day had passed. His feet kicked something hollow and he looked down to see two clear tubes running up the porch into the house.

He heard a grunt and looked over his shoulder.

Morgana's black coat fluttered and a blade slashed through the air.

Another body crumpled lifelessly to the street, nestled in a small bed of purple moss at the foot of a black glass tree. Morgana carried a gun, Jackson knew, but for some reason she wasn't using it, preferring her knives instead.

She's nuts and we haven't even gotten into the house yet, he thought.

Morgana noticed Jackson ogling her, sheathing the knife somewhere inside her coat and flashing a devilish smile. It looked like she felt right at home.

Enzo stamped past him in a huff, firing off blind shots as the white robes flowed in from the fog, seemingly never-ending. Enzo made eye contact with Morgana, motioning at Scarlett and Jackson. She tipped her head, acknowledging him, then swiftly whirled her body, twisting at the torso and pitching a knife through the air.

A cultist caught it with their head, thrown off the street into the gutter.

"Get inside," Morgana ordered. Enzo didn't bother to argue. He turned and scrambled up the porch steps.

Harper, Park, and Nick had caught up to them by this point, somehow having fought their way to the house's entrance.

"We need to get everyone inside," Scarlett said to Harper. "But we can't—it's not safe."

It was like some type of deranged puzzle, Jackson thought. They would die if they stayed outside. And if they went into the house, at least they might have an eternity to lose their minds to madness before their eventual deaths.

The cultists were everywhere, an army of lunatics brandishing makeshift weapons and crude inventions meant to maim in the worst ways imaginable. Even Morgana was beginning to grow overwhelmed. She leapt into the air like a jumping spider, latching onto a cultist from the front. She snarled, punching two knives into their eyes and riding the body down to the road. She jerked the blades out and Jackson saw two spurts of blood like miniature geysers.

"Shit, shit!" Scarlett said, pacing before the steps. Even the red carpet was there from their induction by Elizabeth Crow during the Seventh Street Lottery, tattered and soiled by the elements.

"What the hell are we waiting for?" Park asked, panicked. Her sleeve was soaked with blood, but it was hard to tell how much.

"We can't yet! You can't just walk in," Scarlett warned. "It does something to you—to your mind. We need to be hypnotized. That was what Vincent told us the last time. That's how we survive."

Harper shook her head. "No, look!" she said, pointing. While the carnage unfolded around them, Willard and Wendy were calmly nestled in their chambers, the long tubes protruding into the house's black entrance. "The rats—they're unaffected."

"What the fuck are you guys talking about?" Nick asked impatiently. "Why are you all standing around? Get inside!"

Nick rushed up the steps.

"No, wait!" Jackson yelled. But Nick was already inside.

Jackson dropped to his knees, sliding up the hatch on top of the chamber. The scientist was right. The rats were peaceful. Calm despite the pandemonium taking place around them. They stirred inside the small container, restless. "Scar—she's right! They're okay!"

"They were inside?" Scarlett asked, skeptical. "They went *into* the house? Like *inside*, inside?"

Harper nodded. "Yes, yes!" she replied impatiently. "I swear."

"I saw it, too," Park added. "They're okay."

A second wave of cultists was coming. Less than fifteen feet away. They appeared from alleyways and gloomy, abandoned storefronts. Jackson looked around hopelessly and saw them watching from windows, rooftops, fire escapes, while the ones on the street rushed them, throwing themselves forward like lemmings.

Scarlett looked out at their endless numbers, closing in with their knives and clubs and axes, and shrugged. "Fuck it, she's got my vote!" she shouted. "Everyone inside!"

Harper and Park dashed up the slant of stairs. Scarlett started up behind them, taking two steps at a time. Jackson remembered being here, remembered the red carpet looking like a long perverse tongue gobbling up flies.

A grunt somewhere in the chaos behind him. He stopped halfway up the steps, one hand on the balustrade. He turned back to see Morgana cornered, worn down by wave after wave of the crazies, ready to die a brutal, painful death as long as it was on her own terms.

Jackson saw movement out of his peripheral. The mountain man was back, battered and bleeding, but alive nonetheless. Jackson imagined that he might look like the men who had spent years in the wilderness, hardened by the elements. He was moving fast, roughing it down the road as quick as he could.

A cultist sprang from a side alley, the flutter of white tackling the mountain man into the side of a car. The cultist swung a knife but the man blocked it with his forearm, stopping the blade inches from his face. He bared his teeth, overpowering the figure and breaking their wrist with a loud *snap!* He grabbed the limp hand holding the knife and thrust it back, driving it into the cultist's neck. Undeterred, he pushed off the car, throwing the corpse to the ground. The man's chest was rising and falling, and Jackson knew it was only a matter of time before he ran out of gas.

"Come on!" Jackson screamed, waving. "Hurry! In here!"

The man made eye contact with him as Jackson took a step down. The *opposite* direction of where he should have been going. Jackson couldn't be sure, but he could have sworn that he saw relief in the man's filthy face knowing he hadn't been forgotten entirely, hadn't been left behind to die by the hand of these crazies. But then again, maybe he'd imagined it.

A plan began to formulate in his head. He looked over his shoulder to glimpse Scarlett disappear into the house's maw. Good. She would be marginally safer there. For the moment at least. If he wanted to set his plan in motion, he needed to do it now. He made a choice then and there that he was going to be a hero. He was done running.

"Fuck it," he said. He leapt over a trio of steps. As he came down his foot caught water; his arms windmilled; his legs shot out from under him, and any grand plans he fantasized playing out in his brilliant mind dissolved into the night along with the air in his lungs.

Jackson had felt a lot of painful things up to that point in his life. Catching a jellyfish across his midsection in Huntington. That time his fingertips got closed in Scarlett's Mustang door. A Yellow Jacket stinger to the eyelid. But taking two stone steps to his spine and skull damn near topped the list. The air rushed out of his body. He skated down the flight of stairs on his back like the star of his own personal *Home Alone* film, spilling onto the sidewalk in a sorry pile of bruised limbs and even more bruised bones.

His skull went numb. His mind turned sluggish.

And then for the second time in twenty-four hours, darkness.

PART 3: THE HOUSE

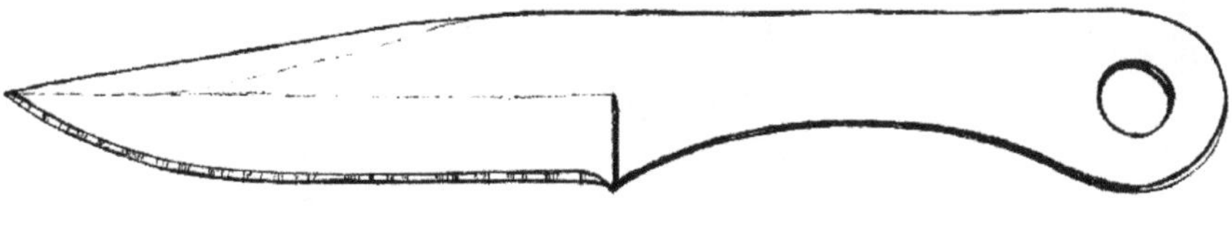

SCARLETT

THE HALLIDAY HOUSE. She was back. The headache. The body aches. The malaise. They were immediate, like contracting a particularly vicious strain of the flu. Her head was heavy, like her skull was forged from lead. A lazy squelching sound rebounded in the distance, the slurp and release of something gelatinous superimposed over the eerie silence of a considerable space.

Scarlett peered around and saw a wash of watery gray light. She held up her hands, looking down at the chipped silver nail polish. Blurry fingers shivered into focus. She smirked. Her nails were grotesque and her hands were filthy, coated with blood and grime, but they were there. They were hers. She wiggled her fingers and felt a swell of pride. Control; that was it. A privilege within the house's endless walls. Some part of her expected her body to make its grand entrance into the house like a Picasso painting, her eyes askew, limbs grossly distorted, perhaps even disfigured. Scarlett found no logical reason for her to think this as it had not happened in her past iterations in the house, but knew there was no real consistency in its winding halls, and her current reality might not be the same one she was in ten minutes from now, if you could even call it that. But alas, she was, as far as she could tell, still one hundred percent unabashedly herself.

She sluggishly lifted her head, finding Harper slumped in a chair across from her, the woman's pointy chin resting on her breastbone and, between them, on a floating slab of triangular stone, was a small gold coin. Harper's chest rose and fell peacefully, tresses of long red hair dangling over her face. It was strange seeing the woman's eyes closed. Scarlett thought them so large and so striking that without them, Harper's face almost appeared featureless. A small round medallion hung around her neck. One of the straps from the field pack Harper had managed to save was wrapped around her forearm. Miraculously she'd managed to get it into the house. Although Scarlett didn't see what was in there that could possibly do any good.

Scarlett admired her a moment, electing to let the woman have a few final moments of peace before waking her to their new reality. She deserved a few more minutes of rest after what she'd been through. They all did.

Scarlett pushed the dull, droning pain from her mind, watching the single gold bullion glint at her from the table like a light. She reached out and took the coin in her fingers, holding it up. The details were fuzzy, twisting into focus like film exposing.

She wasn't an expert on coins. She wasn't an expert on much of anything with the exception of horror literature, procrastination, and a few recipes she'd committed to memory from a cookbook her mother left behind. Dale had collected a few coins after his wife had passed, attempting to take up a new hobby at the urging of a concerned friend, but he lost interest within a few months, always falling back into engines. What was there to fix with a coin? And that was the problem. There wasn't one. No mystery. No moving parts. No complexity. And damn sure no need to get your hands dirty. So what good was it then? Scarlett thought they were alike in that way. *Work builds character,* he had told her once. She would sit on a stool in his garage when she was little while he'd call out for his tools. Not many women she knew could pick out a ball-joint splitter from a lineup, let alone men.

She raised her palm to her eye, examining the coin. The gold was ancient but still maintained a noticeable luster. Scarlett would have guessed it was over a hundred years old, if not more. The edges were smooth save for a nick to the upper rim, the face itself marred by decades of handling. The obverse displayed the sun cresting over mountaintops and what she assumed was the ocean. She turned it over in her palm. The Great Seal laid over a Bald Eagle, one of the bird's wings stamped EB. A decorative leafed border wreathed along the inner edge.

"What's that?" Harper's voice. She sounded like she was half-asleep and in desperate need of some water. Welcome to the club.

Scarlett quickly palmed the coin and looked up to find the psychologist stirring to life, those doll-like eyes wide open, blinking at her. She had two fingers pressed to the side of her long neck, and the other hand braced on the stone wedge to stop herself from falling out of the chair.

An urgency was working itself up in Scarlett's stomach, telling her to go. To move. Jackson is somewhere in this house right now. But she had to be patient. Neither of them was going anywhere right now feeling the way they did. At least until their minds and bodies acclimated to the temperature of madness.

"Well, I gotta say, I'm glad it's you I'm looking at right now and not that asshole with no neck," Scarlett said. Harper was surprisingly composed as well despite the situation, counting in her head while she calmly breathed in and out. "What're you doing?" she asked Harper.

"Checking my pulse."

Harper didn't look great. She was even more pale than she had been outside in the street. The blood vessels in her face were darker than before. Her forehead was damp with a sheen of sweat. Scarlett imagined she didn't look much better herself. She felt a chill ooze out of her pores like her essence was bleeding out of her body.

"What's the verdict?" Scarlett asked. "You gonna live?"

Harper let out a weak laugh, removing her fingers from her throat. "Sixty-five. Low. But alive." She touched her forehead and winced, no doubt feeling a migraine taking root in her skull. "My head…I feel…"

"Like shit?" Scarlett said, finishing her thought.

Harper laughed weakly, then broke into a cough. "For lack of a better word."

"It's the house," Scarlett said, standing up. "All the fun of a hangover, none of the fun from the night before." She stood up from the chair and a spell of dizziness passed through her. Her body swayed. She felt herself begin to topple. Harper's hand shot out and seized her arm, anchoring her.

Scarlett pressed her palms onto the table, stabilizing the world around her while it warped into razor-sharp focus.

"Oh my God," Harper said.

Scarlett turned and saw Harper's mouth hanging open, something she doubted happened very often in the woman's life.

The room—if that's what it was—was massive. They stood at the edge a stone cliff overlooking a black ocean. Scarlett guessed it wasn't unlike standing high atop an ice shelf in Antarctica. In front of her: a sheer drop-off into a sea of the same black ooze she recognized so well, the same kind that coursed through the house's arteries like blood. Only they weren't outside. They were in the house.

Weren't they?

Scarlett tilted her head up. A limitless coffered ceiling. Incredibly intricate. She squinted, but the ceiling was too high. Without a pair of binoculars, it would be impossible to make out any of the details. The corners of the room where the ceiling met the wood panels appeared to warp, as if the room were spherical in design.

Harper inhaled deeply, staggering to her feet, the two women using each other for support. They stood together at the foot of the great abyss, gazing upon an endless alien ocean contained within the house, and Scarlett noticed how much taller Harper was, the woman nearly a foot taller.

Harper gaped at the obsidian sea, overwhelmed, her mouth moving but no words coming out. Scarlett put a hand on the woman's shoulder and she quieted.

Scarlett had that effect on people. Vincent had taught her that. She looked down at her hands and remembered how she had always detested the scars, the Celtic knots seared into the fleshy tissue of her palms. But she didn't hate these beautiful gifts anymore. How could she? Especially after they had saved her, pacified the Oblivion Stone long enough to allow them to escape. Her very own superpower, in a way.

Harper was still staring into the abyss, watching the languid black oil below, a nervous hand massaging her neck where the necklace hung.

"This isn't possible," Harper said.

Scarlett fought the urge to say something smart but didn't. She could tell the woman was having a moment.

"Nothing ever is in here," she replied.

Scarlett looked skyward to find a panorama of weak ashen light pouring in through skylights cut intermittently into the paneling. Was it the world she knew beyond? Was Winterview somewhere on the other side of those windows? Or was it somewhere else altogether?

"Park…" Harper muttered. She turned to Scarlett, looking at her as if Scarlett would know where to find her.

"Don't worry—they're here. The question is *where*," Scarlett said. "If Jackie isn't here, it means he's with them, which means we'll find them. This is how it always starts."

"And who is *them*, exactly?" Harper asked. "That man and woman you were with, who are they?"

Scarlett sighed. This was bound to come up sooner or later. Better to get it over with now. "Jackie and I—they kidnapped us. Brought us here."

Harper looked at her as if she'd misheard.

"They work for some woman. Some type of high-powered rich bitch working with organized crime. She says her daughter's plane crashed here a few days ago."

Harper's ears perked up. She blinked, her eyebrows dipping.

"You know something?" Scarlett asked.

Harper cleared her throat. "We found a plane on our way to the house. On the east end of Seventh Street."

"The plane? You found it?" Scarlett asked. Titillating as that news was, she couldn't decide if she wanted to hear the rest. She asked anyway. "Was she… I mean, did you find anyone?"

Harper shook her head. "The wreckage was burned. Looked like it had been that way for a couple of days. But my intuition says she wasn't inside."

Scarlett held there alongside the stranger, digesting the lead, gazing out at the infinite expanse of black slime as far as the eye could see. Her mind drifted to what could be lurking below. She remembered the Void, a plane of nightmares where colossal things drifted in the dark, hidden away from the light. A shiver worked its way through her.

"What is it—the substance?" Harper asked. Not a bad question. Of course, Harper would assume she would have the answer being the authority on the house and all.

Scarlett got down on knees, peering over the ledge. "I don't know what it is, but it's all over the house."

"The substance coating the exterior walls?" Harper asked.

Scarlett nodded, her imagination running wild, conjuring all manner of creatures hidden below the surface. "Yeah, that's the one."

Harper reflected on this, studying the slime from afar. "Park and I found something similar. We analyzed samples taken from the wall surrounding the Dead Zone, but all were ruled inconclusive."

Scarlett turned to her. "Dr. Harper, right?"

"Harper is fine."

"Okay. Harper. Look, we didn't have much time to talk with everything that happened back there. You heard my side. Maybe it's time we talked about why you're here."

"Mhmm..." Harper said, her attention focused elsewhere. Scarlett looked behind her to see Harper drop to her knees, finding no means of support for the levitating stone slab.

"You're a scientist, right?"

"A psychologist more specifically." Harper waved her arms under the stone, then over the top, half expecting to find invisible wires attached like it were some type of illusion.

Scarlett chortled. "What? You're a shrink?" She ran her fingers through her greasy hair, pulling a hair tie from her wrist and securing it into a short ponytail. "What the hell is a shrink doing way the hell out there?"

Harper looked up at her, annoyed. "*Skeptical* is what I am."

"Skeptical?" Scarlett chewed her lip. "What do you mean? Skeptical of what?"

Harper got to her feet, using her weight to press down on the table. "Phenomena like this," she said, pushing down with her weight.

Scarlett arched an eyebrow. "Of all the things happening *that's* what you're having a hard time believing? That the stone table can float?"

Harper gave one last shove before surrendering, standing up.

"Uhhh… You *did* see all that other shit floating outside right? In the streets? The cars and the…" Scarlett swallowed, "bodies?"

Harper put her hands on her hips, craning her head to the great white blizzard above them. "You knew Vincent Velladex, yes?" Harper wasn't asking.

That was when it hit her. The coin in her pocket. The same one Vincent had carried with him. But what did it mean?

Harper stared at her expectantly, waiting for a reply.

Scarlett nodded.

Harper started pacing away, following the ledge.

Scarlett trudged after her.

"Back when I was an undergrad, a friend of mine took me to one of his shows," Harper recounted. "He was touring the States before leaving for Europe and she thought it would be fun way to celebrate the semester ending."

"You met him? Vincent?" Scarlett asked, mystified.

Harper shook her head, deflating Scarlett's hope. "No. I never met him. In fact, I didn't even want to go to the show, but my friend—she was very, very convincing." She stopped suddenly and Scarlett almost ran into her. Harper dropped to the ledge, peering down below.

"What in the hell are you doing?"

Harper got back to her feet and turned to Scarlett. "I saw things I would never have believed that night, Scarlett. Things I couldn't explain. Things that were absolutely impossible."

"Dr. Harper—*Harper*. I'm happy you enjoyed his show, but what does that have to do with anything?"

Harper leaned in, a sly look in her eyes. "What it *means*, Scarlett, is that if an ordinary man, some charming stranger in a dashing suit can make Mount Rushmore disappear in front of a *live audience*, then I have to ask myself: What else am I willing to believe is real?"

"But you're wrong," Scarlett said.

Harper cocked her head. "Wrong about what?"

"Vincent wasn't *just* a man."

"No?"

Scarlett shook her head. "No. He was a friend. But more importantly he was a hero." She shouldered past Harper, taking the lead.

"That may be so," Harper called out to her. "But it doesn't mean I'm wrong, Scarlett. There's always a logical explanation. Always."

Scarlett laughed. "*Logical?* Look around you, Harper. Does any of this look even remotely logical to you?"

"There are traces of unknown pathogens in the city's air. All originating from *this* house. It's been known for some time to cause deliria. Depression. Even psychosis in some. But, we can't prove it yet." Harper spouted off rationalizations one after another, unwilling to accept the truth that was laid out right in front of her, and Scarlett wondered if it was her own way of protecting herself from the things she wasn't ready to accept. "This isn't new information, Scarlett. It's been all over the news lately. Haven't you seen the papers?"

"More than I'd like lately." Scarlett grumbled, marching on.

"Okay," Harper said, catching up to her. The two walked side by side, following the path. "So, what is it, then? Surely you have your own theories?"

Scarlett scoffed. "How the hell should I know?"

"You've had plenty to say over the years since you came here, and now all of a sudden nothing?"

"And I'm sure you didn't believe a word I said."

"In my line of work we deal in facts, Scarlett. And facts require proof. I mean…your stories…they're impossible."

"And there's that word again." Scarlett abruptly stopped, throwing up her hands. "What the hell do you call all this?!" she shouted. "You want to see how real this is? You want to find out? Why don't you jump off that cliff? And when you wake up in a completely new room, maybe worse than this one, maybe not, then *maybe* you'll start to believe me."

Harper shook her head. "You're impossible."

"According to you that's everything we've seen tonight," Scarlett said. "Fine then. So what are you doing here then, Harper?"

Harper stared at her. "What do you mean? I told you, I'm a scientist—"

"Yeah, yeah, you're a scientist. You came here to study the house, and save the city blah blah. But are you?"

Harper stared at her.

"Because I only can think of one type of person that would come her of their own free will. And that's the kind of person that's got a death wish."

"You're here," Harper countered.

"And that's because of *someone else's* death wish."

Harper wasn't impressed.

"You *are* with the Red Sky, aren't you?" Scarlett prodded.

This got Harper's attention. She exhaled, nodding. "Yes. As a matter of fact, I am. And you know this information how?"

"A friend," Scarlett said, using the term "friend" loosely.

Harper waited for her to elaborate but Scarlett offered nothing.

"What is it? The 'Red Sky'?" she asked, air quoting.

Harper looked her up and down, considering her, and Scarlett wondered if she would refuse, tell her it was classified information reserved strictly for government officials. A closed book, this one.

"After the disaster with the lottery, the government tasked the Red Sky with observing the house. Initiating containment. Researching the disturbances to the city's ecosystem." Harper began walking again and Scarlett kept pace. "The military grew concerned after they noticed a decline in Winterview's population. A *significant* decline."

Maybe not so closed off after all, Scarlett thought.

Scarlett laughed to herself. "Creating an entire branch of the government specifically for the house—*wow*."

Harper cocked her head. "I'm afraid you've been misinformed. The Red Sky has been around a lot longer than the house has been here."

"What? Seriously?"

Harper nodded. "Indeed. They've been operating for decades. I believe the division was founded after the appearance of the Great Suttershade Anomaly, something which, as you know, is still debated to this day."

"And you're here to find out what's going on with all the weird shit happening in Winterview, is that it?"

Harper nodded. "More or less. Our team is only the most recent in a long line of researchers tasked with investigating the house."

Scarlett was quiet. The corner of Harper's lip curled into a smile. "Aren't you going to ask me why we're not carrying guns? Why they didn't send soldiers in here instead of us?"

"No," Scarlett said. "With the physics of the house, they'd have a better chance of shooting each other than anything they found in here."

"You think so, huh?" Harper asked.

Scarlett slowed, peering past her, and nodded. "Oh, I know so. I've already seen it."

A wooden door embedded in the floor, less than ten feet away.

"What?" Harper uttered. "When?"

"The last time I was here. The Crow Corporation," Scarlett replied. "They were here long before I ever went inside. Hannah and Jackie and I, we found them in another room. Big, like this one. Bullet holes everywhere. Blood. The works." Scarlett could see this was new information to Harper. "You didn't know that. Did you?"

"What were they doing here?" Harper asked.

"Hannah said they were after the stone. Killed each other trying to get it. It does something to your mind, makes you do crazy things." Scarlett squatted and twisted the knob and the door was ripped away in a rush of air like they were in an airplane, revealing a bottomless pit. Scarlett looked up at her and grimaced.

"I hope you're not afraid of heights."

JACKSON

HE FELT WEIGHTLESS. That same ethereal feeling you get right before your body jolts itself back to consciousness. Jackson remembered Scarlett talking about it once. What did she say that sensation was again? Your body thinking it was about to die? Or maybe it was falling asleep too quickly? Either way, that was how he felt right now, careening into depths so deep you couldn't tell where they began or ended.

A solid darkness, heavy and damp. Air rushed past him. He felt his hair fluttering like he'd abandoned a plane, plummeting to Earth.

His eyes shot open; he gasped.

Something was wrong. He was looking at a room from the top down, almost like he was seeing a blueprint in real-time.

He barely had time to scream. His arms and legs flailed. His weight drove him straight down, leveling an ornate end table in a spray of wood slivers and dust.

He groaned, laying there in sort of a quiet shock, breathing in the woodsy smell and the musty air that was like a room full of taxidermy. *Falling. Always falling*, he thought. He languidly flipped onto his back and let his eyes roll around the room. A cough racked his body, spraying motes of dust into the air.

The arcade? The same one he'd met Vanessa Halliday and watched her head spin around like in *The Exorcist*?

He squinted his eyes.

No. This was something else.

A study.

There were worse places he could have ended up, he supposed.

He leaned forward, propping himself on his hands, shaking the splinters of wood off him like a wet dog.

Ebony wainscoting. Two floor-to-ceiling windows overlooking a stone courtyard peppered with an odd variety of switch grass.

He shook his head. What difference did it make? He wasn't going out there no matter *what* it was, arcade or not. He turned back to the room. An oiled wooden desk sat across from him with a dark object resting on top of it front and center. It wasn't a computer sitting there, that's for sure. But definitely...*something*. His sight was a little hazy. Probably his brain getting jostled from the fall, he thought. He waited, watching it, but whatever it was didn't move an inch. To each side of the desk was a smooth black door. Almost as smooth as glass. The rest of the room was surprisingly ordinary. He wasn't sure what he expected at this point, but ordinary wasn't it. One small detail that stood out was the wallpaper: a purple and emerald paisley. He couldn't help but think of Vincent then. He'd seen enough posters of those emerald eyes and Vincent's elaborate suits during his lifetime to imprint them in his brain permanently. A dull ache throbbed in his heart, the same way it did when he thought about Tommy and Hannah sometimes. And it hurt worse knowing he'd never have friends like that again.

They went home is all.

And as for Vincent, well...he'd been their guide the last time they'd found their way to the house, but who did they have to guide them now?

Him? Scarlett?

Jackson coughed a nervous laugh. "No, definitely not you."

God, his neck was stiff. Maybe from his swan dive into the table. He rotated his head until the vertebrae in his neck crunched. His head was woozy but not nearly as bad as last time. The air was thin here though, in the house. That much hadn't changed. It was like being on the summit of Mount Everest. Something about the air pressure, he remembered. His eyes began to sting and he mashed his palms into them to wring out the sweat. The house had started on him already. The old bitch worked quickly, he thought. He could feel that weighty pull in his bones like gravity was trying to suck him down to the Ninth Circle of Hell. *We're on an express elevator to hell—going down!* He couldn't help but chuckle a little despite himself. *Aliens.* Him and Scarlett must have watched it at least two dozen times.

He looked across at the desk, listening to a quiet tapping. The black shape sat dead center, tempting him. Only he could see now that it wasn't a lone shape. But many. He held his breath, crossing the room, padding over a carpet so elaborate he couldn't find any one place to focus on.

He stopped. He was a foot away. Maybe two.

A typewriter. Only it wasn't. Not yet at least. The antique was exploded, all the individual pieces frozen in midair. It reminded him of furniture instructions, showing you all the parts before they're screwed together.

A moan.

His eyes bulged.

He wasn't alone.

He turned, searching the room.

He leapt over the ruins of the end table, circumventing a leather couch. A lamp toppled over and instead of smashing in a clatter of ceramic it hit the wood and burst into a puff of smoke. Or maybe it was dust?

Before he could give it another thought, he realized he'd found her: One of the women from outside. What was her name again? It was a short word. One syllable. Doctor…Palm? Pear?

He got down on one knee, softly shaking her. "Hey," he said. "Hey, are you all right?" He looked around the room like someone was going to shout out the answer. "Doctor…?"

"Park," the woman croaked. Her voice was soft. She smiled weakly, and Jackson smiled back. "It's Park." Park blinked, letting her eyes wander. "Where the hell are we?"

"The house," Jackson replied. "We're inside."

Park's brows flattened like she didn't believe it. "Yeah?"

Jackson nodded. "Afraid so. The belly of the beast." He climbed to his feet, leaning back on the couch's headrest.

Park stood up too fast and Jackson reached out to steady her. He kindly guided her against the wall like he was handling a drunk at Rowdy's. Jackson looked closer at the woman. Nearly her entire sleeve was stained red, the field jacket's fabric sliced open straight across her upper arm. "That looks pretty bad. You all right?"

Park looked down as if seeing her arm for the first time, soaked with blood, and gave a short, nervous laugh. "Flesh wound. Isn't that what I'm supposed to say?"

Jackson stared at her.

"You know—in the movies and what not?"

Jackson smiled. "Oh. Yeah, I guess so."

Park surveyed the room. "I've got to tell you, it's not quite what I imagined."

Jackson sputtered a short laugh. "Don't let it fool you. Might not look like much but...it's full of surprises. And I don't mean the good kind, either."

"Where're the others?"

Jackson shrugged. "I don't know. You're the only one I've seen so far," he said. "That's how it always starts. It likes to separate you. It's more disorienting, I think."

Park nodded. She made a sour face, massaging her throat. "God, I'm thirsty. I feel like I got hit by a train." She wobbled over to the window, shoving the curtain aside and peering into the courtyard.

"It's the house," Jackson said. "Sucks the life out of you faster than you can say haunted mansion."

Park didn't answer, glued to the window.

"What are you doing here, Dr. Park?"

"Just Park."

She paused, the silence in the room smothering.

Park suddenly began to sob quietly. "He's dead."

The other scientist, the one with the wild white hair. *Poor bastard*, Jackson thought. "Yeah. He is. I'm sorry, Park."

"He's dead because of me," Park said. She turned around, looking at him. "Those fucks practically cut his head off," she said crying harder. "Because I had to—"

Jackson took a step toward her then stopped. What was the protocol here? Should he do something? Give the woman a hug? A back pat? Console her somehow?

"It was quick," Jackson offered. It was all he could think to say. Then: "There's nothing you could have done. Nothing anybody could have done. There were too many of them."

Park seemed to agree, nodding, wiping the tears from her eyes.

"What are you doing here, Park?" he repeated.

Park sighed, sitting down on the windowsill. "Harper and I, we were hired to come here and investigate what's happening in the Dead Zone. The house. Everything."

Jackson's eye twitched. "All the stuff happening on the news. The people getting sick. *That* everything?"

Park nodded.

"Why would they send people here? What good is it going to do?" Jackson couldn't fathom it. Had they learned nothing after what happened here? "Scarlett told them there was no point. She told everyone."

Park laughed. "Yeah, yeah she did. She definitely tried."

"You saw her? On the news?"

"Didn't everyone?"

"Yeah, I guess they did, huh."

"People are assholes," Park said.

A pause between them. It was true. While Scarlett's vlogs recollecting her stories of the house made her channel the biggest sensation in YouTube history, the more formal interviews she'd given weren't quite as successful. She had her fair share of critics. And some of them made her life a living hell. Men and women in fancy suits grilling her about the afterlife and what happened to Tommy and Hannah and Vincent. Most were unrehearsed, and Scarlett wasn't exactly the best when it came to articulating her thoughts on the spot. Improvisation. He counted his blessings she was a fucking suit of armor when it came to other people's opinions.

"Yeah..." Jackson said.

"I thought she was great, though. The girl has a big personality." Park lifted her hand, inspecting the wound. "Shrinking folks is more Harper's department, but I think the majority of the public can't appreciate people that are different. But in my opinion, I think that's what makes her so great." She sounded sincere.

"She is that," Jackson said.

"Although to be fair, I discovered her *before* she was famous."

Jackson looked at her, intrigued.

"I had this phase," Park confessed, grinning. "Stephen King for breakfast, lunch, and dinner. 'Sinister Scarlett' was my go-to for a minute there. At least until my dissertation rolled around." She stood at the window a moment more, then turned around, a confused expression set into her face. "Are you *sure* we're in the house?" She was skeptical. If he hadn't been here before he might have been too. After all, it wasn't anything like the original foyer he and Scarlet had awoken in.

"Yeah, Park. I'm sure," he said. God, he wished he wasn't.

Park took a step forward, clutching her bloodied arm and surveying the room. "But it all looks so...*ordinary*. Like we're in someone's house."

"It is someone's," he said, more to himself than to her.

Park walked to the couch, perching herself on the arm. "So, how do you know?"

"How do I know what?"

"How do you know we're in the house? I mean, it doesn't look much different than any other house I've been in."

Jackson arched an eyebrow. "You hang with a lot of swanky socialites back home?"

Park leveled her eyes at him. "You know what I mean. I mean seriously, though, how can you tell? There must be some kind of giveaway, right?"

Jackson nodded over his shoulder.

"What?" Park asked curiously.

Jackson stayed silent, tipping his head to the side.

Park looked at him suspiciously, then stood up, walking past him to the desk.

"Holy shit," she uttered.

The typewriter.

Park got down on the heels of her combat boots, taking in every intricate piece of the typewriter—hovering a foot off the desk no less.

"I know," Jackson said. And in comparison to the shit he'd seen, the typewriter was small potatoes. Just wait until she saw the other things. The things he wished he could forget. *If* she lived long enough to see them.

"There were cars in the street. Things floating just like this," Park said. She was coming to life minute by minute, second by second, although he could see she was going to be holding on to the guilt for a long time. Maybe forever. She was distracted by the typewriter parts for now, though, like seeing the inner workings of a human body via x-ray. Park saw with the same childlike wonder he remembered having himself once. A zest.

Where had it gone?

Jackson stood beside her, leaning on the desk. "Any theories?"

Park chortled, shaking her head.

"I thought you guys were scientists?"

Park leaned closer and tapped one of the typewriter keys, watching it drift away.

"That was Dirac's department," she said soberly. "I'm a biologist."

Park tapped the type lever, and they watched as it went spinning off across the room. If the sickness hadn't gotten to her yet it would soon. But for now, he let her enjoy the moment. "How is this possible?"

"Anything's possible in here. Dreams…*nightmares*. Anything."

Park turned, looking over her shoulder at him. "Harper."

Jackson nodded.

"I have to find her."

Park gasped, her face twisting in terror. She started and lost her balance, her upper back bumping into the desk. The shockwave rolled through the wood; the typewriter parts collapsed uniformly, falling onto the wooden desk like dozens of black teeth.

Jackson spun around. His heart lurched in his chest.

Outside the window, a gigantic bloodshot eyeball stared in.

NICK

A COLD SLAP brought him to life.

"I thought that was you, Nicky," a gruff voice said.

A sunbaked face that looked like it belonged to a giant was inches away. Leathery skin. Crazed, dark eyes. Yellow stained teeth black at the gums. He'd recognize that caveman brow anywhere.

Enzo "The Beast" Astley. Of all the rotten luck.

"You aged a bit, but I knew it was you," Enzo said, squeezing Nick's cheek and twisting his skull side to side. Enzo's breath reeked of coffee and brandy, and Nick made to get away but found he couldn't move. "I told ya it was him," Enzo said, rising to his full height. Nick wouldn't be surprised if he blocked out the sun.

A woman in a tight black coat was over his shoulder leaning against the wall, her arms crossed over her chest, watching them.

Nick groaned. The room was wobbling like he was drunk. Only he wasn't drunk. He hadn't touched the stuff since Rachel was born.

"You know, I didn't have time to say hi out there—crazy religious fucks in the robes and what not. Maybe it's time for a proper hello."

Enzo pitched forward, throwing his weight; all five fingers of the beast's oversized right fist collided with his head and he was surprised his neck didn't snap then and there. A burst of Fourth of July fireworks in his vision. His ear exploded into a high-pitched ring. The world began turning on its side and he realized that *he* was the one turning. He made a feeble attempt to move but his hands and legs were fixed to the chair with zip ties.

His head smacked the ground with a hollow thump. Hardwood floors. Thank God his head was already numb from the punch or that would probably have hurt like a bitch.

Enzo seized his boot and gave a hard jerk. The world snapped upright again, giving him a front row seat to the horror show that was Enzo Astley's face.

The giant grinned, and Nick could see all the small chips in his rotten teeth. From countless brawls, he assumed. You could only get pummeled in the face so many times before your skin started to resemble wrinkled leather.

"That was for Atlanta," Enzo said. "Two years I spent in that sardine can because of you. Your girl mighta gotcha off the hook last time, Webster, but your reputation in this city is precisely *dick* now."

Nick felt a string of blood stretching down from his mouth. This seemed to please the man. Enzo's grin widened.

Too many teeth, Nick thought. He shook his head, hoping to wake up.

"You're looking a little rougher than the last time I saw ya, Nicky. I guess leaving behind your family is bad for your health, huh?"

Nick gazed around the room, finding he was in some sort of a foyer. The walls were a flat, stark white. Flourishes of ornate molding traced the edges and four emerald columns rose to a high ceiling. The space couldn't have been wider than fifteen or twenty feet. The ceiling, however, went on and on, and if there *was* an end, he didn't see it. Nice and intimate for their little reunion. How charming.

Another punch cracked him across the face and his head bounced on top of his neck like a Jack-in-the-Box. He spat a mouthful of blood on the floor, looking up to find Enzo getting fuzzy, the lines engraved in his face starting to blur. The last hit had taken something out him. His eyeball throbbed in the socket. He ran his tongue over his teeth and felt one of them wiggle.

Enzo grunted, waving his hand in the air like it was on fire, snickering. He looked down at his hand and squeezed his fingers into a fist with a dusty crack.

"That's enough," the woman said. She slipped past Enzo and a shiver ran through him.

Morgana got down on one knee, her split pupil boring a hole into Nick's soul. The pink scars crisscrossing her face looked darker in this room, almost red, like someone had driven her face through a sheet of glass. "We haven't been formally introduced," she said. "My name is—"

"Morgana," Nick said weakly. He found the strength to straighten himself out, locking eyes with the woman. "Morgana 'Nightmare' Venditto."

Morgana smirked. "Clever boy. And you are?"

Nick sighed, hacking up syrupy blood onto his chest. "Nick. Webster. Ask him, he knows me," Nick said, nodding at Enzo.

Morgana blinked, and it felt like he was looking at a snake. "What are you doing here, Nick Webster?"

Nick regarded her a moment, then looked over her shoulder at Enzo.

"Don't look at him," she said, taking his chin and redirecting his gaze. "It's just you and me right now. Whatever business you and he had is irrelevant to me. Now, I'm going to ask you again, and I want an answer. What are you doing here?"

He couldn't tell her. Couldn't tell Enzo. Not the truth, anyway. He had to protect Rachel. She was here somewhere, in the house. She had to be.

Morgana stared at him, awaiting an answer. Her tone was pleasant enough, but he knew that would be short-lived if her moniker was any indicator.

"Took a wrong turn back there somewhere," Nick said coyly. "Guess my GPS isn't quite working. You know, electronics and all." He flashed her a smile of bloody teeth.

Morgana didn't react. Didn't hit him, or scream in his face. She merely stared at him with her horrible eyes, considering him.

"It's a big city," Nick finished.

Enzo laughed hoarsely while he worked out the ache in his hand. Apparently punching Nick in the face had hurt him, too. *Good*, Nick thought. Hopefully he'd broken a finger or two.

"This structure is interesting," Morgana said, gazing at the foyer. "These patterns on the columns—do you know what they say?" she asked.

Nick shook his head. "I have no fucking idea." Who cared what they said? He sure as hell didn't. He had one thing on his mind and that was finding his daughter and getting the hell out of Dodge.

Morgana stood up and strolled over to one of the jade columns, running her delicate fingers along the stone. "These markings…they're in Arabic. They speak of life and death. They describe a story rich with history. A history lost with time." She strolled back and stood in front of him. "Much like your history with the city, Nick Webster."

"That was a long time ago," Nick said. "That's not my who I am anymore. I'm done with that part of my life."

Morgana ran a hand along the battered side of his face, smearing the dried blood. "You might be done with it, but it is not yet done with you." Her hand slid from his face to his shoulder, then down his torso around to his back, their faces cheek to cheek. He could smell her pale skin, sweet like vanilla. She exhaled and her breath was cold, like she had a glacier inside of her.

Her fingers slipped into the wound in his back and he shrieked so loud his only working ear popped. His body jolted like he'd been pumped with two million volts of electricity.

The pressure abruptly retracted and it was like two eels sliding out of his body.

His body fell limp in the chair, then snapped taut again. He looked up at Enzo and the man turned away, pretending to be fascinated by the scripture decorating the columns even though he clearly couldn't read it.

Even Enzo "The Beast" Astley was terrified of her, and that was saying something.

Nick was panting now. The puncture in his back was liquid napalm. Whatever the man had used to seal it up, Morgana had split it right back open with her bony fingers.

Morgana's fingers slid into his skin again.

Nick screamed, so hysterical with pain he started laughing, his chest heaving with big, obnoxious sobs.

Enzo looked at him like he'd lost his mind while Morgana remained indifferent.

"Hmmm," she said. "Perhaps you're used to more pain than most. Perhaps not. I guess we'll find out, won't we?"

She was thinking. And giving this woman time to think was not a good thing. He used the adrenaline pumping into his blood to tug at his restraints, the plastic cutting into his wrists.

Morgana looked at him with pity. She coolly reached into her coat, sliding out a brushed metal knife. A throwing knife. He'd seen what she could do with them first hand out in the streets. She'd singlehandedly dispatched more of the cultists than the rest of them combined, including pretty boy Enzo and his hand cannon.

Morgana sighed. "Ordinarily I'd take my time, but, regrettably, time is something which we do not have tonight." Morgana held her hand up and spread her fingers, using the knife to casually dig under a nail. "I'm going to give you one more chance to tell me what I want to hear."

"You better tell her, Webster," Enzo warned. "You don't wanna know what she did to the last prick who wanted to play hero."

"Ugh," Nick groaned. "That why you're letting her run the show, Enzo? You scared of this little thing? C'mon man, surely you've got some balls left after all those steroids."

Enzo glared at him. Morgana half smiled, amused.

"This is your last chance," Morgana said. "Where is she, Mr. Webster?"

Nick stopped laughing and the room went quiet. Did they know about Rachel? Was that why they were here? Did they find out about her somehow?

Enzo walked closer, waiting for him to answer. "Don't be stupid, Webster. Just answer the question."

"What?" he asked, genuinely confused. "Who?"

Morgana lowered her eyes. She began to move around back of him and his body went rigid again.

"No, wait! Hold on a second! Who are you talking about?"

He bit down, trying to shake his body loose but to no avail. He felt her icy hands take one of his own, holding it rigid.

Enzo shook his head, disappointed.

The nail of his middle finger flared with white hot pain. He let out a sharp, piercing scream as the blade bit under the nail, separating the soft fleshy tissue beneath. Morgana steadily wedged the stainless blade up and he heard a faint crack as the nail popped off. He screamed and flailed, tried to get free, but he couldn't.

His heart was thundering, punching the inside of his chest harder than Enzo had punched his face. He'd bitten down so hard that the loose tooth in his mouth had been pushed completely free. He looked up to see Enzo's stupid face staring down at him. He pooled the blood in his mouth and spat it at the man. The blood arched down, splatting on his fine Italian leather shoes.

"You dirty little cocksucker," Enzo sneered. He took a step forward but Morgana stepped between them, the woman's stare enough to stop the charging rhino in his tracks. "You better count your lucky stars Belle is here, Webster, otherwise you'd be fuckin' dead for that. You hear me? *Dead!*"

"Belle?" Nick groaned. "Isabelle? She's here?"

"Before you do that, you may want to look at this," Morgana said.

Enzo was crazed, possessed with rage, a mad gleam in his eye.

Morgana coolly held the blade up to his face, pressing the cool steel against Enzo's cheek, offering out her other hand.

Nick's wallet. It must have fallen out when he'd been trying to break out of the chair.

"Hey!" he shouted, caught in the restraints. He could feel the plastic digging into his wrists and ankles. The air was rushing over the bloody stump of his fingertip.

Enzo reached into his jacket, taking out a small pair of reading glasses.

"Are you fucking kidding me right now?" Nick said.

Morgana flipped open the wallet, holding it up.

Enzo's eyes went wide.

Tucked behind a small window of crinkled plastic was a picture of Rachel.

"Sonofabitch," Enzo uttered. He looked past Morgana, grinning. "You got a kid, Webster? You sneaky little prick."

Morgana yanked the picture out and turned around, tossing the wallet at him; it bounced off his chest and flopped to the floor. She stepped closer, holding up the photo. Rachel's school picture from last year. The only school picture he'd ever seen her smile in. He remembered wondering what had done it, what had gotten her to laugh. Had the photographer made a joke? Told her something funny? Maybe he'd used a prop. One of those stupid little puppets. He'd seen them do that sometimes for kids' pictures.

"The resemblance is uncanny," Morgana said. "How old is she?"

Nick glared at her. "Fuck you, you crazy bitch."

"Little bit too much of a coincidence don'tcha think?" Enzo asked. "First Isabelle crashing here in her goddamn plane and now him," he said, jabbing a finger in Nick's direction. "And now their *kid?* Something stinks here, Morgue."

A fitting nickname.

"Isn't it obvious? They had her in secret." Morgana deduced, grinning. "Katya has no idea she even exists." She leaned in close, dragging the blade across his cheek. He winced, felt his bruised skin splitting under the razor-sharp edge, blood seeping from below. "Does she, Mr. Webster?"

Nick squeezed his eyes shut, feeling the edge of the blade sink into his face, doing everything in his power to block the pain out. A scream climbed in his throat.

"Where is she now?" Morgana asked, raking the knife down to his jaw while she studied the picture, Nick's agonized screams like music to her ears. "It's late, no?" And then: "Ah, the woman from the street," Morgana said, putting it together, her eyes widening with glee. "You both came here for her, didn't you? Your daughter...she's lost too. And that wasn't your companion in the street. It was the *help*."

Morgana had a wicked glint in her eyes. She smiled impishly. "It's time to go, Mr. Astley. The night is young and we have much blood to let." Morgana tucked it into her coat.

"We're going to have ourselves a little family reunion tonight."

Without warning, a flare of blinding white light bit into Morgana's neck. A shriek of electricity cackled like a banshee had flown into the room. The woman's body snapped rigid, twitching viciously and going down hard. The knife went skating across the tile in a metal grind.

It was the most beautiful sight he'd ever laid eyes on.

Sandi stood tall, his own personal super hero. Chunks of skin were missing from her knees but she was upright, a chunky stun-gun in her hand. Sandi flashed him a smile and he exhaled a *thank Christ!*, feeling a spill of air rush out of him. Sandi was missing one of her bottom teeth, and a few of the others were chipped, and he made a vow to himself that if he got out of this alive, he was never going to let go of her again. He had thought her dead the second she went flying off into the fog, but here she was with a mountain of unfinished business and a pissed off look that would make God think twice.

The next seconds happened fast. As fast as Nick could process them at that point, anyway.

Enzo had rounded the corner, a shocked expression on his face. His hand was dipping into his jacket, awkwardly fumbling for his gun. Without hesitating, Sandi ran straight up to him and jammed the stun gun into his crotch.

Enzo's eyes blew up in an OH FUCK kind of way as Sandi threw the switch and lit him up like a Christmas tree. Nick screamed and cheered as Enzo's body contracted violently, spasming as Sandi unloaded all twelve hundred volts into his groin in a flaming crackle of brilliant, heavenly color. Sandi kept at him as he danced, pissing his pants and making all sorts of funny noises. He made a sharp squeal like he'd been kicked in the testicles and Sandi let off.

The hulk collapsed to the floor, wispy smoke billowing off him like Sandi had put out a fire.

Sandi spit at Enzo's lifeless body, kicking his designer shoe, then turned to Nick. He was sure he had tears streaming down his face but between all the blood and sweat he couldn't tell anymore.

"The help," Sandi said, dropping the stun gun, "has arrived."

HARPER

HARPER WAS WEIGHTLESS. Her breath rushed out of her like she'd went over a drop on a roller coaster.

A pair of arms shot out and wrapped her from behind seconds before her face hit the floor.

"Gotcha!" Scarlett said, grasping her from behind.

A whole world of black-and-white checkered tiles filled her vision. If Scarlett hadn't been waiting to catch her, she'd be short eight front teeth about now.

Harper breathed steadily, calmly flattening her palms on the floor and pushing herself up. Scarlett tugged her from behind, helping her get back on her feet.

Harper looked around, then craned her head up, a cutout of white light glowing above.

She looked at Scarlett. "Where are we?"

Scarlett shrugged. "Beats me," she said, looking around.

Harper laughed.

"What?" Scarlett asked.

"You've been here before. I assumed you—"

"What?" Scarlett interrupted. "That I'd have this place mapped out in my head?" Scarlett scoffed. "Why does no one listen to anything I say about this place?"

"I don't—"

"As far as I can tell, this house has no fixed rooms. You walk out of a room, it changes when you get back. Everything changes. Always. Even if I had a piece of paper and a pen there *still* wouldn't be any way to map it."

"Ah," Harper said, snapping her fingers. She released the pack slung over her shoulder to the ground. She got down on one knee, unzipping it and rifling through.

"Oh, what, you *have* a pen in there?" Scarlett mocked.

"No," Harper said. She looked up and flashed a proud smile. "I have something better." She took out a small device with a small crank attached to the side, holding it up.

"What in the hell is that?"

Harper stood up. "A camera."

Scarlett ogled the thing, noticing a mischievous smile on Harper's face. "A camera?"

Harper nodded, winding the crank on the side. Scarlett shook her head and began walking away. "I guess you didn't get the memo," Scarlett said, "but electricity doesn't work in here, *Doctor*. You're wasting your time."

"Scarlett."

Scarlett turned around and flinched as a flash hit her across the face.

An electronic *beep!*

She stood frozen, her eyes fluttering. "*Ow*," she said, exaggerated. She was about to start yelling but stopped, realizing, quite inexplicably, that the camera had indeed worked. Scarlett ran over, snatching it from Harper's hands. "It works?!" Scarlett said excitedly. "But how?"

Harper pried it from her hands, using her shirt to wipe the smudge off the view finder. There was a chirp and the camera spit out a small, thin metal slate from the top.

"And it's a Polaroid?!"

Harper held the photo up while Scarlett attempted to reach it, leaving a short window of time for the film to properly expose. When it finally did, she offered it to Scarlett, who snatched it from her fingers.

"Ugh. I guess that looks about right for someone that feels like they're dying. Again." Scarlett groaned. She thoughtfully ran her fingers across her forehead, brushing aside the loose strands of hair. "How can a camera work in here? Nothing electrical ever works once we're inside. Our watches. Our phones. Nothing."

Harper took the slate, wiping Scarlett's fingerprints off with her shirt and holding it up to the light. "After listening to your testimony, the researchers monitoring the area ran dozens of experiments. A man named Loren Ormand is convinced that the house's electromagnetism is what's causing all Winterview's power issues."

Scarlett stared off into space, remembering the night the house had come. "Even that first night. I remember the power went out. Our entire block. The whole city. Took a while to come back on."

Harper slipped the camera into her jacket pocket for safe keeping. "Yes, well, it didn't come back on at all for a lot of people."

"You mean the people in the Dead Zone?" Scarlett asked.

Harper nodded. "The city's electrical issues thus far have mainly been localized to the Dead Zone, but the Red Sky says it's spreading to the other side of the wall now. And soon it'll be beyond the Fringe."

"That's why they sent you? Because it's spreading and they don't know how to stop it?"

Harper nodded. "Yes. And if Park and I can't figure out how, it won't be long before it reaches outside the city."

Harper was rummaging through her pack again. Scarlett was bent over at the waist, her head between her knees. Harper pulled out two L-shaped brass rods, placing them on the tile. She looked up at Scarlett, noting the girl's shallow, steady breaths. "Are you all right?"

Scarlett waved her away with a wan smile. "Just trying to catch my breath." Scarlett looked down at the rods. "What're those things?"

Harper went to reach for the rods and lost her balance, teetering over and catching herself. Scarlett went to reach for her and Harper shrugged her off.

"Looks like I'm not the only one feeling like shit," Scarlett said.

"I'm fine," Harper replied.

"Sure you are."

Harper grabbed the rods and stood up.

"All right. I give up," Scarlett said. "What are they?"

She opened her mouth to speak but a voice cut her off.

"Dowsing rods."

They both looked up to find the mountain man standing across from them, his shirt stained with blood, his face and hands positively filthy.

"That's right," Harper confirmed.

Scarlett stepped closer and the man didn't move.

"What're you lookin' at?" he asked.

Scarlett moved slow, and it was like watching her try and walk up on an animal in the wild.

"You're alive?" Scarlett asked, shocked.

"Looks that way," he said.

"But how?" her voice went up an octave that made her sound ten years younger. "We saw you crash. And those…people, they were all over you."

"Don't matter. I'm here—they're not." The man seemed to grow uncomfortable with Scarlett staring at him, like he didn't want anyone to remember his face. He stepped past her like she was covered in boils, walking up to Harper and grabbing the rods out of her hands. "What the hell you gon' do with these stupid things?"

"They're for research," Harper said. Her brow flattened and she snatched them back from his hands.

The man scoffed. "*Research*? Who the fuck you think you are, the goddamn *Ghostbusters*?" He laughed snidely, shaking his head.

"Dowsing rods?" Scarlett echoed, scratching her chin. "Why does that sound familiar?"

"For finding ghosts and shit. Ain't that right, Doc?"

Harper turned to her, ignoring the brute. "Since our options are limited in the Dead Zone, we've had to turn to more...*rudimentary* means of investigation. In theory, dowsing rods are supposed to allow us a means to communicate with the dead."

"Crock a shit is what it is," the man said. "Don't work on those stupid TV shows and it sure as hell ain't gonna work in here. You wanna see a ghost, all you gotta do is open your eyes and look."

"Well, since you're such an expert on the subject, perhaps you can share some your thoughts with us, mister...? I didn't catch your name." Harper glared at him and he took the hint, starting away.

Scarlett saw him going and looked at Harper. "Aren't you gonna stop him?"

Harper laughed. "And why would I do that?"

The man continued down the hall, rounding the corner.

Scarlett gaped at her, appalled.

Harper exhaled a sharp breath. "What?"

"What do you mean *what*? We need his help," Scarlett said, raising her voice. She paced a few steps away, watching the man grow smaller and smaller. "We're losing him, Doctor!"

"What could he possibly do to help us, Scarlett? I mean, besides offer crude, unsolicited opinions and bash our skulls in?"

Scarlett held her hands up, shaking her head. "Did you or did you not see him take out like five, of those freaks back there in the street with his bare hands?"

"He was *looting*, Scarlett. Didn't you see his truck? It was loaded to the brim with stolen goods. I don't know about you, but where I'm from we don't steal from the dead."

"Irrelevant. Completely irrelevant," she argued. "He might be a little rough around the edges—"

"A *little* rough?" Harper said.

"Well, you're a shrink, right?" Scarlett said. "So shrink him!"

Harper ignored her, holding up the rods. What should have been two L-shaped rods were now an S and a C. She sighed, her eyes falling closed while she cursed the mountain man. Her pack must have been jostled when she had been attacked in the street.

"Harper," Scarlett began. She thoughtfully removed the rods from Harper's hands, putting her hands on her shoulders. "I know you don't know me, but you have every reason to listen to me, so trust me when I tell you that we are going to need his help. He might be the biggest asshole on the face of the planet, but he is going to an invaluable asset in here. *Believe me.*"

Harper pondered her request. "Fine. But if you want him around, then *you* are his wrangler," she said, poking a finger into Scarlett's chest.

"Fine," Scarlett said. She rushed off down the hall, chasing after the man while Harper went to put the dowsing rods back in her pack. She held them up, the sad misshapen things dangling from their handles, and shook her head. "Best laid plans," she muttered. She took the rods and hurled them across the room.

She zipped her pack up, a defeated look on her face. "Where are you, Park?"

She caught up with Scarlett and the mountain man five minutes later. They were standing at the end the hall and their conversation was going surprisingly well for how standoffish he had been only moments ago.

Harper approached and the man looked at her out of the corner of his eye.

Scarlett turned and smiled. "Harper, I'd like you to meet Beau."

"Beau…?" Harper repeated.

"Winchester," the man said. Harper could see he was straining. Even this much civility was a stretch for him. She guessed he had very little contact with the world unless he was in town to steal or fence stolen property. "Anything else you dames wanna know? My birthday? My favorite color maybe?"

This is never going to work, Harper thought. The man was far too unpredictable. And a killer, no less.

Scarlett forced a smile and Harper did too. They must have both looked deranged.

"Great. Nice to meet you, Beau. This is Dr. Harper, and I'm

Scarlett."

"Yeah, I know," he said. "Your face has only been plastered all over the news for the last year. Hard not to."

"Right..." Scarlett said.

Harper looked at her and snickered.

"Harper's a researcher," Scarlett said.

Harper's body relaxed. *Well, at least she didn't say—*

"And a psychiatrist," Scarlett added.

Harper frowned.

The man turned and looked at her.

"A *psychologist*, actually," Harper corrected.

"Oh, right. Sorry," she said, grimacing.

"Well, don't be tryin' any of those fuckin' head games with me," the man said. "Don't need no one tryin' to get in my head."

"As if there would be anything in there anyway," Harper muttered under her breath.

He began walking away and Scarlett followed, waving Harper to come along.

Beau moved fast, and Harper had to jog to keep up.

Scarlett was caught somewhere between them.

"Do you know who they were?" Scarlett called to him. "Those people in the streets?"

"Nope," he said.

"Oh."

Scarlett slowed and Harper caught up with her, the two keeping within Beau's line of sight, far enough away to talk amongst themselves.

"I've got a confession to make," Harper said.

Scarlett chuckled. "Ah, is this the part where you tell me that I was right and you were wrong?"

"Something like that," Harper replied. They walked, watching the odd specimen of a man. Seeing someone so out of their element yet so comfortable at the same time was wild, like you could have dropped him anywhere on the planet and he'd adapt. Harper harbored a whisper of admiration hidden under ample layers of loathing.

"I didn't think there was anything you could have said that would make him want to help us," Harper said. "You must be more persuasive than I took you for."

Scarlett slowed, looking at her. She smiled, and it was almost like a friendship was blooming if the house didn't stamp it out first.

"What?" she asked. "Oh, you mean how did I get him to agree to be our own personal bodyguards for the foreseeable future?"

"Yes, that's exactly what I mean. What'd you say to him?" Harper asked. "How'd you do it?"

"Easy," Scarlett said, grinning. "I just offered him fifty grand."

MORGANA

THEY'D GOTTEN AWAY. Her blood boiled. Her left eye twitched. Her hand trembled, the steel chilled by a thin layer of frost. She felt a tingle where her shoulder met her neck, the muscles spasming in a residual shudder. The sizzling electric shock had done some damage to the muscles. At least temporarily.

She seethed, her pride humiliated almost as much as her ego. A feeling Morgana hadn't experienced in a long time came surging back like it had never left at all, searing all those delicate parts of herself like molten lead.

Weakness.

The strings of humiliation swirled inside her head like a cyclone, whirling into a rage so pure it was almost euphoric.

They were as good as dead.

The only thing she had to decide was how she was going to do it.

Enzo was lying at her feet, a telling wet stain spilled over his groin and down his thighs. The offensive stench of urine permeated the air. She had to fight every impulse in her body not to slit his throat then and there. He'd left her rear unguarded and she'd paid the price for it. If Nick and his savior had been smarter they would have killed her. Killed Enzo. But they hadn't. It was because they were weak, she knew. Couldn't do what needed to be done. And now they were going to pay the ultimate price for it.

Something was different now, though. She heard a light rainfall and looked up to find a set of double doors at the other end of the foyer propped open, the outside world bright with pale light.

Wait a minute.

What doors?

They hadn't been there before. Had they?

And daylight? It couldn't be. It was hours until dawn.

Enzo gasped, springing to life. He groaned, then rolled over, holding his groin. "Goddamn it!" he snapped. "That bitch—she fuckin'—" But he couldn't get out the rest, keeled over in the fetal position whimpering like he'd been castrated. He squirmed across the tile floor and all Morgana could think was how pathetic he looked.

She swung down and mounted him, sliding the blade against his throat, the other hand snatching a fistful of greasy hair.

Enzo froze.

"Mr. Astley. When I accepted this job I was led to believe that you were the very best at what you do," she said. "As you know, our reputations are all we have in this business, and based on the last half hour I'm beginning to have serious doubts about your abilities."

Enzo was holding his breath. "It wasn't my fault," he stuttered. "I heard something, out in the—"

"Shhh…" she whispered.

She leaned in close like she was going to kiss him then stopped. She blinked, staring down at him with that horrible black slit of an eye, then reached out with her fingertips, gently stroking Enzo's eyebrows.

Enzo stared up at her, a grown man trembling beneath her. She reveled in his fear, savoring it like a fine wine.

"I removed a man's eyelids once," Morgana said casually.

Enzo gulped, and the blade nicked his skin, a bead of blood rolling over the cords in his neck.

"You'd be surprised how simply one can get a message across when one has to. Sometimes even the smallest cuts can do the most damage."

Morgana lifted the knife, dangling the blade over his eye like a mobile. "The next time you have a problem keeping watch, I'll take yours. You'll be guaranteed to see everything happening then," she said with a callous smile.

Morgana slipped away from him like a shadow receding into the night.

Enzo's brow flattened. He grabbed his handgun and awkwardly stumbled to his feet, bracing himself on the wall. He glared at her, massaging his groin, his face contorted in pain. His pride was hurt, but he kept his mouth shut. He knew what she was capable of. They all did.

A light winter breeze tossed Morgana's black coat.

Enzo sniffed at the air, turning toward the sound of the rain.

He spotted the open double doors, surprised to find the city beyond. He waved his pistol at the exit, tabling their feud for the time being.

"How long was I out?" He ran his tongue along his lips, then wiped the sweat from his brow with the back of his hand. "I don't know what's worse, this fuckin' headache or my…" his voice trailed off.

Morgana was silent.

Enzo went to check his watch, tapping the face with the barrel of his gun. He cocked his head at an angle. "Eight grand and this fuckin' thing doesn't even work."

"The battery is dead," Morgana said. "It has been for hours." How the man hadn't noticed this long ago was a mystery. She'd first noticed the watch's hands frozen shortly after they'd exited the underground tunnel. She thought it curious, but had anticipated it. She hadn't been to Winterview in years. Not since long before the house had come. She had done mild research to prepare herself for the excursion, memorizing every street and alley and manhole before they had come. After all, strange things were reported to happen near the structure, and thorough preparation could mean the difference between life and death. Or more importantly, a successful job or a failed one. She had predicted electrical disturbances. Strange illnesses the closer in proximity you were to the building. But nowhere in her studies was there mention of the murderous cult that combed the streets surrounding the house.

A glaring flaw in an otherwise flawless plan.

The others were a surprise as well, but they would be easier to manage. The sheer numbers of the cultists would be difficult to deal with.

"Sonofabitch," Enzo scoffed, snapping his wrist like it had caught fire. He took out his phone, flipping it open. His face scrunched. He snapped it closed and whipped it at the wall, the device shattering in a confetti of glass and metal.

A growl of low thunder rolled in from outside, drawing Enzo's attention. He walked over to the exit, listening to the rain pour.

"This isn't what I signed up for," he said. He turned around, meeting Morgana's eyes. "Sure as shit ain't what I signed up for."

She watched him stand there, hesitating, and she didn't doubt that had she not been there, with her eyes pinning him to the floor, he'd have already ran out the front doors.

"I will find them," Morgana said, without a hint of trepidation. "With or without you."

Enzo seemed to reflect on this, turning to the glowing box of light before him and gazing out at the rain, a mere step from freedom.

But what waited for him beyond?

The cultists? Hiding behind every wall and window with a weapon in their hands. Waiting. Biding their time.

The light was curious, though. She was absolutely certain that dawn was hours away. But, then again, the house was full of tricks. Maybe it was an illusion to make them *think* it was morning. To trick them into believing the cultists would be safely removed from the Dead Zone, grown tired of waiting, only to spring out the second they stepped foot outside the door.

A delicious idea came to her then.

"The house is larger than I initially anticipated," she said.

Enzo shrugged. "Yeah? And?"

"I have a plan."

"I'm listening," Enzo replied.

"It'll take us hours to search all the rooms. Even then they outnumber us. It would be too great a risk."

"So, what'd you wanna do?"

Morgana came closer, closing the space between them.

"Do you have any associates in the city?" she asked.

Enzo looked away, digging inside his head. He nodded, looking at her. Determined. "Yeah. I do. I know a couple guys that work the docks. Friends of my brother. They're on the payroll. I can have them down here in an hour to help us sort out this mess."

"Good," Morgana said. "Get them." She stepped beside him and they gazed out at the fog, two strangers in a stranger land.

They must have been at a different exit. The porch steps were gone. No red carpet or charred helicopter husk. No limousines or news vans overgrown with plants. No skeletal vault doors.

Morgana stepped right up to the boundary, taking in a deep breath. Something smelled different in the air. The winter was gone.

Impossible, she thought.

Outside the threshold of the exit, a quaint cobblestone street wound away into the fog. It seemed worse now, somehow, then it had been at night. The rain slowed, turned to sleet, lazily slipping down from dark clouds. About fifteen feet from the doors were a pair of asymmetrical slate columns rising out of view, covered in short ceramic barbs. Hideous architecture by today's standards, but beautiful in its own right.

Enzo breathed in, a rush of air in his lungs coming out in a short burst of white smoke. "What're you gonna do, Morgue?"

Morgana gazed out at the street, peacefully admiring the gray world.

"You think those crazies are still out there?" he asked.

"It looks clear," she said, lying through her teeth. There really wasn't any way to know what was waiting out there. She had trained herself for years to detect even the smallest discrepancies, but somehow the ghosts that roamed the streets had eluded her. Eluded them all.

"Easy for you to say. Ain't your ass that's gonna get hacked up," Enzo sneered. He ejected the magazine from his gun, checking the bullets, then slapped it back in, chambering a round with a hearty clack.

"Just move fast. The fog has thickened; it should give you enough cover. Stay out of sight and keep moving."

"I don't get it," Enzo said, scratching the back of his head with the butt of the pistol. "What gives? I thought this place was supposed to lock up come mornin'?"

Morgana's eyes skimmed beyond the entrance, suspicious. He was right. Everything she had read said the house seals at dawn. So then why were the doors still open? It was peculiar. Morgana shook her head. "I don't know. I suppose they were wrong."

Enzo looked at her like he knew something was off but couldn't say what exactly. "One hour. One hour and I'll be back." He turned his eyes to the streets, the two of them watching the rain fall, the fog sweeping past in the road like ghostly tides.

She wondered how many of the cultists might be watching right then. How many were waiting in the veil, axes in hand waiting to lop off a body part the second they were within reach.

He was nervous. Even with his gun and his brawn the man was scared. Enzo swallowed, stepping forward. Sickly gray light swept down his face like sunrise.

And then he was out.

He wandered forward a few more feet, peering around, the gun down at his side. His chest seemed to deflate a little; his shoulders sunk down, and he looked back over his shoulder at her.

"It's clear," he said, his mouth relaxing into a relieved smile.

Enzo gave her a thumbs up and, for a fleeting moment, she thought he might actually make it out of the Dead Zone alive.

The sky suddenly darkened, like a chain of clouds had blotted out the sun. A heavy whirr, something large cutting through the air.

The columns: they were moving. And that was when she realized; they weren't columns at all—they were appendages. Appendages of something so vast only Enzo would ever truly see what it was.

The man looked up just as an enormous pincher swung down and snapped closed over his torso, biting down in a spray of blood. The gun reflexively went off in his hand in a sharp blast and Enzo shrieked so loud his voice cracked along with his ribs. The claw reminded her of a lobster, armored and wet and strong, with crevices of glistening black fibers like quills that reminded her of hair.

Enzo looked up and his eyes shot open in horror. He whimpered, sobbing, screaming her name, and Morgana's heart sped up. Her pupils dilated; her chest flushed with heat. Never in her wildest, darkest, most perverse fantasies had she ever been able to elicit that level of fear. It was absolutely glorious.

She drew her gun fluidly, training it on Enzo's head. She held it out in front of her, drawing in steady breaths, watching Enzo writhe in agony while blood spewed out of his mouth. She briefly considered putting a bullet in his head and ending his misery, then lowered the gun.

There would be no mercy tonight. The time to atone for his failures was nigh; fate had claimed him, she decided. His life was not hers to take.

Morgana couldn't see exactly *what* had seized him, only that it was so colossal it passed well beyond the doorframe into the sky.

The hulking claw shifted, like whatever it was attached to had drawn a great, shuddering breath, and Enzo lifted off the ground. He screamed, thrashing his arms and legs while Morgana watched him be carried into the sky, disappearing in a curtain of dreamy fog.

She took a step back and calmly reached out and seized the double doors, one with each hand, and swung them closed.

She took a deep breath, blinking her eyes, and exhaled.

She had work to do.

SCARLETT

THEY'D STOPPED TO rest in an immense conservatory, the walls and ceiling comprised solely of green glass frosted with lines of elegant script. Unreadable, of course. In the middle of the floor was a sprawling willow tree rife with stunning violet leaves and black glass bark, at least forty feet high. Beyond the refined glass walls, glowing insects buzzed past in a moonlit marsh, leaving sparkling contrails behind. Swampland, by the looks of it. Louisiana, maybe. Like the Blue Bayou from *The Pirates of the Caribbean*, Scarlett thought. A peaceful night paradise with a hint of danger.

Harper was inspecting the glass shards coating the tree's surface, sketching them in a notebook she carried in her backpack.

Beau was watching the winged things whirr by as he polished the long bowie knife he carried in a leather sheath on his belt, and she wondered if he'd ever felt so close to home and so far all at once. That maybe the dark world outside was something from his memory the house had recreated special, just for him.

"You're a walking cliché, you know," Scarlett said to Beau, gazing out at the beautiful wetland. Pulses of warm light flickered in the darkness between the trees.

Beau didn't look up.

"Big hunting knife. Greasy rag hanging out of your back pocket. Cut-off sleeves. You are the quintessential mountain man, my friend."

Beau grunted.

"At least that's what you *want* people to think."

Beau stopped polishing the knife.

"You're covered in dried blood and grease. Probably from working on engines, right?" she said. "But there's also little itty bitty flecks of color on your hands. Under your nails. On your boots. Even your shoe laces."

Beau looked down at his boots. Tiny freckles of color were speckled across them. Pinks. Yellows. Blues. Even red. But not the color of blood, like he had everywhere else. A brighter red, the color of a fire engine.

"Paint?" Scarlett asked. "But you don't strike me as the type to paint your car, so the question isn't *why* were you painting so much as *what* were you painting? And what were you doing with all that scrap metal? You had enough copper back there to rewire the whole city."

Beau's brow flattened. "You're an annoying little shit, you know that?"

Beau started away and Scarlett followed after him.

"That actually reminds me, I saw this thing on the news a few years ago. One of those 'feel-good' humanitarian pieces. People were finding these copper statues out in the woods all over the East Coast. Like, just doing random things. Reading books. Running. Some of them were leaning on trees. Fishing—"

"Do I look like I give a flying fuck?"

"Sorry, sort of off-topic, I guess. But not really. It reminded me of that, though, when I saw all that pipe in your truck and—"

"Christ, kid, what's it gonna take to shut you up?" Beau said.

"Do you always answer a question with a question?" Scarlett smirked, folding her arms. She wasn't going to let him deflect. If he was going to be part of their group, she wanted to know something about him. Something that would make him seem a little more human and a little less like the monster Harper took him to be.

"All right, small fry," Beau said. "You really think you're so fuckin' smart?"

"Well, no, but I have my moments."

"Yeah? Then how come you ain't noticed that kid standing there for the last five minutes?"

"Huh?" she said.

Scarlett spun around. Harper's attention caught too. She stopped sketching, closing her notebook and zipping it back in her pack.

Standing across the room, staring out at the marsh, was a little girl.

HARPER

A WALKING GHOST. That was what she reminded Harper of. Her feet were bare. Filthy. She was pale but her cheeks were flushed with blood. If she didn't know any better Harper would have guessed she was sleepwalking.

"A girl," Scarlett said. She turned to Harper. "Is that her? What does she look like?"

Harper shrugged. "I don't know. He didn't say."

Scarlett exhaled. "He didn't say," she repeated. "Of course, he didn't say."

Oddly enough, Beau was the first to speak to the girl.

"Hey," Beau said, moving closer. "Kid."

Harper grabbed his arm, keeping him close.

"What the hell?" he said.

"Shhh! We don't want to scare her and *you* most definitely will," Harper said quietly.

"What the hell is that supposed to mean?" Beau asked.

"Look at you," Harper said. "You've got blood all over your shirt and your hands. You're filthy."

He looked at Scarlett.

"You kinda are," she said.

"A little tact might be in order," Harper said. "I'll go."

Scarlett stepped back, holding out her arms. "By all means, Doctor."

"You?" Beau sniggered. "I wouldn't trust you to treat a dead body."

"Thank you for that vote of confidence, Mr. Winchester," Harper said. "Now if you don't mind."

Beau folded his arms. "This oughta be good."

Harper ignored him. She unslung her pack and set it on the ground.

The girl wasn't moving. She was simply standing there at the other end of the conservatory in the dark, staring at the night marsh. Odd behavior, but not entirely alarming.

Harper treaded with care, keeping her footsteps light on the tight carpet. Something about this whole thing felt…off? Like they were being setup.

"Hi there," Harper said calmly. "My name is Dr. Miranda Harper. I'm here to help."

The girl didn't respond.

"Can you hear me?" she asked.

But still the child didn't move.

Harper approached, mindful not to scare the girl.

"What's your name?"

When the girl still didn't respond, she laid a hand on her shoulder.

The contact did it. The girl's eyes blinked as if she were waking from a dream.

"Hi," Harper greeted. "Are you all right, sweetie?"

The girl blinked again, nodding her head.

She turned to Scarlett. "She needs to be evaluated."

Beau found them a nice space not far away. A place with stainless steel counters and cabinets and a bizarre appliance from a Salvador Dali painting that might pass as a refrigerator. Harper thought it was a kitchen but realized there were pullout chambers in the walls and then realized it was closer to a morgue. The smell definitely felt right. Chemicals like bleach and antiseptic permeated the room. Harper thought she perceived a note of formaldehyde somewhere in there, too. The space had a certain barren quality about it. A sterility that made her feel more at home than she would have thought.

Rachel sat slouched on a large island in the center of the room, Scarlett perched beside her.

Beau leaned in and sniffed the air near Rachel, his face going sour.

"She stinks," he said.

Scarlett stared daggers at him. "So do you."

"Hey," Beau said, snapping his fingers in the girl's face. "You in there?"

Harper brushed his hand away. "Don't do that."

Harper had performed a brief physical examination, checking for any bruises, cuts, or scrapes. Combed her fingers through the girl's oily hair for lesions or bumps and come up with nothing.

Beau rummaged through the cabinets on the walls, not caring about the noise he was creating. He slammed one drawer closed then jerked open another, and the cacophony of racket he could make all on his own was oddly impressive if not immensely grating.

"Will you *please* be quiet," Harper snapped.

Beau scoffed, insufferable, then slammed the drawer closed. "Sure, anything for you, Doc."

Rachel's head lolled. She blinked lethargically and wiped the back of her hand across her forehead. Scarlett reached out and put the back of her hand to the girl's forehead, brushing a few greasy strands away from her face and tucking them behind her ear.

"She's burning up," Scarlett said worriedly.

Harper took Rachel's wrist between her fingers, counting down in her head. Her pulse was steady. Not fast. Not slow. Steady.

"What's wrong with her?" Scarlett asked.

"I don't know," Harper replied briskly. She dropped down on the heels of her military boots. "I need to run a few tests."

Harper leaned in. "Rachel?"

Rachel stirred, her chin lifting. Harper gently lifted Rachel's eyelids one at a time, discovering the girl's eyes were mapped with dozens of dark blood vessels, but overall, relatively normal.

Eye tracking. Pupillary response was impossible short of blinding Rachel with the camera flash but she sure as hell wasn't about to do that.

"Follow my finger," Harper instructed. She waved it horizontally back and forth, then continued in a star pattern. Rachel followed it, albeit blearily, to completion.

"Good," Harper said. She looked at Rachel and the girl's eyes widened like two mouths, black as space.

Harper gasped, mashing her eyes shut.

"What's the matter?" Scarlett said, jumping off the countertop.

Harper forced them open again, but when she did, Rachel's eyes were blue again.

Had she imagined it?

The room flickered. She looked up at a nervous set of fluorescent bulbs on the ceiling.

A trick of the light. That's all.

Scarlett said, "If you're not up for this—"

"I'm fine," Harper said, composing herself. "Let's get on with it."

"All right," Scarlett replied.

"What's your name?" Harper asked.

"Rachel," the girl said, but her voice was slow, churned out like cold molasses. "My name's…Rachel…Webster."

"What day of the week is it?"

A cupboard banged closed and Beau chortled. "Shit, I don't even know that. What makes you think a kid—"

"Thank you, Beau!" Scarlett interrupted. "That'll do."

Harper gave Scarlett a look that said THANK YOU and then trained her attention back on the girl.

She needed to work her way down her list.

Retrograde amnesia.

"Where do you live?" Harper asked.

Rachel blinked, thinking, then said, "Our house."

Anterograde amnesia now.

"How did you get here?"

"I walked," she said.

Scarlett and Harper exchanged a look.

Concentrate.

"I want you to try and count backwards from a hundred—"

A hollow thump and Harper spied Beau out of the corner of her eye leaning against the cupboard, shaking his head.

"Kid ain't old enough to count."

"Are you speaking from experience?" Harper asked, and Beau's face went beet red.

Scarlett scratched her head. "Harper, I really don't think she's going to be able to do that right now."

"Are you a doctor?" Harper asked.

"No, but—"

"Well, I am. So let me do my job."

Scarlett was floored. She threw up her hands and pushed off the counter, moping to the other side of the island. Beau flashed a childish smirk at her.

"Try for me, Rachel," Harper insisted. "Can you try?"

"I don't think so," she replied. "I'm too tired right now."

"That's okay," Harper said, and Scarlett looked at her. *I told you so.*

"Do you have a headache? Or hurt anywhere?" Harper asked.

Rachel was silent.

"Do you feel nauseous?" Harper asked. "Sick?"

Scarlett rolled her eyes, growing impatient. "She means do you feel like you might throw up?"

"No," Rachel said. "It doesn't hurt anymore. I feel fine."

"That's good, Rachel. That's real good." Harper exhaled, standing up. "She seems to be all right for now."

"All right? What're you talking about?" Scarlett asked, concerned. "She's clearly not. It's like someone spiked her chocolate milk with valium or something." Scarlett took a deep breath, pacing, and Beau was basking in the tension. "And if she *does* feel fine that's even more concerning because the rest of us feel like utter shit right now."

"Nancy Drew is on to something," Beau said, swinging his feet off the counter and landing on the tile with a heavy thud. "Maybe you're gettin' a little rusty, Doc."

"Physiologically," Harper explained, "she's fine. Her memory seems to be intact. Her reflexes. All of it. Her emotional response *is* off, but there is nothing that I can do about it in here. We have got to get her out of the house and to a hospital where she can be properly evaluated *and* monitored. And that's *if* we can get past the madmen that lie in wait outside in the streets."

Scarlett nodded. "Yeah, okay, you're right. Agreed."

"So," Harper said, expectant.

"So?"

"Where is it?" Harper asked, pointblank.

"Where's what?"

"Dr. Quinn is askin' where the exit is at, genius," Beau said.

"The exit?" Scarlett echoed. Scarlett looked at her, clueless. "How should I know?"

"You got out before. Surely you must know where the exit is?"

"Oh, must I?"

Harper crossed her arms, taking a step closer. "Scarlett, do you or do you not know how to get out of this house?"

"The exit sort of just…appeared," she said, clearing her throat. "We didn't 'find it,' I wouldn't say. More like it found us."

Beau erupted into a fit of laughter.

"Shut up!" they shouted in unison.

This was getting them nowhere. If Scarlett didn't know where the exit was, they were simply going to have to keep looking. Harper slipped the backpack over her shoulders, starting away, and Beau watched her storm off, entertained like he was watching his favorite sitcom.

"Harper! Where are you going?" Scarlett shouted.

She looked at Beau, a pleased grin on his face.

"Guess I'm not lookin' so bad about now, huh?"

And she said, "Get bent."

JACKSON

WHERE ARE YOU?

That was all Jackson could think. The thought looped on end in his head, whipping over and over. Scarlett was here somewhere. He could feel her somehow, the same way he could feel if someone had been in a room right before him. Like they'd only just missed each other.

He and Park were moving quickly, as fast as they could as far as they could from that room with the arched windows and the giant eyeball ogling them from outside.

Park was quiet. They hadn't spoken two words to each other, only proceeded to calmly exit the room and slam the door closed behind them. He could tell Park was intrigued. How could she not be? But her fear of the unknown had trumped any desire she had to get a closer look.

Jackson, however, knew what would happen if he died; he'd wake up somewhere entirely different in the house, maybe with someone else. Trapped in an endless cycle of life and death.

Maybe with those two psychopaths. He remembered the way Morgana had looked up at him and smiled, a pile of white robes laid out before her, soaked with blood. She didn't need the house to drive her mad because she was already there.

He shuddered. His chest went tight.

Scarlett.

She's fine, he told himself. *She's here. She can take care of herself. Focus.*

The sconces on the walls blinked by one after another, a ghostly lick of flame fluttering as they passed.

He could hear Park behind him, hear her labored breaths as they rushed into the unknown.

"Jackson," she called. "Hang on."

He slowed, turning back to find Park pitched over by the wall.

"I think we're okay," she said, out of breath. "We left giant eyeball monster like five miles back."

Jackson turned and glanced back from where they'd came.

A funnel of blackness.

"What in the hell was that thing?" Park asked.

Jackson shook his head. "I don't know. But whatever it was looked pissed off." He took a minute to let his jack-rabbiting heart slow to a normal pace.

Park's complexion had lightened considerably.

"Are you sure you're all right? You look sort of…pale?"

Park laughed weakly. "Yeah, I think I lost some blood. And all the running probably didn't help." She carefully slipped off her jacket, tying it around her waist.

The cut was deeper than Jackson had thought. "Holy shit, that looks pretty bad. I think you need stitches," he said. He leaned closer. Buried under all the dried blood a fine line ran straight across her shoulder.

Park moved her arm to inspect the wound and the layers of skin stretched apart, exposing a fissure of raw muscle below. "Holy shit that hurts," she said, wincing.

"Here," Jackson said. He grabbed the end of his shirt and ripped off a long strip.

"You some kind of doctor?" Park asked.

"Me?" Jackson laughed. "Hell no. A bartender. At least I was." Jackson smiled halfheartedly. "I'm sort of in-between jobs right now."

"Do you have even the slightest idea what you're doing?"

"You'd be surprised how many times I've had to patch someone up. I'm pretty good now with a needle and thread. No shortage of brawls once the alcohol starts flowing."

Park looked up at him.

He swathed the fabric around her arm, looping it around several times. "The bar I worked at, Rowdy's," Jackson explained, "most people were cool. Some were dicks. But the majority just wanted to have a good time. Have a drink and forget about all the shit going on in their lives, ya know? Things were usually pretty quiet…" his voice trailed off.

"Until they weren't?" Park said, raising her eyebrows. "Right?"

"Until they weren't," he echoed. He took the two ends in his fists, pulling it tight.

"OW!" Park yelped. "Jesus! How about a little warning next time?"

"Sorry," Jackson grimaced. He stood back, proud of his makeshift tourniquet. "It's not pretty, but it should be good enough until we can get you to a hospital."

"That's assuming we get out of here at all."

Jackson chuckled. "I took you as more of a 'glass half-full type.'"

Park groaned, straightening up. "Wait until you get to know me." She looked down the hall, the lamps trailing away. "Where are we? Any idea?"

Jackson shrugged. "Why are you asking me?"

"You've been here before, haven't you?"

"Well, yeah. But it changes. Things are always shifting around. It's like a giant Rubik's Cube."

A beat passed.

"We need to find the others."

Jackson agreed.

"Who were those people with you?" Park asked. "I'm going to guess by the guns and the knives that they're friends of yours?"

Jackson shook his head, leaning against the wall. "They're looking for someone. They think Scarlett and I are going to be able to tell them how to navigate this place. Like it *could* be navigated." Jackson laughed. "Joke's on them, I guess."

"Who're they looking for?"

"A woman named Isabelle. Some mafia kingpin—or rather *queenpin's*—daughter. They think she's here somewhere, in the house."

Park went quiet. She squinted in the gloom, her eyes narrowing.

"What is it?" Jackson asked.

Park pointed. "Look."

The floor ahead was awash with a flood of orange light. Jackson noticed it beaming from under a set of metal doors in the wall. He started forward, moving to one side. Park stood next to him.

"What'd you think?" she asked him.

Jackson looked down at his shoes. "I don't see any other doors."

Park went to push it open and he grabbed her hand.

"What?" she whispered. "What's the problem?"

"Hold on a minute," he said. "We don't know what's in there."

Park gawked at him. "And that's exactly why I was trying to open it."

Jackson stepped in front of her. "You don't know what it's like in here. You don't know what's in there," he said, hooking a thumb over his shoulder. "We could walk off a cliff if we're not careful."

Park rolled her eyes. "Fine. Then what do you want to do?" she asked, poking a finger into his chest.

"All I'm saying is we should maybe think about this for a minute before rushing in, that's all. We made some…*mistakes* last time we were here, and I died and Scarlett died and I don't feel like reliving that again."

"I remember her talking about that in interviews. Dying here over and over," Park said. "Wild shit." Park took a breath. "Fine."

Jackson moved out of the way and Park shoved the doors open anyway.

"Wait!" he shouted, reaching out to try and stop her.

A dazzling spectacle of neon lights beamed into the hallway. Park turned and looked at him, shrugging her shoulders.

"Oops." She stepped past him, eyes widening. "What in the world?"

A theater lobby. Right here in the house.

"The movies?" Jackson muttered.

Park and he wandered through the entrance together. The tight carpeting had cartoon-like illustrations of theater concessions. Popcorn and sodas and movie stubs. A long glass counter ran from one wall to the other. All around were neon signs and lights welcoming them to the experience of a lifetime. Only that wasn't quite what they said.

"Jackson," Park said. "Look at that."

Jackson took a step closer, noticing the glowing signs were written in gibberish. A few letters speckled here and there, but other than that, the characters were completely unknown to him. And judging by Park's reaction, unknown to her too.

They wandered forward, taking in the high ceiling, where a glass skylight displayed a fantastic lightning storm. He listened as thunder growled low and deep while the popcorn popped. Jackson could smell the butter. Taste the salt.

"The time," Park said, her gaze on a clock above the entrance to the stretch of halls. "The numbers—they're all wrong."

Jackson knew them. "Those are the same symbols on the clock on the front of the house."

"What do they mean?"

"No idea. I don't think anyone does," he answered. "I think they had some theories, but nobody knows for sure."

Jackson stopped in the middle of the lobby, standing in the center of a large nautical star. Something wasn't sitting right.

"I don't get it," he said, taking in every gleaming piece of metal, every twist in the vivid light fixtures.

Park slowed, turning back. "Don't get what?"

Jackson scanned the theater lobby, searching.

"It wasn't like this last time," he said.

Park walked closer. "You're going to have to help me out here, Jackson? This is my first time here. Wasn't like *what*?"

"Everything we saw before, it had this look to it, almost like it was an antique. This *used* look. Even the things that shouldn't have. It was all old. Dull. But this..." He approached the glass countertop, running his finger along the chromed trim. "...it's like it's been restored. Like it's brand new."

Park was quiet.

"Why doesn't it look the same, Park? What's changed?"

Park shrugged. "You tell me."

Jackson exhaled, trying to figure it out, then said, "But that has to mean something. I mean…doesn't it?"

Park smiled somberly. "We need to go."

Jackson nodded.

They walked together down the short track to an empty podium, passing it by. It was like being back in the Starlight in Silvers Hollow. The same yawning black corridor. The same haunting glow spaced evenly along the walls. The same dotted track lights following along the floor.

Whereas the Starlight's auditorium doors were off in an alcove, these were instead like any other doors, placed intermittently, trailing away in the darkness. Above each door was a marquee of more nonsensical glyphs.

He and Park looked down at the same time. The lights on the floors reminded him of a runway. And, where most lights had an end, these didn't; they simply carried on and on, and Jackson wondered if they ever ended. A dread he could only begin to describe as hopelessness started to cloud his mind.

He reached up, patting his jacket pocket.

Whew. The ring. It was still there.

"How long have you had it?" Park asked curtly.

Jackson looked at her, surprised; he'd been caught.

"A couple of days," he said.

"Ah," Park nodded. "All right. Spill it."

Jackson smiled. "You know, Park, there really isn't much to tell."

"Bullshit," Park mocked. "It's for Scarlett right? You've been carrying that thing around with you this *whole time*?"

"How did you—"

"Because I'm not blind, dude, that's how." A beat. "*So?*"

"What?" Jackson asked modestly.

"Can I see it?" she asked.

Jackson mulled it over. He groaned, then fished the box out of his jacket pocket, handing it to her.

Park flipped open the lid and smiled warmly. "It's beautiful," she said. She snapped the lid closed, handing it back to him. "You did good. She's going to love it."

"Yeah," Jackson said, unconvinced.

"Let me guess," Park said. "You want to propose, but you don't know how, or when."

"You know," Jackson said, sliding down the wall to his butt. "I'm starting to question whether you're actually a biologist. Am I really that transparent?"

"People in love usually are," Park said. "They can't help it. I think we're just hardwired that way." A few seconds passed. "So, you've got the ring. You've got the girl. What's stopping you?"

Jackson sighed, combing his fingers through his hair. "Haven't found the right moment, I guess."

"Ah, the 'moment,'" Park said. "Let me tell you something about that 'moment,' Jackson. It's complete and utter bullshit."

Jackson laughed. "Yeah?"

"Scout's honor, hand over my heart. It absolutely is."

Then he said, "Have you ever been…"

"In love?" Park asked.

Jackson nodded.

"Once." Park reached up, twisting a strand of her hair. "My hair was a lot shorter then. It was my second-to-last year of grad school and I didn't expect it to happen and it did and… It feels like a lifetime ago," she said wistfully.

"What happened to him?" he asked.

"*Her*," Park corrected.

"Oh, sorry," Jackson said.

Park shrugged it off. "Don't be. I'm not. We can't help who we fall in love with. I guess that's one of life's great ironies, huh? The people we want so badly are the ones the world works the hardest to keep apart."

"What was her name?" he asked.

"Abby," Park said. She gazed up at the glowing marquees, the reflection of dying dreams in her eyes, tortured by a lifetime of what could have been.

"What happened to her?" Jackson knew right away it was the wrong thing to say but his curiosity got the better of him. Park was clearly still in pain despite her best efforts to hide it, and he couldn't help but remember the unrequited love he'd suffered with most of his adult life.

The sparkle in Park's eyes dimmed like a dying sun. "We had just gotten back from Alaska. I'd surprised her for our anniversary, rented this picture-perfect cabin out in the wilderness, only the two of us and this amazing thing we had and no one and nothing else for miles."

"That sounds nice, Park." And he meant it. Every word.

"My parents were waiting when we got back to the apartment." A single tear rolled down Park's cheek, glistening like a diamond. "They'd made the trip a couple days early for my graduation—to celebrate. My family...they couldn't...they're old-fashioned, which is putting it mildly." A beat passed. "I tried to talk to them, but it was no good. The damage was already done."

The house creaked all around them, and it was like they were passengers on the Titanic, sinking to the bottom of the frozen Atlantic.

Park used the back of her hand to wipe the tears from her face. "So instead of celebrating the most important day in my career, I lost my family and the love of my life all in one fell swoop."

Jackson looked at her soberly. "I'm sorry, Park." Because that was all he *could* say. No amount of talking would ever make things right again or mitigate the agonizing pain of losing your entire future in one day. Of losing everything important to you. He prayed he never had to know that feeling.

Park got on her feet and Jackson followed suit. His headache had evened out slightly, the up and down throb in his temples had shifted to the base of his skull. The contrast of marquee lights and the dark theater halls brought a glassy haze to his eyes.

"I used to think my parents were the villains in that story," she said.

"I never defended her, Jackson. Not once," she confessed. "I never even tried. I just stood there, listening to them spew their hate and their bullshit and I didn't do anything." She looked at Jackson impossibly, her eyes sparkling with tears. "She walked out the door and never came back. And to this day I still don't know why I didn't try and stop her from leaving."

They walked to the first door, and Park took the handle.

"There's a million doors in life, Jackson," she said. "We just have to find the one we're meant to walk through."

She looked at him and he nodded.

"And that is why our time is so, so precious," Park said. "There is no 'right moment.' No perfect time. Don't waste a single second of your life on 'what ifs,' Jackson. Not one. Because if you do, I promise you that you will spend the rest of your life wondering what could have been instead of living it."

And with that, Park pulled the door wide while countless others trailed into the darkness ahead of them.

A wash of dappled light came roaring out at them. Jackson and Park threw their hands up to dull the glare.

His breath hitched; his mouth went bone dry and he nearly passed out from sensory overload.

A world of candy.

NICK

SANDI WAS HURTING. She stood across from him on the other side of the hall, her back pressed flat against the wall. They'd heard some sort of sound coming from around the bend and stopped without saying another word.

The side of Sandi's jaw was swollen. She had a smear of blood at the corner of her mouth like lipstick and her lip was split right down the middle. She'd lost a chunk off her tongue, too, when she'd hit the street with her face.

Yet here she was. Fighting for him. Fighting for Rachel. She may have lived in the kitchen, but she was as tough as any woman he'd ever met. Maybe tougher.

"You all right?" Sandi mouthed.

"Huh?"

Sandi slid down the wall onto her heels. "You look *dead*, Nick. Like you literally *died* and are walking around this house with me."

"Oh, yeah," he said weakly. "I think that punch took something outta me. But I'm good. Just need to catch my breath."

But he wasn't good. Not even close. He could feel the cold air creeping over the dried blood on his back. His skin was gradually turning to ice. The glue had peeled right open since Morgana had gotten the urge to feel his insides, and ever since he'd felt the warmth escaping his body. Every time he breathed the crusted blood would stretch and move with his skin, tugging at the wound. He had a raging headache and at least one of his ribs was cracked. And he was trying his best to pretend like he still had all ten of his fingernails.

"You need a doctor," Sandi said.

Nick waved her away. "Not until we find Rachel."

Sandi thought for a minute, wetting her thumb and scrubbing the dried blood from the corner of her mouth. She ran her tongue along her bottom teeth and winced, feeling the space where her tooth was missing.

Nick grimaced, blindly touching the wound in his lower back to assess the damage.

"Let me see," Sandi said, reaching for his shirt.

Nick politely waved her away, keeping her at a distance.

"Really?" Sandi gaped at him. "It's like that?"

"Really."

"Why do you have to be so damn stubborn, Nick?"

"Why do you?"

Sandi smiled, and laughed.

"There's nothing you can do, Sandi. At least not right now. Let's just find her and get the fuck out of here. Then we can worry about me."

"Fine. But the second we find her we're getting you to a doctor," she said, "and you are getting your shit put back together because *damn*."

"Do I look that bad?" Nick asked.

"You look like you got dragged behind a fucking car."

Nick chuckled. "I've had worse."

"In Cheshire?"

He nodded. He hadn't, but he lied anyway. He'd gotten in a few small scuffles inside, but nothing even approaching the magnitude of danger they'd been thrust into that night. Most brawls in Cheshire were over before they had a chance to begin. And he especially never imagined surviving that living hell only to get shanked *outside* the pen. That was his luck, though. The world was flipped upside down. Lies. White lies. What did it matter? Besides, he wasn't lying for his own sake. He was doing it for her. Maybe his little fib would set Sandi a little more at ease, help her feel a little less anxious about him and a little more about herself for a change.

"Chef?" he said.

Sandi looked at him.

"I never thanked you," he said.

Sandi smiled at him, and he could see the worry there.

"For saving my life."

"You're welcome."

Sandi smiled, and he smiled, too.

A creak, long and loud.

A streak of silver light bounced over Nick's eyes.

They both turned and peered down the hall.

Sandi exhaled, wary, her mind already conjuring up a million potentially horrible things lying in wait. Nick painfully got to his feet and padded across the hall, standing beside her. He flattened himself and slid his body along the wall, drawing closer.

The light brightened.

He arrived at the threshold of an open doorway and heard a sound inside like wind chimes and lazy, hollow metal whirring.

Sandi was right behind him. He turned and looked back at her, but the fear he'd seen that night was gone, replaced with something else. Acceptance? No. He was the pessimist of the two of them. That much he did know about her.

He stepped out from behind the corner and his face glittered with shards of yellow light.

Sandi crept out behind him with a hand on his shoulder.

The resonating hum of metal held steady in the room.

"What in the hell is this?" he asked, starting forward.

No monsters. No cultists, or killers. No plants. Only wood and glass and metal.

More specifically mirrors. And plenty of them. Suspended from chains that shone with a polished coppery luster. Flawless panes of glass as tall as he was, maybe taller.

"It's like a funhouse," Sandi muttered.

They wandered forward until they were in the middle of it all, a giant room with high walls in the shape of an octagon.

Nick craned his head up but couldn't see where the ceiling ended, only that the mirrors went up and up until they disappeared into the shadows.

"Mirrors," Nick said. He stopped directly in front of the mirror nearest and looked closer at the frame housing the glass. He ran his scabbed fingertips along the wood, noting strange shapes carved into the surface.

His eyes snapped open.

They were people.

Bodies.

Flourishes of viscera, and God only knew what else. His stomach went tight.

"What is it?" Sandi asked.

Nick didn't answer.

A seemingly infinite amount of naked human bodies, their faces contorted in agony like prisoners on their way to hell. The realism, the skill it would have taken, it was all so astounding that he couldn't help but wonder if they might have been real people somehow manipulated by the house, absorbed into the painting. But that was crazy, wasn't it?

Absorbed... or eaten?

"Nick," Sandi said.

No. That was ridiculous. Wasn't it?

"Nick!"

He blinked, fluttering his eyelids, prying his eyes off the mirror and the horror.

He turned around to find Sandi on the other side of the room.

Only it wasn't the Sandi he knew.

The real Sandi turned and looked over her shoulder at him.

"What is this, Nick?"

Sandi turned back to the mirror image of herself, trembling.

Her doppelgänger flashed her bleached white teeth at them and waved, and Nick saw something insidious hidden behind that smile. Idealized Sandi wore a double-breasted white cotton coat accented with eight white buttons, her hair pulled back and secured in a tight bun. Her olive skin was immaculate. Her dark eyes sparkled. Everything about her appearance was calculated, thought-out, put together. The version of herself that was successful, and admired. Revered. Celebrated.

And after a moment of them looking at the mirror and the mirror looking back, Nick realized the reflection standing before them was everything Sandi yearned to be. The idealized version of herself that she gave up when she moved back to Winterview. Nick knew a little something about dreams. They were dangerous the same way hope was dangerous. You get a taste for it and suddenly you're ravenous.

As luck would have it, he'd never gotten a taste of the good life the way Sandi had, never been afforded the same opportunities, taken chances on his own dreams. But he was glad. Especially now, looking at all these mirrors. He glanced around at the other mirrors but couldn't find himself in any of them. Maybe because he'd never had any dream except to be a good father, and that was all right by him.

A tear streaked down the side of Sandi's face and Nick felt a pang of sadness for this woman who asked for nothing and got nothing in return.

"Sandi?" he said softly, putting a caring hand on her shoulder.

Sandi nodded, taking in that perfect mirror image of herself like she was coming to terms with what she'd given up.

"It's funny, isn't it?" she asked.

"What do you mean?"

"The things we hide from ourselves." Sandi swallowed, rubbing the soft nape of her neck, paralyzed by a vision of herself that was more dangerous than anything she could ever find in the house.

"When I was in my mid-twenties, I worked at the greatest restaurant in the world," she said, and Nick assumed she was embellishing for the sake of her story. Then she said, "*Literally*. I didn't know it then, but… It was in Denmark. This amazing restaurant in Copenhagen called the Noma."

Sandi looked at him like she was expecting him to recognize it by name, and when he didn't, she smiled, and it was like one more punch to the gut.

"I'd worked in some of the biggest kitchens in the world by that point. I studied my ass off, learned everything I could from people who didn't see food when they cooked; they saw *art*.

"I spent *years* of my life making sure everything was perfect, Nick. Every temperature. Every cut of meat down to the millimeter. Every glaze and truffle until it was all I could think about. Even when I was asleep I dreamt it. I practiced and I practiced until every tiny *excruciating* detail was fucking perfect. Because that's what it was…this perfect machine. *I* was perfect."

Sandi stared at her reflection but the phantom's smile had faded.

"They appointed me head chef within a year, which was unheard of at that age, never mind the fact I'm a woman. People had their opinions about it, but it only made me push harder. Hearing all their bullshit made me hungrier. Angrier. I was there to do what I set out to do, and nobody was going to tell me that I couldn't."

Sandi stepped closer to the glass and the imposter did too. She pressed her palm down on the mirror and the imposter did the same. The vibrations stirred in the glass, growing louder.

"I made it my personal mission to make the Noma the greatest restaurant in the world. I was going to take this two-star Michelin restaurant and elevate it to a level they'd never fucking seen, and then all those pricks would understand that I wasn't a joke. That I wasn't some talentless washed-up cook from the slums who didn't know what she was doing. I was going to get them that third star."

"Wait," Nick said. "Michelin? Like the tire company?"

"Actually, yes," Sandi half-laughed, half-sobbed.

Nick stepped in front of her, shutting out the imposter in the mirror.

"So, the year comes and goes and they come, these faceless, anonymous critics, judging my entire life on a plate. And after work, I'd go home every night and drink a glass of chardonnay, just waiting for the news that I'd changed everything. We'd got the star and I was the hero and everyone would eat their words just like they ate my food."

A moment of silence settled in, even the unnerving vibration of metal calming to a standstill.

"But we didn't. And I wasn't. Because that's life. That is our shitty, fucked-up reality and we have to live through it because that's what we do. We keep going, full of holes. Full of pain and…suffering. Regret."

Sandi's eyes shut and she turned her back to him, ashamed.

"I left after that. I moved back to the States and got a job working at a *Denny's* of all places. Jesus Christ," she said, and she began sobbing harder then, taking the pieces of her shattered dreams and seeing them again for the first time in forever. "So, imagine my surprise when, the year after I leave, the Noma is named 'The Best Restaurant in the World.' But they never got their star," she said, strangely relieved. "They never got their star."

"You *were* the star, Sandi," Nick said. He might never understand the intricacies of cooking foie gras (much less know what foie gras *was*), but he understood what it meant to be human, the expectations that came with that, and what it was like to have the world kick the shit out of you when you were already at your lowest.

Sandi began sobbing harder and Nick tenderly wrapped her in his arms, letting her head rest against his chest. Her body was racked with shudders and he held her tighter.

"I was in Manhattan once," he said, and Sandi stayed there pressed against his chest with her eyes squeezed closed, listening to the beat of his heart, relishing a moment that was long overdue. "This was before Rachel was born. I had a job in the city, and I found this little place when I was walking down the street. This little hole-in-the-wall called Serendipity 3."

If Sandi knew what it was, she didn't tell him.

"It's the middle of summer and it's scorching hot outside and I'm covered in sweat and this guy standing in line next to me, he leans over to me and he whispers something," Nick said, lowering his voice. "He says, 'Hey, kid. They have a sundae here that's a thousand dollars. Maybe someday, huh?' he says. A *thousand dollars*, Sandi. I stood there with that asshole and his smug smile, sweating my ass off mind you, and I know it sounds crazy, I know it sounds absolutely fucking ridiculous, but in that moment, that sundae sounded like the most delicious thing on the entire fucking planet. And the fact that I couldn't have it only made me want it more."

Sandi was quiet now, and he felt her steady heartbeat against his as it calmed to its regular pace.

"The 'Golden Opulence Sunday' it's called," Nick recounted. "I guess they serve it in this fancy crystal goblet. It's got—"

"Tahitian vanilla ice cream," Sandi said, much to his surprise. "Vanilla beans from Madagascar. Amedei Porcelana Chocolate—the rarest, most expensive chocolate in the world, straight from Tuscany." She recited the ingredients from memory, her tone somber yet invested. "A gold, sugar-forged Orchid that takes eight hours to prepare. Candied fruit flown in from Paris. Grand Passion Caviar," she said, looking up at him, the light coming back to her eyes. "And last but not least, actual 23-karat edible gold leaf covering every inch of it."

"That's right." Nick smiled, nodding his head. "There are a lot of things I regret in my life, Sandi. Things I wish I'd done differently. Moments like those I wish I could do over again. But you..." he said. "I never took chances because I never wanted to know what it's like to fail. I mean, if you don't try to do something, you can't fail at it, right?"

Sandi looked at him, hopeful, drawn to this new side of him.

"But you...you *did* everything. You took every chance, made every mistake that you could and you kept pushing. You're fearless in a way that I've never been. And this reflection," he said, stepping away from the mirror, revealing Sandi's imposter, "is *not* you. It's not even fucking close.

"And when we get out of here, I'm going to take you and Rachel and we're going to take a little vacation to Serendipity 3, and we're going to eat a thousand-dollar sundae because I want to know what that tastes like. But more importantly, we *deserve* to have good things in our lives. We're not dead—not yet—and I am not wasting one more second of my life being scared to do all the things that I want to do, whether it's eating ice cream or fixing a mistake I should have fixed a long time ago."

Sandi smiled sheepishly, blinking her sparkling dark eyes, and said, "It's a date."

SCARLETT

HARPER WAS AT it again. Scarlett and Beau watched as she crouched down, waving her hands at an invisible barrier. Her backpack was laying on the ground next to her, and Rachel standing next to that, her face fixed in a dream-like state. Harper looked ridiculous, but as far as Scarlett could tell, she couldn't have cared less. She might as well have been alone in the house at this point. She'd hardly said two words to Scarlett or Beau since Rachel had joined their group.

The winding hall they'd made their way through had transformed somewhere in the last quarter mile, going from a rigid Tudor home to something out of the dream world. None of the lines or contours made any sense. Shapes were distorted. Colors were ashen and diffused. Scarlett had even seen a door at one point that bore no hinges nor knob. And with the exception of a rat, not much else could have made use of it, the door barely twelve inches tall. She imagined a tiny mouse walking around the house in a suit and tie and found herself giggling at the thought. Was it so crazy though? She'd seen stranger things. Floating lanterns. Rivers of blood. Colossal horrors drifting in the cosmos.

She shuddered.

They'd found their way to an archway. Strings of the black viscous substance slinked down, pooling on the floor below. They'd been careful not to go near it and Harper had quipped something about not having her sample kit. Scarlett assumed she was referring to the other bags lost during the attack.

Beau quietly watched Harper work, his face a cross between disgust and contempt. His arms were folded across his chest, a tanned triangle of skin peeking out of the top of his button-up. He was leaning against a doorframe that looked like it was sculpted out of soft cheese.

"Harper?" Scarlett asked. "You know, I thought maybe if you saw us staring at you long enough, you'd tell us what you were doing."

Harper didn't look up, only kept feeling the air.

"So…what are you doing?"

Beau shook his head, fishing out a pack of cigarettes and tugging one free with his teeth. He snapped open a lighter and Scarlett snatched the cigarette out of his mouth before the flame could touch it.

"Hey, what the hell you think you're doin'!" he said.

"We've got kids in here," she said, smacking the cigarette to his chest. "Give it a rest for a minute, will you?" She turned to Harper. "Harper, what're you doing? We need to keep moving."

"I'm checking for cold spots," Harper said. She slid her knees across the floor, careful not to touch any of the black goo from the ceiling. "I felt something when we crossed through this threshold."

"Jesus Christ," Beau spat. "Look. I wasn't gonna say anything—"

"Oh good, what a relief," Harper said.

"Ain't it obvious what's goin' on here? You bringin' all your fancy rods and knickknacks thinkin' you're gonna find something when the truth is starin' you right in the face."

Harper waited for the punchline.

"It's aliens," Beau said, serious as cancer. "Same kind that come from outer space."

Harper looked at Scarlett, lost for words.

"A sound theory, Mr. Winchester," she said.

Scarlett looked at Beau and he shook his head. She flashed him a nervous smile, walking over to Harper.

"Harper, I know that you're 'having a moment,' or whatever—after what happened to your friend outside. I think we all are. But we don't have time to sit around playing ghost hunter right now."

Harper's hands dropped and she exhaled sharply. "As inconvenient as it may be, since you can't seem to remember how to get out of here, we've got all the time in the world. So you'll have to excuse me while I try and get done the one thing I came here to do rather than engage in a dialogue with a brute marginally more intelligent than a chimpanzee."

"Who you callin' a chimp?!" Beau said, rushing forward.

"Whoa whoa, relax!" Scarlett said, shoving him away. "Walk it off, big guy."

Scarlett shook her head, clearly frustrated. "Really, Harper?"

Harper's head fell back and she exhaled, looking up at her like she'd caught herself being ill-mannered. Bad form, she thought.

"I watched every single one of your interviews, Scarlett. Did you know that? Every YouTube episode. Every post, or tweet. Everything."

Scarlett shook her head.

"I've studied them. I've studied you." She ran her tongue across the back of her teeth. "I've read every research paper. Every shred of information and every half-baked theory there is about this place, including your own."

"Ummm...thank you?"

"Until there is undeniable proof, your claims are never going to be substantiated. *That* is what I came here for, and that is what I intend to do."

Scarlett frowned. "Your friend is out there somewhere. Jackson is out there too." She reached up and pressed her palm into the wall, the surface indenting like dough. "There are a lot worse places in this house, Harper, and you do not want to see them. *Believe me.*"

Harper began tracing her hands through the air again like a conductor, composing her very own symphony for the dead.

"Don't you even care?" Scarlett asked. "Don't you give two shits that that woman, a 'friend' of yours, is lost in this house right now?"

"No," Harper said. "And do you want to know why?"

"Why?"

"Two reasons." Harper stood up, dusting her hands on her thighs. "You said you died here?"

"Yes."

Beau scoffed somewhere behind her, and Scarlett said, "Shut it."

"You said you lived so many lifetimes in this house that you lost count," Harper said.

"I did," Scarlett said.

Harper gazed around the room and it was like she was disappointed. Like something was missing that she thought she would have found by now.

"What's your point?" Scarlett asked.

"If you did die all those times, if you really do think you died in this house, over and over again, then according to you, we should have all the time in the world. That's number one."

"And number two?"

Harper bent over, tugging her pack off the ground and sliding it on. "Park came here for the same reason I did: to find proof." Harper walked past her and Beau, venturing to the end of the hall.

"Look," Scarlett said, jogging up beside her. "I'm all for your little 'saving Winterview party,' but if we're going to do that, we need to find the others first. Our best chance of surviving this place is *together*. I learned that the hard way."

Harper stopped at a set of double doors. She grabbed the handles and threw them open. A powerful breeze rushed out like a flood of ice water, fluttering her ruby-red locks.

Harper was a black silhouette in front of a wall of gray light, her stringy arms stretched out at her sides, propping the doors open.

A library. Only it wasn't any library. It was the exact same one she'd stood in only a year earlier. The same nautical star. The same towering bookcases. Tall arched windows. And a rolling ladder fixed to the higher floors.

But more importantly: proof.

Of everything. The architects. The house. The Oblivion Stone. Dante Greystarr. The journal. Everything she needed to prove she wasn't the basket case everyone in the world seemed to have her pegged as.

She sprinted past Harper, cutting over the nautical star and swinging around the first corner, her Converse skidding across the tile. Her shoes hit a wet patch and sent her skating into a wall of hardcovers. The jolt jarred a few books loose; they rained from the shelves, one of them smacking the back of her head with a thump.

"Scarlett, wait," Harper shouted behind her.

She shrugged it off, screeching to a halt to find the same wooden desk waiting exactly as she'd left it.

Only it wasn't.

She rushed forward, horrified to find it completely barren. She gawked at it, confused. The wood; it had changed. The grain shimmered, polished with a high luster.

Harper and Beau cautiously approached from the hall, stepping into the light. Rachel kept back, hidden behind Beau.

Scarlett jerked open a drawer.

Empty.

Then another.

Empty again.

She pulled out the last, finding not so much as a dust bunny.

"What is it?" Harper's voice.

Scarlett turned to find the woman leaning in over her shoulder, searching the desk with her large eyes. "The same one where you found the photo? The one of the Hallidays?"

"It's gone. Everything's gone," she snapped, slamming the drawer closed.

"What is?" Harper asked.

"There was a journal here, Harper. That man—the same one Hannah said built all of this, his diary was here. That picture I found, it was here, in *this* desk."

Harper looked down at the desk and ran her finger over the surface. "You're sure? This is the same desk?"

"Positive. Everything looks different, though."

"What do you mean?" Harper asked. "Different how?"

Scarlett's gaze drifted about the room. Beau was standing near the entrance, studying a book he'd taken off the shelf. "I can't explain it. Everything looks the same, but it's not. It's changed. I can feel it." She inhaled, then breathed out, frustrated. "Have you ever walked into a place, a room, a house, whatever, and you know something's changed but you can't quite tell what?"

"Yes, I suppose," Harper said.

"This was old." Scarlett reached down and tapped her fingers on the desk. "It didn't look like this before."

Harper blinked. "What did it look like?"

"An antique for fuck's sake!" Scarlett barked. "And there were people floating in here. Bodies."

"Someone was here?" Harper asked, interested.

"YES!" Scarlett shouted. "That's what I've been trying to tell you!"

Harper flinched, composing herself. She put her hands on Scarlett's shoulders. "Whatever is going on here, Scarlett, you said yourself that things change in the house. That they're not consistent."

"Mighty Mouse ain't wrong." Beau slammed the book closed with a spray of dust, chucking it over.

Scarlett caught it. Harper leaned over her shoulder to get a closer look.

The hardcover was bound in a grainy leather, the cover free of any markings or blemishes. Scarlett turned the book over in her hands to find the spine blank. She flipped open the cover with a leathery creak.

Inside, the parchment was inked with bizarre symbols.

"What is all this?" Scarlett asked, scanning the characters. "Some sort of code?"

Harper took the book from her hands, turning the heavy pages over. "No, it's not a code…"

"Hope you two don't plan on doin' any readin' anytime soon," Beau said, peering down at another book. "Shit might as well be written in fuckin' Greek."

Scarlett looked at Harper and rolled her eyes, flipping through a few more pages. "Look—there's letters," Scarlett added. A crude *M* among the sea of symbols. Other letters from the modern alphabet were peppered throughout the hundreds of pages.

"And there," Harper said, pointing. "Numbers. Some of these glyphs are cuneiform."

"Cuneiform?" Scarlett asked.

"The oldest form of writing in the world. Older than Egyptian hieroglyphs." Harper explained. "Even older than Jesus Christ. The majority of the samples archeologists have unearthed are engraved on clay tablets. And some are carved into stone."

Beau scoffed, much to Harper's chagrin.

Harper looked up from the book, cross. "Did you have something constructive to add to our conversation, Mr. Winchester?"

"Just think you're wastin' your time is all. Unless you can read languages a thousand years old, there ain't no answers in these things. Just a whole buncha nonsense."

Harper closed the tome. "I'm not all that surprised you'd think history is a waste of time. I can't imagine a person looting a restricted area would see much use in books let alone language."

"You don't know me," he said.

"You're right. I don't. I doubt anyone does."

Scarlett could see where this was going and she didn't like it.

"Harper?" she said. "You're the stick—he's the bear. You know what that makes me? The *bear spray*. Please don't make me be the bear spray, Harper."

She hoped by some small chance it would end there, and assumed it did when Beau went back to wandering the aisles, letting his fingertips run over the leather spines.

"But I know your *type*," Harper pressed.

"Don't poke the bear, Harper," Scarlett said. "Seriously."

Harper ignored her. "Should I make an educated guess?"

Beau stopped walking and turned around, standing tall.

"It was your father, wasn't it?" Harper said. "He had an affinity for the finer things in life. Cigarettes. Alcohol. Bourbon maybe. He'd start in the morning, not long after he'd awoken, and by the evenings he was totally gone."

Beau glared at her.

"Harper, I don't think now is such a—" Scarlett began.

"He'd hit you sometimes," Harper continued. "You'd go to school, and when the teachers would ask you what happened, you'd lie. The ironic part is that you'd cover it up out of pride. Because you didn't want anyone to think you were weak. And then you'd go home, scared, and it would start all over again. Eventually, you got the itch too. So, you started hitting other boys so that people would feel what *you* felt. Before long you got expelled, and things got worse. *He* got worse. He'd put cigarettes out on your skin," she said, nodding to a molted scar on his forearm, "tear into you any way that he could. And every day you'd have to come up with a reason not to kill him.

"Years went by, seasons came and went, and eventually you left, or he *died*, whichever came first. Until it was just you. Only you."

Beau marched forward, and Scarlett's eyes went wide. *Goddamn it, Harper.* Now she'd done it. "Hold on a minute, Beau," Scarlett said, inserting herself between them. "Clearly she isn't thinking straight," Scarlett snapped at Harper.

Harper didn't react. Didn't attempt to extinguish Beau's blistering anger. She only stood there, waiting to see what the deranged mountain man would do.

Scarlett threw up her hands, shoving an incensed Beau back.

"How'd I do, Mr. Winchester?" Harper asked, smug.

"All right, Dr. Phil," he spat. "What about you?"

"Me?" Harper asked.

"Yeah. You. You and your diplomas and your ivy league this and that, slinging your psychobabble bullshit everywhere those giant bug eyes look."

Harper snickered, folding her arms.

"You might have everyone else fooled around here with your little 'ghost hunt' alibi in this haunted house spaceship or whatever the fuck you wanna call it, but you and I both know that's not why you're really here."

Scarlett looked at Harper. Huh?

"What's he talking about, Harper?" she asked.

Harper's laugh wore thin. A crinkle formed between her eyebrows.

"Oh, what, you think I didn't know?" Beau said. "You think you're some sort of 'expert' on people, lookin' down your nose at the rest of us like we're shit stuck to the bottom of your boot. Well, I got news for you, lady, you might think you know people, but *I've* gotten to know them pretty damned good, too, over the years, Doc. And the one thing they all got in common? They're *fucking liars*. And that starts with *you*," he growled. "I ain't ever been nothin' I don't claim to be. But you...well, don't take some fancy degree for me to see you're not here to help nobody but yourself. So why don't you cut the bullshit and tell us what it is you're really doin' here."

Harper was silent, her face turned to stone.

The corner of Beau's mouth pulled into a smirk. Justice was served as far as he was concerned. He looked at Harper with disgust, then turned his back on them, wandering back into the aisles.

"What's he talking about, Harper?" Scarlett asked. Had she missed something? What exactly was going on here?

"Nothing," Harper said. "He doesn't know what he's talking about." She took the volume and set it back on the shelf, sliding it in.

Beau laughed, shouting out, "Keep tellin' yourself that, Doc."

"I don't know why you have to provoke him," Scarlett said. "Aren't shrinks supposed to help people feel better about their feelings?"

"Not this one," Harper dismissed.

Scarlett rolled her eyes and walked to the wall, sliding another volume off the shelf. She opened it, sorting through the pages hastily. Page after page of a seemingly endless array of obscure characters.

"It's the same. They're all the same," Scarlett whispered.

An eerie silence settled over the library and that was when she noticed it.

The sound of rain.

It was light, but she could hear it clear as day.

"The breeze," Scarlett said. "Do you guys smell that?"

"That's the rain, Einstein." Beau's voice echoed from the aisle nearest them. "Door must be open somewhere."

She looked up to find Rachel pointing around a bend on the other side of the library. The girl stared at them, emotionless, like a signpost anchored in the floor.

"Harper, look," she said.

Scarlett smelled the water and thought of home. She smiled, rushing over to find a spill of leaden light washing in through a pair of double doors that had been pried open.

Harper stumbled up beside her, shocked.

The city. The exit.

But how?

"Winterview?" Harper said. "I don't understand."

Scarlett stared at the two open doors, not trusting her own two eyes. Was the house mocking them? Showing them what it wanted them to see only to rip it away at the last second? Stripping them of their hope?

Beau rounded the bend with a book in his hand. He looked up and saw the exit and dropped the book on the floor.

Scarlett looked at each of them, wondering why they hadn't sprung for the door. But she knew the answer already. It was because the others were still here. Jackson. Park. And if they didn't come back with Isabelle, they were as good as dead. Dale, too.

"We need to get help," Harper said.

Scarlett took in the mist while it swarmed and flowed and danced for them, giving them glimpses of the gray city.

"No," Scarlett said, shaking her head. "It's too dangerous. They could be out there still."

"It's day," Harper said.

"So what?"

"Hate to say it, but Hannibal Lector's right," Beau said. "I'll take my chances in the streets."

"And what about her?" Scarlett said, gesturing at Rachel. "Are we just going to leave her here in the house?"

Beau was silent.

An engine. Loud. Out in the street.

"Tell me I'm not the only one hearing that?" Scarlett asked. "It sounds like a truck?"

Harper took a step forward, cocking an ear to the gray, then held there at the threshold, waiting.

Rachel waited patiently behind the trio, curiously watching the fog crawl through the streets, the rain drizzling down in needle-like droplets.

The fog suddenly swirled to life out in the street. A streak of black exploded from the mist outside. Scarlett couldn't see much other than a neon glow along the roof. She got the impression of a heavily fortified R.V., a vehicle straight out of the apocalypse, but it was gone before she could know for certain.

"A vehicle! There!" Harper shouted. She broke into a sprint, dashing outside.

"Harper, wait! Don't go out there!" Scarlett reached out to grab her and only managed to pull her scarf off.

"God dammit, Harper!" she screamed. She smacked the door with an open palm as Harper was engulfed in a puff of fog.

She turned around to find Beau eyeing the fog.

"Watch her," she ordered, jabbing a finger at Rachel. "Do not let her out of your sight. You hear me?"

"You stay with him," she said to Rachel. "Right here until we get back. Got it?"

Rachel blinked at her, completely vacant.

"What do I look like, her damn babysitter?" he sneered.

"You want your fifty grand?" she snapped. "Okay, then shut up and do it."

Beau glared at her and turned, starting away.

Scarlett reached for him, putting a gentle hand on his shoulder.

"Please," she begged. "*Please*."

Beau exhaled, exasperated, and she took that as his indication of approval.

Scarlett spun on her heels and began running.

The musty scent of parchment and leather whisked by, giving way to rain and stone and wet earth, and before she knew what was happening, she was out of the house, speeding into the rain.

Into the fog.

Back in the house, nestled high on the ceiling in a lattice of wooden supports, something stirred.

Something that had crawled in from the rain.

Something hungry.

JACKSON

"IS THAT…*CANDY?"* Park asked, her eyes bright with elation. An entire world of sweets lay before a papery, bright sky.

Park went to take a step forward and Jackson grabbed her arm.

"Don't go out there," he warned. "It might look like candy, but it's not."

"Jackson," Park said, "how are you not even a *little* amazed by this? I mean look out there!" she shouted, the excitement in her voice evident. "We're never going to have another chance to see something like this again in our lifetime."

"You're right," Jackson said, nodding. "And I would like to *continue* that lifetime for as long as I can."

"Doesn't this mean something, though? Us finding all these doors here?" She twisted her head, taking in all the doors vanishing into the endless dim hall. "What if they're all gateways? What if each of these doors leads to a whole other world?"

"I don't think they're meant for us, Park."

"How can you say that?"

"I like to think I'm a little wiser than the last time around. And being wise means not taking *unnecessary risks*. Candyland is first on that list."

"Ah, c'mon," Park said. "Where's your sense of adventure?"

Jackson looked at her. "I left it back in Winterview, where the streets have potholes, not peppermints."

"Don't you understand what this means though, Jackson? It's the discovery of the century. Maybe the biggest ever." Park turned back to the dazzling panorama of sweets. Floating islands shaped like strawberries reflected in Park's eager eyes. "It means we're not alone. It means there's infinitely more out there than we ever dreamed of. It's—"

"Not for us," Jackson said, dashing her hopes. "We have a home. *I* have a home. And she's running around here somewhere."

He grabbed the door handle, about to pull it closed.

The wooden frame between them exploded in splinters.

Jackson fell back on his butt and Park lurched the opposite direction, tumbling down a short hill.

Jackson whipped his head to the right to find Morgana at the mouth of the theater hall, the gun trained on him. Half her face was bathed in pink neon light from the lobby.

"Get up," she ordered.

Without thinking, he dove through the open doorway, landing hard on his stomach and rolling down the hill.

He crashed into Park's legs.

Chocolate.

He could smell it. The sugar. The milk. He opened his eyes to find the ground was chocolate. He fumbled for a piece with shaky fingers, finding a small chunk that had broken free when he'd hit. He blinked, holding it up to his eyes, and ran his tongue over it.

His eyes fluttered. He shoved it into his mouth and chewed, and goddamn if that wasn't the best chocolate he'd ever had in his life. For a second, he imagined he'd died and went to heaven, that maybe he would be content to live out eternity here in a house made of gingerbread.

And then he heard Park's voice.

"Get up!" She grabbed at his jacket, trying to pull him up.

Jackson groaned, stirring.

"Jackson! We need to move!"

He pushed himself up sluggishly, his head spinning, and then he was on his feet.

A crack of lightning and him and Park ducked. Winged things scattered into the pastel sky. Birds? No, not birds. Then what?

"Come on!" Park screamed.

He was tripping forward, Park towing him like a dinghy. He watched the chocolate trail, glimpsed marbled rocks embedded here and there, thinking how impossible it all was.

He could hear Park panting in front of him and he slowed, the two sidestepping behind one of the gingerbread houses.

Park pressed her back to the wall, poking her head out and looking behind them.

"I don't see anything," she said, breathing hard. "Where are you, you crazy bitch?"

Jackson took the opportunity to look up at their new world, his view completely unobstructed for the first time.

An ominous black castle sat atop a sprawling mountain range, perched atop cliffs formed of pure chocolate. Some of the landscape below had collapsed as if there had been a mudslide. Lengths of crimson ropes crisscrossed high above their heads, disappearing out of sight. He spied more houses on the floating islands, and wondered if anyone dwelled in them.

His head was beginning to calm. He felt a throb in his temples, but he wasn't sure if it was the house or the fall.

Park crouched down, slinking to the other end of the wall and peering out. "I don't see her," she hissed.

Jackson stepped over and looked out from behind the house, finding the trail they'd taken deserted.

He listened to a slow, gelatinous squelching. He looked over the hill to find a river of chocolate sluggishly passing by below. A stream? No, definitely a river. At least twice as wide as a house.

"Park," he said. "A chocolate river," he whispered.

Park grinned and began to creep back.

A sugar window exploded behind her.

A pair of arms flew out and grabbed her, dragging her inside.

Jackson rushed forward in time to see Morgana hurl Park onto a table. The surface cracked in half (graham cracker?), the legs buckled, and the whole thing collapsed to the ground.

Park was unfazed. She scrambled to her feet as Morgana slid a knife from her coat, plunging it down with her whole weight.

Park quickly grabbed part of the broken table and threw it out in front of her, wielding it as a shield. The cracker cushioned the blow but the tip punched through and jabbed Park in the chest, drawing blood. Park shrieked and kicked out, catching Morgana in the stomach with a hollow thud, knocking her back.

Jackson braced himself on the broken window frame, awkwardly climbing through. A shard of sugar glass raked across his stomach and he yelped.

Morgana saw him out of the corner of her eye and drew the pistol from her belt, pointing the barrel in his direction.

Jackson's pant leg snagged on a shard of glass from the windowsill. He heard a tear; he lost his balance, crashing to the ground as two bullets blew chunks out of the gingerbread wall.

Click. Click.

Jackson looked up to find Morgana's pale hand slipping into her coat. She was out of bullets. Her crazed eyes burned into him.

No time. He looked around, his eyes landing on a candy cane lamp. He scrambled to his feet and jerked the lamp from its place, ripping a cord of licorice out of the wall. He took the giant candy cane solidly in his hands. He roared, breaking it over his knee to form a makeshift club.

Morgana snapped in a magazine as the candy cane exploded across her face in chalky peppermint fragments. The impact snapped her head so hard that her body spun, crashing into a pretzel rocking chair and topping over.

Park was on her feet, her chest heaving, a hand clutching the fresh blood on her chest.

Morgana shot up from behind the chair.

A blade whizzed past Jackson's head, thudding into the wall.

He ducked, diving behind the counter as another blade cut through the air.

Park sidestepped it and charged.

Morgana saw her coming and stood up, unwavering.

Park roared, tackling her like a linebacker. They hurtled into the front door, exploding it open and spilling onto the chocolate trail. They screamed and grunted, clawing at each other before rolling over the hill toward the river.

Jackson dodged the edible debris sprinkled throughout the living room, launching himself out the front door in time to see the women spill onto the riverbank below.

Park strained, taking Morgana's throat in her hands while Morgana gasped for air, staring up at her with her split pupil, her face reddening. Morgana slid another knife from her coat and arched the blade through the air.

Park caught her wrist, holding it inches from her side.

She strained, the blade inching closer as Morgan's face contorted into a wicked grin.

Park abruptly released Morgana's throat with her hand. Her eyes narrowed, fierce.

Jackson watched the madness unfold as he descended from the side of the hill, carving a path through the dark chocolate as he got closer.

Morgana's eyes went wide as Park threw a hard punch, mashing the woman's porcelain face. The impact caused Morgana's knife-wielding hand to go limp; Park reached over while she was stunned and snatched it from her, taking it firmly in her hand and pitching her whole body's weight down behind it.

The blade punched into the Morgana's upper chest and a vein of red squirted across her white neck like blood on snow. Morgana's eyes shot open, bloodshot and wet. She let out a bloodcurdling scream, throwing her knees up and launching Park over her head.

Jackson tripped, sliding the rest of the way down the hill.

Morgana ripped the blade out of her chest and flung it out of view. She flipped over, climbing to her feet and rushing Park. She dropped low, getting leverage, and threw a hard uppercut, knocking Park out cold. She reached down and grabbed the woman from behind, dragging her into the shallows of the chocolate river.

Park stirred. She reached out, attempting to grab onto something, anything. She bucked her legs, splashing dark chocolate.

Morgana swung around and slapped Park's arms away, straddling her. Her fingers snaked around Park's throat, easing her down.

Park's face disappeared under the opaque chocolate, and Morgana's smile widened.

A lash of green lightning streaked across the sky.

Morgana looked up while Park flailed beneath her.

Jackson didn't think; he wrapped his arms around Morgana's thin torso, throwing his weight and flinging her off Park. Morgana rolled like a cat, landing on one knee, her arms out at her sides, glaring at him.

Another spectacular crash; the sky dimmed like the sun was dying. Jackson looked up to see a black blur racing through the clouds. He didn't want to know what it was, didn't care. He waded through the shallow of chocolate to find Park laying in the river, hacking out her lungs. He bent down and carefully pulled her from the chocolate with a long squelch, heaving her away from the river.

Morgana watched the blur flit past the castle, mesmerized.

It was coming this way.

"Time to move, Park," he said, and he doubted his urgency was getting through to her. The woman looked half dead, covered in chocolate and blood head to toe, her hair like seaweed.

And then it was there.

He and Park shuffled away from Morgana, back toward the base of the hill. He decided to circumvent the hill altogether, opting for ground that would be easier to climb. He shepherded Park along, the two of them shambling like zombies, cresting the hill while Morgana studied the shape rocketing through the eerie sky.

Another sonic boom. The earth shook beneath his boots.

The blur struck like a bolt of lightning, cratering the shore and turning the chocolate sand to sheets of muddy glass.

Jackson and Park looked back and the threads of reality unraveled a little bit more.

A witch. The same kind he'd seen in fairy tale books his mom used to read him long before she left. Dressed in all black with a tall, pointed hat, the bizarre creature held some type of a wand down at her side, and a small tattered cape slung over her shoulder flapped in a breeze that smelled of vanilla. Her ghastly white skin glistened with a sheen like a snakeskin, and a shiver ran through him. He was glad they were way over here, far away from the horror from the sky.

Morgana eyed the witch, in her pointed hat and intricate black dress, and shook her head. She chuckled, like she couldn't believe what she was seeing, and then calmly slid a knife from her coat.

Jackson and Park watched as Morgana, more fearless and perhaps more stupid than anyone he'd ever met, twirled into a concise spin, maximizing her momentum.

She pitched the knife through the air; the blade whirled end over end, over and over, and it was like watching a scene unfold in slow-motion.

Morgana's smug smile faded.

The blade hung in the air inches from the witch.

The witch raised her hand, her palm up, curiously examining the knife. The witch ran her finger along the razor's edge and her skin separated. The witch held up her finger and watched as the cut worked itself back together, healing.

The witch stared at Morgana with her dead, silver eyes, and blinked.

The knife, suspended in midair, began to vibrate. The blade hummed. The tinny sound of metal crunching. The knife began to shred, threads of steel folding, then knitting together as if it was alive.

"What the hell?" Jackson muttered.

The steel filaments coiled together. Morgana watched as the metal began to glow white, simmering with blinding heat. Tendrils of smoke drifted into the air. The steel buckled, snapping taut, and then the mass simply dropped out of the air, spearing the dirt below.

Morgana's eyes narrowed. She went to reach into her coat and the witch burst into a smoky shadow, solid one minute and vapor the next.

She rematerialized, seizing Morgana by the throat and lifting her off her feet. Morgana went to swing the blade and the witch squeezed her throat.

Morgana's eyes watered; the blade slipped out of her hand and stabbed into the shore. She grappled at the witch's hand, powerless. Morgana's fingers suddenly wilted; she watched in horror as they began drooping like melted taffy. Jackson and Park gasped as her skin darkened, turning more and more red, spreading to her wrists.

She finally met her match, Jackson thought.

"Do it," Park urged, hungry for revenge.

Jackson looked over and Park had a crazed look in her eye. He would have been more surprised if she didn't; she'd nearly been drowned in a river of chocolate.

Her hands transforming to taffy, Morgana fought while the witch choked the life out of her.

The witch hauled her closer, and Jackson saw that Morgana's body was nearly a foot off the ground, her feet dangling.

The witch's silver eyes glinted like mirrors. She breathed in long and slow, as if taking in a delicious dessert, carefully studying Morgana's bone structure. The monster blinked once, dreamily, and then released her.

Morgana collapsed to her knees in a splash of chocolate, cradling her sad, misshapen hands. She glared up at the witch, ready to accept her fate.

The witch leveled the wand at her. The spike began to hum audibly, pulsing with brilliant emerald light.

Morgana's eyes closed, exhausted, as her elongated fingers retracted, reforming themselves. Jackson watched as muscle wrapped bone, Morgana's pale skin sheathing over the muscle. She opened her eyes to find her hands fully restored. She looked up at the witch in awe, wiggling her fingers. She clutched at her chest, feeling for the puncture from Park, but it was gone.

The witch had restored her.

"What. The. Fuck," Park uttered.

"We need to go—now," Jackson said.

Morgana watched as they turned and ran, disappearing back into the house. They'd escaped—for now. The witch, or whatever she was, stared down at her, emotionless. The twin moons that served as her eyes glowed, and Morgana had never seen anything so beautiful. She admired the creature before her, thought maybe she'd been like her before she became whatever she was now. Morgana had no idea why, but for whatever reason the monster had elected to spare her.

The monster stood against a world of candy, her stark black clothes a powerful contrast before all manner of candy stripes, gumdrops, and decorative frosting. The witch held there a moment longer, gazing down at her, and then simply turned and began walking down the beach, her cape fluttering behind her.

Morgana looked beyond the witch's shrinking silhouette and beheld a castle high on the mountain of chocolate, and wondered if maybe that was the witch's destination. Her home. She wondered if there were more of them. Maybe a lot more.

An adventure for another time, perhaps, she thought.

Morgana shook her head like she was waking up from a bizarre fever dream, then collected the knife from the sand, tucking it back in the sheath on her vest. She ran forward to find the other knife, the one the witch had transfigured, and pulled it free from the shore. The blade glimmered in her hands; the handle engraved with unknown symbols.

Morgana took in her reflection as the blackened blade glimmered with destiny, a gift from one monster to another, and began her trek back to the house, new and improved.

HARPER

AN ARMORED VEHICLE.

"Hey!" she called, waving her arms. "Over here! Please!"

But the vehicle kept on like a passing train, rumbling away, its length absorbed by the thick spell of fog draping the street until only a mirage remained.

It was some variety of heavy military escort. She'd glimpsed a large turret on the roof and steel bars over reinforced windows. Heavy armored plating. Basically, a roaming fortress. Was the Red Sky conducting another operation here?

"Goddammit, Harper!" Scarlett was running out behind her. "What the hell are you doing?!"

Harper pointed, her lungs burning. "It's gone. Down there."

The rain was relentless. Sections of the road were partially underwater. Her hair was wet; her clothes soaked through with bone chilling water. She felt the squelch of water in her socks and boots. Storm clouds growled overhead, hungry, and Harper beheld veins of lightning in the distance over the serrated mountaintops.

Scarlett stamped through the water, coming to a stop beside her. "We need to get inside," she advised, and her voice was nearly drowned out by the storm. "Those freaks in the white robes could be crawling all over this place right now."

"No," Harper argued. "What we *need* is to find help and get that little girl out of here so I can resume my research and find out what's happening to Winterview."

"Screw your research!" Scarlett snapped.

"And the truth shall set you free." Harper looked at her, taken aback. "You think I'm wasting my time? Is that it?" It wasn't a question.

Harper listened to the rain falling in droves, watching the droplets slip down Scarlett's face.

"You can't..." Scarlett began. "I know you think there has to be some sort of explanation for all of this, but there isn't. At least not one you or I can understand. Sometimes bad things just happen. You can't change them, no matter how badly you wish that you could."

Harper turned her gaze skyward, shutting her eyes and feeling the angry patter of the rain on her face.

You can't change them, no matter how badly you wish you could.

Katie's face came to her. The strawberry curls that fell over her shoulders. Her kind, innocent blue eyes. Doing homework. Playing board games at the kitchen table.

Harper felt herself begin to fall apart and drew in a long breath of cold air, grateful her tears were lost in the rain.

"I don't know why you're doing this," Scarlett said. "But whatever it is, you need to let it go before you get yourself killed."

Scarlett's words struck a chord with her.

She looked at Scarlett, strangely comforted to have the girl at her side despite the mountain of skepticism she felt toward her. "I'm sorry, Scarlett," she said. "They were wrong about you. I know that now."

"The cultists—"

"There is no one here, Scarlett," she smiled. "They've gone."

Scarlett rattled her head. "You don't know that."

Harper looked back but couldn't see Rachel or Beau in the house.

"Tell me something, Scarlett," Harper said. "How is it that the entrance to the house is open yet its currently daylight outside?"

The low rumble of thunder shook down from the mountains.

Scarlett looked around, noticing the sky darkening.

"I thought the house seals at dawn?" Harper said, and she was almost yelling now. The rain was getting more intense by the minute.

"It does," Scarlett said.

"Well, apparently not, because we're standing here and as you can see," she said, waving her arm, "the house is still wide open. And not just that, but according to everyone else *including* yourself, anyone that leaves the house doesn't survive it without hypnosis yet here we are."

"And I *told you*," Scarlett said, "things are different now. You think we could have walked out that front door and still have our heads screwed on straight if something hadn't changed? Not everything is happening the same way it did last time."

Harper rolled her eyes.

"I've been thinking about that. About what happened to Brent. The guard."

"I'm listening."

"I think it wasn't that they went into the house that was the problem," she said. "I think it's the *when*."

"Elaborate."

"It's like a roller coaster. You have your highs and your lows. Loops. But when it's first being constructed, the track isn't finished. And what happens if you're on a roller coaster with an unfinished track?"

"You fall off," Harper said.

Scarlett nodded. "Bingo." She leaned in closer. "Everyone who has gone crazy from going inside that place walked inside right after it appeared in the city. I'm talking *days* after it came, Harper. What if in between wherever it came from and here it didn't have enough time to reform itself? What if Brent and that guard went into the house when it was still being realized in this reality before it had a chance to finish?"

Harper began to speak and then stopped, her mouth agape.

"What's wrong?" Scarlett asked.

Harper lightly nudged Scarlett's face the opposite direction.

The buildings; they weren't familiar. They were tall, but not as tall the skyscrapers surrounding the house in Winterview. These ones were only five to eight stories, max.

The fog stretched apart and that was when Harper realized: they weren't in Winterview.

She drew in steady, controlled breaths, watching the environment around them materialize before her eyes.

"Where in the hell..." Scarlett murmured.

Bizarre Gothic and Victorian buildings encircled them. Blood-red oriel windows looked down on the courtyard like spiders' eyes. Harper's gaze fell to the road and she realized these weren't the streets of Winterview at all, with their cracks and potholes. These streets were of a more eloquent variety, assembled with cobblestone, the sidewalks dotted with towering iron lampposts flecked with gold.

A heavy metal grind was coming from somewhere to the left.

"What's that?" Scarlett asked, peering around.

A few feet further, embedded in the road, was a golden disc made up of circular rings. The two women took a few cautious steps closer.

"I've seen one of these before," Scarlett said.

Harper crouched down on her haunches, taking the camera out of her bag and winding the crank.

"Where?" she found herself asking.

Scarlett paced to the other side of the disc, then dropped to one knee, watching the segments spin independent of each other. "The last time we were in the house. There was this..."

"Gallery," Harper said. She remembered Scarlett describing the gallery in one of her YouTube episodes.

Scarlett nodded. "Yeah. There were paintings, and a statue. And this was there, in the middle of the floor."

Harper let off the crank and held the camera up. A wash of blue light brightened the ground and the camera chirped, spitting out another slate. Harper tucked it into her pack, then handed the camera to Scarlett.

"Hold this."

"Harper, no. I'm not doing this with you. We need to get inside *now.*"

Harper's hands fumbled around inside the bag. There. She took the pencil in her hand and spread open the mouth of the bag.

"I'm serious, Harper."

Harper stopped writing and looked up at Scarlett. "These symbols could be critical to figuring out what's going on here, Scarlett. The faster I get them, the faster we go back to the house and find the *actual* exit."

Scarlett crossed her arms, shaking her head. Rain was dripping down both their faces while lightning lashed the sky.

They'd reached an impasse. Harper knew Scarlett wouldn't leave without her, and Scarlett knew Harper wouldn't leave without her research.

"Look," Harper said, "after that spectacle you made of yourself, you of all people could stand to benefit from our discoveries here."

"I don't care about any discoveries, Harper. Don't you get that?"

"Is that right?" Harper asked. "Because I think there is some part of you in there—a very scared part—that wants to know what's going on here as badly as I do. Maybe more."

Scarlett frowned.

Harper continued, "The only difference is that I will do *whatever* it takes to get the answers we need."

A moment of silence passed between them.

"Fine," Scarlett said. "You want to die out here, that's your problem. I'm helping that kid and I'm taking that hick and we're getting the fuck out of here."

Harper looked at her, and her face softened.

Scarlett started marching away through the rain.

"My daughter died," Harper said, and hearing herself say it out loud brought a pain so potent up from the depths of her soul that her entire body went rigid.

Scarlett stopped, looking back over her shoulder with sadness in her eyes.

Harper turned her gaze skyward, watching the black clouds braid together, wringing out dull, cold rain.

"She was thirteen," Harper said, and she felt a tremble in her voice. "She didn't have many friends."

Scarlett listened.

"She liked to read, like you. She always had a book with her." Harper sighed. "I asked her once why she watched your videos, and she told me that they brought her comfort…like you were her friend." She smiled, bittersweet.

Scarlett was standing over her now, the small camera in her hands, looking down at Harper with sadness in her eyes.

"I was asleep and…I didn't even," her voice trailed off. "I woke around three," she said. "I heard this…*sound*—in the bedroom. This creak, like she'd dropped something. I thought maybe she had gotten up to go to the bathroom," and suddenly she was sobbing. "The next morning, when I went to wake her up, she was—"

Harper fell apart sobbing. Scarlett wrapped her arms around her and held her while the rain kept on and the golden disc whirred in the ground.

"I *heard her*, Scarlett," Harper screamed, and it was like she had lost her all over again. "Oh, God, I heard her when the chair had fallen—and I didn't get up. I was so exhausted and I just laid there and went back to sleep and she fucking died in that closet because I didn't have enough sense to check on her and help her!" Harper felt herself withering away to nothing, wilting like a plant in a barren landscape.

Scarlett hugged her harder the harder she cried, until eventually Harper's sobs were lost to the peaceful lull of the rain. Scarlett didn't say anything, only held her, this poor shell of a woman, her head resting on Scarlett's shoulder like she had been vindicated. She was grateful for Scarlett in that moment. She understood then what the rest of the world had seen in her, this quirky yet strangely brave woman.

After a time, Harper removed herself from Scarlett's shoulder, looking at her with tears in her eyes. "I am not leaving here without this, Scarlett. Your reputation may not matter to you, but it's all I have left now. If you really want to help her," she said, motioning at Rachel in the house, "then help me find out how to stop this before it's too late."

Scarlett considered her, and Harper could see the decision came with a heavy toll.

Scarlett relented with a sharp exhale. "You've got *two minutes,*" she said.

Harper smiled, grateful, and Scarlett got to her feet and began winding the camera, wandering away.

Harper wiped the tears from her face, digging her hands into the backpack. She took a moment to breathe, to let herself calm, pushing the sorrow and pain down into that black void in her stomach. She found the pencil, folding open the leather-bound journal and crudely sketching the symbols.

A blue flash went off in her peripheral followed by the camera's mechanical chirp.

"Harper!" Scarlett shouted. "I've got something weird over here!"

The heavy grind of the golden rings slowed.

Harper looked down as the outer of four rings stopped spinning.

Then another. And another.

Harper stumbled back, grabbing the strap of her pack.

The last ring ground to a standstill, and Harper observed a single string of glyphs aligned perfectly across all four rings.

"Harper! Are you listening to me?!" Scarlett shouted.

Harper reached out, stretching her fingertips toward the weathered brass surface. Her hands tingled; adrenaline pumped into her body.

Out of nowhere, the ear-piercing drone of a storm siren tore across the Gothic city, ricocheting around the plaza in painful waves.

Harper's heart skipped a beat; she quickly looked at Scarlett and their eyes locked.

"It's time to go!" Scarlett shouted. She waved her arm and Harper broke into a run.

The sky dimmed to black.

The siren shrieked, rattling her bones.

"What the hell is that?!" Scarlett shouted.

"Some sort of alarm," Harper replied, her voice lost in the wind.

For what, though?

The journal tumbled from Harper's pack as she ran, splashing into a puddle. Harper slid across the cobblestones to a stop.

"Leave it!" Scarlett yelled.

Harper doubled back, diving down and scooping up the journal.

The sky flickered, chased by a roll of heavy thunder. Harper stumbled back as an impossibly long arm crested the rooftop of the nearest building. Something vaguely resembling a giant hand slapped down against the side, knocking loose a rain of shingles.

"Move it, Harper!" Scarlett screamed.

The alarm cut out, replaced by the gentle wash of the rain. Harper was frozen in place, stuck between running for her life and her duties as a scientist. The air turned colder, and she realized her feet were going numb.

A crazed demonic laugh boomed from the other side of the structure. Harper threw her hands over her ears and saw Scarlett doing the same.

Scarlett stood near the entrance to the house, about thirty yards away. She glanced toward the sound, panicked.

Another spell of bizarre laughter echoed over the buildings and the hand shifted on the slanted roof, the fingers tearing into the shingles like a junkyard claw.

A hideous pale face the size of a Winnebago rose like the moon, the mouth fixed in a demented smile, lined with teeth the size of yardsticks. *Humpty Dumpty sat on the wall.* And that's exactly what he looked like. Humpty Dumpty brought to life straight from a child's worst nightmare. Wood crunched as the inside of the building buckled under the thing's massive weight. A second hand emerged, sliding over the roof. The monster chuckled again, apparently enjoying itself, tugging its enormous mass up over the rooftops. Harper saw movement in the shadows and realized something scurried along with the creature, climbing over it like an entourage of cockroaches.

The monster crooned, and Harper saw the glass windows vibrating.

Giant red eyes slid over in its head, settling on her.

"Oh, shit," she said.

"HARPER, RUN!" Scarlett screamed.

And run she did.

BEAU

THEY'D BEEN GONE too long.

He paced the library floor like a nervous dog with too much time, tracking wet boot prints across the six-foot nautical star.

He stopped, chewing his filthy fingernails, and looked over.

The little girl was sitting quietly in a wooden chair, her hands folded in her lap, staring up at him like a doll.

"They shoulda been back by now. This whole thing is fucked," he said, spitting out a nail.

He strode to the doorframe and braced himself there, gazing out at the streets into the silver veil.

"Where the fuck are they?" he said. "Can't see shit in all this fog. Fuckin' idiots should have stayed inside."

He shook his head and paced back and forth, keeping one eye on the girl who had somehow become his problem.

His skin itched. He raked it with his clawed nails hard enough to break the skin. He wondered if Scarlett had gotten in his head. By some fluke of time and space the girl seemed to be light-years more intuitive than the shrink. Maybe because she seemed to be less concerned with the house and more concerned about her new companions.

A thought came to him. The same one that never really left, even when it wasn't at the forefront of his train wreck of a mind.

The Copper Man.

He didn't know why he was so shaken up by the revelation that Scarlett had seen it on the news, the blink-and-you'll-miss-it segment about the metal sculptures. They'd been popping up for years now. Nearly two decades now. They'd found the first in the Chattahoochee National Forest. Then Hightower. Tongass. Even the Painted Mountains. Dozens of them, all simple in design yet painstakingly crafted. Brilliant statues of ordinary people immortalized in solid copper. Sometimes other metals, too. But most were copper.

Beau held his hands up, studying them. Flecks of oil paints covered his hands and forearms. Most people would have been hard pressed to have noticed, but somehow Scarlett had detected them buried beneath smears of dried blood.

His mind raced, but his hands were solid.

He didn't have time for this. He didn't have time for any of it.

He walked over and planted himself in front of Rachel.

"Where's your parents, kid?"

She stared at him, but didn't respond.

"Hey!" he said, snapping his fingers. "You hearin' me in there?"

Rachel blinked, lost in a daydream.

Beau scoffed, pacing away.

"The mind hangs by a thin thread," Rachel said, "these unknown things, forever lost, upside down."

He turned around.

Rachel was standing now.

"What'd you say?" he asked. He walked back, fishing a cigarette out of his pocket. He popped open the lighter, cupping his hands around the end of the flame.

A string of mucus plopped into his hands, snuffing out the flame with a hiss.

Wood creaked.

Rachel craned her head up and Beau followed suit, raking his eyes over dozens of shelves.

The first floor.

Second.

Third.

And that was when he saw it there, perched in the wooden beams holding the ceiling together.

"Fuck me," he said.

He'd seen things like it before when he'd pulled up the floorboards on the front porch. *Creepy crawlies* his ma used to call them. Only this one wasn't quite the same. The thing was easily ten feet long, maybe more. It had a pale exoskeleton like an albino centipede, and legs like furry sticks, its back was covered in long serrated black quills.

Out of nowhere, a storm siren began blaring from outside.

"Now what?" he said.

The sound startled the horror to life, he saw it twitch, stirring above, and it was like they'd been spotted. The thing sprung to life, scuttling across the ceiling, and he realized it must have crawled in from outside.

He stepped in front of Rachel, throwing an arm out and ushering her back.

"Don't. Move," he said coolly.

Snap!

Beau looked down to find a splinter from the chair under Rachel's shoe. His eyes shot up to find the creature swinging its body from the wooden beams, throwing itself to the wall and latching onto the bookcases with nightmarish legs.

"Move!" he shouted. He took the girl in one arm and made a run for the door to the hall.

Books rained down as the creature scuttled along the shelves, tearing across the walls and crashing into the floor in front of the doors with a weighty thump.

He set Rachel on the ground, throwing himself between her and the horror from the storm. "Hey!" he said, waving his arms. "Over here!"

The creature tracked him with a pair of red eyes attached to two long stalks, like a snail. Beau lurched to one of the bookcases and snatched a book out, lobbing it at the creature.

The book bounced off its head, the eyes retracting into its body. It shrieked, something between a chirp and a rattle, scurrying after him on a dozen impossibly long legs. The thing ignored Rachel altogether, giving chase.

He swung around the aisle and shouted to her, "Get outta here!"

Rachel disappeared through the doors, slamming them closed behind her.

Beau ripped the knife from the sheath on his belt and bolted straight down the aisle, running for his life.

The creature snapped into the air, the wiry legs wiggling, the sheer weight of the creature toppling over entire sections of bookshelves.

Beau hit a wet patch and he went down hard on his ass.

The knife went skidding across the tile.

He scrambled to his feet right as the monster reached him.

It stretched its body between two bookcases and the weight brought them both down over his head, a dump of large hardcovers crashing down on top of him.

One of the monsters' legs was caught between the wooden shelves, squirming wildly. One of the milky barbs hooked the meat in his shoulder and he screamed, dropping down to the floor.

A glint of metal caught his eye; he reached for the knife and wrapped his fingers around the handle and swung.

The blade cut the leg clean off; the stump dropped down and he swatted it away. The creature shrieked and the bookcases shifted, one of them dropping down and nearly crushing him.

The horror skittered toward him, impossibly fast. He got to his feet and ran, grabbing the bookcase at the end of the aisle.

It was coming right for him.

He waited, watching it charge at him like a gigantic centipede, its crazed red eyes ravenous for blood. The stump gushed black blood, dowsing the floor like an oil spill.

The crazed thing screeched and Beau winced, but held his ground.

Now!

He shoved forward, throwing his weight. The cords in his arms bulged and he roared, taking the entire wall of bookcases and pitching them over.

The monster reached him; the wall of hardbacks spilled over; he couldn't have timed it better if he'd wanted to. Hundreds of pounds of weight collapsed down on top of the thing. A sickening *CRUNCH!* punched the quiet and a splatter of dark blood spurted out of the horror like someone had stomped on a cockroach.

Beau Winchester stood panting, his shirt dark with rings of sweat around the neck and arm pits, his tanned skin covered in a light sheen of sweat but heavy with blood and grime. He looked down and saw the creature's head loll to the side, the serrated mandibles opening and closing, reaching for his ankle even in its final seconds.

He dropped down without thinking twice, slamming the blade into the monster's skull with a sharp crunch. He used his other hand to throw his weight down, and he felt it break through, sinking into the soft tissue inside.

"Beau! Shut the door!" It was Scarlett.

He ripped his knife out of the dead thing's head and a gush of blood spewed out. He made for the door to the city.

Scarlett and Harper flew through the entrance, running for their lives.

"Close it!" Scarlett screamed.

The women spun around, grabbing the doors and swinging them closed.

"What the hell is goin' on?!" Beau shouted.

The women ignored him, hastily trying to fasten the locks.

"Hey!" he yelled. "Somebody better start giving me some fuckin' answers 'round here!"

Scarlett turned around. Her eyes went wide.

"Beau—what the hell is *that?"* she said, pointing at the remains of the ten-foot-long creature and a half-destroyed library.

Harper hustled over, studying the monster, then asked, "Where's the girl?"

Scarlett glanced around the destroyed library.

They stared at him, waiting for answers.

"I don't know," he said bluntly.

Scarlett scoffed. "You *don't know*?"

"No," Beau said. "I was a little busy."

"Busy?" Scarlett snapped. "Doing what?!"

"What the hell do you think?!" Beau yelled, hooking a thumb over his shoulder at the creature. "Savin' her skinny little ass!"

Harper jogged for the door to the hall and jerked on the handle. "It's locked—from the outside. So, unless someone has a key, we're trapped."

"How 'bout a fuckin' thank you?!" Beau yelled.

Scarlett looked at him impossibly. "For what?! I told you to watch her!"

"*Excuse me?*"

"You had one job!"

"That's it," Beau said. "You can keep your money. I hope you fuckin' choke on it," he snarled. "You're on your own." He stormed past her and Harper stepped aside.

Beau threw a leg out and the double doors exploded open.

He turned back, a scowl on his face.

"You're all gonna die here."

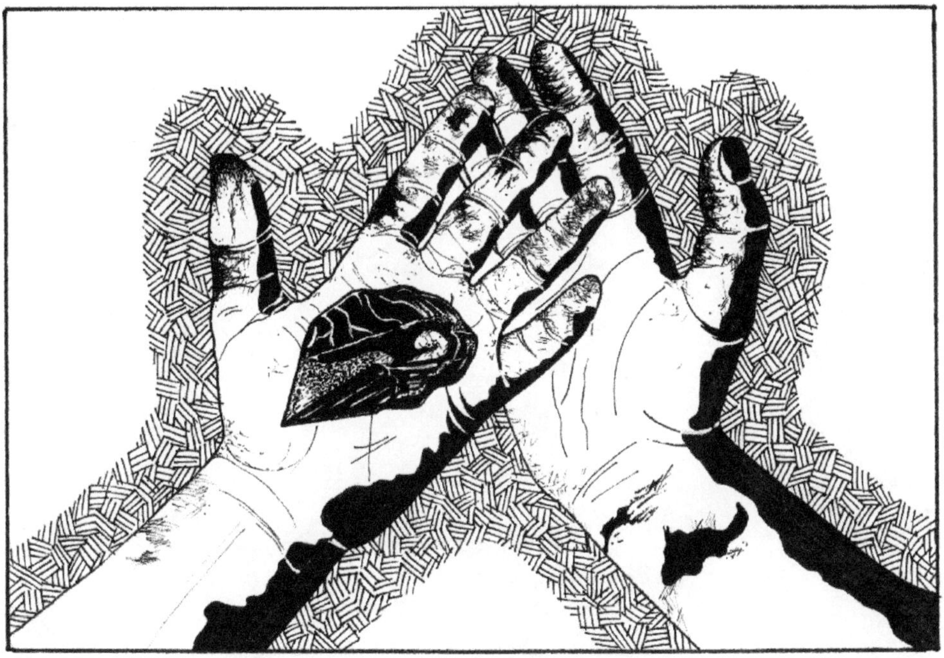

PART 4:

MAGICIANS and MONSTERS

MORGANA

THE GIRL WAS standing at the end of the theater hall.

When she'd gotten back to the doorway exiting the land of sweets, she'd pushed it open, spotting a trail of chocolate twisting down the dim hallway.

She'd stood there, taking in each of the endless doors, and wondered how many other worlds there could be on the other side.

How many other universes.

How many other monsters.

Didn't matter, she decided. She had a job to finish in this one.

But which one? They could have gone through any of them, and without her gun she would be taking a big chance. The biggest.

Her clothes were covered in filth, and her skin was appalling, but the pain was gone. The witch had seen to that. Her mind raced, processing a chain of events so extraordinary she couldn't quite believe them herself.

She saw no way to find them. There were too many possibilities. They could have run to any of the doors. And when she decided to call off her search and exit the lobby, she'd found the girl watching her from the other end of the hall.

She was short. Maybe up to her hip. The girl's face was concealed in shadow. She wore pajamas but her feet were bare.

Morgana took a step closer, careful not to scare her.

"Hello," she offered.

The girl didn't reply, only watched her.

"Are you lost?" Morgana asked.

But still the girl did not speak.

Morgana crossed through the wash of neon light, and the girl became clearer.

Webster's daughter, no doubt.

The blue eyes. The blond hair.

"Rachel," Morgana said.

The girl cocked her head and blinked.

"I'm a friend of your father's."

Rachel was quiet.

"I can help you find him," she said. "If you come with me, I can help you find them both."

Rachel reached up and held out her hand.

Morgana looked at her strangely, as though she couldn't figure her out, then took it.

"Did you see anyone else come through here?"

The little girl bobbed her head.

"Where?"

Rachel raised her tiny hand and pointed down the long corridor connecting to the theater lobby.

Morgana smiled.

NICK

SANDI WAS STROLLING beside him, carefully surveying the courtyard. The path and walls were constructed from some sort of large stone blocks streaked with veins of emerald and flecks of silver. Strange ivy glowed like radioactive waste, twisted around the top of the two walls like barbed wire. The vines spilled down to the ground in coils, invading the lone path through. *The path will be gone soon*, Nick thought, oddly sentimental. *Soon it'll only be plants and nothing else.* Overhead: a glass dome of pure black, like the sky was a sea of oil. It moved the same, too, like it was swaying with the rotations of the Earth. God, he *hoped* it was sky.

Sandi shivered. Nick listened to her teeth chatter. She didn't seem to have noticed the strange otherworld above. Hopefully she didn't.

"I don't get it, Sandi," he said. "We've been walking for hours."

"Don't I know it," she said.

"Where is she? Shouldn't we have found her by now, even *accidentally*?"

Sandi shrugged, pulling her arms tighter and looking up at the skylight. "Maybe she's hiding somewhere."

"Hiding?" Nick parroted. "Why would she be hiding?"

"She's a scared little girl, Nick. That's what I would do if I was her."

Nick agreed.

They looked up and saw two tall glass windows, bright with light the shade of honey.

"It seems strange, though, doesn't it?" Sandi asked.

"What's that?"

Sandi nodded her head at the lights coming from inside the house. Nick had seen her make that same face when a recipe hadn't worked out and she was trying to figure out where it went wrong.

"For a place with no power, the house sure does have a lot of lights on," she said. A moment of silence. "You'd almost think someone was home."

It *was* curious, he thought. Nothing else worked here. Not the phones. Not watches. Car batteries for a few hours, max. And certainly no electronics of any kind.

So why did the house have electricity?

"Something's not adding up," Sandi added.

Voices. They were hushed but unmistakable.

"Wait," he said, interrupting her. "I hear someone."

Sandi turned toward the house.

The voices conversed quietly, coming from the shadows at the opposite end of the courtyard.

Nick crouched down into the vines, mindful of his wound, sneaking closer.

"What about that thing out there?" a voice hissed.

"I don't see it. Maybe it's gone." A woman's voice.

Nick poked his head out, breathing a sigh of relief.

"Jesus, you guys almost gave us a heart attack," he said, rising from the foliage.

"Who's that?" a man said.

Nick waved, beckoning Sandi over. "It's okay. It's the guy from the news and that scientist."

Jackson and Park looked marginally worse than he and Sandi. Jackson's pants were ripped down the leg as well as a gash in his stomach that was crusted over with blood. Park looked like she'd been doused in sewage. Her face was marked with dark bruises.

"What the hell happened to you two?" Nick asked.

He and Sandi approached, but Jackson and Park didn't move from the doorway.

"Ummm, what are you guys doing out there?" Park asked.

"We're looking for my daughter. Rachel. Have you seen her?" Nick replied.

"No, I mean, why are you outside?" Park clarified. She poked her head out from the house, peering around. "You haven't seen anything out there?"

Nick and Sandi shared a look.

"Like what?" Nick asked.

Jackson frowned. "Nothing, apparently."

Sandi leaned forward, sniffing at the air. "Is that...*chocolate?*"

Park groaned. "Don't ask."

Twenty minutes later and everyone was up-to-date on current events. They walked together; Nick optimistic with the two new additions to their search party. The old adage "power in numbers" came to mind. They crossed through an opulent foyer that looked like it may or may not have belonged to a certain Count. Brass candelabras hung in the air, flickering with warm candlelight. Their shoes clacked across the marble tile. A wide staircase rose to a platform that could fit a small jazz band.

"Wait a minute," Park said, stopping. "You're telling me that you actually used to work with that psycho bitch?"

"Me? No." Nick shook his head. "She's a contractor. Works for Isabelle's mother from time to time when she's needed. She's done jobs for her for years."

"Jobs?" Park repeated. "Wait. Like *job* jobs?"

"What kind of jobs?" Sandi asked, reticently.

Nick reached out and ran his fingers over one of the candelabras and the light danced animatedly. He'd given up on trying to figure out the house at this point and decided to let the magic be magic. "The kind where people punch out and never punch back in. I only heard stories about it."

Park exhaled, cradling her arm. "Great. So not only is there a bloodthirsty cult here, there's also some sort of *Sopranos'* family reunion going on, too?"

"I've heard of her," Jackson said to everyone's surprise. "My pop—I heard him talking on the phone once. He mentioned her a couple times to his buddies down at the precinct. I remember the name; Morgana. He said she's killed a lot of people but I guess they never could get any solid evidence to connect her to any of the crimes."

A moment of silence filled the time as they walked.

"So, what's with the knives?" Park asked.

Nick glanced over at his shoulder at her. "Nobody really knows for sure. She's a legend even among the other contractors. Some people say her parents were gypsies who traveled Europe working as entertainers. Last I heard she had a twin brother. They say she grew up performing, that her parents taught her everything they know, traveling around Europe doing shows. Others say she lived down in Antarctica for years with some sort of guru hunting Polar Bears. Some kind of extreme training or some bullshit. I guess there's more honor in it if you use a knife instead of a gun." He went quiet for a moment. "But if you ask me, she's just a fucking psychopath running around with a coat full of knives."

Nick slowed, his head light. He coughed into his arm, feeling the wound in his back send a flood of pain throughout his body.

"And then one day, last I heard, she'd given it all up, left that life behind. That was years ago now. Obviously bullshit, though, or she wouldn't be here now."

"What about her employer?" Jackson asked. "That lady with the gold fangs and the museum of heads?"

Nick sighed. He turned around and started walking again. "Katya Carlisle. Isabelle's mother."

"Who is she?" Jackson pressed.

"Katya?" he asked. "She's responsible for ninety percent of the deals going down on the East Coast. Take your pick. Drugs. Prostitution. Trafficking. Money laundering. That's not including her own personal hobbies." Nick said. "And she is not a person you want to have on your bad side."

"Quite the crowd you used to run with," Sandi said. "No wonder you never wanted to talk about your old life."

Nick laughed dryly. "Yeah, well. I guess we all have parts of our lives we'd prefer to leave in the past."

"So, this one who's after us—the Nightmare. She knows?" Park said.

"Knows what?" Nick asked.

"Your daughter and your ex, the one who crashed in that plane we found out in the street. They're both here in the *same* house on the *same* night. Tell me that doesn't mean something."

"You're the scientist here," Jackson said. "Don't you have a theory or something?" he teased.

"Isn't that a line from *Tremors*?" Park asked, and she seemed tickled by the reference. "And this is your friendly reminder that I am a *biologist*. That doesn't qualify me to know anything about the supernatural happenings and hauntings taking place here. I should be asking you these questions."

Jackson cleared his throat. "Ahem. Excuse me now? What about your show?"

Park feigned ignorance.

"Ah, you thought I didn't know about that, huh?" he said. "What was it again…Ghost Hunters?"

"Ghost *Stalkers*," Park corrected.

"What's that?" Sandi asked.

"Nothing," Park answered curtly.

"Park," Jackson teased. "She's being modest. They were a pretty big hit a few years back. Definitely had a decent following, too."

"Funny, but not even remotely accurate," Park said.

"They used to go to haunted places, check rooms for cold spots, tell ghosts to knock three times, all that jazz," Jackson said.

"Oh, shit, that's right!" Sandi laughed, clapping her hands together. "I remember that show! Weren't you that one chick who said she met the Boogeyman one time and—"

"I *did* meet the boogeyman, yes, and no, I don't want to talk about it."

"Enough, guys," Nick said, killing the vibe. He turned to Jackson. "I don't understand. We've been in this house for *hours*. Shouldn't we have found her by now? Shouldn't we have seen her? Shouldn't we have found some trace of her?"

"It doesn't work like that, man," Jackson replied.

"Like what?" Nick asked.

"The house gives you *what* it wants *when* it wants. You don't get to pick and choose."

"You got separated last time, though, right?" Nick asked.

Jackson nodded. "Yeah? So?"

"Then how did you find the others? How did you get everyone back together?"

The others had crowded around, waiting for Jackson to answer.

"Whenever Scarlett or one of us died, we'd wake up again. And the house changed around us every time. The furniture would look different. The paint. The wallpaper. Everything. And the last time it happened, the last time she died, everyone was there when we woke up. Everyone except Tommy."

"Great," Park said, slapping her hands on her thighs. "So one of us has to die now?"

"Hell no," Sandi said. "Nobody is going to kill themselves, at least not while I'm around. We're doing this the old-fashioned way and *looking* until we find that little girl."

"Yeah. Right," Nick said begrudgingly.

"Hey, look—over there," Park said.

"Do you guys smell that?" Sandi asked. She looked at Nick. "Food?"

Nick turned around to see a large stone archway surrounding a passage in the wall.

He started forward and the others followed.

The hypnotic dance of flames cast an eerie glow on the walls, throwing long shadows. Dozens of candles were peppered across a long wooden dining table that could easily sit twenty. The table fit the aesthetic, like something you'd find in a medieval castle, but the wallpaper was off, made up of disorienting patterns and bizarre geometric shapes. Dozens of high-backed chairs were tucked under the table, as if awaiting an entourage of dinner guests.

"It looks like they were expecting company," Park said. She leaned over one of the chair backs, carefully stretching the neckline of her shirt away from her chest and inspecting the wound.

"How's it look?" Jackson asked.

Park eased the top of her shirt down and shrugged. "I can't tell what's chocolate and what's blood, so that's something."

Jackson stopped in front of the wallpaper, feeling along the raised paisley pattern. "This looks familiar…" he said. "Why do I know this pattern?"

Sandi skirted the length of the table, passing before the steady orange flames while Nick eyed an assortment of empty plates and unused utensils.

Nick laughed, sighing. "We're striking out every which way tonight." He reached back, massaging his wound.

"I can smell it, Nick," Sandi said, and he could hear the frustration in her voice. He felt it too. "I can practically *taste* it. I'm so thirsty. So fucking thirsty."

She was starting to unravel.

"We all are, Sandi," Nick said softly. "We've just gotta hang on."

"You can't see it?" Jackson asked.

"See what?" Nick said.

"The food," Jackson said, pointing. "This entire table is overflowing with food. You guys don't see it?"

Nick did a double take. Sandi did, too.

"Man, I don't see shit," Park said, smacking a wine glass over.

"This is what the house does," Jackson said. "It plays tricks on your mind. Makes you see things that aren't really there."

Park pulled out a chair and nearly fell into it.

Jackson said, "Vincent said you never truly see what's here. He said it was all an illusion. That if we could see what was here, that if we could see what the house's true form looked like, we wouldn't survive it."

The room went silent. Morale had reached an all-time low.

Nick and Jackson shared a look, like they both knew time was inevitably counting down. That soon, they'd all become permanent residents of the Halliday House if they didn't find a way out.

A set of maple double doors burst open at the far end of the room.

A rush of lively voices roared to life.

The group recoiled, scattering to the sides and corners of the room as a man and a woman dressed in Victorian-era clothing led an entourage of partygoers into the dining room.

They all froze.

The phantoms couldn't see them. At least they didn't appear to. Sandi was across from him, ducked down behind a tall wingback chair while Jackson had slipped behind the thick drapes on the opposite wall. Park seemed to have vanished into thin air before he noticed her eyes peering out from underneath the table.

The man and woman sauntered to opposite ends of the table with stars in their eyes, smiles as if they hadn't a care in the world.

Nick looked around to find the room brightening, the drab walls and decor taking on a more vibrant appearance, brimming with golden accents and deep reds, like going from black and white to rich, beaming Technicolor.

He noticed Jackson watching the process as it unfolded, like seeing a house being built before their very eyes.

Once all of the guests had been seated, the man stood, taking in the room of elitists, feeding off the excitement, a sparkling glass of champagne in his hand.

"My friends," he began. "Tonight marks the completion of something extraordinary. Tis a day that which will be remembered by humanity as the day our kind was not forgotten in the shadows of greatness, but propelled into greatness itself." He paused, smiling at the woman admiring him across the table. "A legacy, if you will," he said, his mouth hooking into a grin.

That was when Nick realized; he was watching a scene play out before him, only a hundred times more vivid.

"And like all great legacies," the man continued, "they are not built on the shoulders of a single man, but rather an idea. With all of your generous contributions, brick by brick, we, *together*, have built what shall be known to the world as humanity's greatest legacy."

The man's voice raised, oozing with charisma, his eager guests unable to pry their eyes away from glory.

All except one.

A single man in a worn derby lingered in the shadows, his arms folded across his chest, his eyes hidden in shadow. Nick saw him check his watch and knew it must have been before the house had been ravaged by whatever had happened here.

The host continued, "My friends. When we began this journey, I realized not long after that we would not succeed based on your plentiful donations alone. Because, the truth of the matter is that even in a place where time equates to nothing, where the physical laws of man can be broken, and where we can aspire to seize our dreams, we were *still* restricted by factors beyond our control.

"Then how did we accomplish this you might ask? How did we dare extricate a dream and manifest it here, in our own reality?" His voice climbed to a mad pitch, blinded by delusions of grandeur. "Him," he said with a proud grin and a tip of his head.

A collective gasp.

Heads swiveled. Silverware rattled. Bodies shifted.

At the other end of the table was a pale man in a long black coat. The man looked out on the room, his piercing blue eyes studying each of the guests. He was beautiful the same way a portrait was beautiful and, somehow, in a way Nick couldn't quite understand, he was able to sense immense power hidden in that pale man.

"May I present to you, Dante Greystarr. An individual not bound by the chains of humanity, but powered by the will of the gods themselves. Capable of feats others dare not dream." The host paused, admiring the pale man. "He is our savior. And he is our host in this place that we have come to call the Grey World."

The man paused. Nick noticed Dante Greystarr and the man's wife eyeing each other. A look passed between them. It was subtle, but it was there.

"Please," the host said. "Raise a glass and join me in a toast. To my lovely wife, Constance. To Mr. Greystarr, a god of gods. And lastly, to our undying legacy."

A tremor jolted the room. The crystal glasses violently rattled, the massive table juddering.

The lights flickered once.

Then twice.

And the third time, they didn't come back on.

SCARLETT

THEY WERE LOST. They'd been working as a team, moving hastily from room to room, investigating briefly before moving on to the next. Most of the rooms were fairly ordinary. Old timey furniture. Dated décor usually from the late nineteenth century. One room was more akin to a cave than an actual room, mostly rocks and a few sparse weeds.

But there were others that were far more interesting. Once, they'd opened a door to a dark room full of stark white mannequins. They'd popped their heads in the room and heard a long creak somewhere in the darkness. She'd thought of that time at her old work where she and Jackson had been trapped in a store full of corpses and that was enough to deter her from venturing further. Scarlett couldn't see how far back the space went, but she could see the mannequins carrying on into the dark far enough to know it was easily the size of a football field, maybe bigger.

Another time she'd nudged open a door to find a corridor that looked like the inside of a cockroach. Amber colored walls coated with hard resin and a stench that could knock out a horse. They'd seen something vast scurry by at the other end and slammed the door before they could get a better look.

After a brief argument, they'd agreed to try one last door. Harper had been the one to pull it open.

It was hard to describe what was on the other side. The room was opulent. Dark. Almost like being inside of an old museum. A sprawling wooden table ran down the center of the room. A cross between a dining table and a makeshift laboratory. There were platters of strange insects. Severed limbs of the nonhuman variety. Bits of sallow flesh. Purple mold and exotic, alien plants like the kind growing in Winterview. And some things Scarlett couldn't even begin to describe. Seated around the table were three humanoid figures in deranged porcelain masks. Metal mesh covered the eyeholes. Each ghoul was dressed in black Victorian garb, donning their own unique hat and a pulsing emerald stone fastened to their ascots.

The door had opened and the ghouls' heads had swiveled toward her and Harper in unison.

They'd both gasped, then stood there silently, frozen in a combination of fear and curiosity and disgust, interrupting the dinner party of three highly sophisticated ghouls.

The tallest of the three, one in a comically tall top hat, stood up, and Scarlett grabbed the handle and slammed the door closed before she could see what it did next.

"I think that's enough for now, don't you?" she'd said.

Then they'd walked. And walked. On and on for hours.

Scarlett's mind reeled with all sorts of possibilities since they'd gotten back inside the house.

Rachel was gone.

And now Beau was gone, too.

Harper remained silent while Scarlett rattled off theories on the Gothic city they'd left behind.

"Maybe it's some sort of alternate dimension," Scarlett said. "Or maybe it's some other planet in the universe, and the house is like, some sort of doorway to get there. You know, like *The Gate*."

"The Gate?" Harper said.

"Yeah. You know, that movie where the two kids find that hole under their tree in the backyard and it's a portal to hell."

Harper furrowed her brow.

"Didn't you say you've been there before? I thought I remembered you mentioning it in one of your interviews," Harper said.

"No, but I've *seen* it before."

Harper inspected the decaying walls as they walked, nodding.

"And that alarm," Scarlett added. "I heard it the last time I was in the house. It was loud, and I saw that old Victorian city outside the window with all the rain and the fog. And the sky got dark just like it did this time and some sort of gigantic leg walked by in the street."

"The creature from the roof?"

Scarlett shook her head. "Something bigger."

Harper stroked her chin, thinking. "Why didn't you recognize the city when we were out there?"

"It was darker this time. The fog was way worse."

They started walking again.

"What do you think that siren was?" Scarlett asked. "That's usually for tornados, right? Or like, floods or something?"

"Yes. That creature appeared right after the siren began, so it's safe to assume it's a warning."

Scarlett kneaded her eyes with her knuckles. "But who was warning us?"

"Someone who knew what was coming," she said. Harper turned and looked at her. "That vehicle we saw driving away from the house—did it look familiar?"

"No," Scarlett replied. "Why?"

"My intuition tells me it was your Crow Corporation."

"That doesn't make any sense," Scarlett said. "If the house is the only way to get there, how could Crow Corp have gotten there, let alone that motorhome they were driving? There's no way it would have fit through the front doors."

"I don't know," Harper said. "But they did."

"Spoken like a true scientist." Scarlett smiled. She pushed open a door in front of her and a flood of pale light shone in.

Jackson's face flickered in her head like a spark.

The foyer.

The *original* foyer.

"I remember this," Scarlett muttered.

Harper looked over her shoulder.

It was just like Scarlett remembered it. The waterfall of black slime. The stone walls carved out of immense Cyclopean blocks. Engraved railings twisting all over the floors and walls, arching into the air like mangled roller coaster tracks.

"More of that substance?" Harper asked, her gaze on the slime.

Scarlett moved into the room, mindful of the drop-offs on the sides while Harper held back, shrewdly inspecting the tracks.

She remembered when she'd first awoken in the house and found Jackson looking down at her. How she'd been relieved that he'd been there with her. How she wasn't alone. She glanced over her shoulder and saw Harper sketching more of the markings and missed Jackson more. But all she could do was tell herself he was fine and focus on finding Rachel.

"Where are you, kid?" she said to herself.

"It's only been a few hours. She couldn't have gotten far," Scarlett said. "I can't believe that freaking hillbilly abandoned us. What an asshole." She cursed Beau for losing Rachel and then cursed herself for losing him.

"We'll be fine without him," Harper said.

Scarlett watched the waterfall of slime ooze into the bottomless pit below. "Will we, though? Because I'm not so sure."

Harper zipped her sketchbook back in her pack and walked over, grimacing at the filth below. "People like him only know one thing. And violence is never the answer."

"Oh yeah? Because it looked like it worked pretty well on that thing in there."

Harper wandered through a passage in the wall, and Scarlett followed.

They were greeted by the stained-glass panel at the foot of a set of stairs. At the top, two double doors were framed with decorative floral carvings.

Harper stood in front of the sign, playing the cryptic phrase over in her head while Scarlett gazed up at the murky light high above their heads, wondering if the sun was somewhere up there, or if it was another world altogether.

"The mind hangs by a thin thread," Harper read, "these unknown things, forever lost, upside down."

A chill wormed down Scarlett's spine. It always did.

"What do you think it means?" she found herself asking.

Harper's brow pinched together.

"That we're all on the edge. That we're all on the verge of breaking like fragile little porcelain dishes," Harper said.

Scarlett stared at her with equal parts sympathy and loathing. Harper reminded her of Vincent in that way. He had a way of speaking his mind too, regardless of whether you wanted to hear what he had to say or not. The only difference was Vincent always spun it in a way that seemed charming, like he could tell you that you were dying of cancer and you'd still be happy about it.

Harper took out the camera and wound the crank, snapping a picture of the panel of glass. The camera spit out a slate and Harper held it out in front of her, watching the image develop.

"Do you believe in the afterlife, Scarlett?"

Scarlett frowned, sitting down on the steps, wiping the sweat from her brow and running her tongue over her cracked lips. "Wow, you go right for the throat, huh?"

"I'm sorry," Harper said. "You don't have to answer that."

"No, it's all right." Scarlett waved the notion away. A warmth bloomed in her chest and she smiled. "I think I do, yeah."

"Why?" Harper asked, and it didn't seem like she was interrogating her but was rather genuinely interested in her rationale.

Scarlett looked at Harper, her heart heavy, and said, "When Tommy and Hannah died, I thought a lot about that question. The 'why.' Why everything happened the way it did. Why it was them and not me. Was it just luck of the draw? Or was it part of some grand design?

Was it our fate? I mean, after all, I'm here and they're not, right?" Scarlett said sadly. "And then I realized that it didn't matter, because there was no right answer. I realized that people believe what they *want* to believe. I want to believe that I'll see Tommy pitch another game. I want to believe that I'll be able to hug my best friend again, tell her that I miss her so badly that I can't fall asleep sometimes. And I want to tell Vincent that he was right about me. So, I guess what I'm saying is that, yes, one day, maybe sooner than later, I'll see my friends again. And we'll laugh and we'll cry, and things will be like they were before."

Harper nodded solemnly, waving the picture in her hand. "I read once that sometimes the dead can communicate through the living. That they can use us as vessels to carry messages through to the other side." Harper tucked the slate into her pocket.

"What do you mean? Like possession?"

"Some might call it that. But there's other ways, too, to communicate with the ones we lost."

Scarlett looked up to find Harper down on one knee, removing a board from her pack and setting it on the ground in front of her.

Scarlett bolted upright, shocked to find Harper unfolding a thin wooden board in two halves. The face was simple, engraved with the letters A through Z along with a YES and NO and the numbers zero through nine.

"A *Ouija board?"* Scarlett asked. "You're joking?"

Harper fetched a metal planchette from her pack and slapped it on the board as if she and Scarlett were going to play a board game right then and there in the enormous stone foyer. "I know it's crude, but you know the limitations here. Photographs are one thing, but keeping a steady supply of electricity for any other devices is impossible in here. And according to my research, some very well-known paranormal researchers consider Ouija Boards a useful tool when communicating with the dead."

"Wait. You actually believe these things work?" Scarlett asked.

"No," she said. Harper's bluntness caught Scarlett off guard. "I don't believe in the afterlife, or ghosts, spirits, or anything else. I only believe in what's right in front of me. But if there *is* an afterlife, this house is going to be the best conduit to find out once and for all."

"I didn't mess with those things *before* I knew about all this supernatural shit. Do you really think I'm going to mess with them *now* knowing what's possible?"

"Come on, Scarlett. You've dabbled in the dark side of the world. You know how this works. Remember what President Roosevelt said? 'The only thing we have to fear is fear itself.'"

Scarlett scoffed, folding her legs and sinking down across from Harper on the stone floor. "Umm…I'm pretty sure there's a lot more to fear around here than you think."

"I'll start," Harper said, positioning her fingers on the planchette. "Now you."

Scarlett shook her head, reluctantly putting her fingers on as well, chuckling to herself. "This is so stupid. I cannot believe the United States Government gave you a Ouija Board."

"It's Park's."

"Why did she own a Ouija Board?"

"She was formerly with a team who dabbled in the supernatural. Any more questions before we begin?"

"If you say so."

Harper took a breath, her eyes skimming the room, and called out, "Is anyone here with us right now?"

Scarlett gawped.

"What?"

"Seriously?" Scarlett said. "You're in the only genuinely haunted house in the world and that's what you're going to ask it?"

"All right, fine," Harper said. "What do you suggest?"

Scarlett thought for a moment, scratching her head. She smiled, coming up blank. "Is someone there?"

Harper smirked. "Much better, thank you."

The two women looked around the cavern, taking in the wash of cold light like they were underground in an ice fissure.

Silence.

"I told you," Scarlett said. "This isn't going to—"

The planchette suddenly yanked across the board, flying out from under their fingers.

YES

Harper looked mortified. She scrambled to her knees and dropped down, examining the heart-shaped piece of metal.

"Holy shit!" Scarlett yelled. "Did you see that? It worked!"

"Say something," Harper urged.

"Why me?"

"Because it responded to you," she hissed.

Scarlett sighed. "Fine." She paused, biting her lip. After a moment, she asked, "Is that you, Tommy?"

The planchette came to life, slipping over the wood.

NO

Harper waved her hand in the air impatiently. Hurry up, she was saying.

"Where's the kid? Where's Rachel?" Good. Cut to the chase. Scarlett's voice echoed off the stone walls.

The planchette didn't move.

"Is she all right?" Scarlett asked.

The planchette smoothly glided across the wood, working over to each letter and stopping before moving on to the next.

"Danger?" Scarlett asked. "Rachel's in danger?"

The planchette sprung to life again.

NO

"I don't get it," Scarlett said. "Are you following any of this? What the hell is it talking about, Harper?"

Harper was silent, entranced.

"I don't understand," Scarlett said, as if addressing a child. "What're you talking about? *Who's* in danger?"

The metal dial feverishly sped across the wood, and Scarlett could see little grooves being scored into the surface.

Scarlett leaned down, squinting while the thing worked.

"Everyone," she whispered. "Everyone?"

The planchette slowed, its movements sluggish.

"I think it's running out of juice," Scarlett said.

Harper was sitting across from her, a grimace on her face. It looked like she'd aged ten years in a matter of seconds.

"Harper? What is it?"

She didn't answer, only kept staring at the board.

"Someone's coming?"

A grind of wood.

YES

The planchette sputtered across the board in short, jerky movements.

"Who?" Scarlett quickly shouted. "Who's coming?!"

The planchette flew across the board while Scarlett memorized the letters, putting them in order in her head.

K

I

N

G

The planchette spun wildly while Scarlett followed it with her eyes, her heart racing.

I

N

"King in…" she read aloud.

Y

E

L

O

W

Scarlett started as the planchette whipped through the tail of the final W, nearly flying off the board.

"Shit!" she said, flinching. She reached out and nudged the planchette back toward the middle of the board with her sleeve like it was a hot coal.

"The King in Yellow," she whispered. She looked up to find

Harper's eyes wide.

"What's wrong?" Scarlett asked.

Harper shook out of her daze. "What?"

"Are you all right?"

Harper stared at her, glassy eyed.

"Does that mean anything to you? The King in Yellow?"

Harper shook her head. "No."

Scarlett got to her feet, facing off with the double doors waiting at the top of the stone steps.

The Red Room. The same one where a river of blood passed through the center and a skylight of cosmic horrors swam in the darkness.

"Katie?" Harper's voice.

Scarlett turned around, finding Harper leaning over the Ouija Board, her fingers resting on the planchette.

"Katie? Honey? Are you there?"

The misery in Harper's voice put a knot in Scarlett's chest. Her face fell, heavy with sadness for the woman.

Harper stared hollowly at the planchette. Willing it to move. Praying for it to slide across the board like it had for Scarlett even the tiniest bit.

"Harper…" Scarlett said softly.

And that was when it hit her. Harper's daughter. That was why she was here. Why she'd come to the house.

Harper looked up, blinking her big eyes, then looked down at the planchette, like she didn't recognize who she'd become.

"I don't believe in the afterlife," Harper confessed. "I never did. Even before what happened."

Scarlett let herself sink down on the steps again.

"When the house first came to Winterview, it was all Katie could talk about. Anytime they would talk about it on the radio, or the television, she always wanted to know what was going on."

"Everyone did," Scarlett said. "Like it was magic."

"After a while," Harper said, "she started having these…*dreams.*"

"Dreams?"

Harper nodded, her face long. "She said that she'd seen herself here. This beautiful paradise where dreams and reality met somewhere in the middle, and life was finally bearable. That it was her true home. A world that was kinder. Happier. It tricked her. Made her feel like the only way out was in."

Scarlett sighed. "Hannah thought the same thing. That the house was the answer to all her problems. That it would bring some sort of closure to her life. To the loss."

"How could I not have seen it? Every sign was there. This is my job for Christ's sake," she snapped. "How could I not have seen what she was planning to do? What kind of mother am I, Scarlett?" she sobbed quietly.

Scarlett gently laid her hand over Harper's, covering the planchette, and said, "The kind that loved someone once, and *still* loves them."

Harper looked at her, her eyes wet. "She said I didn't listen to her. That I never listened to her. She told me so many times about this place but I never listened. I dismissed her, told myself she'd grow out of it. That she was bewitched by it like everyone else was."

A beat passed.

"But I'm listening now," Harper said with a glint in her eye. "I came tonight because Katie believed that this house meant something profound. And I'm going to find out what."

MORGANA

THE GIRL HADN'T said a word, and Morgana made no attempts to converse. Rachel kept a few steps ahead, her feet bare on the tile floor, her eyes lost in a dream. She kept a pace that was unshakable, and wandered with a purpose. Morgana trailed back and to the left, letting her dark eyes scan the halls as they progressed through a labyrinth of passages and corridors. Morgana stopped and scored the walls every so often with an X but never came across them again. She let the girl wander far enough ahead and worked quickly. Her coat was full of tempered steel but she kept her hands empty mostly; she didn't want to scare the girl. Rachel had gone willingly enough, and Morgana saw no reason to show she intended her anything other than assistance. At least not for the time being. There had been a moment when they'd seen something pass in front of them in the hall, but it was too far ahead to get a clear look.

Rachel had stopped.

Morgana peered into the dark and the dark peered back.

They waited.

Then waited some more.

Eventually Rachel decided it was safe and they resumed their trek. The girl moved swiftly, and while Morgana couldn't understand it, she knew Rachel was leading her somewhere, and she trusted her own intuition.

A haze of light grew in front of them. A draft from deep in the Earth gusted by, greeting them before continuing down the hall.

They turned the corner and the corridor opened upon a hollow.

Morgana put a hand on the girl's shoulder and she slowed.

Her jaw went slack. Her breath hitched. Her fingers curled around the cool metal in her coat.

The laws of physics had gone right out the window. They had a long time ago, she thought, when she had gazed upon a world formed of pure candy and nearly drowned that bitch in a river of chocolate.

The hall opened to a sprawling cavern chiseled from beautiful white stone. The texture reminded Morgana of the Statue of David, the way the light touched the stone and drank the shadows. She'd seen it once in Florence with her parents for her twelfth birthday. She'd been drunk on jealousy that day looking up at that marvelous sculpture, taking in the flawless contours and anatomy, imagining the discipline it would take to utilize a skill so masterfully.

Inside her coat, her delicate fingertip ran along the edge of a blade and she felt the outermost layer of her skin split.

She grinned.

She had mastered blades. And then she'd mastered murder.

Morgana shifted her gaze up and saw a high ceiling covered in pulsing green stalactites. The light throbbed and she wondered if they beat to the rhythm of her own heart, or if she merely imagined it.

A flicker of bright light and an ear-piercing shriek.

Morgana squinted her eyes to find an elaborate gold conduit chasing along the ceiling, carving a path through the emerald rock, a housing of glass coils feeding unstable electricity toward the other end of the cavern to an immense circular track on the wall. Thousands of ancient cogs rolled over above them like a tiny city dipped in gold. Morgana saw arcs of blistering light raining sparks down on them, and wondered if it was the first time she'd ever seen true magic in her life.

She looked down at the girl and noticed her admiring them, too, smiling without a care in the world. Morgana pondered why the girl didn't seem panicked, or even reasonably worried. Why she hadn't asked for her mommy or daddy. But she had learned early on in life never to question a good thing lest you regret it.

Rachel took Morgana's hand and started forward. The floor welcomed them with a glistening path of black-and-white checked tiles running the length of the long room. Their very own Yellow Brick Road. The hollows in the cavern walls made her skin itch. Anyone could be hiding there, she knew. But she *did* have the upper hand, after all. The young girl was all the bargaining power she needed.

They walked along the path hand in hand, following the checkered trail toward the massive ring of light at the other end. They passed along artificial cutouts in the stone enclosed with glass. Inside were elaborate displays of exploded human bodies, their nervous systems suspended in crimson strings, their skeletons bleached and varnished like prizes. Dozens of species unknown to her were vivisected, arranged in various poses, exhibited in a demented gallery. Beyond that the side of the path became bottomless fissures.

Their footsteps clacked across the tile. She breathed in the air, tasting the salt and brine, and she thought she heard waves on the precipice of her thoughts.

They came to a circular platform before a face of smooth black stone encircled by the ring.

The end of the cavern.

Morgana's eyes slid down to Rachel, who stood staring at the wall rock face as if seeing a brilliant painting.

They both watched as the electricity cycled around the ring, moving faster and faster, singing with profound power.

A draft was picking up, tossing Morgana's raven hair, breathing new life into the enormous cavity sunken into the Earth.

Rachel looked up at Morgana with a blank expression, then released her hand, tiptoeing across the platform and stopping in its center. While electricity sizzled and effervesced behind Morgana in a feast of sound and light, Rachel fell to her knees, and it was then that Morgana noticed the immense platform was etched with the symbol of the crown.

Rachel extended her small hand out, blinking dreamy eyes, and flattened it against the platform.

A colossal boom and a concussion of explosions shook in the walls.

The wind gusted and Morgana's coat flapped behind her.

The light was almost blinding now.

The electricity screamed and she recoiled but remained steadfast.

The low grumble of a howl faded, and it was as if all the oxygen had been sucked out of the room.

The wind cut like wire; her hair fell over her shoulders.

The cavern settled into an eerie silence.

Rachel looked back over her shoulder, her eyes gone, replaced with a blackness as slick as oil, and smiled.

BEAU

HE'D BEEN WALKING for hours. Following through the endless halls like a rat in a maze. At one point he realized he'd gone in a complete circle, arriving back at the library, finding the doors hanging off their hinges. He'd seen the creature smashed under the collapsed bookcases. Seen the double doors at the far end, secured.

He felt something tugging at him inside, drawing him to the dark world beyond by a sort of nostalgia he couldn't quite place. He'd marched across the ruined library and twisted the deadbolts in the doors, unlocking them with a hefty *click!* and taking the two knobs in his hands.

For a brief moment he thought about opening them, seeing what was outside for himself. Maybe when he did he'd find an entirely new world outside? Maybe the world he knew rather than the one he didn't.

His hands had been on the knobs, and his mind was made up.

And then the house had shuddered beneath his feet and he'd let go, just like that.

Beau looked around and watched as the shelves began collapsing like he was inside a tomb, raining down leather hardcovers by the thousands.

He broke into a run, found himself zigzagging through a minefield of oiled leather and parchment, the tomes pelting him from above.

The walls and the entire room began collapsing in on itself.

He dove like he had into the lake so many times before, flying out the doors and into the hall, crashing into the wall.

He spun around and scrambled to his feet in time to watch the entire library sink past like watching a building falling through a window.

A heavy crash sprayed a blast of dust into his face.

He lowered his arms away from his face in time to see a few more books topple at his feet.

"Ain't my fuckin' day," he said. He got to his feet again, same as he always did, and started walking again.

Music. He heard it clear as day on the other side of the gold door. Old timey music. "Ragtime blues" his daddy used to call it. The music had that tinny sound the keys made back then, like hearing a piano in a dream.

The Entertainer.

He'd recognize that old tune anywhere. He remembered seeing the record in his old man's collection before everything was boxed up and moved to the attic.

He listened closer.

Voices. Lots of voices. Like someone was having a party.

"What the fuck?" he muttered.

He pulled away suspiciously, thinking, then pressed his ear to the door again, squinting his eyes.

They were celebrating. He was sure of it.

"People?" he said to himself.

He twisted the handle and pushed the door open.

He thought the music would cut out, that the voices would die away and he'd be left standing there staring into an empty room.

But they didn't.

Quite the contrary. They only got louder.

It was a bar, that much was for certain. Only it wasn't like any bar he'd ever been to, no. This bar was for the elite of society. The crème de la crème. People that lived in a different world than him, filled with silver spoons and luxuries he'd only ever heard about in stories.

In other words, people with a lot of fucking money.

He'd never seen so many people in his life. The men wore tuxedos and tailcoats and the women glittered in sequin dresses and extravagant jewelry. They laughed and drank and danced, and a few of them eyed him curiously while he made his way through the sea of bodies like a fly on a wedding cake.

Polished gold glimmered from every accented surface. Rich mahogany wainscoting shone like a mirror. Dozens of tables dotted the room and a man with armbands worked a grand piano like it was his only purpose in life. A long counter ran across the far end of the room, canopied with a gaudy overhang of gold veins that chased into the room like webs.

Christ, it was hideous, he thought. Everything was so shiny it hurt his throbbing eyes even more.

Ahead, the barstools were swarming with lively patrons.

His eyes scanned the room with a glare that could kill a mule.

Several of the partygoers eyed him up and down, then went back to their drinks while others were more curious, a bald man raising a monocle to get a closer look.

"The fuck you lookin' at?" Beau said. He slapped a crystal glass out of the man's hand and it went spinning into the crowd with a roar of voices. The man's female companion gasped like she'd stumbled upon a circus attraction, nearly fainting.

Beau moved through the room like he owned the place, a walking testament to all of life's hardships and miseries boiled down to grease and blood and all of the filth these rich assholes would never know.

Men cowered. Women hid behind their withered lovers, terrified of the stranger yet unable to look away.

Beau stopped.

The bodies parted like the Red Sea, revealing a single woman at the bar, her back turned to him, the backless dress exposing a canvas of glistening skin.

"What took you so long?" she purred, and her voice was one of the sexiest things Beau had ever heard in his life, rich bitch or not.

Beau slowed. His heart picked up its pace.

The woman finally turned around and his breath caught.

Her brilliant eyes sparkled like the sunlight catching the shore of Lake Lanier. Her skin was flawless and silky, and a small beauty mark above her lip gave her the look of an actress from the golden age.

"I knew you'd find your way," she said.

Beau considered her, then realized all eyes were on him.

"Don't mind them," she said. "They've never seen anyone quite like yourself. Someone so…*untamed.*"

The woman sighed, easing down on a stool and crossing her legs. She snapped her fingers with a wink, and when Beau looked around the room again, everyone was gone.

The music played on, still, apparently by a ghost now.

He turned back and the woman stared up at him.

"Who are you?" he asked.

The woman's face melted into a smile, and her teeth were white as pearls. "Constance Halliday, at your service," she said, doing a half curtsy from her chair and offering a satin-gloved hand. "And you are?"

Beau was silent.

Constance blinked, her hand dangling in the air, and Beau found himself lost in those beautiful blue lakes she called eyes. "Aw, what's the matter? Haven't you ever met a lady before?" Constance pouted.

Beau finally relented, taking her hand and giving it a gentle squeeze.

"I always liked the strong silent type." She chuckled, tickled by his reticence, and he caught a note of her perfume then, fruity and sweet. She twisted at the hip and lifted a glass of bourbon from the bar counter, sipping it casually. She set it back down and Beau noticed the imprint of her lips on the rim.

Lipstick…or blood?

"Party really died," she said, with a giggle. "Care for a drink, stranger?"

Beau shook his head. "Ain't no booze here," he said. A beat, then, "Is there? It's not real. None of it."

"Real, fake. Alive, dead. Who can tell anymore?" Constance's smiled faded. "You're not as simple as they take you for." She gulped down the last of the bourbon, wiping her mouth with the back of her hand.

Beau's face was stone. "People like to assume a lot of things. Don't make 'em smart."

Constance folded open a mirrored cigarette case, setting one on her lips. "That they do. That they do." She hadn't taken her eyes off him since they'd met. "Got a light?"

Beau reached into his pocket and took out his Zippo. His father's. The same one he'd set the house on fire with. He flicked open the lid and spurred the wheel with his thumb, the flame sparking to life.

Constance smiled. She leaned forward, sucking in a long drag. "You remind me of someone I knew a long time ago. He was the strong silent type, too. All smoldering eyes and more attitude than I knew what to do with." She took another sip. "He was a better dresser, though, no offense."

"What is all this? The people? The party?" he asked. "You celebrating those things runnin' around out there? Maybe toasting to those fucks outside watching this place right now?"

"I'll tell you what," Constance said casually, breathing out a cloud of dark smoke. "I'll answer your question, but first, you have to answer one of mine."

Constance leaned back, spreading her arms along the counter. She wore a string of hefty pearls that hung down to her cleavage, her sequined dress refracting shards of light like a disco ball.

"Fine," Beau agreed.

"Why did you come here?" she asked, and the simplicity of the question took him by surprise.

"Had to."

"Tsk tsk tsk," Constance said. "But that's not quite true now, is it?"

Beau stared at her. "What?"

"You could have escaped anytime. You could have run. You could have taken your things and fled, but instead, you came here—to the house."

A surge of power in the walls, like a freight train was passing on the other side.

"Even now you're thinking about them, aren't you?" she asked, twisting her head to the left. Beau followed her gaze to find the two skeletal doors leading to Seventh Street.

The exit. The bodies had been cleared, no doubt by the cult, but the wreckage was still there. He could even see the tubes running down to scientist's rats waiting at the base of the stairs.

"You can lie to the others," Constance said. "You can even lie to yourself. But you can't lie to the house."

"Who are you?" he asked again.

Constance finally tore her eyes away from him, gazing into the world beyond the doors that Beau knew so well. She took another long drag off her cigarette and blew the smoke out of her nose in two plumes.

The house shook, short and violent, and they looked at each other.

"You came here because it's fate," she said finally. "Just like it's *my* fate to spend eternity in this house, tortured by my past. My mistakes."

"This is your house, then?"

Constance ran her tongue over her lips. "*This* house? No," she said, shaking her head. "Not anymore. Once maybe, but now…it belongs to *him*."

"To who?" Beau asked.

Constance went quiet. Another tremor rocked the foundation, the ceiling spraying motes of dust.

"Who?" Beau repeated, grabbing her wrist. Constance giggled like a child, grinning.

"*Who?*" he demanded, and this time the warning in his voice was enough.

Constance looked up at him, and the fear in her eyes made his blood run cold. She held a finger up to her lips. "Shhh… He'll hear you," she whispered.

Beau held her gaze and Constance's eyes softened.

"You're here because it's your fate. Those people—all of you—are meant to be here on this night. It's your destiny."

"I don't believe in destiny," Beau said.

"Yes, you do," Constance said. "You just don't know it yet."

"You're as crazy as the rest of 'em," Beau said, releasing her and starting for the exit. "You don't know what the fuck you're talkin' 'bout."

"He's coming!" Constance shouted, drunkenly standing up from the stool. "He's coming, and the only way you stand a chance is *together*. It has to be all of you, otherwise there is nothing anyone can do to stop him."

"Do I look like I give a shit, lady?" Beau snapped. He paused at the threshold to Winterview and drank in the moonlight and the fog beyond the entrance.

"Wait! You can't leave," she pleaded. "They need you!"

And he said, "Watch me."

JACKSON

THE EARTHQUAKE HAD shuffled them about like a deck of cards. The ghostly reception had literally gone up in smoke and the details of Scarlett's ravings had finally begun to come in clear.

But that wasn't all that'd changed.

The entrance they'd come in through was gone, replaced with a hall like all the others before it.

Jackson stepped out from behind the curtain, Sandi rising from behind the chair and Park army-crawling out from under the dining table. Nick was already at the entrance to the hall, listening to the same shrieking electricity they all heard now.

Erratic light pulsed, throwing shades of white and blue and yellow on the paisley wallpaper.

Jackson and the others stood beside Nick, and he saw then that the hall opened up on a gigantic white cavern. Like it had always been there if only they'd looked.

"What in the hell is that?" Park's voice.

"Sounds like someone is having one hell of an electrical problem," Sandi added.

Jackson looked at Nick and saw the determination on his face.

"She's down there," Nick said.

"What?" Jackson asked.

"I don't know how I know, I just do. Rachel—she's down there."

They watched the blinding light strobe and hiss as if a mad scientist was conducting the experiment to end all experiments. They held there together on the edge of the abyss, and just like Nick knew his daughter was down there, well, Jackson knew they had all been put there for a reason.

"Well?" Sandi said. "What're you all waiting for, an invitation?"

Jackson exchanged a look with Nick.

"She's a firecracker," Jackson said.

"You have no idea," Nick said.

Sandi started forward.

And together, they followed, one after another toward the light, and toward their destinies.

Nick's heart sank. He rushed forward but Jackson and Sandi seized him by the arms, holding him back.

Rachel was a short distance away, standing on a platform, a towering ring of light burning behind her on the wall. Morgana waited patiently at her side, a blade held down at her side.

"Rachel!" Nick screamed.

Morgana smirked.

"Whoa, hang on a second!" Jackson said, corralling him. "We need to think of a plan, goddammit!"

"Get the fuck off me!" Nick snapped.

Sandi stepped in front of Nick and slapped him across the face, hard. "Nick! Get ahold of yourself! We need to think before we go running over there."

Nick glared at her and, after a moment, his face softened.

"Uhhh…guys?" Park said, pointing up. "There's something happening here."

They all looked up and saw the stalks of unstable power coiling across the ceiling, pouring into the conduits built into the cavern.

"What the hell is that?" Jackson asked.

"It looks like some sort of generator funneling the electricity," Park added.

"What the hell for?" Nick said.

"Why do you keep asking me?" Park said.

The reference wasn't lost on Jackson.

"Everything's going to be okay, honey," Nick reassured, but Rachel didn't hear him.

They all moved in, carefully approaching the platform. Jackson saw bizarre scenes in glass cubes embedded in the stone walls but made a conscious effort not to look.

Nick took a step forward. "What do you want?" he called to Morgana, his words echoing.

Rachel was motionless, standing on the platform, complicit.

"Something's wrong," Jackson said quietly to Sandi.

"What're you talking about?" Sandi asked.

"I don't know," he said. "Something feels off. Look at her."

And look Sandi *did.*

She saw everything he saw. Rachel's emotionless face. Her empty eyes. The way the life was gone from them. Jackson watched her and wondered: *Is she even breathing?* He'd seen one too many possession movies to know the signs.

Jackson put a hand on Nick's shoulder, raising his voice over the hiss of the electricity. "She doesn't look so good, man. Maybe we should think this through—"

But Nick was having none of it.

He shoved Jackson hard and he toppled over onto the rocks connecting the path to the cave walls.

Nick broke into a run.

"Hey!" Jackson shouted, reaching out and grabbing fistfuls of air.

"Nick, wait!" Sandi said, and then she was running after him, too.

Park had disappeared altogether.

"Ah, shit," Jackson said, scrambling up. His eyes darted around, noticing hollows cut into the cavern walls like Swiss Cheese.

He dashed behind one of the glass displays, hoping that Morgana might lose track of them if they split up.

"That's far enough," Morgana said. She calmly rested her hand on Rachel's shoulder with the blade facing away.

Nick skidded to a stop at the edge of the platform, panting, and Sandi collided into him to break her fall.

"What part of *wait* do you not understand?" Sandi asked, out of breath.

"Let her go," Nick ordered.

"Katya has no idea, does she?" Morgana asked. "You took her and you ran," she said. "Some people might call that kidnapping."

"My daughter is not a part of this. Do you hear me? She is not a part of any of this!"

"Oh, but she is," Morgana said, stroking Rachel's hair. "Isabelle might be dead, but her daughter is not. She will be reunited with her true family, and there is nothing you can do about it."

Dead? But how? The only people that die in the house were the ones murdered by another human being.

"Goddam you," Nick said. "Why'd you do it? Why'd you kill her?"

Morgana shrugged. "I didn't."

Jackson did a double take.

Nick tilted his head, and Jackson could tell something wasn't adding up. "Then who did?" Nick asked.

A blue flash. A chirp.

Morgana whipped her head to the left to find Harper tucked in one of the alcoves in the wall.

And that was when he heard her.

Scarlett shrieked with a battle cry Jackson never thought her capable of, and then she was there, swinging out with a piece of stained-glass and bringing it down over Morgana's head.

Morgana gasped; the sheet of glass shattered into a million colorful shards and the sound was louder than the shrieks of electricity filling the room.

Park was there in an instant, having climbed up from the other side of the platform, grabbing Rachel and pulling her out of harm's way. She ushered her forward and Nick dipped down, scooping her up in his arms.

Morgana went to raise her arm but Scarlett caught her wrist with both hands, using her leverage to steer the blade away.

Sandi saw her struggling and rushed forward, throwing a hard fist.

Morgana's head snapped right from the force. Her fist went limp and the blade clanged to the platform.

Morgana stood in a daze, barely upright.

"You had this coming," Park said. She turned back and threw her body weight into it, landing a punch square in Morgana's head. Her head jerked and she went down on her back right there in the middle of the platform like a fallen angel.

Scarlett turned and it was like he was seeing her for the first time. She smiled at him the way she always had, her cheeks flushed red, a mist of sweat on her forehead, and he felt warm, like he was watching the sunrise.

Jackson rushed forward and she rushed forward, two friends turned lovers, colliding in an embrace where sparks flew and magic was as real as everything else they knew.

He realized he was crying then, and when he pulled away, she was crying, too. He laughed and she laughed and they kissed and he could taste the salt of her tears but they kept going anyway like it was their last.

Harper slid down from her position to the platform, and Jackson saw that she had a picture in her hand.

"Scarlett!" she said. "Look at this."

The woman ran over, handing the picture to Scarlett.

The others gathered around, looking down at the slate.

Morgana and Rachel.

Only it wasn't Rachel at all, but another little girl.

Which meant she'd been with them all along.

SCARLETT

THE ELECTRICITY WENT SILENT. The spitting coils above them stabilized. The electric current cycling through the ring on the wall went unnervingly quiet.

"Vanessa Halliday," Scarlett whispered.

"Who in the hell is that?" Park asked.

Scarlett jerked her head up as the electricity feeding through the glass coils hummed, brightening to an unnerving shade of green.

She'd solved it. She finally understood.

"The power..." she murmured, and Harper and Jackson both looked at her.

"What?" Jackson asked.

"It's the power," Scarlett repeated, mystified, and Harper blinked, shaking her head, astonished she hadn't figured it out sooner herself.

"It was this place," Harper said. "The conduits?"

Scarlett nodded. "That's why nothing works in Winterview," Scarlett explained. "The house has been syphoning the city's power. The house has been taking it, channeling it here. Using it for..."

Jackson furrowed his brow, putting it together himself. "That's why the house looks new... That's why everything look different. The furniture. The walls. The house has been restoring itself, bringing itself back to life piece by piece. Regenerating."

"We found doors. A lot of fucking doors," Park said to Jackson.

"But why?" Jackson asked. "Why *steal* all that electricity to look new again? What would be the point?"

"To create more doorways," Scarlett explained. She quickly turned and looked up at the glowing ring on the wall.

The others followed suit.

Veins of electricity webbed across the circle on the wall, turning the surface to a perfect white mirror for a split-second.

Then…silence.

The survivors waited in suspense, the frontline of humanity against the oldest evil in the universe, staring up at a hole torn in front of them, giving them a glimpse to somewhere else. Somewhere that had been lost, but was lost no more.

The roar of waves crashed into the cavern.

"Until you find the one you're looking for," Scarlett muttered, and the realization of everything that had come before made sense then. "The only door that truly matters to the house. The only one left to open."

The stone within the ring was gone, cutaway like a hole in reality itself.

Scarlett took a step a forward. Her eyes went wide. A rush of air expelled like the cold vacuum of space taking a breath. She beheld a burning green sky and twin black suns. Endless dead oceans crashed with violent waves. They were green, too, reflecting a horizon she'd only ever imagined in nightmares. The silhouettes of mile-long tentacles dangled from an infinite expanse of ashen clouds. And below it all, an ancient castle where geometry and sanity had no place.

A high-pitched metallic sound cut through the air, and something like a tuning fork chimed. Scarlett and the others winced as the noise grew shriller, more painful. They clapped their hands over their ears, taking in the great beyond.

Blood dripped from Scarlett's nose in two bright streaks.

She saw Morgana begin to stir, crawling away from the portal.

Scarlett grabbed Jackson's hand, squeezing it tighter, her heart galloping on the verge of seizing.

"Make it stop!" Sandi screamed, and stop it did.

A thunderous rumble could be heard on the other side, and the collision of two waves collided like walls of fire, the spray spilling into their world through the gateway.

Scarlett watched as it misted the platform like acid, eating away the tile in blisters of smoke. Some of it caught the tails of Morgana's coat and it caught fire. She turned back and slapped it out, crab walking back on her palms and heels to escape the overspill.

The survivors watched the hellscape in awe.

The sound of chains, heavy and slow.

Scarlett's gaze went up as a device of iron lowered from a shadowy cavity in the ceiling. A mechanism of black steel lengths and barbs began to stir within the cavern itself high above their heads.

Nick gasped, pulling Rachel into his side, recoiling from the ghastly sight himself. Scarlett saw the hopeless look in his eyes. The dread. And she had to fight not to look away herself.

A shudder rolled throughout the cavern as the mechanism slammed to a halt right above their window into another world, the chains snapping taut with a weighty clack.

"Holy shit," Park asked, sickened. "Is that…?"

"Isabelle?" Nick gasped.

What was left of her, anyway. Her naked body had been pulled apart surgically, folds of skin peeled back revealing organs and muscle that had been petrified with some sort of artificial glaze. A preservative, Scarlett assumed. Her face had been left untouched. A small mercy. Her heart ached for the woman. Tears slipped down her cheeks thinking about the unimaginable terror Isabelle must have endured, a fellow human being, taking solace only in knowing the pain was finally over.

Nick doubled over and vomited all over the platform.

Harper took a step closer, mesmerized yet horrified all the same.

Sandi didn't look up at all.

Scarlett stared into that other world. Prisms of dead light glittered in the sky, like every part of the world was layered in glass. Jagged sections of the clouds swayed against each other like sheets of ice, and she beheld monsters hidden in the clouds so vast they had no end.

A horn blew, low and alien, and she imagined it sounded much like dread manifested in physical form.

"Scar," Jackson said, and his voice was nearly lost among the sound of her own beating heart. "What in the hell is that?" His breathing was picking up. All of theirs was, Scarlett included. She squeezed his hand tighter.

Harper had pushed to the front of the line, watching with obsessed, wild eyes, eager for front row seats to an opera of madness.

Below the dead sky in a doomed emerald castle, buried beneath layers of unholy prisms, and sitting atop a black throne carved from the same cursed mineral as the Oblivion Stone itself, was the King in Yellow.

SCARLETT (cont'd)

"WHAT THE FUCK is that thing?" Sandi said, but her voice was lost among the waves and the low primordial wail preaching from the clouds.

But Scarlett already knew the answer. She watched a snow of black ash drift over the emerald castle, coating the throne room like it did in Winterview, and if she hadn't been thinking of the apocalypse before, she sure as hell was now.

The others watched with baited breath, petrified.

This was it. The one behind it all. The house. The suicides. The Grey World. The land of candy. Not just her story, but to *all* stories. Everything that had come before and everything that would come after.

It all started here.

The low sound of the horn blew again, and a mass of golden robes stirred from the black throne. The thing stepped to the transparent glass floor and it was like the weight of two slabs of stone colliding with the Earth.

"Not good," Jackson uttered. "Definitely not good."

The sigils painting the air shifted like clockwork, burning with a grisly light, and the monster reappeared, closing half the distance between them, following along a protracted yellow carpet. Three golden devices hovered in the air around the monster like vultures, shuffling and restructuring themselves as they morphed into various sequences. A mass of oily vines blossomed at the bottom of the monster's frayed robe as it strode forward with heavy, lumbering steps. Scarlett watched in amazement as sharp mouths sprouted into existence like Venus Fly Traps, yawning with needle-like teeth before abruptly withering away, as if life cultivated wherever the monster walked and then died moments later.

Scarlett gasped and staggered back a few steps, ushering the others away.

The great thing drew in a breath, shuddering with a wet cough, webs of electricity flickering over its enormous body. Neither female nor male, the creature was easily ten feet tall, and seemed more beast than man, although of what variety, Scarlett couldn't be sure. Swathed in a patchwork of filthy yellow robes scorched with burns, soot, and blood, the monster was grossly deformed, a nest of dark spines torn through the rear of the cloak, shielding a severely hunched back. The beast's two elongated hands dangled from the tattered sleeves like coils of snakes, the pale, scabbed fingers brandishing an assortment of ancient rings, some of the jewels containing entire universes within. The creature's deformed spine curved down to its head like the drop of a rollercoaster, a substantial soiled yellow hood draping a pallid ivory mask rusted with age, enchanted by spells that had been forgotten since the beginning of time.

This is the way the world ends, Scarlett thought to herself. The beginning of the end for life across this universe and all others.

The survivors held there, staring up at the towering entity in awe, trapped somewhere between a dream and a nightmare.

The monster shuddered again, hacking while the ash fell dreamy and slow, two oddly human eyes behind the mask panning across each of them, studying them hard and long.

A scream tore through the cavern. Everyone whipped their heads up to find Isabelle's eyes open wide, staring down at them. The corpse coughed and a spurt of blood spilt down her chin, running over the petrified organs and muscle.

"*Isabelle?*" Nick muttered, and the agony in his voice was evident. If he hadn't lost his mind by now, seeing his child's mother in this state would surely finish the job. Rachel couldn't be bothered to notice, staring up at the thing on the other side of the universe, bewitched by its majesty.

Isabelle hacked again and more blood sprayed out of her mouth. She groaned, as if whatever was left of her knew what was happening, experiencing every excruciating detail.

And then she spoke, "Universes old and new. Travelers from near and far. All hail Terrilax, the King in Yellow," the corpse announced. Isabelle's mouth morphed into a deranged grin, cackling hysterically, and that laughter echoed throughout the cavern, and Scarlett wondered if they'd all gone mad.

"Oh, Jesus!" Nick screamed, shrinking away from the horror.

"We have to figure out a way to close it!" Scarlett shouted.

But Harper was too transfixed by the spectacle to move. She stepped forward while the others shrank back, withdrawing themselves from the platform.

And when the King in Yellow spoke, the sound of the creature's voice flooded Scarlett's body with a sorrow as dark as death and a hopelessness no amount of light could ever reach.

"All of the dreams. All of the nightmares," it said, its voice primordial, and strangely wise. ***"All of the havens you could have chosen, and yet somehow, rather serendipitously, you've managed to bring yourself right to me."***

The oceans lulled to a calm.

"Who are you?" Scarlett asked, her voice trembling.

Jackson turned and looked at her, his eyes wide. "Scarlett? What are you doing?" he hissed. "Don't talk to it."

"I am the endless," the thing bellowed. ***"The eater of worlds. The conqueror of the Twelve Realms. The magician of Aiv'aale. The curator of death. And the end of all things."***

A third and fourth hand, yet unseen, emerged from the folds of golden fabric. Spidery, ashen fingers of one hand uncurled to reveal an orb in its palm pulsing with light, while the other wielded an archaic scepter ornamented with bleeding black jewels and forgotten etchings.

"It's you," Harper said, enraptured. "You're the creator?"

The monster turned to her, amused, its fingers squirming.

"No, child." A pause, then, ***"The destroyer."***

"What do you want?" Scarlett asked, and she couldn't help but feel inferior, like an ant before the Sun.

"Scarlett!" Jackson snapped. "Will you please *stop* already?!"

Scarlett watched as the haze of ash fell in that horrible other world, watched as the alien plants with their hungry mouths blossomed and withered in a span of seconds, finally realizing that the plants weren't dying quickly at all, but rather that time was passing at a rapid pace. Seconds in the other realm appeared to be days, weeks, months, as if they were all watching a movie play out on fast-forward.

The monster shifted on his haunches, the golden boxes speeding through various amalgamations like a halo circling around its head.

"I have traveled across time and space, traversed the great unknown, seen the unseeable, and drank from the forbidden fountain. I've created what should not be and reclaimed all that was taken from me."

The monster raised a long, crooked finger, the glistening nail pointed in her direction, and said,

"Scarlett Vantassel, descendant of Life, I have come for you."

"Me?" Scarlett asked. "I don't understand. I'm a nobody."

"But you're so much more," the monster said.

Jackson was looking at her like he noticed something that he had never noticed before.

Scarlett looked at him hopelessly.

"You held the stone, and I felt you as I felt magic for the first time. You are touched by the divine. And you must be destroyed."

Scarlett noticed movement and turned.

Dozens of cultists.

And they were everywhere.

HARPER

THE TIME HAD come for her part. And not only that, but the chance to find out why. Her one chance to ask, "What's the point?"

She glanced over and saw Scarlett whispering something to Jackson. Planning something. She needed to act quickly.

Then she noticed the cultists. Filling in the spaces in the cavern walls, creeping out into plain sight like they'd been there all along and had merely been waiting for an invitation.

The being on the other side of the portal seemed quite taken with Scarlett, almost acting as if the others weren't there at all. The monster's blatant disregard irked her.

"Divinity had no place in the old dream, and it has no place in this one," the ancient thing said.

The others were getting uneasy, watching as the cultists filled the cavern, waiting patiently as they had before in the streets. Nick swung down and picked up Rachel, taking her in his arms. Sandi's eyes were zipping around, searching for some type of weapon. And Park, well…she was drawn to that other world just as much as Harper itself. Maybe even more.

This was it. Everything she'd worked tirelessly for and now she was going to be slaughtered before she could get any real answers. Any absolute truths. Offed by a crazed cult of all things.

Harper looked around, watching the robed fanatics close in on their tight-knit group, the same primitive weapons as before in their hands ready to dismember them in the most horrific ways imaginable.

Morgana was the only one armed, a gleaming blade in each hand. She slashed out, tearing a streak of red across one of the white robes.

"What are we doing here, guys?!" Nick asked.

"Working on it," Scarlett said. Her eyes darted about, searching for a solution. Anything that could save them.

But Harper saw nothing because there *was* nothing.

"If you're gonna do something you better do it fast!" Jackson said.

A cultist swung a dagger and Nick twisted his body to spin Rachel away; the edge cleaved through his forearm and the girl tumbled out of his arms.

"Shit!" Another cultist plunged a knife down and Sandi caught them by the wrists, slowing its descent as she fell backward, landing on her back.

Another raised a baseball bat over their head and Jackson launched forward, tackling them to the ground.

Scarlett dove on top of them, trying to wrestle the bat away. She grunted, jerking the weapon out of their hands. A different cultist raked a blade over her shoulder and she yelped, cracking them in the side of the head.

Harper watched as the cultists jabbed and slashed and maimed, taking their time, knowing their prey had no escape. Hopelessness was setting in as they were overwhelmed, all while the King in Yellow looked on, still as a demented portrait.

Harper looked up and found one of the masked lunatics in front of her, a machete high over their head, the expressionless mask speckled with blood, a rusted blade about to cleave her in two.

She braced herself, turning her head and holding her hands up because it was all she could think to do.

A gunshot went off loud as a cannon blast.

The sound of a bullet whizzed through the cavern.

A heavy thud.

Harper opened her eyes as the cultist's head arched back in a spray of blood, the limp body tumbling off the platform and sailing into the pit of darkness like a ghost.

The cultists ceased their assault.

The survivors scrambled away from them, checking their wounds, tearing off makeshift strips from their clothing and fashioning tourniquets where they stood.

A room full of murmurs and angry ocean waves.

The throngs of cultists covering the path parted, the black and white tiles splattered with blood.

At the other end, Beau Winchester stood with a smoking pistol in one hand and an ax in the other.

HARPER (cont'd)

"BEAU?" SCARLETT SAID, astonished, straining to catch her breath.

"The hillbilly?" Jackson said, panting. "Oh, thank God."

Beau's presence gave the survivors a second wind.

The cavern settled into the brassy roll of the ocean waves.

Harper turned and looked over her shoulder at the King in Yellow, who had taken an interest in Beau Winchester, their apparent savior.

Perhaps she'd misjudged him after all.

The cultists changed direction, swarming in the mountain man's direction.

Beau was ready for them. He took a few steps back but held his ground, watching them charge at him. What was he up to?

Sandi screamed and Harper turned to in time to see Nick collapse to the platform, a knife lodged in his stomach. Before Sandi could react, Morgana coldcocked her across the face, knocking her out. Rachel made no attempt to run; Morgana grabbed the girl, ushering her toward the passages in the cavern walls.

Park rushed after them, giving chase up the sides of rock, careful to avoid the drop-offs into the abyss.

"We need to shut this thing off or we're all dead!" Scarlett shouted, pointing at the conduits on the ceiling feeding electricity to the gate.

"With what?! We don't have shit!" Jackson said.

"Harper, I'm going to try and cut the power off!" Scarlett said. "Get the girl!" She sprinted from the platform, scurrying up and over the rock while the monster tracked her with its eyes. Park was scrambling up the opposite side, chasing after Morgana and Rachel.

"Scarlett, wait!" Jackson shouted. He rushed after her, and Harper knew her one true chance was finally within reach.

She had got it all wrong. She knew that now. Monsters. The supernatural. Even God. All of it was real. As real as the pain she'd felt every morning since she'd found Katie hanging from the end of that rope. And if all of those things were real beyond a shadow of a doubt, then that meant that there was still a chance Katie was waiting for her. She still had time to do what was right for her. And not *just* her, but the others too.

She knew what she had to do now. Distract the ancient thing. Create a diversion. Demand answers to the questions that had haunted her for her entire life. Give the others the only thing in the world that could save them: time.

Harper spun around, finding herself face-to-face with the King in Yellow, and it was like she was standing at the foot of a giant theater screen. The thing towered over her, the tattered yellow robes blowing harshly in the stormy world beyond, and the beast's gaze slipped down to her.

While pandemonium ensued, Harper cautiously approached the gateway, mindful of the wash of acid spilling over the threshold of the alien world, eating away at the platform. A cacophony of screams echoed in the cavern. She heard her friends crying, pleading to stay away from it. To run.

But her mind was already made up. She realized then that it had been since the moment she'd set foot in the house.

"If you're real," Harper said, "then that must mean there's a god. There has to be."

"There is no God," the thing said callously. ***"Only the reckoning."***

A shiver ran through her.

"You say you're a magician," Harper said. "What do you know?"

The creature's head dipped down to her own height, the pale mask peeking out beneath the golden hood.

"Everything," it hissed.

Harper considered it, then reached into her back pocket, taking out a worn photograph of Katie. She took a breath, unfolding the picture and holding it out, mere feet away from the monster.

"My daughter, Katie…she died."

Harper held the photo up and the monster's head lowered, its pale blue eyes examining it. One of its fingers breached the portal, then a whole hand, a black nail running over Katie's smiling face as the monster rumbled like it had thunder in its gullet.

"You seek answers," the King in Yellow said.

"Yes," Harper said, listening to the screams filling the cavern. She took a step closer, and with more conviction, "*Yes.* I want to know the point. I want to know why she's dead and I'm still here. Why I'm still trapped here in this fucking house and my baby girl is gone," she sobbed.

"Life's only purpose is to be annihilated."

The monster took the picture in its spidery fingers and withdrew its hand, rising to its full towering height. Harper watched as the paper aged before her eyes, fading yellow, then brown, disintegrating before her eyes to dust, carried away in the storm raging in that other world until only the monster's hideous fingers remained.

Harper eyed Scarlett and Jackson climbing down near the edge of the platform, a steep drop-off below. They'd managed to circle to the far edge of the ring. That was when she noticed: the device wasn't close enough to the ledge. They'd never be able to reach it. She could see Scarlett mouthing something to her, but couldn't make out what.

"If it is knowledge you seek, then it is knowledge you shall have."

Harper's eyes glazed over.

This was it. Everything she'd waited for. Years of misery. Years of sadness. Years of trying to find any reason she could to go on.

Her fingers went to her neck, seeking solace in the single possession that had brought her comfort in her darkest moments.

And that was when she realized it.

Katie's necklace; it was gone.

The King in Yellow extended a hand, the orb in its hideous palm pulsing, flickering between rose and orange and deep red. The three golden devices floating above the creature's head began transforming, mechanically revolving while they interlinked themselves, locking into the shape of a substantial golden crown, mirroring the cultist's crude symbol she'd seen depicted all over Winterview.

"Did you know that time has a sound?"

Harper watched as the crown hovered above the monster's head. The King in Yellow reached its hand through the portal, the glass sphere vibrating, and it was like she could hear the sound of time in her ears.

"For eons I searched the twelve realms. Traversed endless planes in search of a melody. A dream," the King in Yellow said. ***"Until all that remained was madness."***

The sound rose in her mind, distant at first, like she wasn't sure it was there at all. It was droning, cycling in her ears, her head spinning into a daze. Before long it went ultrasonic, like a noise only an animal could hear.

"All of those tiny, imperceivable moments stretched by the wheels of time until they're taut as obsidian strings."

The sound folded over, piercing her brain, violating every part of her mind. Harper fell to her knees before the King in Yellow and the cursed Emerald City.

"But even strings have their limits."

She could see Scarlett screaming something to her, straining to destroy the ring, Jackson holding onto her from behind to keep her from falling. She blinked and Scarlett was back on the ledge now, shouting.

"And like all things, eventually they tire. They strain."

Then Scarlett was gone and Katie was there and it was Christmas morning. The memories were playing out in the belly of a tornado. Debris was belting around them, whirling in a violent gray wind. She saw herself in the street teaching Katie how to ride her first bike, watched as she lost her first tooth. She smelled her hair and her skin, felt her heartbeat the same way she had for the first time when she'd held her on her naked chest in the hospital.

"They unravel, thread by thread."

Then Katie looked at her and frowned and she was gone.

The memory in her was sucked up in the tornado whirling around her. She was flying now, transported through a vortex of swirling lights and sounds. She heard the haunting melody of death and the music of new life, experiencing in a span of seconds all of the greatest joys and excruciating pains life had to offer. She saw worlds she could only dream about. Marvelous new places awash with light and sun. Faces she didn't know yet somehow did, like she was connected to everyone and everything in the universe all at once.

The cosmos faded away, and suddenly she was falling.

She crashed face first into a sea of oil, pulled into dark depths.

Horrors glided around her that were so vast and so monstrous that her mind couldn't fully rationalize them, only revealing fragments. Mile-long tentacles lined with hungry mouths. Pale, scaled flesh scored with rotting sores.

Back on the platform, she felt tears slide over her cheeks.

Blood trickled from every orifice.

"Until one day, when they can't hold on anymore, they break."

And her final thought was Dirac's words echoing in her head, hollow and empty.

Save us from hell.

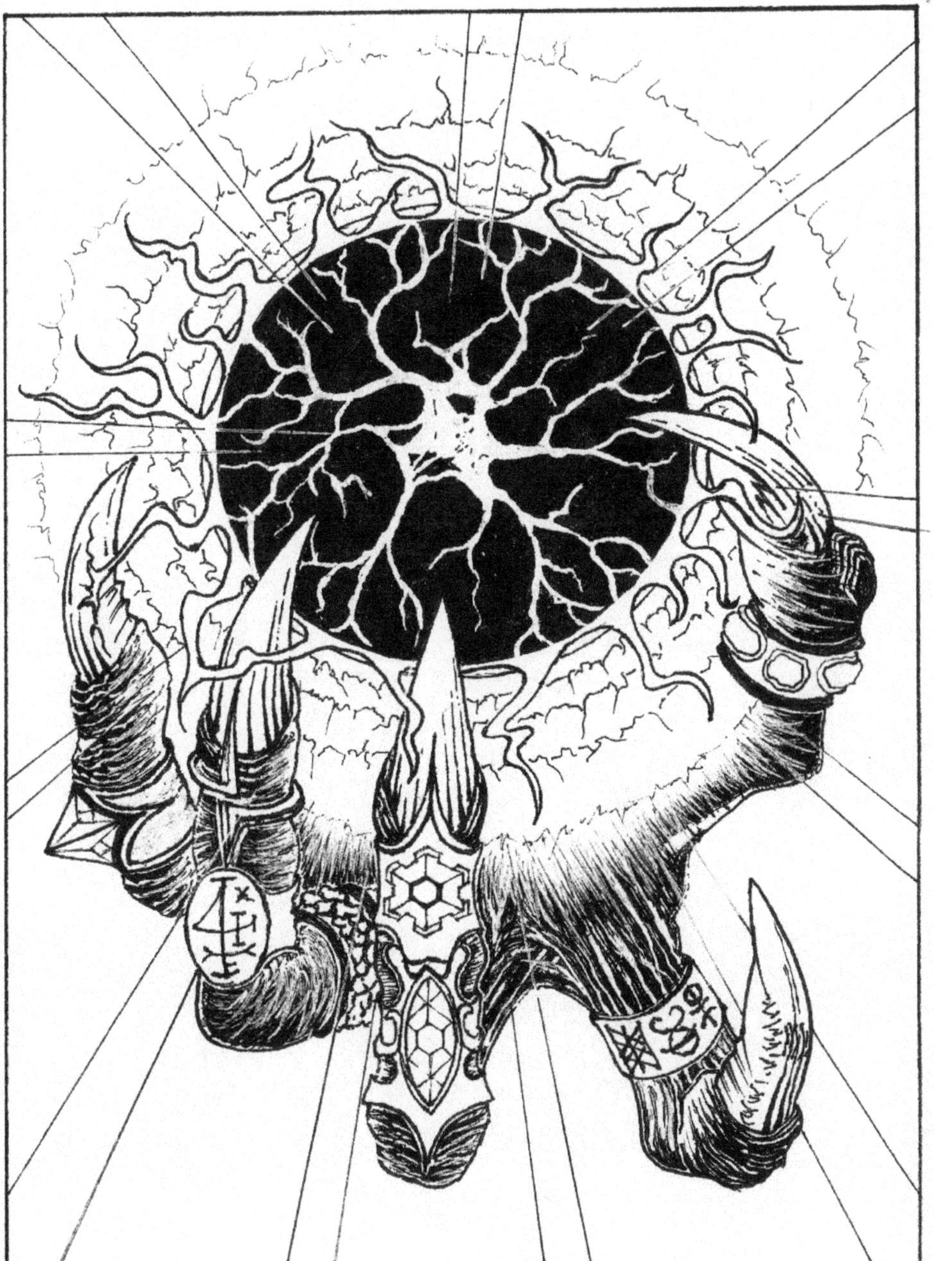

SCARLETT

"A LITTLE FURTHER!" Scarlett said.

She was hanging over the precipice of the abyss—one hand clinging to the rock, Jackson clutching the seat of her pants from behind—desperately trying to shatter the glass coil burning with power.

She had the baseball bat extended out, swinging clumsily in a poor attempt to shatter the glass.

It was no use; she simply didn't have the leverage.

"Shit!" Jackson shouted.

Scarlett lurched forward over thin air and her heart launched into her throat.

She glanced over her shoulder and Jackson's eyes looked like they were about to pop out of his head.

"Sorry," he said, straining. He was near his breaking point; he couldn't hold on much longer.

Scarlett shook her head, determined.

We need more time.

And that was when she noticed Harper standing mere feet away from the portal, handing something to the King in Yellow.

"Harper!" she wailed. "What're you doing?! Get away from it!"

Jackson was yelling behind her, screaming to get away from the monster, but their cries fell on deaf ears.

"Jackie," she shouted. "Something's wrong!"

Nick was barely moving, his crumpled body lying on the platform behind Harper, bleeding out, and Sandi was out too.

"Nick! Get up! Wake up!" Scarlett pleaded. But he didn't. "Nick!"

Scarlett screamed out in frustration, hucking the bat over her shoulder, the wood bouncing off the rock back on the ledge.

"Pull me back!" Scarlett ordered, and Jackson did.

Back on solid ground, she took one last look around, desperate for a way to dismantle the device. The ceilings were too high; she'd never be able to reach it.

Out of nowhere, a high-pitched note erupted into the cavern like thousands of steel strings, raking over her mind. The wires cut at her ears and Scarlett screamed, falling to her knees. Jackson was beside her, immersed in his own private hell.

"What is that?!" Jackson yelled, the capillaries in his eyes bursting in a bloody cascade.

Scarlett looked toward the platform and her heart sunk.

Trickles of blood oozed from Harper's nose and ears, her gorgeous eyes gone, rolled so far back in her head they were nonexistent.

"HARPER!" she screamed, and it was so piercing Nick finally jerked awake on the platform, barely hanging on himself.

The metallic sound abruptly cut out and Harper's body jolted like her soul had been sucked out, drunkenly swaying on the platform.

"Harper?" Scarlett said, her voice wavering.

Harper fell to her knees. She turned and looked at Scarlett, and blinked just once. She smiled, collapsing to the black-and-white tile and dying right there on the platform.

Scarlett squeezed her eyes closed, waited for the inevitable moment when she'd reopen them and be somewhere else in the house. Somewhere she didn't recognize with people she didn't remember, the same as before.

Only when she finally did, she was still there, tears cutting over her face, a battle scene of epic proportions playing out before her in a hollowed-out part of the earth.

Harper's body was still there, too, and Scarlett cried harder then, because she knew Harper was gone and she wasn't coming back.

NICK

A SCREAM IN his ears. His eyes shot open and he bolted upright on the platform. Searing pain flared in his stomach. He looked down and saw the handle jutting out of his abdomen, blood sluicing down his side.

Harper was stuck in a trance of some kind, frozen like a statue before the monster, her head convulsing like she was having some sort of seizure.

"Harper!" Nick shouted, and then he screamed because the pain in his nerve endings caught, setting his stomach on fire. He gritted his teeth, fighting through the pain.

"Get the fuck away from it!" he yelled.

But it was no use. She couldn't seem to hear him. He began to pull himself along the platform, and the pain in his side roared to life like fire. He screamed, biting his teeth down and slapping the platform with an open hand.

A shrill scream cut through the cavern.

Rachel.

He turned and watched Morgana climb up to an opening in the cavern wall with Rachel. They disappeared inside, Park not far behind them.

Sandi was lying near the edge of the platform unconscious.

"Sandi!" he said. "Sandi, wake up! Come on!"

He went to stand and a bite of white-hot pain flared in his gut. He screamed, looking down to see the silver handle of the knife jutting out.

Without thinking, he reached down and tore it out. He screamed louder, nearly passing out from the pain.

He clamped a hand to his side and stood up on wobbly legs.

His vision went hazy, then clear. His limbs trembled. He held his palm up to find it smeared with blood. He looked down and found it running over his boot, pooling on the tile below.

He was losing blood, fast.

BEAU

EVERYTHING WAS SET. He'd made sure of it.

He'd marched outside to his truck. Stopped in the middle of the road, finding a gleaming Colt Python at his feet. He figured one of the others must have lost it earlier in the encounter with the loons. He'd picked it up because a gun like that could fetch a pretty penny and walked to his truck. He'd even made it as far as getting in and closing the door. But no matter how hard he tried, he couldn't bring himself to start it. He wasn't sure why, couldn't understand why he'd suddenly decided to grow a heart right when he was home free.

He'd put the keys in the ignition, ready to throw the truck in gear and floor it like a bat outta hell.

"Just go, you stupid sonofabitch," he said to himself. "Just drive the fuck outta here and never look back." And that was *if* the battery still worked, the chances being nil. They never did last long in the Dead Zone.

But then he thought of the Copper Man, thought of how one day he'd walked out to that blissful clearing in the woods and his friend was gone. He remembered how much it hurt, being left behind, alone with his thoughts.

And something remarkable happened then.

He looked up through the cracked windshield, gazed at the twinkling stars peeking through the blanket of clouds and thought about how happy he would have been if the Copper Man had come back for him.

"Or never left at all," he whispered, coming to his own realization.

He exhaled, shaking his head, marveling at how dense he had been, realizing that *he* had become the Copper Man in the end.

He'd abandoned the others, left them to die.

He let his forehead fall against the steering wheel, chiding himself.

"Well, shit."

He popped opened the Python's cylinder, counted the bullets (four), then palmed it closed. He popped open the glove box, scooping out a cache of filthy rags stained with oil. He carefully unwrapped them, revealing a grenade circa World War 2 courtesy of an abandoned Army Navy Surplus nearby (the owner had left behind a whole stash of the stuff).

He felt the weight of the grenade in his palm and the corner of his mouth hooked into a smirk.

"For a rainy day," he said. He climbed out of the truck and slammed the door, shoving the grenade in his pocket and the Colt tight in his waistband. He hustled to the back of the truck, reaching over the side and throwing up one side of the tarp. He reached inside, pulling out a rusty tin of kerosene.

He turned and took one final look at the façade of the house.

"You ready, you old bitch?" Beau snarled.

The wind howled back at him in response.

"Time to paint this motherfucker red."

Minutes after he'd marched back through the entrance doors there had been a blip in the house's atmosphere. A charge. He felt the change the same way he could feel the electricity in the air during a storm. The fine hairs on his arms stood at attention, a tingling wavered through his body. His brain felt like it reset itself, like he should have forgotten something but didn't.

He turned and noticed a painting on the nearest wall. A handsome man with wavy blond hair and striking gemstone-green eyes. The man was fitted in a three-piece suit and the textures reminded him of the house's strange decor. He dangled a polished pocket watch from one hand, as if trying to hypnotize the viewer, and had a gold coin rolling down his knuckles in the other. The man wore an odd smirk, like he had a secret that you could know if only you were smart enough. Beau thought he recognized him. Thought the man might have been an entertainer. An actor maybe.

Or a magician.

He continued on without giving the stranger another thought, stopping in the middle of the hallway and sniffing at the dank air. Most people wouldn't have paid notice. But he wasn't most people.

A cross between salt and rock.

He drew the gun from his waistband, moving quicker through the halls, passing through the warm glow of countless sconces fixed to the walls. He slowed as he passed an oil painting of a small cabin in the woods, and it reminded him of home. Not of the shitty house he'd been raised in, no. But rather the small cabin anchored at the edge of the Copper Man's meadow like a Bob Ross Painting. And damn if it didn't look identical.

Not similar, he thought. No…the same exact fucking cabin! Was he losing his mind? His eyes examined it harder, closer, searching for the Copper Man on that old fallen log he used to sit on.

A scream broke out around a bend in the hall.

No time, he thought, and he had to fight the urge to turn back, get a closer look at the painting.

He rounded the corner and that was when he noticed it; to his far right the hallway transformed to a gaping maw of white rock.

He held there, listening to the impossibly loud roar of the ocean and a voice so unsettling it made his mind want to collapse in on itself and die.

He cautiously approached the opening, flattening his back against the rock and peering into a room that was physically impossible to fit inside the house. The entire thing looked like it had been chiseled from stone, and he marveled at the feat. He didn't give it a second thought, couldn't if he wanted to. That otherworldly voice was like rusty nails in his head.

That's when he saw the others. They were all there. Everyone that had went into the house. They were down on the platform at the far end of the cavern. On the wall in front of them was a gigantic ring at least thirty feet high blazing with neon power.

The room was crawling with cultists. They poured from passageways in the walls and, somehow, none of them had noticed him enter from this end, too preoccupied with the ghastly figure speaking to them from—as far as he could tell—another world.

The cultists sprang into action.

He heard screams as they swarmed the others, hacking at them with blades of every shape and size.

Fortuitously, the lunatics seemed to be taking their time, trying to prolong the other's terror, gradually wearing them down while they tried to defend themselves. Giving them barely enough time to feel every cut and stab before they struck again.

He needed more time.

He jogged down the black-and-white checkered path, ignoring the gallery of horror and sliding to a stop. He popped the lid off the tin of kerosene and angled it over, one hand on the bottom, pouring a zigzagging trail across the pathway and setting the can on the ground and kicking it over. The canister sluiced gulps of the liquid, dousing the tile. It ran downhill toward the platform at the other end.

He looked up and saw the scientist, Harper, frozen in shock, a cultist with an ax ready to bury it in her head.

He urged her to do something, anything, but she was paralyzed.

"Shit," he said.

He raised the Colt, squinted his eyes, and fired.

The skirmish died down. The cultists withdrew.

The survivors gaped at him in amazement, hanging on by a thread.

The cultists changed direction, and suddenly they were an army. He'd become Leonidas against an infinite army of Persians, swarming right at him.

The little girl.

Morgana had her by the arm, dragging her toward one of the passages in the walls, Park giving chase. Nick was on the ground with a knife in his belly laying in a pool of his own blood with Sandi laid out next to him.

Beau coolly took out his pack of cigarettes and pulled one with his teeth. He popped open the Zippo and lit the end, taking in a long drag as the cultists sprinted in his direction.

"Come on, you fucks," he said. "I'm right here."

Beau watched the army of cultists flutter in his direction, the white robes like a legion of ghosts. His hand tightened around the Python and he thought of the grenade in his pocket.

He sucked in one last drag and smiled, flicking the cigarette.

It whirled through the air in slow-motion, doing a swan dive to the tile. The glowing cherry touched the kerosene and caught, sending a shockwave of flame rolling across the tile pathway, completely engulfing it in fire.

The monster in that horrible other world looked at him then and it was like he'd been marked for death. A shiver of dread wormed its way through his body.

He was a dead man walking. The only question was when?

MORGANA

UP UNTIL THEN, the girl had put up little resistance, if any. So, imagine her surprise when the little brat jerked her arm free and gave her a hard shove with both hands.

Morgana sincerely believed that had it not been for years of training her body, honing senses, her reflexes, she would be dead.

But she did. And she had. When she toppled back, watching the ceiling of white stone pass before her eyes, her instincts kicked in; she dropped the knives and fell back into a roll, praying that her timing was right.

She threw her arms out just in time to fold the upper half of her torso over the edge of the crag, her legs dangling over the abyss below.

She grunted, looking up to find the girl gazing down at her coldly before wandering away.

Morgana's eyes darted over the precipice for something to grab on to. She felt her weight shift; her body dropping an inch or two. Her eyes shot open as her upper body began dragging over the rock, through a layer of dust and pebbles. Her fingers narrowly hooked onto a shallow fissure shaped like a lightning bolt and one of her nails was torn away.

She shrieked, her face showered with white pebbles as they whizzed past her face into the pit below.

She grunted, anchoring herself securely on the ledge and swinging her legs for momentum. She screamed, throwing her weight and rolling onto the ledge to a stop.

She quickly clambered to her feet and looked around.

Before she could get her bearings, a woman screamed, plowing into her like a car, their bodies tumbling through the air.

Morgana slammed onto the ground on her back and the wind left her.

Park was on top of her, her eyes crazy with rage, raining blows down on her face, and it was like they were back in the land of candy.

Morgana kicked a knee up and caught the woman in the spine with a hollow thud. Park's back arched from the blow and Morgana used the opportunity to throw her aside.

She scrambled up, straddling Park. Her eyes darted about.

One of the knives was gone, but the other was still there.

Park saw it, too—but she was too slow.

Morgana quickly snatched it from the rock, taking it solidly in her hand and plunging down.

Park threw her hand up and it punched through the center of her palm. Park shrieked, using her other hand to brace against the attack.

"There's no one here to save you this time," Morgana said with a grin, pressing her weight down. "No more doors. No knight in shining armor. And no witches."

Park whimpered, the blade edging closer.

An explosion rocked through the cavern, quaking the walls and floor, throwing Morgana off balance. Stunned, she tilted her head to the side and saw the mountain man across the cavern on the ground with his hands clapped over his ears, the pathway in front of him cratered by a blast of rock, licks of flame burning, the scent of kerosene in the air. Body parts attached to white, bloodied robes littered the once pristine black and white trail.

Park took advantage of the opportunity to shove the knife handle backward, striking Morgana in the nose with a crunch of blood.

Her vision went blurry. Her grip slackened. She reached up in a daze, touching the blood gushing from her nose.

Park screamed, throwing a left haymaker into her face.

Morgana's head snapped to the right.

The knife still fixed through the middle of her palm, Park roared, slapping Morgana in the face. The blade punched through the woman's cheek, spearing out the other side in a spurt of red.

Morgana groaned painfully, and rivulets of blood dripped down on Park's face. She felt the cold metal above her tongue, felt her broken teeth and torn gums and the coppery flavor of her own blood.

Park abruptly retracted the blade and Morgana gasped, staggering back in drunken shock. She stumbled about a moment, a wounded animal, one hand clamped to her marred face, the other to balance herself on the wall.

Morgana winced, smiling through a mouthful of blood at Park. She fell back against the cave wall, sliding down to the ground. Her chest rose and fell as the chaos unfolded around them. She felt the blood escaping her body along with the fight, finally resigned to her fate.

Park got to her feet and slid the blade from her hand. The woman held the thing up, looking at it in disgust, and then tossed it over the cliff. She cradled her bloodied hand, gazing down at Morgana with pity.

"You're going to die here," Park said.

Morgana laughed painfully, coughing up more blood, her arms and legs limp.

"I hope it was worth it."

And then Park simply turned and walked away.

NICK

RACHEL HAD RETURNED. He watched her carefully make her way down the slope of rocks to the platform, fragile as ever.

She slid the last few feet on her butt, and when her dirty bare feet met the tile, she looked up at him the same way she had the other thousand times.

Park hadn't come back with her, but he prayed the woman was okay, and if they made it out of this alive, he vowed to buy her a beer for saving his little girl.

He was sitting upright on the platform, bracing himself on one arm next to Sandi, the other clamped against his belly while blood oozed between his fingers. The cultists in the room were preoccupied with Beau. Screams rang out in the stone hollow, the swarm of bodies rushing after him like moths to a flame. At one point he'd even heard an explosion at the other end of the cave, watching some of the ceiling crumbling down in giant slabs.

Rachel arrived and he smiled, tears of joy cutting through the dirt and blood coating his face.

He reached out and took her in his arms, and everything that had transpired that night felt worth it.

"I've got you," he said, and he meant it.

He let her go and Rachel stared down at him.

"I love you, kid," he said.

A blade punched into his throat. He gasped. His eyes shot open.

It was an odd sensation, hot and cold at the same time. He felt the bite of the cold metal, the rush of cool air with it, but somehow felt the warmth of his body fleeing him at the same time.

His eyes watered. His breathing snagged. His fingers pawed at the knife lodged in his throat, his eyes going wide with horror.

"What—did you—" he wheezed.

Rachel stared at him with the same blank expression she'd had for the last three months, completely indifferent as he choked to death on his own blood.

He heard Scarlett and Jackson shouting somewhere in his peripheral. He turned and saw the King in Yellow watching him, looking down on all the blood and carnage, pleased.

He coughed, falling on his back, gazing up at Rachel, betrayed yet strangely grateful. Grateful that she'd saved him once but couldn't save him again. Grateful for the honest life he'd lived after she'd been born, experiencing things he never would have had the chance had she not been born. Love. Fatherhood. And now death. He reached out for her and saw a flicker of humanity register in her eyes.

"Rachel…" he uttered. He hacked blood onto his face, dying, his fingers straining to touch his baby one last time.

Rachel crouched down, leaning in close.

As their fingers began to touch, Rachel lurched further, seizing the blade in his throat and jerking it upward.

He felt his throat tear wide open, the skin and muscle now a gaping hole pouring steaming blood onto the platform.

Rachel blinked, staring down at him.

"I…love…" he choked, "…you…kid."

"NICK!"

Sandi had come to. He heard her scrambling across the platform, and then she was there, her lovely face filling his waning vision, her wounded eyes raining tears down on him.

She sobbed, taking his hands in her own.

"NICK!" she sobbed. "Oh my God, Nick, oh my God!"

"Hey, Chef," he said weakly.

"Hey," Sandi said, fighting back a rush of tears.

Nick could feel the warmth leaving his body.

"I guess…we're gonna…have to take a rain check…on that sundae," he said, smiling, and whatever Sandi held back she completely let go, erupting into loud, uncontrollable sobs. "Take Rach…for me… please."

He couldn't feel Sandi's hands anymore.

"Hey," he said feebly. He put his palm on her cheek and she held it there, staring down at him hopelessly. "It's…okay. Don't…be…sad. It's…okay. Everything…will…"

The light faded from his eyes. They slowly fell closed, the world dimming, Sandi's devastated face fading to blackness.

And then nothing.

JACKSON

SCARLETT WAS RUNNING, and he was sprinting behind her, trying not to fall off the ledge and kill himself. The cavern was filling with smoke. His throat burned, his chest filling with burning air.

Harper was dead. He could see her body out of the corner of his eye, sprawled out like a beautiful snow angel.

They'd watched in horror as the monster had given her a glimpse into eternity, overloading her mind with the history of the universe, giving her answers to questions no one should have answers to.

Harper held on for as long as she could, but alas, her mind could take no more. Despite a prickly demeanor, she was still, after all, a human being, never meant to see beyond the scope of humanities' capabilities.

Scarlett had nearly leapt off the platform and Jackson grabbed her around the waist, wrestling her back as she screamed for Harper.

The orb floated back to the Emerald City, dreamily landing in the King in Yellow's palm, the monster storing it away in its filthy robes.

But the strangest thing of all was that they were still here. The day hadn't reset, hadn't taken them back to the beginning like it had all those times before. Scarlett knew this as he knew this, which meant the stakes had changed. If Harper was dead, that meant there *were* no second chances anymore. No dying and waking up again, over and over again until you got it right. The house, for whatever reason, was operating the same inside now as it was outside. At least to a degree. Which meant things had become exponentially more dangerous.

They were moving again. Backtracking through the passages in the walls to get back to the platform. He saw Rachel through windows cut into the rock; she was climbing back down to the platform.

Good. Park had gotten her back. He breathed a sigh of relief.

Scarlett suddenly skidded across the rock, ducking, but Jackson's momentum kept him going. He flipped over her, crashing into the legs of one of the cultists, taking them down with him.

Metal clanged off the ground.

Jackson rolled over and saw a dagger within reach. He went for it but the cultist got there first, taking it in a fist.

Before they could swing, Scarlett's bat smashed their hand, breaking the blade free.

The cultist grunted.

Scarlett chopped the bat through the air a second time.

Jackson heard a thwack and the white robes went down hard in a mound of white fabric.

They dashed forward, emerging from the cave at the edge of the platform, skidding to a stop.

"Oh my God," Jackson said, horrified.

Nick was sprawled out next to Harper in a pool of blood, a gaping hole in his throat.

Rachel stood looming over him.

"NICK!" Scarlett screamed.

Sandi was down at his side, bawling her eyes out.

Rachel's face turned up to find them at the top of the slope.

They rushed down the side of the rock, watching Rachel pad toward the portal.

She stopped short of the threshold and turned to face them.

And for the first time that night, she smiled.

Only it wasn't the innocent, childlike smile of a young girl, but rather something demonic. Something ancient. Something that made his blood run cold.

Rachel held her tiny hand out in front of her in a fist, opening it.

The air was sucked out of the room.

All the chaos filling the cavern fell silent.

Nestled in her palm was a shard of black gem.

The Oblivion Stone.

SCARLETT

THE OBLIVION STONE.

But how?

Rachel's grin widened. The jewel pulsed with emerald light, vibrating in her palm, the girl's skin riddled with infected veins.

"She has the stone," Scarlett said.

"This whole time?" Jackson asked. "But how?"

"It doesn't matter how," she said. "She's using it to keep the portal open. We have to stop her!"

"HARPER!" Park slid down the opposite slope, racing across the platform. Her feet hit the layer of congealed blood and she went down on her ass. She didn't seem to care. She sobbed, throwing her arms around Harper and cradling the woman's head. "Goddamn it, Harper, why couldn't you just leave it alone."

Park whimpered, turning her gaze up to find Rachel staring down at her, grinning. Park saw Nick's body, the blood seeping out of his neck, Sandi pressed down against his chest.

Rachel held herself upright in front of the portal. In front of the King in Yellow. The Oblivion Stone beaming with ghastly green light.

"*You*," Park snarled.

Rachel giggled demonically, and when they looked back, the girl's physical form started to peel away like smoke, coiling into a swirling plume, her soul dragged twisting and screaming into the other realm, her essence absorbed by one of the King in Yellow's rings. The final layer of the illusion whisked from the little girl's body, whirling through the air like a genie into a magic lamp. The monster groaned like it had devoured a hearty meal, then gazed out at them.

And when Scarlett looked back, an entirely different girl stood before them instead.

"Vanessa?" Scarlett said, her voice wavering.

The girl smiled. "Hello, Scarlett."

Vanessa Halliday stood on the platform, as if not a day had passed. She recognized her from the photograph. Vanessa held up her small hands, studying them, watching her fingers wiggle and bend. Her alabaster skin was laced with black veins, her transparent blue eyes bright as winter ice. She wore a grimy linen dress but no shoes.

Scarlett didn't know how she'd done what she'd done, but somehow her physical form was here, like it or not.

A scream loosed toward the entrance and they all turned back to find Beau a short way down the path, working his way closer. He was ready to charge forward but Scarlett held up a hand, ordering him to stand down.

Scarlett took a step forward, Park reverently setting Harper's body on the platform, rising to stand with her friends. Sandi stayed with Nick's body on the platform, cradling him in her arms.

The cavern started to shake, and massive chunks of the ceiling fell away, narrowly missing the path and whizzing past them into the darkness.

"Where is she?" Scarlett asked. "Where's the girl?!"

And the King in Yellow answered,

"Damned."

Jackson looked at her hopelessly.

And suddenly, quite miraculously, Scarlett had a plan. She couldn't take the monster head-on. She needed a workaround. To take the one thing powering everything and strip it from the equation.

She set her sights on Vanessa.

"The stone—it's done something to you. Corrupted you," Scarlett said.

Vanessa eyed her as she circumvented the bodies in the center of the platform.

"This isn't who you are. It never was." Scarlett took a step forward, and Vanessa took a step back. "The stone: we have to destroy it—it's the only way to stop this."

"*Stop it?*" Vanessa asked in her stern English accent. "*I* was the one who opened it. *I* was the one who brought it here."

"No!" Scarlett argued. "That's the stone. Herbert Bell. But it wasn't you. It was never you. You're sick. The stone's infected you. Infected your mind. Don't listen to it!"

"You're wrong," Vanessa maintained.

"I'm not! You know I'm not!"

"This stone is *nothing* without me." Vanessa held open her palm and the Oblivion Stone sang a chorus of madness.

Now was her chance.

She kicked out, swinging her leg as fast and as accurately as humanely possible.

Vanessa realized what was happening a second too late.

Scarlett's foot collided with Vanessa's hand and the stone went flying.

SCARLETT (cont'd)

THE OBLIVION STONE sailed through the open space, passing high above their heads in a dreamy tumble.

Scarlett's eyes narrowed. She turned to Beau and he nodded.

Now!

"This is for you, Hannah," she said.

She whipped the bat through the air, smashing the stone like she was hitting a home run, and she could feel Tommy there watching her, proud.

Beau grit his teeth and fired.

Time might as well have stopped.

Scarlett's breath hitched.

The bullet cut through the cavern, a one-in-a-million shot, zipping over the bodies of countless dead cultists while everyone looked on in amazement.

Over the cratered checkered pathway.

Over plumes of billowing black smoke.

Over ribbons of dying flames and ragged body parts.

The bullet passed over Jackson.

Then Park and Sandi.

Then finally Scarlett.

Vanessa tried to intercept it and the bullet exploded through her hand in a splash of blood.

Scarlett twisted her head, watched as the black stone broke into the world beyond, passing through the iridescent shimmer that separated one realm from another.

The bullet punched through after it, unstoppable, and she thought it strange how calm the monster seemed to be in spite of everything happening, almost unconcerned, like it knew the outcome before it had happened.

The bullet collided with the gem dead center and it shattered like a super nova, raining a confetti of black shards in all directions. She caught glimpses of Tommy and Hannah in the blinding light, saw them smiling at her, tucked away in the light just how she remembered them.

A violent shockwave rolled through the cavern. The bleached stone walls began to splinter; cracks ran rampant, fracturing the ceiling and walls, sending hefty chunks of the roof whizzing past.

The immense ring powering the gateway groaned, the light flickering, losing power. Scarlett craned her head up to find the electricity in the tubes growing unstable.

"Beau, the glass!" she screamed. "Shoot it!"

Beau looked up, determined, and fired again, shattering a length of glass tubing running along the ceiling. The electricity shrieked, tendrils of white-hot power webbing along the cavern's roof like a Plasma Ball.

"You'll ruin everything!" Vanessa screamed.

Her cries caught Beau's attention. He turned to her and scowled as the electrical system went haywire.

He fired one last time, the Colt bucking in his hand, a white muzzle flash as big as his head erupting out of the barrel.

Vanessa's eyes shot open.

The bullet caught her in the shoulder, punching into one side and exploding out the other, spinning her like a top. Her body swayed toward the King in Yellow, the shimmering veil separating worlds welcoming her with open arms.

Vanessa landed hard on her back on the soiled golden carpet and rolled. She flopped to her stomach, breathing hard, a bloody hand pressed to her shoulder.

She got to her feet, a little girl before a towering monstrous being, and it was clear she did not fear the King in Yellow, but quite the contrary, acted as though she had known all along what waited in that horrible other world.

Vanessa blinked, confused by the displacement, then curiously reached for the veil. Her hand met with an invisible barrier and the shimmer flickered like a giant bubble stretched thin.

They'd done it. Their plan had worked: the door was closing.

Vanessa looked up at the King in Yellow sadly, a petulant child furious at losing a game, and the pallid mask gazed down at her, ancient and wise.

"They've ruined it," she cried. "They ruin *everything*."

Vanessa's face grew long; her body withered away before their eyes. Crow's feet stretched from the corners of her eyes. Her youthful skin turned ashen, began to sag and wrinkle. Her cheeks sunk in, deflating. Tears slipped down her face. She aged decades in a span of seconds.

The King in Yellow ran a clawed finger along Vanessa's liver-spotted cheek, gazing down benevolently at an unrecognizable old crone.

Vanessa sighed, tired and dying, and her milky, cataract-laden eyes fell closed. Her skin flaked away like ash, caught in the harsh winds of the nether world, carried out of the Emerald castle into the dead sky and past the twin black suns, and before long, she was gone too.

The King in Yellow took a step toward the barrier, taking in the survivors and their world with fascination, watching it break apart in hard, vicious tremors.

"Enjoy this victory. It will be short-lived."

The monster's eyes scanned over each of them, bloodied and bruised, and Scarlett took a step forward, fearless.

"We've beaten you," she said unsteadily. "We won."

> ***"No,"*** the King in Yellow replied. ***"You've only bought yourselves more time. There is no undoing what has already been done."***

The colossal ring flickered, the power shuddering. Veins of electricity crept across the wall like ivy, restoring the smooth rock face, closing the gateway to the other world.

The King in Yellow shuddered with cruel laughter, standing before them in the endless storm, a hulking mass of tattered golden robes in a pale mask and said,

"You have already lost."

SCARLETT (cont'd)

TENDRILS OF ELECTRICITY sealed Terrilax back in his immemorial city once again, the area within the giant ring restored to a sizeable patch of smooth slate stone.

Scarlett looked at Jackson and he smiled, relieved yet strangely defeated.

Vanessa was gone.

The Oblivion Stone was gone, too, finally, but at a great cost.

Park stared down at Harper's body in disbelief. Or shock. Maybe both, Scarlett thought. Park knelt down and closed Harper's eyes, sobbing quietly, and Scarlett knew the feeling all too well.

Beau, in contrast, was more or less the same. He stood stoically in front of the wall of stone as if he couldn't make heads or tails of the whole thing.

"Fuckin' aliens," he finally grunted, with a shake of his head. He turned around, facing the others. "I knew it."

The others chuckled wearily, and right when they thought they could catch their breath, the cavern quaked.

A heavy whirr.

Beau's head snapped to the right.

An ax flew her way, end-over-end.

"Watch it!" Beau threw his arm out, shoving her back as the ax went hurtling by. The wind wafted across her face, the weight of the steel head fluttering her bangs.

Morgana stood across from them, surprisingly *not* dead, a knife in each hand, her face a hot mess of blood.

New scars, Scarlett thought.

"What the hell happened to her face?" Jackson asked.

"I thought you killed this crazy bitch?" Beau spat.

Morgana shook her head like she had grown exasperated of him. Like she had grown tired of them all. She exhaled in annoyance and her hand dipped into her coat and pulled out a pistol.

Beau's face hardened.

A flash of white sent her ears ringing. The bullet caught him in the side of the head, dropping all hundred and ninety pounds of him instantly.

The others looked down at him, aghast.

"I've lived many lives, Scarlett. But before I was a killer, my family and I traveled the world. I was an entertainer," Morgana admitted. "Even a magician's assistant once upon a time."

"Magician's assistant?" Scarlett whispered.

Vincent flashed in her head.

His fateful final act. The accident. The death of his assistant.

His subsequent disappearance.

And finally, his death.

"He's been here all along, hasn't he? You see him, don't you?" Morgana asked. "The wallpaper. The carpeting. He's influenced this house the same way he influenced people. Lies to them. Shows them what they want to see. Tells them what they want to hear."

Scarlett couldn't speak, couldn't fathom Morgana's words.

"He changed you, didn't he? Made you believe you were someone else. Made you believe you were special. Important."

Was it possible? Could Morgana be who she claimed?

"He spun those same lies with me my whole life. And I believed it, too. That I was special. That I didn't have to be this person I've become.

That I could change, be someone else," she said. "I believed him right up until the moment a thousand pounds of glass collapsed on top of me." Morgana ran her fingertips over the scars crisscrossing her face. "I think he knew, deep down, what was going to happen that night, but he let it happen anyway. Because he knew that he couldn't fix me, and it killed him."

The cavern rumbled in its walls, and the world swayed.

"When I woke up, months later, he'd gone. He'd abandoned me like he always does. Disappeared here, to this place, like the coward that he's been his whole life."

The others were getting restless, watching the world fall apart around them.

"But that's the thing about Vincent, isn't it? He's never truly gone."

"That's why you're really here?" Scarlett asked. "To find Vincent?"

Morgana grinned. "Of course. Katya's contract merely gave me access to this wonderful place. Shown me other worlds. Other universes beyond our own. Other possibilities."

"Vincent's dead," Scarlett said, and even she wasn't sure she believed it. "He died. I saw it myself."

"You saw what he wanted you to see."

"You think he's alive?"

Morgana suddenly began hacking up blood. "This is the second time I've been left for dead." She glared at Park, who was standing beside Scarlett. "You should have killed me when you had the chance."

Without missing a beat Park said, "Third time's the charm."

Morgana charged forward, silent and graceful, wounded but agile regardless.

Scarlett got a running start. She grunted, pitching her weight and whipping the baseball bat through the air.

Morgana ducked, nimble as ever, and slashed out with the knife, catching Scarlett across the midsection in a ribbon of blood.

Scarlett screamed. Morgana slammed the knife's hilt into her face, knocking her off her feet.

A right hook came out of nowhere and battered Morgana across the face, staggering her back a couple steps. She shook it off, finding Jackson across from her, spectacularly unarmed.

She tossed the dagger into the air, catching it by the tip of the blade and pitching it at Jackson.

He instinctually raised his arms to shield himself and the blade bit into his forearm.

"Fuck!" he shouted.

Another section of the cavern the size of a sedan crumbled away, crashing to the checkered path and collapsing the side.

Park quickly grabbed a discarded machete from the platform. She lifted it over her head, dropping it down like a sledgehammer.

Morgana easily sidestepped it, kicking the machete out of Park's hands. Park held up her hands defensively and Morgana hacked the knife down.

Park let out an agonized scream. She held her hand up in shock, the blade embedded between her middle and her ring fingers, chopped nearly halfway through her hand, rivulets of blood dripping over the twine bracelets Abby had given her.

Morgana wasted no time; she dashed toward Jackson as he wrenched the blade from his forearm. She slashed at him but he flinched, narrowly avoiding her and throwing another clumsy right hook. She blocked it, punching him square in the face and knocking him off his feet.

Park jerked the blade from her hand and squealed, falling to her knees, the wound bleeding profusely.

Morgana grinned her mouthful of bloody teeth, taunting Park.

"You think you know pain?" Morgana said. "I'll show you pain."

Park roared, crazed with rage, and sprang forward.

Morgana lobbed one of her knives but didn't have enough time to wind up; the handle smacked into Park's chest rather than the blade. Park slammed into her, tackling her to the ground.

"YOU FUCKING BITCH!" Park snarled, digging her fingers into the lacerations in Morgana's face and working them apart.

Morgana shrieked, grabbing Park's split hand and crushing it.

Park howled and Morgana rolled out from under her, scrambling to her feet. She kicked Park in the face, knocking the woman to her back, then dropped to her knee, arching the knife down.

Scarlett's bat caught her in the forearm before the blade could reach Park; there was a snap of bone and the knife went sailing by, metallically clanging onto the tile.

Scarlett swung again and Morgana caught the bat, hitting Scarlett in the face. Scarlett's eyes crossed and she went woozy, falling back on the platform.

Park grabbed the knife and rolled, impaling Morgana's boot.

Morgana shrieked, kicking out her other foot, catching Park in the face, throwing her back down. She bent over and jerked the blade out of her boot, struggling to get her bearings back.

Sections of the fractured stone walls broke away, crumbling into the abyss. The platform jolted and they swayed on their feet, struggling to stay upright.

"We need to get out of here!" Scarlett said.

A curtain of steely light beamed toward them from across the cavern, throwing a spotlight on Morgana.

Her mouth hung open; her eyes widened.

Scarlett's body might as well have been struck by lightning. The silhouette of a man in a three-piece suit stood before the exit, his wavy blond hair tousling in the wind while chunks of the roof whizzed by, his face hidden in shadow.

"Vincent?" Scarlett muttered. No. He was dead. Wasn't he?

Morgana remained paralyzed, seemingly astounded, staring across at the phantom.

"The exit!" Jackson said hurriedly. "Let's haul ass!"

Scarlett looked at the others, wanted to confirm they saw him too, but when she looked back, he was gone.

She shook herself out of the stupor and dropped down, grabbing Sandi by the elbow and tugging her up. "Run! The exit!"

Sandi was caught in a daze, but a chunk of marble exploded next to her the size of a basketball and she got on her feet and made a break for the exit.

"Go go go!" she yelled.

Park was up in a flash, a knife in her hand and a crazed glint in her eye.

Morgana roused from her stupor a second too late.

Park plunged the knife through the air, lancing it straight into Morgana's eye. There was a squishy *pop!* and Morgana let out a blood-curdling scream.

Park retracted the knife and a spurt of blood as dark as black paint shot out of the woman's eye socket. Morgana wobbled, in a daze, her face a battered mess, the reptilian eye all she had left, and she still refused to die.

Scarlett and Jackson got to their feet, half dead.

Morgana looked at each of them and blinked her one good eye.

"You think you've won?" she said with a wheezy laugh. "You haven't won. You. Can't. Kill. Me—"

A sharp whistle cut through the air.

There was a hard thud and Morgana's reptilian eye shot open. She coughed blood onto herself and found the handle of Beau's knife jutting out of her chest.

Scarlett turned to find Beau alive, sitting up on the platform, one side of his hair matted to his head with blood.

Morgana fell silent, caressing the handle with shaky, bloody fingertips. She looked confused, like she didn't know where she was and, for a very brief second, Scarlett almost felt pity for her.

Morgana's eyes closed. Her head dipped to her chin as she collapsed backward, off the platform and into the blessed dark.

EPILOGUE

A SLIVER OF light was cresting the horizon, peeking between the towering downtown skyscrapers. Scarlett stood in front of the house's skeletal entrance doors as Sandi, Jackson, Beau, and Park burst into the muddy light, covered in copious amounts of blood, sweat, and grime. The gears and cogs inside the doors worked flawlessly, counting down to dawn with immense, shuddering movements.

A layer of mist crawled through the streets. Scarlett smelled the rank scent of blood covering their bodies and clothes but the street was suspiciously empty. The weapons were gone, and the bodies were gone, too. All of the cultists. Even the corpse of the scientist they called Dirac was nowhere to be seen. The tongue of red carpet running down the porch steps was a shade darker now, soiled and beaten by the elements.

The five turned back, watched as the doors creaked to life right on cue, swinging closed like a bank vault, the cogs inside turning over with a thunderous *CLACK!* as the house sealed once more.

Panting, Scarlett raised a hand to inspect Beau's head as he passed, a streak of blood cutting through his hairline.

"That looks pretty gnarly, man, you should probably—"

"Get bent," he said, brushing her hand away, and even she was too exhausted to bother reasoning with him.

Jackson looked at her and shrugged, letting out a long yawn.

Sandi was inspecting Park's mangled hand, tenderly holding it up.

"This looks pretty bad," Sandi said, grimacing. "You're going to need surgery."

Beau walked closer and yanked Park's hand toward him.

"Easy, you jackass!" Park snapped. "That fucking hurts, watch what you're doing!"

"Seen worse," Beau said. He reached into his pocket and took out a small roll of gauze, tossing it to Sandi. "Wrap it tight or it's useless."

Park and Sandi looked at him like he was a stranger.

"Thanks?" Park said with a pained smile.

Scarlett took in the entirety of the house, strangely sentimental. She reached into her pocket and pulled out the gold coin she'd found inside, reflecting on everything that had happened that night.

"I don't get it," Jackson said. "Isabelle? Nick? Why'd Vanessa do it, Scar? I mean, why bring them here?"

Scarlett shoved the coin back into her pocket.

"I don't think *Vanessa* did. I think Rachel did," she said. "Even with the Oblivion Stone, I think she was still in there somewhere. I think she called them here, her mom and dad. Called all of us."

"For what?" Jackson asked.

"For help."

"Lotta good it did," Beau said.

Scarlett saw Sandi looking at her out of the corner of her eye as she unrolled the gauze and draped it over Park's mutilated hand.

But something was still bothering her about the whole thing.

"Did you see anything in there, Jackie?" she asked.

"See anything? I saw *everything*, Scar. We all did."

"Well, yeah. I mean, yes, but did you see anything else? By the exit? Before we…"

Jackson hitched an eyebrow.

"Never mind," she said. "Probably nothing."

But it wasn't nothing. She'd seen him. It had to have been.

"Scar, wait," Jackson said.

She turned around.

Sandi was dressing Park's had, wrapping it in gauze. She stopped, and then they were staring at him, too. Beau was leaning on the balustrade, gazing out at the gray morning.

"Uhhh…what's up?" Scarlett asked.

"I, uh," Jackson said, apprehensive. He looked at Park and she gave a nod of support.

"Marry me," he said, his voice suddenly strong.

Her head went light. Her heart was suddenly a hundred times louder, galloping in her chest. Her fingers tingled and her mouth went dry.

"Wha—what?" she stuttered.

"Scarlett," he said. Jackson took her hand and dropped to one knee, pulling a small box out of his jacket and opening it. "You've been my best friend since the day we met. You've always believed in me, even when I didn't believe in myself. This world is…there are so, so many horrible things in this world, Scar. Things I don't understand. Thing I don't want to understand. But you…" he said, looking into her her eyes, "*you* make everything that I've seen, everything that I've been through, make sense. I don't know how, but you do. These last few years have been a nightmare, but I would go through it all again if it meant I'd get even another second with you. I don't know what's going to happen. But as long as you're with me, I don't care. Because that's all I need, and everything else is…it doesn't matter."

Scarlett's face lit up, and it was like she was her old self again. She dropped down and kissed him on the mouth, wrapping her arms around him.

"Is that a yes?" Jackson asked, beaming.

Scarlett chuckled, sniffling, and said, "Yes, you idiot! Of course I will." They kissed and, for a moment it was like Tommy and Hannah were there again like old times. They laughed and cried, and in spite of everything that had happened that night, Scarlett couldn't remember being that happy in years. Maybe in forever.

Park forced a smile. "Congratulations," she said. "I was hoping you'd get your shit together by the time we got out of here. Glad to see I wasn't wrong."

Scarlett noticed Beau was already at the bottom of the porch steps. He hit the street and went straight for his truck, throwing up the tattered blue tarp to find all of his stolen goods right where he'd left them.

Scarlett and Jackson exchanged a look, like he hadn't changed and nothing could ever make him, and smiled.

To thine own self be true, she thought. And he was.

Beau sighed, relieved, as if everything that had happened that night had been worth the trouble.

"Battery is probably shot by now, Winchester," Scarlett said.

Beau leaned in the driver's window, twisting the keys.

The engine clicked. Long dead, Scarlett guessed.

"Told ya," she said.

"Sonofabitch," Beau said, slapping the wheel. He rested his thick arms along the bed, shaking his head. "Fuckin' figures."

"Don't think you would have gotten far with those tires anyway," Scarlett added.

"What?" Beau took a step back, noticing all four tires were flat, the treads shredded. "You gotta be kiddin' me," he said, kicking the deflated rubber.

"At least you have your health," Scarlett said.

Beau nodded, taking out his pack of smokes and lighting up. "I'll cheers to that." He stood there for a moment with his sad, rusted truck, puffing on his last cigarette, letting the thick fog roll by while he scanned Seventh Street for signs of danger. "Religious nuts are gone," he announced. "You four better clear out before they come back."

He turned back while he sucked in another long drag, the cherry glowing, noticing Park easing onto the porch steps. She bent over and lifted the hatch to Wendy and Willard's carrier.

Park froze, a confused look on her face.

"What is it?" Jackson asked.

He and Scarlett walked over, bending over and peering inside. Sandi was already there, squatting down next to the transport.

The rats were dead. But not just dead. They were nothing more than bones now, more like fossils than living breathing rodents.

"What happened to them?" Scarlett asked.

Park stared down inside the box, incredulous, shaking her head. She massaged her temple with one hand, struggling to figure out what had happened.

"They're dead?" Jackson asked.

"But how?" Sandi added.

"It doesn't make any sense," Park said, closing the hatch reverently. "They were alive. They were fine. But now they're…they're goddamn bones."

Scarlett sat down next to her, draping an arm over Park's shoulders. "I'm sorry, Park. I don't think things in the Dead Zone work like they do out there in the rest of the world. Either way, they're in a better place now."

Beau exhaled, smothering his cigarette on the truck and walking over. Park looked up at him, poorly trying to hide the fact she was wiping away tears.

Beau held out his hand and opened his fingers. "The Doc—she dropped this inside."

Harper's necklace. The one Katie had given her for Mother's Day. The metal twinkled and Park blinked away tears, taking the chain and stretching it over her head.

"I figured she'd want you to have it," Beau said. "I know it don't mean much comin' from me, but wherever she is, she's with her kid now. Where she wants to be."

"Yeah…" Park nodded. "Thank you," she said with a sad smile.

"We'll expect you at the wedding," Scarlett said. "All of you."

"When hell freezes over," Beau said.

Scarlett looked up at the gray sky. "By the looks of it, that may not be far off."

"You ain't serious?" Beau asked.

"As a heart attack. Jackie doesn't have many friends," Scarlett said, nudging him with her elbow. "Besides me."

"No shit," Beau replied, shaking his head.

He started away but stopped midway to his truck and turned around. "Hey," he called. "You know the difference between marriage and prison, don'tcha?"

Scarlett shrugged. "What?"

"Better food," Beau said with a smirk.

She and Jackson shared a chuckle.

Beau reached into the back of the truck and grabbed as much copper pipe in his arms as he could carry.

"Hey," Jackson called. "So that's it? What about your truck? You just gonna leave all that stuff?"

"Ain't mine," Beau said, and Scarlett didn't know if he was talking about the truck or the stolen goods filling the back of it.

He went to start down the street with the lengths of pipe and Scarlett remembered the slate in her pocket.

"Beau, wait!" she called, jogging after him.

Beau slowed in the street, turning back, the morning sun rising behind him, smothered by an ashen sky and a blanket of fog.

"That was a good thing you did there," she said, glancing over her shoulder at Park, who was staring down at the mummified rats.

Beau laughed dryly. "Well, shit, don't go gettin' no ideas about me bein' a nice guy. World ain't changed a damn bit."

"No, it hasn't," Scarlett agreed. "But you have. For the better. Thank you."

Beau nodded, squinting in the morning sun like a hardened gunslinger from the Old West.

"Kid's gonna need to toughin' up if he wants to survive," he said, tilting his head in Jackson's direction. "But I guess if he's got you the dumbass did something right."

Beau began walking away again and she reached out, grabbing his shoulder. "Wait. There's…something else."

He stopped, looking over his shoulder, more suspicious this time around.

Scarlett reached into her pocket and fished out the single slate she'd taken in the Grey World, offering it to him.

"What's that?" he asked.

"It's for you. Take it."

Beau took the slate, holding it up.

His eyes widened in disbelief. The copper piping clanged onto the street in a clatter of hollow metal.

"It's him," he whispered. He looked at Scarlett, his eyes glassy for the first time that night. "That's him!"

Scarlett nodded.

"Where'd you get this?"

"When Harper and I were outside in that city, I saw him in the street," she explained. "He was standing under one of the awnings. I took it with Harper's camera."

Beau's hands were shaking, whether from an overload of happiness or confusion or nostalgia she wasn't sure.

"A copper man," she said.

Beau dropped down on his haunches, his eyes burning a hole in the picture, overwhelmed with emotion. "After all these years," he said, sniffling. "I looked everywhere. And I mean fuckin' *everywhere*. For *years* I searched from the Cape to Ferry's Island and back, lookin'. Searchin'. But he was gone. Just…gone."

The photo of the Copper Man was grainy, from a distance, but there was no mistaking the metal man. Beau rubbed the flecks of blood off the slate with his dirty thumb and it was confirmed: it wasn't just any copper man, but *his* Copper Man, the same one he'd sat next to for hours. The friend he'd confessed his darkest secrets to, and shared his hopes and dreams when there was no one else.

Scarlett saw a grainy metal photograph, but Beau saw something more. The Copper Man was frozen in time beneath a ragged striped awning in the Grey World. Scarlett saw more emotion in Beau then than she had the entire night, like the picture meant more to him than anything else ever could, this single precious thing that he'd searched for his entire life.

"You never let me finish, back in the house," she said.

Beau seemed to be at peace, almost like he was trying to will himself into the picture to be with his long-lost friend.

"That's why you steal the copper pipe, isn't it?" Scarlett asked. "You're not trying to fence it. You're not trying to sell it for scrap metal."

Beau looked at her hard, but somehow the edges had dulled a little, his sharpness softening, making him somehow less threatening.

"Those metal sculptures they found all over the East Coast, those metal people…that was you," Scarlett said.

The copper. The woods. He wasn't a criminal. He wasn't some psychotic hillbilly. He was an artist. Misunderstood. Emotional. And like any artist, his emotions got the better of him more often than not.

"*You* made them? All of them?" she said, amazed. "But why?"

A beat passed. Jackson and Park and Sandi were waiting back at the bottom of the porch steps, quietly watching them.

"The loneliness can kill you," Beau said. "The Doc knew it."

Scarlett nodded soberly. Damned if he wasn't right.

"He saved my life," Beau said. "Thought maybe mine might do the same for some lonely asshole that gets lost in those woods like me."

Scarlett smiled at him but he couldn't bring himself to look at her, his attention focused only on the picture.

"He was the only real friend I ever had," he confessed.

Scarlett put a hand on his shoulder, smiling down at him.

"Not anymore," she said.

Beau laughed like he didn't really believe her, then climbed to his feet, shoving the picture into his pant pocket. He gazed at the house, noticing the same ill fog rolling down the street, the same black oil glistening over the house's exterior walls, and sighed, like he'd lost his chance to see the Copper Man again and would never get it back.

"One day, good buddy," he said. "One day."

Beau looked at Scarlett and smiled, grateful for her kindness.

And before she could say anything else he was gone.

A wild man in a concrete jungle.

The group started away, making their way back toward the entrance, Park cradling her bandaged hand. Scarlett trailed behind them.

She stopped and turned back, taking one last look at the house, letting her eyes touch every window, searching for anything and coming up with nothing. She sighed, a hollow ache in her chest.

"See you around, Vincent."

"What happens now? Jackson asked.

The quartet limped back toward the entrance, marred by more cuts, bruises, and punctures than they could count. Floating cars. More exotic, alien plants. Black glass trees. All of the bizarre spectacles found in the Dead Zone remained, but they were too exhausted to care.

To their surprise, the gigantic door in the perimeter wall was wide open, as if they were expected. The Red Sky, Scarlett thought. Their rendezvous with Park. They must have opened it.

The foursome emerged from the entrance, wandering into the intersection like survivors of a world ended. They slowed, Park setting the carrier-turned-casket for Wendy and Willard's remains down in the road, carefully checking the bandage on her hand.

Sandi eyed the stoop to Nick's apartment where she'd been just yesterday and noticed pieces of plywood had been nailed over the door and windows, a string of faded graffiti running down the side of the porch steps.

"They sure didn't waste any time," Sandi said.

But that wasn't all that had changed.

"Holy shit, guys," Scarlett said.

"It's spreading," Sandi said. "It's everywhere. On everything."

The plants from the Dead Zone: they were invading Winterview. The foliage had spread over the perimeter wall and down the streets. Wispy crimson weeds poked out of the cracks in the road. Vibrant, strange new species scaled skyscrapers and apartment buildings alike, enveloping entire sections of the Fringe.

Maybe more.

Scarlett glanced over at the security both and saw what looked like pink webbing filling the interior like cotton candy.

"Look at that," Jackson said, pointing.

Parts of the street and perimeter wall were scorched black.

"Looks like someone tried to burn it in a hurry," Sandi said.

"When?" Jackson asked. But nobody had a good answer.

"Park?" Scarlett said. "How is this possible? How could it have spread this fast? It's only been one night."

"I don't know," Park said, and the tone in her voice was grave, like she knew this was bad but couldn't be sure of the extent.

Scarlett put her hands on her hips, sucking in a deep breath and gazing around the overgrown city streets, watching the ash drift through the bleak sky while Jackson looked back on the Dead Zone with relief in his eyes.

Scarlett cocked her head, listening.

"That's weird," she said. "It's so quiet. So peaceful."

Thunder rolled low in the silvery clouds, the sky pregnant with rain. Scarlett felt the first few droplets tickle her skin, and it was fucking fantastic in spite of the transformed landscape. The vegetation was cause for concern, but they were out of immediate danger and that was all that mattered.

"Sun's coming up, Scar," Jackson said. "People must still be waking up."

Scarlett sighed, putting her hands on her hips. "Yeah, you're right."

"What is it?" Sandi asked.

Scarlett shook it off. "I don't know. Just a feeling, I guess."

"What're you going to tell them?" Jackson asked Park.

"The Red Sky?" Park asked.

Jackson nodded.

"I don't know," Park said. "I guess I'll tell them the truth. That Harper and Dirac are dead. That our research was lost in the house. That the Oblivion Stone was destroyed."

"For good," Scarlett said. "They're finally free. Hannah. Vincent. Tommy."

Jackson pretended like he didn't hear her. She didn't blame him. After everything that happened, getting on with her new life was all she could think about now. Her future with Jackson. Thinking about all the possibilities outweighed everything else, and that was a good thing. A great thing, as far as she was concerned.

"Hopefully they'll be able to tell me what the hell is going on." Park picked the carrier back up and slung it over her shoulder, exhausted and aching but young enough to shake it off.

"What do you think it meant?" Jackson asked, much to Scarlett's surprise. "The King in Yellow. It said that we had already lost."

Park shook her head, taking in the morning sunrise. "I don't know. And I don't want to know. I hope I never have to look at this place ever again."

Park looked around, squinting down the connecting streets. "I guess they're running late—someone was supposed to pick us up here."

"Since when has the government ever done anything on time?" Scarlett asked.

Park smiled at Jackson, offering her hand. "Take care of yourself, Jackson. And treat that girl well, otherwise I'm going to have to come back here and kick your ass."

Jackson looked at Park's hand hanging in the air and frowned. He always did hate goodbyes, Scarlett thought, and she realized now that she did too. Because this wasn't only farewell. It was goodbye forever to a stranger who had become family in a matter of hours. And saying goodbye felt like losing family the same way she'd lost her best friend and her brother.

To Park's surprise, Jackson wrapped his arms around her, squeezing her tight. "I will. I don't think I'd be here if it weren't for you. Thanks for everything."

Park groaned, giving him a couple of cursory pats on the back. "That makes two of us."

She looked at Sandi and nodded, and Sandi nodded back.

"If you ever come to California, look us up," Scarlett said. "It'd be nice to have some company out there." She hugged her and then Park went on her way, strolling down the sidewalk alone, disappearing into the fog just as Beau had before her.

Sandi looked at them, her arms folded over her chest, and Scarlett knew what she was thinking.

"I'm sorry for your loss," she said. "He seemed like a good guy."

"No," Sandi said, shaking her head. "He wasn't. He wasn't a 'good guy,'" she said. "But he was a good father, and that's all he cared about." Sandi shivered as the rain fell. "Do you think Rachel is…"

"Alive?" Scarlett said.

Sandi nodded.

"Honestly? I don't know," she said. "But I hope so."

Sandi nodded soberly.

"Are you going to be okay, Sandi?" Scarlett asked.

"No," Sandi said. "I don't think I am. But I'm gonna keep going. Because if there's things like that out there, people like that girl with the knives and bloodsucking monsters from beyond… Well, then the world is gonna need good people like us."

Scarlett smiled.

And without so much as another word, Sandi began walking away, down the sidewalk. Before the fog took her, she turned back and looked at them like she wanted to say something else, but didn't.

And then she was gone, too.

"Do you think she's going to be all right?" Jackson asked.

"Are any of us?" Scarlett said.

"Yeah…" Jackson said with a sigh. "I guess it's just us now."

"I'm okay with that."

A clap of lightning roared and it was like the world opened up, dumping down frosty rain in sheets. They watched as the leaden sky lit up with veins of lightning, the rain filling up potholes in the broken streets, water rushing by in canals, flowing past their feet along the sidewalk. The Dead Zone's signature moss coated portions of the sidewalks and streets. Multicolored vines dangled over awnings and from light posts.

"C'mon!" Scarlett said. She grabbed Jackson's hand and they splashed through the overgrown intersection, soaked down to their bones, giggling like kids without a care in the world. Was this what it was like to be in love? Scarlett wondered. Because if it was, she could get used to it.

She pulled him under a tattered awning and kissed him on the mouth. She tasted the rain and his hot breath, allowing herself to be in the moment for the first time in her life without worrying about the house, or roads not traveled or opportunities lost. Regrets or what ifs. None of it. Just her and Jackson and the huge diamond on her finger and their future. She gazed at his beautiful brown eyes and he smiled with that boyish charm he had so much of. And against all odds, in spite of everything they'd been through, she found herself hopeful.

Scarlett threw her arms around him and raised her hand over his shoulder to admire the sparkling ring on her finger, giddy with life and excitement and optimism for the first time since forever.

A papery flutter behind him.

She squinted down at a perforated waste bin bolted to the sidewalk overflowing with garbage and weeds. A crumpled newspaper was smashed against the side, pinned by the wind. The pages flapped in the wind like a dying bird. Miraculously, the rain hadn't managed to breach the area beneath the awning.

She released Jackson and he looked at her. "What's wrong?"

She didn't respond, only took a step past him, letting the bold headline shape itself before her eyes, one black letter coming into focus after another.

She quickly snatched the newspaper from the trashcan, holding it up and stretching the paper taut.

"'Electrical Storms Ravage East Coast,'" she whispered. "'Strange Creatures Sighted in Atlantic.'"

Jackson leaned over her shoulder.

"This is impossible," she whispered, recalling her earlier conversation with Harper.

"'New species wash up on Florida beach'?" Jackson recited.

Scarlett was silent, reading and rereading the headline over and over again, appalled by not only the article but the fact that her one small moment of joy was over before it had even started.

"The date, Scar," Jackson said.

"What?" she asked in a daze, her mind reeling a million miles an hour.

"Look at the date," he said.

"Oh my God," she said. "November first—"

Jackson looked at her in disbelief.

Scarlett furrowed her brow. "But that means..."

The soft rumble of an engine. Coming straight toward them.

The newspaper fell to the sidewalk.

It was getting closer.

Scarlett stepped out from under the awning into the rain, felt the water running through her hair, dripping down her face, the cold sinking into her skin.

Two hazy green beams cut through the fog.

Jackson wandered out behind her, the two standing in the middle of the road while the storm crashed around them.

The mist twisted in a puff of white smoke and an old VW bus skated out. The kind from the days of hippies and peace and love. Only it wasn't. The vehicle had been heavily modified, spray-painted gunmetal gray, and outfitted with all sorts of strange equipment. All terrain tires. A reinforced grille guard with a winch. And a roof full of things Scarlett couldn't even begin to speculate on, including a small radar dish aimed at the sky.

The screech of brakes.

The VW rumbled to a stop.

Scarlett and Jackson had their hands up, shielding them from the burning green headlights.

The driver's door creaked open.

Heavy footsteps stamped through the water.

A silhouette moved through the light, coming closer.

Scarlett lowered her hands. Her eyes widened.

A tall man stepped forward, a drab scarf pulled up over his nose.

"Who are you?" Jackson asked.

Layered in tactical gear, the man was nearly indistinguishable. But

Scarlett recognized something about his squinty eyes. Something oddly familiar…

Wait.

The man tugged down the scarf and held up a baseball card sealed in plastic and it all came rushing back.

The trading card had yellowed a bit. A few creases through the face. Rounded corners. But it was the same.

Daryl Duke of the Winterview Watchers.

"No. Fucking. Way," Scarlett said.

"Holy shit," Jackson said. "Nelson?!"

He was older now. Faint lines in the papery skin around his eyes. And heavier. He'd gained at least twenty pounds or more. But the same curious, sedated eyes. The same frizzy red hair (flattened by the rain). Gangly arms like broomsticks with significantly more muscle.

Nelson smiled his bright white teeth, and that confirmed it.

"You're here," he said, rain falling down his face, and it was like he didn't believe what he was saying. "I knew you'd come. Everyone told me you were gone. That you were dead…but I never gave up hope. Not once. Even after all these years."

"What in the hell is going on, Nelson?" Jackson asked.

Nelson was silent, staring at them with the same shock and awe while thunder clapped and the clouds lit up in ghostly white patches.

"Nelson—the newspaper—the date," Scarlett said. "It said it's been—"

"Five years, give or take," Nelson said.

The torrent of rain began to pick up; needlelike drops fell harder, faster. Puddles were becoming ponds; cratered, sunken sections of the street were filling. Soon the entire street would be underwater.

A sound broke out then, infinitely loud and equally horrible. Then she remembered: the things she'd seen in the house before, the same ones that haunted her nightmares, gliding through time and space in a hellish realm with an ocean (space?) of black oil. Ancient horrors so terrifying reality couldn't contain them.

"What in the hell was that?" Scarlett asked, alarmed.

“A lot of bad things happened while you were gone,” Nelson said.

The trio looked toward to the coast as the sound crooned again, supremely horrible, finding a violent wave of dark clouds rolling in from the ocean, high above the horizon.

“Guys,” Nelson said, a grave glint in his eyes. “We need to talk.”

A NOTE FROM THE AUTHOR

People ask me oftentimes what my favorite book is of all my stories, and I always have the same answer. *The House that fell from the Sky*. I've written many stories, but for some reason, Scarlett and Jackson and her friends have always held a special place in my heart, which is why I was so excited to bring this second chapter in the series to all of my readers. I loved the idea of ending this story on a cliffhanger, much more so than the first book. *Back to the Future* is one of my favorite film series, and that little nod to those movies was just too fun not to do.

Okay, so, acknowledgments. Thank you so much to Wofford Lee Jones for his incredible illustrations and cover design. You're a great friend and a talented artist and one of the nicest guys I've met in this business. I've always enjoyed your writing and look forward to working on some projects again in the future. A special thank you to Soliz Mayer for your help on tightening up my manuscript. Thank you for catching all the little details that slipped past me. Your help and your time are greatly appreciated. Also, a big thanks to Mal for your valuable feedback on the beta read.

On to the juicier, behind-the-scenes details. My biggest relief after finishing this book was that the "big bad" has finally been revealed. Not just for this story, but to all my stories. Coming up with an antagonist fit for my brutal world was just as hard as saying goodbye to some of my favorite characters. I explored many options for what felt like years until now, finally arriving at the corroded doorstep of Terrilax, the King in Yellow. While the King in Yellow is not a new concept by any means, it is often thought of as a figurative concept, something analyzed and studied and researched. Whispered and generally shrouded in mystery.

Terrilax, on the other hand, is quite literal. He is the twisted king of an ancient magic that has terrorized the known universe and beyond, and I'm so thrilled to finally be able to reveal him to you all.

By now readers will have noticed that cosmic horror is my favorite subgenre of horror. John Carpenter's *The Thing* is probably my single favorite horror film of all time. Making us question our place among the stars invites so many intriguing questions. What is our purpose? Is our existence insignificant in the grand scope of the universe? Does God exist? Cosmic horror carries with it a weight of hopelessness, and a dread that looms over us as we devour the pages. Which is why it's so important to me that these characters are able to connect with readers, to be a beacon of light in what is quickly becoming their darkest days. Stories are all about stakes, and I can say without a shadow of a doubt that the stakes have never been higher.

While it is true that Scarlett's tales concerning the house that fell from the sky can be read as a standalone series, all of my books are meant to complement each other, sharing people, places, and a mythology that I meticulously crafted to ground their world so that it feels as real to you as it does to me.

It's no accident that one of the infamous witches (who appear to be a fan-favorite) from *Witch 13* appears in this story. Nor is it a coincidence that the Collector's (my personal favorite trio of monsters) make a blink-and-you'll-miss-it cameo during Harper and Scarlett's journey through the house's winding halls. Dante Greystarr. The Copper Man. The Grey

World. Every single character and every single idea were put to page to build to the epic conclusion I've wanted to write my entire life. Unfortunately, there are still many years to come before that massive tome arrives in your hands. But when it does, I guarantee you it will be the greatest story I have ever told.

So, until then, sit back and enjoy the ride, because I'm just getting started.

Patrick Delaney
12/11/2023

Printed in the USA
CPSIA information can be obtained
at www.ICGtesting.com
LVHW040627020424
776092LV00021B/93

9 781735 525198